Praise f

"My choice for the year's best. . . . Profound and suspenseful. . . . A sensitive, original, unpredictable, and extremely moving novel . . . [*The Late Man*] goes against conventional expectations. There is a heightened credibility derived from the sense that we haven't been here before and that we are in the presence of characters we know well, care about, and are not likely to forget very soon."
—*Los Angeles Times*

"With skillful writing, an original plot, and characters so real they'll be hard to forget, *The Late Man* is my nominee for the best mystery novel of the year. Get a first edition and save it. James Preston Girard will be a big name in the writing business."　　　　　　　　—Tony Hillerman

"A mesmerizing novel [that takes] readers so deeply into a killer's mind that we share the madness. . . . With unusual depth and feeling, Mr. Girard verifies the amazing flexibility of the genre by creating . . . psychologically rich characters . . . and elevating a sordid crime story into a powerful existential drama."
—*The New York Times*

"Full of insight . . . real people . . . tough in the right way. A very accomplished piece of work and a highly intelligent novel."　　　—Ruth Rendell

"Excellent . . . a probing novel about the delights and dangers of obsession."　　　—*Chicago Tribune*

"This is a wonderful novel about three unforgettable people, about grace and love, solitude and hope."
—Andre Dubus

continued . . .

SOME SURVIVE

James Preston Girard

AN ONYX BOOK

ONYX
Published by New American Library, a division of
Penguin Putnam Inc., 375 Hudson Street,
New York, New York 10014, U.S.A.
Penguin Books Ltd, 80 Strand,
London WC2R ORL, England
Penguin Books Australia Ltd, Ringwood,
Victoria, Australia
Penguin Books Canada Ltd, 10 Alcorn Avenue,
Toronto, Ontario, Canada M4V 3B2
Penguin Books (N.Z.) Ltd, 182–190 Wairau Road,
Auckland 10, New Zealand

Penguin Books Ltd, Registered Offices:
Harmondsworth, Middlesex, England

First published by Onyx, an imprint of New American Library,
a division of Penguin Putnam Inc.

First Printing, January 2002
10 9 8 7 6 5 4 3 2 1

For my sister, Mary

ACKNOWLEDGMENTS

Neither this novel nor my previous novel would be even as good as they are, had it not been for my late editor, Lee Goerner, and my agent, Phil Spitzer.

Prolog

The young woman sitting on the edge of the large round bed was tall and slender, not beautiful but not plain, either. She wore a simple white blouse and a tan skirt, black medium heels, and panty hose in the shade called nude. Her dark hair was clipped short on the sides and in back, brushed away from her eyes. She looked neat and trim and nervous. She looked like someone applying for a job she needed badly.

When the door opened, she sat up straight, tensing, her hands twisting in her lap. The man who entered was short and bald, well past middle age, walking with a straight black cane. His bearing was militarily erect, even a bit exaggerated, as if to suggest that the cane was only an adornment. He wore only a pair of white tennis shorts and leather sandals. Despite his posture and his deep tan, his belly hung out a little in front over the elastic band of the shorts. He took two steps into the room, and closed the door behind him, before appearing to notice the woman on the bed. Then he stopped and looked at her with an expression of surprise as exaggerated as his bearing.

"Hello, Daddy," she said.

He gave an overloud bark of laughter. " 'Daddy,' " he repeated, his voice high-pitched to mimic hers. "You never called me that when I was married to your mother, my dear." He frowned, glanced around the room. "How did you get in here?"

"I still had a key. I'll give it back to you. I just needed to see you."

He stood silent for a long moment, regarding her, his expression changing from surprise to contempt. "Well, what is it?" he asked at last. "I suppose she has run out of money and has sent you to squeeze more from me, no? Half of everything would not be enough for her."

"She kicked me out." The young woman hesitated, then said, "I didn't know where else to go."

"How touching."

She gave him a sharp look. "I couldn't just sleep on the street. Don't worry, I'll get a job and—"

He laughed. "What sort of job could you get, Diane? You are a frivolous person without any skills. The street is probably where you belong." His eyes suddenly widened. "Perhaps you do have some skills . . . the same as your mother."

She looked away, her chin lifting slightly, her lips pressed together. When he didn't say anything more, she gave him another sharp look, and he gave a start, as if he'd been daydreaming. He took a couple of stiff steps toward her, the cane swinging with his unbending leg, only stopping when the waistband of his shorts was inches from her face. She turned her head farther to the side and leaned back on her arms.

"It wouldn't be right to just turn you away," he said. "Perhaps I can employ you here for a time. Of course, I will have to see a sample of your work before setting your rate of pay."

She swung her legs to one side and tried to get to her feet, to step around him.

He lifted the cane and used it to block the movement. She pushed at it but seemed unable to move it, as if the strength of his arm were immense, his balance solid. She sat back again, still not looking at him.

He lowered the cane, leaned on it again and put out his other hand to grasp her chin, turning it toward him. He looked into her surprised eyes for a second, then pushed her back onto the bed. She gave a kick as she fell backward, but it missed.

He leaned forward and gave her a light slap, which made her stiffen, staring up at him. "Now behave and do as you're told," he said sternly.

She struggled to raise herself, seemed unable to do more than get her elbows beneath her. Her voice came in a hiss: "You can't—"

"Can't what?" he barked, cutting her off. Then he smiled. "My dear Diane, don't you know by now that I can do whatever I like in this house? And a person as worthless as yourself . . . if no one ever saw you again, who would notice or care? Your mother? Perhaps for a few minutes."

"She knows—"

"No. You would never tell her you were coming here. She might want you to share whatever you could get from me, not true? No." He shrugged. "But if you would like to scream, please, by all means do so. At most, Miles might send David to see if I am having some trouble with you. You realize, of course, that if your work is not of sufficient quality to suit me, I will be forced to ask my men to dispose of you. Their tastes are less discriminating than mine, so I imagine they would take their time about it. Particularly remembering the insolence with which you and your mother used to treat them when you lived here. But perhaps you would enjoy entertaining them."

Her expression had changed gradually to one of fear, her eyes growing wide. But now she made an effort to regain her composure, relaxing back on her elbows and saying, "At least they'd be able to get it up. Mother told me—"

He lunged forward suddenly and struck her with his fist, making her head snap back. She made no sound but lolled to one side, her elbow giving way, her eyes glazed. The man fought for his balance, clutching the cane and trying to straighten. As he began to topple backward, the girl rose and stretched out a hand to catch his wrist and hold him upright until he had regained his balance. Then she touched her own cheek tentatively with her fingertips.

"Thank you, Celeste," the man said, then saw what she was doing and made a sound of disgust beneath his breath. "I'm sorry. I lost control." He peered more closely at her. "Is there a scratch?" He looked at his hand, made a hissing sound and began tugging at a ring he wore on one finger. Tearing it off, he hurled it into a corner of the bedroom. "Idiot!" he said, clearly meaning himself.

The girl, who was sitting up, waved a hand dismissively in the air. "I'll be fine, Mr. Bannerman. It'll make the finished tape better, more real." She worked her jaw back and forth for a second, then smiled at him. "You still pack a pretty good punch. Maybe you don't need Miles."

He grinned sheepishly, then said, "But I should have better control. I still have much to learn. Are you sure there won't be a scar . . . ?"

She shook her head, getting to her feet. "Just a scratch. It'll go away. In the meantime, I'll have to cover it with makeup, but that's no biggie. Makeup's what I'm best at. I learned it from my mother. Sometimes I think I ought to give up acting and be a makeup artist."

He didn't look convinced. "If you're sure . . ."

She gave him a pat on the arm and went to the videocamera set on a tripod at the end of the big bed. "Get back in character. We still have work to do."

Getting behind the camera, she peered into the viewfinder for a moment. She glanced up at him. "You'll need to move away from the bed for a moment," she said. He turned obediently and walked to the dresser. As he did so, she bent to pluck a small piece of cloth from a gym bag and held it in her hand as she changed the camera's angle slightly. "I'll just do a quick reaction shot," she said.

He leaned slightly against the dresser, watching as she returned to the bed, slumped to one side, her head turned as if she'd just been struck.

"Mein Gott!" Bannerman said. "Blood? Did I—"

She waved a hand at him, looking a little impatient for the first time, then smiling as she said, "It's fake. From my bag. I'll start again."

"Verzeihung," he muttered. She resumed her position on the bed, then pulled herself back up a little, shaking her head, her eyes looking glazed again for a second, then touched a hand to her cheek and stared at it in horror. She looked up at the spot where he'd been standing and hissed, "You son of a bitch!"

She held the pose for a few seconds, then hopped up and went back to the camera and readjusted it. "I think this'll be good," she said. "Okay. Let's get you back in position."

She watched as he moved back to where he'd been, then gently moved him a little, saying "One foot a little forward . . . that's right. Make sure you have your balance." She studied him for a moment, then said, "Why don't you raise your fist, as if you're ready to hit her again? You didn't hurt your hand, did you?"

He shook his head, looking a little sheepish, but then drew back his fist again and kept his eyes on her as she resumed her own position on the bed.

"Remember that you're angry," she said. "Remember that terrible insult. And remember that you're completely in charge. You can do whatever you want. You have absolute power. And you don't feel any guilt at all. You're having a very good time. Right?"

He nodded seriously, then frowned, narrowed his eyes slightly, flared his nostrils, and finally, as an afterthought, curved his lips into a tight prunish smile that made him look demented.

"Good," the woman said. "Hold that expression as long as you can. But don't be afraid to be spontaneous. And don't forget to use the bad words."

He nodded.

"Remember the script," she said. "The hair, the blouse, and then a little oral, to establish control. But not too much."

He nodded a little impatiently, evidently having

some trouble maintaining his expression. "I know," he said.

"Good. Let's do it while the blood's still wet. Action." Her own expression changed back to mixed horror and anger. "You son of a bitch!" she snarled again.

He hesitated, as if not quite certain of what came next, then leaned forward just far enough to grasp a handful of her hair. She jerked upright, as if he were pulling her, although it was obvious that she was actually keeping him balanced as he let his cane fall to the floor beside the bed. Her face pressed for a second against the front of his tennis shorts, where the only discernible bulge was that of his belly. Then she moved back slightly, swinging a fist that landed lightly on his hip without any force.

"Behave!" he barked. "Now take your shirt off." He hesitated, then added, "You little cunt."

"Fuck you," she said.

"Of course," he said. "All in good time, my dear. But now I wish to see your br—your tits. Those tits you used to like to tease me with, with little glimpses . . ."

"Like hell! You old—"

Obviously using her for balance, he slapped her lightly with his other hand. Her head jerked to one side as if he'd hit her with great force. She shook her head again, again looking momentarily dazed as she looked up at him.

"Now . . . Diane," he said. "From this moment, you will do whatever I tell you to do, and only what I tell you to do. You will keep your eyes open at all times. You will not speak unless you are spoken to, and when you do, you will call me 'Daddy,' as you did earlier. Yes?"

She stared at him sullenly for a moment, then looked past him and muttered, "Yes, Daddy."

"A little less sarcasm," he said. "And look at me when you speak. Keep in mind that if you please me sufficiently, I will not want to share you with Miles and the others. Now—the tits, if you please."

*　　*　　*

Bannerman lay naked on the rose bedsheet, breathing hard, his eyes closed. The pillows and the rest of the bedclothes lay scattered on the floor beside the bed. From the open door opposite the doorway by which he'd entered came the sound of the woman gargling and spitting.

"That was very good, Celeste," Bannerman said, not opening his eyes. "Very intense. You have her to a T, that little Diane. That little cunt." He laughed. "Are you quite sure you do not know her?"

Celeste came back into the bedroom. "I do know her, Mr. Bannerman. Not Diane herself, but a lot of women like her. The world is full of them." She carried the gym bag in one hand, the small piece of cloth she'd used to adjust the camera clutched in her other. She used it to reach behind her and switch off the bathroom light. She wore an oversized baggy T-shirt, dark full-length tights and sneakers. The scratch on her cheek had turned into a purplish bruise and had begun to swell. "We've done a good night's work," she said. "You look ready to go to sleep."

"Yes. I will sleep well." He opened an eye and looked at her. "I wonder . . . would you very much mind letting yourself out?"

"Of course not, Mr. Bannerman. Just as long as you're sure the dogs are in their pen. I don't want to be eaten up."

"Not to worry." He opened both eyes, smiling, then squinted at her and shook his head. "I'm sorry for the . . . mishap."

"You're sweet," she said. "I know you didn't mean to do it. And it looks much worse than it is. It really doesn't hurt at all. Really, it's a nice touch. Spontaneous. We probably ought to put it in the script. Without the ring, of course."

He looked abashed. "Of course. That was stupid. I'll never wear that ring again."

"Nonsense." She looked around the floor. "Did you

find it?'' She knelt and began moving the sheets on the floor, looking beneath them.

He waved a hand at her in annoyance. "Please, Celeste, don't concern yourself. It's nothing. The maid will find it."

She straightened and smiled down at him.

"You really think it was good?" he asked.

"Well, it's only a rehearsal, of course, but for a first take . . . yes, I thought it was very good. But of course I haven't reviewed it yet. There are always little problems. We can't always control ourselves—I mean, either of us. No one can be in complete control of the material at this point."

He nodded seriously. "Yes, you're right."

"You have a tendency to be much too hard on yourself, Mr. Bannerman. I mean, I'm the pro, and you're doing—"

"I hate that word!" he said with sudden heat.

She stopped talking, looked at him wide-eyed.

Immediately he softened, looked chagrined. "I'm sorry, Celeste. You know how I bark sometimes when I'm tired." He laughed and she grinned.

"You're worse than the Dobermans," she said.

"It's true. Sometimes I am. I only meant . . . pro . . ." He shook his head. "Why do Americans talk this way, a little bit of the word? Never mind. It only made me think for a second . . . well, I won't say it. It's a great insult. I am ashamed for thinking it."

She bent to pat his arm. "It's an insult to yourself," she said. "The idea that you'd pay for . . . well. A man with your principles."

"But I think a lot of people would look at it that way. Sometimes I—"

"Foolish people," she said, straightening up again. "Anyone who knows anything at all about drama knows that what actors do during a performance isn't their real lives. It's just the character. And besides, look at the things you see in the movies today, even on television—and that's just to make money. It's dis-

gusting. Really, it's much worse than what you're trying to create."

"We," he said. "This work is as much yours as mine,
Celeste. I could never even have begun it without you.
I only hope you will someday get the credit you deserve,
when it is finally possible to let the world see it."

"But first we have to finish it," she said. "Let's not
get ahead of ourselves. Anyway, you yourself said it
will probably have to be kept secret for fifty years,
remember? Before the world is ready for it. I only
hope I live long enough to see that. That would be
my reward."

"I was so fortunate to find you," the old man said.
He closed his eyes as he spoke, his voice fading a bit
at the end.

She watched him for a moment, as if waiting for
him to go to sleep, then asked, "Will you want your
own copy of the rehearsal tape? To review, I mean?"

He jerked awake, blinking in confusion. "What?
Review . . ." He stared at her for a second, then said,
"Oh, the tape, yes . . ." He licked his lips. "I suppose
I'd better have a copy of my own to review. If you
don't mind."

"No, not at all. But that's another five hundred dollars, remember."

He raised a hand just enough to give a hint of a
dismissive wave. "It's nothing." He closed his eyes
again, then suddenly opened them and raised himself
on an elbow. "The money," he said. "Always I forget.
You should remind me."

She laughed. "I know you're good for it, Mr. Bannerman. Want me to get the box for you?"

"No, please, just take what I owe you."

"Don't forget about the dogs."

He looked momentarily annoyed, then said, "No, I
haven't. I'm just very tired."

"You worked so hard," she said, lifting a small
leather box from the bottom drawer of the dresser
with one hand, using the small piece of cloth.

"I'll call Miles right now."

"Great. Thanks." She turned back to the dresser, opened the leather box and took out a stack of crisp hundred-dollar bills. She counted several off the top, put the rest back, then put the box back in the drawer. She turned toward the bed again, fanning the bills she'd taken for him to see.

The old man glanced at her, grimaced, and said harshly, "Put that in your bag!" Then he punched a button on the device he was holding.

A small voice said, "Mr. Bannerman? You need me?"

"My guest is preparing to leave," the old man said, speaking a little too loudly. "Are the dogs in their pen?"

"Yes sir, they are. Want me to double-check?"

"Not if you're sure."

"Yes sir. What about the front alarms? Want me to walk up and turn them off for her?"

The old man hesitated, and for that second the woman's expression froze. Then he said, "No, of course not. I will walk her to the door and do it myself. You go on with whatever you're doing."

The woman's face relaxed again and she took a quick glance at her wristwatch, not in an impatient way. "You know, you're much too trusting," she said. "What if I grabbed your cane right now and hit you on the head and took all that money?"

He laughed, and the laugh turned into a rattling cough. After a moment, controlling it, he said, "You're too young to know what a wonderful thing it is to be able to trust someone, Celeste. So much of my life . . . well . . ." He held out his hand, offering her the remote. "You remember the numbers, don't you?"

"Five, six, three." She took the remote from him, held it in front of her, squinting at it as if she too found it confusing, then quickly pushed three buttons and handed it back to him.

"You know I would walk you down—"

"Don't let that worry you for a minute, Mr. Bannerman. We don't have to stand on ceremony."

He gave a thin smile. "I'm afraid I can hardly stand on anything."

She laughed a little more than it deserved, then bent over the bed and kissed his forehead. "It's so amazing how you can make light of your troubles," she said. "It's an example to me."

"I hope so, Celeste," he said. "But I hope you never have any such troubles."

"It's so good you have someone like Miles to help you. He seems so devoted. You must trust him, too."

Bannerman's lips formed a tiny smile. After a moment he said, "Miles is a good man. But I trust him only to do what is in his own best interests. As long as that is to serve and protect me, I do not worry about him." He looked at her. "That is the way the world really works, you see, my dear. There are very few like ourselves, who can see beyond their own self-interest. Self-destruction and treachery are twins. I hope you will remember that."

"I'm not sure I understand it, Mr. Bannerman, but I certainly will remember it, and I'll think about it. I think about a lot of the things you've said to me."

He closed his eyes and sank back into the pillow. "I'm very glad. When one grows old, when one is . . . let us say, not entirely satisfied with one's life, then one begins to want to leave something for the future. Something important, but also . . . you know, my dear Celeste, I think of you sometimes as the daughter I never had."

The woman was watching him expressionlessly, but now she smiled again. "You remind me of my father sometimes, too." She walked around the bed and reached to retrieve a sheet from the pile of bedclothes on the floor. She shook out a sheet and spread it over him, then did the same with the bedspread. He gave a sigh of pleasure and murmured, "Good night, Celeste."

"Sleep well," she said softly, her face once more

expressionless. She stood watching him for a while, her eyes narrowed in thought, but then gave a shake of her head and bent to the gym bag, dropping the small cloth in and pulling out a pair of rubber gloves. Straightening, she slung the bag over one shoulder and looked again at the sleeping man, her lips twisting once again into a half smile. "Good-bye, Daddy," she whispered.

Outside the door, she pulled on the surgical gloves and checked her watch. Twelve minutes left before one of them would come out to turn the front alarm back on. More than enough. She glanced over the railing at the immense living room below, confirmed that the wide opening to the hallway leading back to the kitchen, where Miles and Dave were, was only a black square, then turned and went quickly along the mezzanine wall. Miles would know she was leaving by herself, of course. He knew that the old crip wasn't really going to get up and haul his lazy, liver-spotted ass down the stairs to see her out. And he would assume that only the front-door alarm had been turned off, because he knew that that was about all Bannerman knew how to do with it, besides annoy the men who worked for him.

But Miles was paid, in part, to do the same kind of thing she did: indulge the old creep's fantasies and clean up his mistakes and his messes without comment. The first few times she'd come here, Miles had come from the kitchen to see her out himself. She'd made a point of stopping to chat with him, all bubbly and effusive, a slightly stupider version of the Celeste Mundy the old man knew. He'd been polite and pleasant. Once he'd asked her some questions about photography, claiming it was his hobby and that he'd like some pointers from a professional, a little smile on his face that let her know he'd seen some of the videos. She'd thought about that, and decided he must have taken a surreptitious look, the way she had at Bannerman's manual for the alarm system. She couldn't imagine Bannerman showing the videos to a younger, stronger man. It would destroy his fantasy.

It was his belief that he was screwing this foolish, real woman, Celeste Mundy, who actually seemed to take his bullshit seriously. Most of her clients were like that. She made each of them buy his own film equipment. They could easily afford it, after all, and it added to the illusion—the one they were really paying for—that she was selling something only a select few could buy. Not just sex, or even sexual fantasy. Any man could buy that. There were whores and call girls aplenty, priced for every budget. But only her clients could get the shameful things they'd always secretly wanted, and get them from a woman who wasn't a whore at all, who provided them with legitimate reasons. That those reasons might be unusual—too "advanced" for the common herd to understand—was one of the things that made it so expensive.

The older and wealthier a man was, the more accustomed he was to getting what he wanted, the nearer he was to death, the better it worked. Because even behind that illusion he didn't know he was buying, there was another—the illusion that maybe even death could be bought off.

Sex, death and money. That's what the books said it was all about, and they were right. Or at least that's what she'd believed before Eddy. She still believed it was true for most people—certainly for her clients—but Eddy had changed her, in a way she hadn't expected. Made her a little weaker perhaps, a little more afraid of the tiger hiding in the brush, but also a little stronger in another way, made her willing to put herself in the tiger's path, to keep him from Eddy. It was a kind of strength she liked better, a kind she'd once had, a long time ago, in another life.

But Eddy also made it necessary for her to get out of this life, close out accounts with the old fools—by her own accounting. And she'd saved Bannerman for last because he wasn't really like the others. He was more like the tiger himself. Or rather, Miles was.

Crouching at the top of the broad, curving staircase, she studied the black rectangle of the hallway opening, glanced at her watch again, and then stood up and launched herself down the marble staircase, the tips of her toes moving quickly, rat-a-tat, one rubber-gloved hand lightly touching the railing for balance. Move quickly without hurrying; that was what her tennis coach had liked to say, and it was true. There was still plenty of time. It wouldn't take long to get it, and she could get from the front door to the gate in less than three minutes at a normal walking pace. If she had to run, she'd sprint straight across the lawn to the nearest part of the fence and be over it a lot quicker than that. But hopefully she wouldn't have to. Hopefully they wouldn't even know she'd taken anything, let alone what it was, until Celeste Mundy had vanished forever. Even if they discovered the theft right now, tonight, Miles would have only a few nighttime hours to look for her. As long as she got away clean, that wouldn't be nearly enough.

The living room seemed even bigger than she remembered it—another telltale sign of fear. It could really have been a ballroom, except for the huge round fireplace at the center, which all by itself was larger than her own bedroom. In fact, Bannerman used it as a sort of auditorium—or rather, the self-righteous nuts who met here to plan their stealth campaigns did. The oversized chairs and sofas and tables and bookcases and all the rest were arranged in little groupings, like half a dozen separate living rooms with no walls between them. That was for when they split up into their brainstorming sessions.

She came to the opposite wall, where a long row of locked glass display cases glittered with all sorts of small, valuable things: jewelry, artwork, objects of gold and objects of clay and bone that might be millions of years old. A lot of it she could have turned over quickly for pretty good value, even in the hours left before she and Eddy got on the plane. But the really good stuff was in the little room with a door that looked like a broom closet except for the little square keypad on the wall beside it. And there was only one thing in there she wanted, which she planned to take on the plane with her. She'd decide later exactly what to do with it, how best to use it. And she'd already raised the amount she'd planned to raise in that way, from the former possessions of her former clients, most of whom didn't yet know that that was their status.

Bannerman had been dumb enough to show her what was in this room, and then dumb enough to fall asleep while she was still there, as he had tonight. The manual in the bottom drawer of his dresser, right beside the leather box with the money in it, had given her the three-digit combination for this keypad, as well as the one she'd already punched into the remote, upstairs, that turned off every alarm in the house. There were things she couldn't know for sure, but from what she'd read in the manual she was reasonably confident that nobody could tell, from either the kitchen or Bannerman's bedroom, that the whole system was off. The guard who usually sat inside the little room off the front hall would have known it, but he wasn't there. She believed that Miles and David were the only employees Bannerman kept around when she came to visit him. Evidently he didn't feel that the rest would see it as being in their own best interests to keep her visits to themselves. The combination to the keypad changed periodically, but Bannerman always wrote it down inside the back cover of the manual, because he couldn't remember it. She'd gotten the current number while getting her fee from the leather box.

She punched it in now, holding her breath for a second, but it worked. She went in quickly and closed the door behind her before turning on the light.

Old fuckface, sleeping now like a baby upstairs, had told her that all this stuff, both out in the hall and in here, was the legacy of his family back in Germany, that he had brought it to this country himself, to keep

it safe from the Nazis, but that his parents had been
sent to a death camp before they could get out. He'd
gotten very emotional telling her the story, the best
bit of acting she'd seen him do yet. He'd obviously
assumed that Celeste Mundy was too young and foolish and ignorant to think that there was anything unusual about a European Jew of his generation not
being circumcised. Or maybe he himself believed it
by now.

All of the paintings in the little room were tiny,
many no larger than a postcard, and many had specifically Jewish themes. One depicted what looked to
her like a bar mitzvah; another what might have been
a seder, although she'd never actually seen one. She'd
learned about them from a couple of clients in the
film community. The one she was interested in was
set on its own tiny easel on a tall wooden table against
the near wall. When she'd first seen it there, she'd had
no idea what it depicted. A big sort of mountain or
plateau with some people on top and some soldiers
scurrying around the bottom, looking like ants, piling
up dirt as if they were making a kind of ramp. Then
she'd seen it on TV and learned that the place was
called Masada and that the soldiers were Romans and
that they had indeed built a huge ramp all the way to
the top, where they'd slaughtered the rebel Jews on
top. It was a big deal in Jewish history.

She lifted it from its easel and tucked it carefully
inside the padded envelope she'd bought at an arts-
supply store, then wrapped the package and the folded
easel together inside a couple of pieces of clothing,
and put the package back inside the bag, zipping it
shut. She moved the remaining paintings closer together to cover the space.

Back outside the room, she moved along the row
of glass cases to the one that contained what Bannerman called the "family jewels." She used a small
tool from her bag to snap the lock with a single cracking sound loud enough to make her glance around for
a few seconds, listening. When nothing happened, she

lifted the glass and pulled out a few diamond pieces—
a couple of necklaces, a gaudy pin and a bracelet—
and dropped them into the bag. She debated leaving
the glass standing open, but then instead closed it as
securely as she could, as if she were really trying to
hide this theft. She went quickly back across the big
room, looping around the fireplace at the center, and
stopped in the dark shadow beneath the mezzanine.

She was trying to read her watch, holding it at an
angle to catch some light, when she heard the door
of Bannerman's room open, directly above her. She
flattened herself against the wall, not breathing as she
listened to the clump-thud of the old man moving out
to the railing to look down. She found herself looking
straight across the room at a display case on the wall
that held a matched pair of shotguns. Great. Just what
she'd needed to see at that moment. She closed her
eyes and listened hard.

"Miles?" Bannerman spoke in a normal tone of
voice, but the slight slurring of the word told her what
had happened. The old man's false teeth had awakened him and he'd gotten up to take them out, as he
usually did. She'd seen him do it twenty times. Why
hadn't she thought about it, reminded him to take
them out before falling asleep? Either he'd heard the
snapping lock or he was just coming out to make sure
the alarm was back on.

She felt a sudden hopelessness, a certainty that this
was it. This was the tiger. She thought of herself as
careful, good at planning. But wasn't there always
something she missed? Wasn't the real truth that she
was a fuckup, who only almost got things right, only
thought of almost everything?

"It's David, Mr. Bannerman. I'm on my way." The
words seemed to wake her up, as if she'd been dreaming. It took her a moment to realize she was hearing
them from right above, from Bannerman's remote re-
ceiver. David was on his way from the kitchen, not
even close to the living room yet. And it was David,
not Miles.

She looked at the front door, took the bag off her shoulder and looped the strap around her hand, gathered herself—and then thought: But where is Miles? Suddenly it seemed quite possible that he was right there somewhere, maybe in that maze of furniture squatting in the dark between her and the exit. Or maybe in the guardroom, whose door stood open. Or maybe just outside the front door, on the steps of the big porch. Or maybe he was at the back of the house, releasing the dogs, while Dave came up to turn the alarms back on. Maybe he was just doing what he usually did, and she was behind schedule. Christ.

She began moving, keeping to the wall, not exposing herself until she had to. If she could get out that door without Bannerman or David seeing her, and if the dogs were still at the back of the house . . .

She looked at her watch again, but still couldn't read it in the darkness beneath the mezzanine. It didn't matter now anyway.

She heard Bannerman move, up above and behind her. He was coming to the stairs, coming down to see for himself. She was nearly to the end of the wall, almost right beneath the staircase. Hide there or go? Then she heard his bedroom door close. Then silence. He hadn't been coming this way. He'd gone back inside.

She bolted for the front door, as quickly as she could in the dark, through the maze, holding the bag against her like a very big football. She dodged a chair, pivoted, hurdled a footstool. Her sneakers were squeaking on the patches of hardwood floor between the rugs, but she couldn't do anything about that. She looped around the end of an L-shaped sofa, leaning inward, as if on a banked track, letting the bag swing out to balance her. And then there was the door right in front of her, with nothing in between.

Except for the little reading table she hadn't noticed. She swerved at the last second and missed it, but the gym bag, still swinging from her hand, brushed it. It didn't topple. It skidded, staying upright, not really making that much noise, not really going very far . . . and then stopped, coming up against a foot-stool, and the small metal sculpture set on it flew off, bounced once on the carpet, and then clanged against the hardwood floor.

The door was three long strides away. Lights came on somewhere behind her. David's voice said, "What the fuck?" She hunched her shoulders instinctively, as if she could get her whole body inside the Kevlar vest she wore both back and front beneath the huge T-shirt. She had a flash of memory, herself standing at the sporting goods store looking at it, thinking it might slow her up too much, that she wasn't really likely to need it . . .

She felt dizzy for a second, remembering how close she'd come to deciding against it, and stumbled, and fell against the door, the handle sliding right into her hand, her face turning toward the guardroom, which was empty except for the panel of blinking lights and the little TV.

More lights came on, but they were still far away behind her. She realized that David was standing at the bank of switches by the hallway entrance, turning the lights on in order, from where he was to where she was. Thank God for morons. She stifled a squeak of joy and darted through the door, leaving it half open. She was across the porch, nearly to the steps, when light spread out on the lawn in front of her, and she hesitated, startled, and nearly lost her balance and fell down the steps. But it wasn't the floods. It was only the widening, lengthening trapezoids made by the house lights that grew gradually brighter, through the tall front windows.

She'd always imagined the big lawn being completely dark, herself disappearing into the blackness, even if she had to run, as long as the floods weren't turned on. But there was nothing to do about it except run. The main thing to worry about now was the dogs, if they were out. And she couldn't really do anything about them, if they were and if they got to her before

she got to the fence. Everything was simple now.
Just run.

Thanks to the house lights, she'd be exposed all the
way to the fence—and even more when she went over
the fence. That was why she'd decided to buy the vest.
She didn't think they'd shoot. They wouldn't know yet
what she'd taken, except maybe for the jewels, and
they wouldn't be worth it to Bannerman. He wouldn't
want the cops showing up, in any case. The nearer she
got to the fence and the street beyond it, the less
chance that even David would shoot.

Had the yard always sloped uphill like this? Why
hadn't she noticed it, all the time she'd spent studying
the layout? Despite her reasoning, she felt more and
more like a target with every stride. And every stride
was a little shorter, a little more labored. In shape,
huh? And the goddamn bag must weigh twenty
pounds. She began to imagine Miles standing back
there on the porch, lining her up in his sights. Even
though she knew he'd know better. Would it be one
of those fancy shotguns from the glass case? No. A
handgun. Or maybe a rifle with a night scope and a
silencer. She could see him standing there, cradling
it in his hands, just waiting, letting her run until he
was ready.

Or waiting to see if the dogs got her first. If that
happened, they could say it was just a terrible
accident.

As she thought that, she heard the first bark. It was
far away. They were out, and they were coming to get
her. It made her stumble, made her feel suddenly as
if she were running in a dream, the kind of dream in
which you can't even make your legs move. And in
that same dream the dogs were flying, their paws
never even touching the ground. Her legs ached, but
theirs were fresh and strong. And she was running all
wrong, because of the bag, because of the slope, because of her fear. A calf might cramp at any second,
and she'd just have to push through it. And the fence
wasn't getting any closer. She'd been running forever

and the fucking fence stayed just where it had been. She no longer knew whether she could really run that far, or whether she could get over it if she did. She'd been breathing correctly, but now she gave a sob and opened her mouth, gasping for air, giving up the last bit of discipline, just staggering and stumbling like any silly, panicky girl. She felt tears coming, too—felt that old impulse to let go and fall and take herself away inside and not care what happened on the outside. But she hadn't done that in a long time, and there was a reason she couldn't do it now. Eddy. Thinking of Eddy brought her back to herself, made her straighten up. Get your ass over that goddamn fence! she shouted at the part of herself that was trying to hide. Guns, dogs—fuck it all. It was just the tiger. The same old motherfucking tiger.

The fence rushed to meet her, so she had to drop the bag and turn sideways, going limp as she slammed into the black metal. Turning, she glimpsed movement in the dark, realized the dogs really were coming. They weren't barking. They were making that low, chuckling sound that Dobermans made when they knew they were going to get what they were after. In some crazy way, the sound reminded her of her clients and actually made her less afraid, more in control.

The floods came on, and the yard was swimming with dogs, more than she'd known he had, their eyes and grinning snouts all aiming for her. She gave a startled shriek and threw the bag way up in the air, not watching to see if it cleared the fence, just throwing herself after it, managing to catch a crossbar in one hand, clutch an upright with the other, the glove and the skin beneath it tearing a little as it slid along the thick cast iron. Something struck the fence just beneath one of her sneakers, and then, somehow, she was at the top, getting one leg over, pulling herself up, perching between a couple of the spikes and looking at the gym bag hanging precariously from another spike a couple of feet away.

She gave a bark of her own, a kind of laugh, and

leaned to grab the bag and fling it on over. The dogs were hurling themselves at the fence, scrabbling at it, trying to climb it, coming within inches of her foot. She drew the leg up, knowing she'd made it. She looked toward the house.

All three of them were standing on the porch—all in silhouette but easy to tell apart. The little shriveled fuck with his cane. Big dumb David raising something to his ear—a cellular phone? Bannerman saw it, too, and grabbed David's arm, yanked the thing away from him and tossed it out into the yard. The movement caught the attention of a couple of the dogs. They started that way, sniffed the air, then turned back again, confused. Miles stood apart from the other two, much as she'd imagined him—calm, motionless, some kind of long gun cradled in his arms. But he wasn't aiming it at her. He knew she'd made it. Now it was a matter of figuring out what she'd done, why she'd been hanging around in the dark, and why she'd run. And whether it was worth Bannerman's time and money to try to find her.

She rested for a few seconds, watching them, getting her breath while the dogs' growls changed to whines of disappointment. Then she held her arm up, in the light from the floods, and gave them the finger, waving it back and forth so they'd be sure to see it. They stood and stared at her.

She swung her leg over, pushed off and landed on her hands and knees, feeling the pain of the scrapes on her palms, which was nothing, which was almost a kind of pleasure. She felt a little dizzy, like being in shock. It was always a kind of shock to survive danger, even just a near miss on the freeway. All she had to do was the last little bit and then go home. Just follow the script.

Bannerman and David had gone back inside, to start looking. Miles still stood on the porch watching her. She opened the gym bag and took out the bundle of clothing that contained the padded envelope with the painting, leaving everything else, including the jewelry, and began stripping off her clothes, making no effort to conceal herself. There weren't many cars along the hillside road that wound between the big houses, and in this area no one would really think very much about a woman taking her clothes off in the floodlights in front of one of the houses. They'd just wonder what weirdness was going on now. And she didn't mind Miles watching her. She sort of liked it. He'd be trying to figure out what she was doing, and why.

She took everything off but the rubber gloves—the T-shirt, the tights, socks and sneakers, the Kevlar vest—and wedged it all into the gym bag, not zipping it up. Most of the dogs were wandering around in circles or sniffing along the fence, looking for some other trail to follow, giving low, frustrated moans. A couple of them were still pushing their snouts through the vertical bars, showing her their teeth, telling her what they were going to do to her when they caught her.

"Here you go," she said to them. "Try this." She'd been planning just to dump the bag somewhere, but the dogs deserved something for their efforts. She swung the bag back and forth a couple of times, then flung it upward, back over the fence. The vest popped out when it hit the ground, and then the dogs swarmed over it, growling and yelping, tearing pieces off, pulling out the stuff inside, their long jaws jerking and snapping, two of them playing an angry tug-of-war with the vest. She watched them with a kind of fondness while she put on the terry-cloth shorts and the T-shirt in which she'd wrapped the envelope. You couldn't blame animals for just doing what humans had taught them to do.

It was over. The thought surprised her, as if she'd never really believed it would be. Not just tonight, but the whole thing. L.A. Celeste Mundy. All of it. It was in the past, which didn't really exist, except in other people's minds.

A couple of the dogs had come back to the fence to look at her, as if curious to see what she'd toss them next. Miles had put down the gun and was walking casually up the big lawn toward her, obviously not trying to catch her, just coming to have a look. She gave him a friendly wave, and after a second he returned it. She looked at the two dogs.

"Here comes the tiger," she said. "If you'd had the sense to be cats, you could have gotten over this fence."

Driving, she imagined being on the plane at last, Eddy asleep on her lap, the last ties to L.A. cut for good. She found that she was humming the old nursery song, and sang a few lines aloud:

> *I'll tell me ma, when I get home,*
> *The boys won't leave the girls alone.*
> *They pull my hair, they steal my comb,*
> *But that's all right, till I get home.*
> *She is handsome, she is pretty . . .*

She drew a deep breath and let it out. Four more hours to get through, and they wouldn't pass quickly. But that's all right . . . *till I get home.* . . .

PART ONE

Part One

1

It was a gray day in November when the two women showed up down below and began unloading furniture from the rental truck and carrying it into the apartment opposite his.

Zach was trying to concentrate on working his way through a spaghetti patch of COBOL code, reading it line by line, practically running his finger along the page and moving his lips, trying to figure out if it had any purpose at all, let alone what that purpose might be. He had a powerful temptation to just redo the whole damn program from scratch. But he'd been hired only to check out the date codes, for Y2K. On the other hand, if they'd had any idea where the author of this piece of shit was, he'd have been glad to track him down and kill him, free of charge.

The women had been working for a while before he noticed the sounds, and the distraction was partly welcome. All he could see from where he was, leaning to peer down through the gap at the side of the window shade, was the top of the truck and a quick glimpse of a hooded head moving toward the front door of the other apartment, which was a mirror image of his own, the back half of the duplex that faced his, separated by a narrow yard split by an ancient, cracked driveway that no one ever used except to move in and out.

He sighed. It had been inevitable. The front apartment on the other side, the one nearest the street, had been vacant for a long time, but the rear apartment never stayed empty long, because of the extra, if tiny, upper room connecting the stairs from the apartment itself to the stairs that went down to the garages at the rear ends of the two buildings.

He swiveled back to the monitor, but he'd lost the thread. He'd probably have to start over.

Time for a break. He lifted his coffee cup, confirmed that it contained about a quarter inch of cold liquid, and headed downstairs, glancing guiltily at the clock. Not even noon yet, but close enough that he was tempted to think of lunch. Which would throw him even further out of the program, make it that much harder to work his way back into it.

This was sure the life, owning his own business, being his own boss. Maybe he'd go out for lunch and then drop in on his old buddy Casey, the programmer who'd urged him to go out on his own. Come to think of it, Casey was also the one who'd told him what a gold mine this Y2K stuff was. He'd have to cut back on the Dr Pepper and tortilla chips, which meant he'd starve to death. That was also why he couldn't afford to do the responsible thing and tell his clients to just go out and buy a program that hadn't been written by a retarded twelve-year-old.

And now new neighbors. Ever since the incredibly stupid young couple from Montana or Wyoming or someplace like that had pulled out in the middle of the night, stiffing Mrs. Metcalf for two months' rent, it had been relatively peaceful. Just him and the elderly Mr. and Mrs. Neuenswander, shouting at each other on the other side of his living room wall. But he was used to that. They weren't fighting. It was just the way they talked to each other, and they didn't really talk to each other all that much.

Count your blessings. He put the coffee cup in the kitchen sink, deciding he didn't need any more, and looked out the window above the sink. Two young women, it looked like. The parkas they both wore made it hard to tell much about them, but one appeared to be tall and white, the other short and black. The furniture they were carrying looked new but rela-

tively cheap. Much like his own. It looked like they'd
driven the rental truck to Sears or Penney's and
loaded up a living room/dining room suite that was on
special. About his own age, he thought—late twenties,
early thirties—or maybe a little younger. Hard to tell.

Two women might not be bad neighbors if they
didn't have a lot of boyfriends. Guys would be worse.
The tall one came back out the door, and for a second
he thought she looked right at him. There was something in the look, though . . . and maybe something
about the way she moved . . . For a second he thought
he knew her, but he couldn't come up with a name,
and the impression vanished as quickly as it had come.
Maybe he did. He'd grown up in Wichita, gone to
high school and his last three years of college here. It
wasn't unusual for him to think he recognized someone but not be able to come up with the name.

Hopefully, if it was true, she wouldn't recognize
him. The last thing he needed was a new neighbor
who *knew* him. Especially if she turned out to be attractive. And if she liked to stroll around naked with
the blinds open. He could keep his own closed, of
course, but Mr. Neuenswander would be hanging
around out in front of his apartment all the time.

He closed his blinds now, deciding to have an early
lunch and then go back to the program from hell.

By the time he'd eaten and gone out to check the
mailbox, the truck was gone. But as he stood there
leafing through the credit card offers, a little blue car
turned into the narrow driveway from the street. He
assumed that it was someone using the driveway to
turn around—its most common use, since this stretch
of street ended unexpectedly a half block from here,
cut off by a bend of the river. But it went on past
him, and he saw the profile of the tall white woman,
her parka hood thrown back, as she went by, not looking at him. Again there was that fleeting impression
of familiarity, and this time it was a little more solid.
She stopped near the end of the drive, just before the
stretch of sand between the facing double garages that

connected to the alley beyond, got out and opened
the nearer garage door on that side, and then pulled
her car in, closing the door behind her. She was already using the stairs from the garage to the overhead
room, instead of walking from the garage to the back
door. He liked that. It seemed to mean she was private, like himself, perhaps even reclusive. An excellent
quality in a neighbor. Before long she'd figure out that
the alley was the better way of driving in and out.

It was a couple of days before he saw the baby, and
before he got a clear look at the woman's face and
realized that he did indeed know her. She was one of
the reporters at the *Mid American*—one of the people
he'd taught to use their new front-end system when
they'd put it in, a job his friend Stu Merow, the systems editor, had wangled for him, knowing he could
use the money.

He happened to be standing on his porch looking
through the mail again when she came out the front
door opposite him, carrying the baby. He recognized
her immediately, and even raised one hand reflexively
in greeting, thinking that she'd had one of those short
names—with a J, he thought, like Jan or Jill . . . he
couldn't quite get it . . .

Then he noticed how she was looking at him. Complete absence of any recognition. More than that.
Complete absence of any desire to recognize.

He realized that he was standing stupidly with one
hand half raised, like he was getting ready to swear
an oath, and he dropped it. She turned away, suddenly
indifferent. He wondered if he'd only imagined what
he'd seen in her expression, if she'd even noticed him
there at all.

He went back inside feeling stupidly hurt, vaguely
mistreated. Part of it was that he'd had some sort of
vague idea that she was someone he'd liked. Just some
general positive feeling. But there hadn't been anything positive in her eyes just now.

Later that same day he called Merow, talked about

computer stuff for a while, and then, very offhandedly, mentioned the woman who'd moved in opposite him.

"Sounds kind of like Jes Wellington," Merow said. "But she doesn't work here anymore. She's gone freelance." He grunted. "Kind of funny she'd move over here and rent a duplex apartment. She owns her own home in Sand Creek. Maybe the freelancing hasn't worked out, and she's had bad financial problems or something. Seems like she'd come back here, though. Cubbage would take her back in a minute, I'm sure. If he could . . ."

"She has a baby, too," Zach said. "Doesn't look very old."

"No kidding. Wow. I'll have to ask Cubbage what he knows. She's a nice kid. I liked her. Hope she's not having too rough a time. You didn't talk to her?"

"No. I, uhh, I didn't get the impression she recognized me. No reason she should."

Merow was silent for a second. "Seems like she ought to. I mean, a week of classes . . . you don't look much different. It hasn't been that long. And she's a reporter. Let me talk to Cubbage a second."

"Huh? Why? It's no big deal."

"No, you've got me curious now. Hang on."

Zach found himself listening to Muzak. He stood there holding the phone, feeling like an idiot, knowing he ought to be working, wondering why he'd mentioned her to Merow. Why he'd called Merow at all. He hadn't really had anything to say to him.

Her own home in Sand Creek. Maybe she'd lost it. But what about the furniture? And he hadn't seen the short black girl since the day they'd moved in. Maybe she'd just been helping.

Merow came back on. "Cubbage says it isn't her. Jes is still in Sand Creek. He talked to her yesterday. And he's pretty sure she doesn't have any baby. I'm pretty sure he'd know if she did. Must be someone who looks like her."

"Yeah, I guess so. Maybe it's someone I met somewhere else. Or a different person from back then."

"Describe her again."

He did so.

"Sounds like Jes, all right. Nobody else around here I can think of. But apparently it ain't Jes. Sorry."

"For what? Doesn't matter to me. Just one of those, you know . . ."

"Yeah. Sure."

"Well," he said. "Sorry to bother you. Guess I'm just avoiding work."

"Hey, no problem. Always glad to avoid a little myself."

After he'd hung up, he sat in front of the computer feeling vaguely like a fool. It ought to be good news that this woman wasn't someone he knew, after all. But he felt stupidly disappointed. He sighed heavily and punched up the COBOL program he was still struggling with.

2

Once he was in the hotel room, alone at last after the airports and planes and taxis and clerks and bellboys and the crowded glass elevator rising far up above the lobby and the flagstone courtyard, Lassiter took off his jacket and walked to the big window with the little decorative balcony outside, sixteen floors above the strange city streets. He was a man who knew his own city better than any taxi driver, who had gotten used to not having to think where or how to find whatever or whomever he wanted. Here, he wouldn't be able to get a bottle of aspirin without asking some stranger's help.

He opened the big sliding window, but the wind that came in was hot and damp, and he closed it again, then closed the curtains as well and sat down on the bed beside the telephone. All he had was the name of a man he'd never spoken to and had seen only once. All he knew about the man was that he was an agent with the federal bureau of Alcohol, Tobacco and Firearms, that he was based in Atlanta, and that he was now living with Lassiter's wife. Lassiter didn't want to talk to him, and he wasn't sure what he'd say if the man answered.

When he picked up the telephone and punched the buttons, though, Kay answered.

"Hi. This is me. I need to talk to you."

"Floyd? Where are you?"

"At the Hyatt, downtown."

"Downtown Atlanta?"

"Yeah."

"You should have called, Floyd."

"I didn't want you to tell me not to come. I need to talk to you in person."

She was silent.

"Not about us," he said. "About me."

"Can't you talk to Jerry?"

"Not about this. You're the only one."

He heard her sigh. "The Hyatt?"

"Yeah."

"Be out front. Green Jeep Cherokee. Thirty minutes."

"Thanks, Kay."

"Better be good." She hung up.

The last phrase stayed in his mind. He knew she meant that what he wanted to talk about had better be worth the trouble, but she could also have meant him—that he'd better be good.

Overall, the call left him feeling hopeful. She'd spoken like the woman who'd been his partner, before their marriage. That was the one he needed to talk to. He missed that woman, and he hadn't known until his wife left him that he'd been missing her for a long time.

The Jeep was dark green and shiny, with a new-car smell.

"Nice," he said, climbing in. "New?"

"New to me."

He decided not to pursue that. There'd be land-mines everywhere, and he wasn't great at spotting them. When in doubt, keep quiet.

She pulled past the entrance to the underground parking lot and on around the curve to the exit, where she leaned out slightly to watch for a break in the traffic.

"So we're gonna ride around and talk?" Lassiter asked.

"No. We're going somewhere."

He digested that. It made him feel vaguely uneasy, but he didn't know why. They rode in silence for a while, and he thought of something else to ask. "What's Atlanta like?"

"Not as bad as I thought. I thought, with the high percentage of blacks, you know, there'd be more tension. More trouble. But it's not like the North. It's kind of friendly and laid-back. 'Course, it's still the South. And the humidity sucks."

They were silent again for a while. "You working?" he asked.

She hesitated, then said, "No. I mean, not a regular job. I did another . . . you know . . ."

She meant an undercover assignment for the feds. That's what she'd been doing, on loan from the WPD to the ATF for a sting of gun traffickers, when she'd met the agent she was living with now. He'd been posing as a buyer for some weirdo right-wing military group, and she'd posed as his wife. The bureau had rented an old house on the west side, near Friends University, and they'd moved in there together, full-time. Kay had made a point of telling Lassiter later that there'd been nothing between them for a long time. He believed her. He didn't see what difference it made. The truth was, it hadn't occurred to him to worry about it, and he knew that was part of the problem. Even when the pretend marriage was still a pretense in every way, it must have seemed to Kay more like a real marriage than the one she had.

"You planning to find something?" he asked.

She was silent for so long he thought she wasn't going to answer, that he'd asked the wrong thing. "I'm working on it," she said at last.

He knew she meant she hadn't decided yet. It was what she'd always said when they'd worked together. It also meant: Shut up about it.

"You left some stuff I thought you might want," he said. "I mean, like some kitchen stuff . . . and there's that little computer—"

"I've got a new one. Keep it all, Floyd. Or do whatever you want with it. Anything I haven't missed by now, I don't need."

He nodded, having run out of topics, and watched the city go by. Through the window of the plane, coming

down, Atlanta had looked to him like a place built in
the middle of a forest, a vast clearing filled with buildings
and people. And at ground level, there was a moist
lushness that penetrated even the air-conditioned vehi-
cle. As if the forest were still right here, waiting to
take back that stolen patch of itself.

"Margaret Mitchell is buried here," Kay said. Lassiter saw that they were turning through a narrow
stone gateway into what looked at first like a park but
turned out to be a cemetery. The road looked more
like a service road than a public drive. It ran up a
short hill, turned sharply and followed the crest for a
while, then went down the other side to a lower level
of older graves, so old that some of the taller ones
were leaning. At one point Kay had to slow down and
edge past a corner of one of them to avoid scraping
the Jeep. The stones were also crowded in so tightly
that there wasn't any room to mow, and the grass was
high and thick in the narrow spaces between them.

Then they curved past a thick cluster of the tall old
stones and emerged into a section so different it was
as if they'd gone through some invisible gate into a
different world. Here, rows of small white markers,
their tops and sides discolored by time and weather,
stretched off as far as he could see, perhaps forever.
The grass here was cut close and neat, like a smooth
green garment lying over the earth.

"This is the Civil War part," Kay said. She pulled
off the road, then turned off the engine and got out.

Lassiter got out, too. The sun was low in the sky,
reminding him that it was later in the day than it felt
like to him. There was a palpable quiet that he didn't
think had existed before, a sort of smothering of the
distant growls and beeps of traffic he could still hear.
A few scattered visitors—the first other people he'd
noticed—wandered here and there, none near enough
to hear anything they said. He understood at last,
and smiled.

He followed her to a bench of white stone facing
the rows of graves, and sat down beside her, a space

between them, feeling a pleasant touch of cool in the wind. He felt again that this was right, that everything could be right again. He found himself looking at a particular gravestone right in front of him. The inscription read: JOHN L. WALKER, SEPT. 1, 1864. And under that: 9 KANS.

"Public but private," he said, taking his eyes away from the stone, looking at the other people wandering among the rows of graves. "Which one is him?"

"He's behind us. Don't look."

He wouldn't have anyway. He watched her raise one hand above her head, hold it there for a split second, then smooth her hair back.

"What was that?"

"Everything's fine, go on home."

"And he will?"

"He better." She looked at him. "I came here to talk about you, not him."

"Right." He looked down at his hands, marshalling his thoughts. He'd thought about how to tell it the whole way, on the plane, but now he thought about it again. "Okay. There's this guy killed his wife, beat her to death. We knew him already, 'cause he sent her to the emergency ward four times before. That we know of. But she'd never cooperate, you know? And the D.A.'s office wouldn't do anything if she didn't. Thing is, these people, they're . . ." He hesitated. "You know the kind of people nowadays, call themselves Christians, and they're all involved in politics."

"They're everywhere, Floyd."

"Yeah. Well, that was part of it, 'cause these kinds of people support the D.A., you know? And they don't like spousal abuse—I mean, they like to think it doesn't really happen. You know. And the D.A. doesn't want to piss them off, unless she's got the goods. So, okay. I know how that works. But now he's fucking killed her. Jerry and me, we really wanted to nail this guy. I mean . . . you know how most of these guys, afterward, they're *so* sorry and they'll *never* do it again and—" He hacked and spat. "But this guy's even worse. He's not sorry. Because he was the master of the house and she did something wrong."

"She provoked it," Kay said.

"Right. Same old excuse. Except religious. God approves. The problem was, the wife bought this herself, which was why she wouldn't help us."

"*That* almost makes you feel she deserved it."

"Nobody deserves that, Kay. So anyway, now she's dead, but to the husband it's just . . . it's not a big difference. Just another beating, just happened to wind up with her dead, instead of just having some broken bones."

"Jesus. Didn't the guy even—?"

"Oh, he *loved* her. Of course. He's very, very sad that's she's dead . . . that God saw fit to call her home, is what he says. But it wasn't his fault. He was just doing what he was supposed to do. And she's not really dead. She's with the angels now. He'll see her again when God calls him home."

"Any jury's gonna listen to stuff like that and bury the asshole," Kay said. "What's the problem?"

"Well, for one thing, they only get to listen to stuff like that if the defense attorney lets the guy take the stand, and anybody who did should be disbarred. But we felt pretty good. The D.A.'s office was with us now. You know. He crossed the line. It's almost all women over there now. So Jerry and me are pretty sure we got him. We're doing all the stuff, dotting the *i*'s, nailing it down. We hear the guy's lawyer is talking negligent homicide, max, and we laugh, 'cause we're thinking that's the minimum, with what we got."

"So . . ."

"So then these fucking so-called Christians get into it. All of a sudden there's this story going around that the doctor on call in the emergency ward that night was an abortionist. Like that has anything to do with anything, even if it's true, which it isn't. I mean, she went to St. Joe's, for christsake. They're gonna have an abortionist on call? In fact, the woman who was on call that night is a pro-lifer. But for some reason she didn't see any need to make any great effort to point out the mistake. Neither did the newspaper, for that matter. Once these things get going, once it's a controversy . . ."

"It didn't used to be that way," Kay said.

"I know. It used to be, somebody says the sky is red, the newspaper and the TV and everybody else would say, well, actually, it's blue. But nowadays it's like, okay, some people think it's red, some people think it's blue. Anyway, all of a sudden everybody in town is arguing about whether she really died from the beating or was actually killed by some mysterious abortionist doctor working in the emergency room of a Catholic hospital, in order to . . . what? Frame the husband and make Christians look bad? It's completely crazy, but everybody's talking about it like it's serious. I mean, yeah, sure, there are some people that write letters to the editor and say, Hey, this is fucking crazy. But right next to 'em is another letter saying the sky is red." He shrugged.

"So the D.A. . . . ?"

"The D.A. backs off big-time. They drop the charge down to assault. Too much 'reasonable doubt' on the murder, one of 'em tells me. Can you believe that? Her husband beats the shit out of her—he cops to that; hell, he's proud of it—and she dies in the emergency room, at St. Joe's, with a doctor who's a pro-lifer. But there's reasonable doubt that he killed her."

"No jury—"

"It ain't the juries anymore, Kay. It's the voters." He fell silent, then shook his head and gave a soft laugh. "I try not to even think about all this shit," he said. "Sometimes nowadays I think maybe I'm not so crazy, after all. Maybe everybody else is."

Kay didn't smile. "So what happened, Floyd?"

He didn't answer for a moment, then sighed and said, "We're having this meeting in Loomis's office. Me and Jerry and Loomis and the ADA they sent over to take the roasting."

"Who?"

"Strickland."

"Oh. She's not bad."

"No. She's fine usually. I really got nothing against Strickland. It wasn't *her* idea. But they sent her over instead of her boss, to let Loomis tear somebody a new asshole, and he's doing it. Actually, he's mostly talking about her boss, but she's the one catching it, so . . . She's sitting there with her lips all tight, you know? And her jaw stuck out. I was kind of feeling sorry for her. Jerry isn't. I can tell he wants to jump in. But . . . you know. It don't mean nothing in the end. Nothing really changes."

"Especially you, Floyd."

He glanced at her, saw that she wasn't being mean, and smiled. "Yeah. So after a while Strickland figures she's taken enough and she starts coming back at Loomis. You know, cops fucked it up. Never really had a case in the first place. You know. I'm not even listening, really. But then all of a sudden, I still don't know why, she's looking right at *me*. I'm like, huh? And she starts saying something about how maybe if we still had as many female detectives—"

"The fucking bitch!"

Lassiter gave a startled laugh. "I know what you're thinking. Jerry and Loomis thought the same thing. But see, it didn't hit me that way at all. I mean, it wasn't until later, when Jerry started talking about it—"

"You're so smart," Kay said. "And you're so dumb."

"Yeah, I know. Anyway, what I thought . . . I mean, the way I reacted, was not like it had anything to do with, you know. You and me. I thought she was saying something about me, like I didn't care about it, something like that. Me in particular. Like I just didn't care about this woman getting killed by her husband, so I hadn't really—"

"Jesus!" Kay said. "She knows better than that. Strickland knows you."

"Well, I guess . . . she wasn't thinking about it that way, either. She was trying to say something like what you first thought, that it was my fault that you weren't here anymore, and so we didn't have as many female detectives as we—"

"It all comes down to the same thing," Kay said. "She was saying that because you're a man—"

"Yeah. But not me. Not Floyd Lassiter personally. She didn't mean it that way. But that's how I took it. I mean, men in general, I might agree with her a little. Overall, you know."

"I know. It was a bad mistake. I'll bet she knew it as soon as she said it, too." She gave him a worried look. "So what did you do?"

He took a breath. "Well, next thing I know, I'm on my feet, yelling. Screaming. I think I just kind of stuttered for a while, but then I got into it, and . . . actually, I don't remember what I said. I don't really remember the whole thing very well, you know?"

"You were having one of your . . ."

"I don't know. I don't think so. Not right then. Later I had a big one, though. Major league."

"The same day?"

"Yeah. That evening, at home."

"But of course you didn't do anything about it. You didn't go see a neurologist."

He shrugged, remained silent. It was an old thing between them. She already knew his arguments.

"Okay," she said after a moment. "I'm sorry. Go on."

"Well, one good thing is, I was backing up all the time," Lassiter said. "All the way to the wall, across from the door. It was like . . . part of me was still just watching, was just as surprised as everybody else. They were all staring at me, you know? Even Strickland. I mean, she didn't say anything back, you know? I mean, she was scared." He stopped, thinking about that. She'd been afraid of him. Then he said, "I don't know. It just seemed to go on by itself, like I was standing back watching . . . but I was moving backward . . ."

"You were getting yourself away from her so you wouldn't do anything," Kay said.

"Yeah, I think that's right. It's almost like three people. There's this one that's shouting and out of control, and there's this other one—which is me—just standing there watching and not able to do anything. And then there's this other one . . . you know, grabbing the one that's out of control and pushing him back." He laughed. "Crazy."

Kay wasn't smiling. "You didn't really do anything, though?"

"No . . . well, I broke Loomis's phone. Threw it against the wall."

She did laugh at that. "Jesus, Floyd."

Lassiter gave a sheepish smile, then sobered. "Really, the worst thing was what happened next, though."

"Happened next? Christ, what was it?"

He found himself looking at the Walker headstone again, thinking about the Kansas boy who'd died so far from home, probably a farm boy. He lifted his eyes from the stone and looked at all the rest of them, the endless rows, like rows of corn or wheat.

"Floyd?"

He looked at her, traced quickly back to what he'd been about to say to her. "All of a sudden I started crying," he said. It didn't have the kind of force he felt it ought to have. Didn't sound like as big a thing as it been, as it still felt like. But he could see by Kay's face that she understood, as even Jerry wouldn't have. This was why he'd come to see her, he realized. Because she'd understand this part. "It caught me completely by surprise," he said. "Just like the shouting part did. One second I'm standing with my back to the wall, screaming at Strickland, everybody staring at me like they don't know whether to call for reinforcements or pull their weapons or what." He smiled, then said, "And then the next second I'm sitting on the floor crying. Sobbing. Hell. And it just went on and on, exactly the same way. I just had to wait till it wore itself out before I could get control again. That's when Strickland left, I guess. She wasn't there anymore when I could see again. I was expecting her to really . . ."

"She knew she'd made a mistake," Kay said grimly. Something in the way she said it made him feel he didn't quite understand it—something between her and Strickland, or because they were both women.

"Anyway, then Jerry came over, but he didn't know what to do, you know?" He laughed, but realized with surprise that there were tears in his eyes now, and that Kay had taken one of his hands in hers. Really crazy, he thought. Maybe he shouldn't be a cop anymore. But then what would he do with the rest of his life?

"So what did happen?" Kay asked.

"Oh, not that much, really, considering. Loomis told me he thought I ought to take my vacation time. I had fifteen days saved up."

"He didn't suggest a doctor?"

"Sure, he did. But you know I can't do that."

"Floyd, I know you have to do it sooner or later. You know it, too."

Loomis shrugged. This was an old thing, and there was no point in getting into it now. "He meant a shrink," he said.

"A shrink. A neurologist. A G.P. You gotta start somewhere."

"Look, Kay . . . What good's it gonna do me to see any of them if I can't tell them everything?"

"It's confidential."

"You know that's not the problem Anyway, sometimes things get out, even when it's confidential."

"Floyd . . ."

"Anyway, I can't afford a shrink, and I'm sure as hell not going to talk to one who works for the department."

"That's paranoia, Floyd. Dr. Alvarez works for the insurance company, if he works for anybody, not the department. But I mean, he works for you, the patient."

"Whatever."

She was silent for a moment, knowing he didn't
want to go any further with that. Finally she said,
"Floyd, did you really come down here to get my
advice, or just so you'd have somebody to listen to
you yap about this?"

He thought about that, smiling a little. Kay always
asked good questions. Maybe it was her questions he'd
come to hear.

Instead of answering what she'd asked, he said, "I'm
supposed to go talk to Loomis when my vacation time
is up. There's a chance he'll say don't come back. But
I don't know what to do about it."

"Yes, you do."

He sighed, not saying anything, looking off at the
rows of graves again. There was something he liked
about them, something that made him feel calmer.
Safer.

"Let me suggest something," Kay said.

"Shoot." It was what he'd have said when they were
working together.

"Okay. I know you can afford to pay for a visit to
a regular doctor. Dr. Dreier . . . or if you don't want
to go to him, find somebody else. Just a regular G.P.
Just tell him about the thing in Loomis's office and
your episodes, whatever they are."

"I know what they are. Temporal-lobe seizures."

"And when did you get your M.D.?"

"I've studied it, on the Internet. And I know what
my symptoms are, better than any doctor. See, they're
all in my head. I mean, a doctor can't see them. And,
anyway, that doesn't necessarily have anything to do
with—"

"Oh, bullshit. You know that's bullshit. You said it
was a bad one."

"Yeah, but . . . it wasn't any different, really. I
mean, it was more . . . pronounced or something. But
it was the same old stuff, like I'm having a dream at
the same time I'm awake, and my mind is trying to
connect all the real stuff together with all the dream

stuff, and make it all make sense. So everything kind of reminds me of something, but then I can't figure out what it is, or if I can, it's more like something I dreamed once . . . and of course the trouble with words . . . but it went away, like they all do. And I was by myself, so—"

"You won't always be."

"Hell, I've had them when other people were around. I've had conversations with people. It always feels like maybe I'm using the wrong words, not making sense. But nobody notices anything. I've asked them. I've said, Hey, I was feeling a little nauseous, or a little dizzy, or something, when we were talking, and they say they didn't notice anything different. I had them with you, and you didn't know."

"I knew."

"Not always. You didn't—"

"I knew, Floyd. I didn't always say."

He shook his head. "I don't think so. I think there were times when you had no idea."

She closed her mouth, then said, "Did you have a blackout?"

"It's not a blackout," he said. "Drunks have blackouts. It's just sometimes there's a little blank place right there, where it was . . . at its peak, I guess . . ."

"Call it what you want. You do things and then you don't remember doing them. Like when you went out to get the mail after you'd already gotten it . . . and when you watched that baseball game and—"

"That wasn't the same thing. Anyway, what difference do those things make? It's just a little tiny spot, and I remember everything around it, and I've never had one on the job."

"All right. The main thing is—"

"The main thing is, if I got diagnosed officially with this shit, I wouldn't even be allowed to drive, let alone be a cop. That's the bottom line. I can't risk that. You know I can't."

She was silent for a moment. "You could drive

again if you were seizure-free for six months. That's the law in Kansas."

"Right. And how many months do I have to wait before the defense attorneys can't ask me about my seizures and memory lapses when I'm on the stand?"

She frowned. "There are other things—"

"Not for me. This is what I do."

She'd argued with him about that in the past, but this time she only sighed. Maybe she'd just remembered that she wasn't really his wife anymore.

"I do appreciate your advice, Kay," he said. "And I will think about everything you say. You know how I am. I like to play the devil's advocate."

She nodded. "There are other things you could stand to talk to somebody about, Floyd. I mean, somebody who knows something—"

"That was all in another life, a long time ago. It doesn't have anything to do with this stuff."

"You sure?"

"Yeah. This temporal-lobe stuff doesn't have anything to do with personal problems. It's just . . . in the brain, you know? It's physical."

"How do you know that what happened in Loomis's office had nothing to do with this other stuff?"

"I told you, later on I had—"

"Yeah. The blow-up caused an episode. But what caused the blow-up? And what were you crying about?"

He didn't say anything. He knew she was right. He didn't remember thinking about anything at all like that when he'd suddenly gone haywire and started shouting at Strickland, but just before he'd started crying, for no reason he could remember he'd had a sudden flash of the boy. The one he'd once been. And he'd suddenly felt terrified, as if what he was doing was making things worse for him, putting him in danger . . . and then he'd started bawling, as that boy had never done. "I don't know," he said.

She didn't push it. After a short silence he said, "It's starting to get dark. You better drive me back."

Riding back to the hotel through the gleaming lights of the nighttime city, he found himself becoming intensely aware of her physical presence, so near to him, in a way he didn't want. They'd ridden together just this way, mostly at night, for four years, and he'd never really felt that, not until after they'd married. Before then, that part of him had still been dormant, numbed, and he wanted to get back to that. He'd been content that way. Never being hurt that way, never hurting anyone else. Any shrink he talked to would try to talk him out of that, persuade him he should try to be normal. And there wouldn't be any way to answer that except by explaining why he wasn't normal, and never would be, and was happier that way.

At the hotel, Kay pulled into a space near the street, behind the taxis that lined the curving drive in front of the entrance, and left the engine running. Lassiter thanked her again and began to climb out, but she put a hand on his arm.

"Floyd," she said. "Are you going back in the morning?"

"Yeah. I just have to call the airline and get the flight time. No reason to hang around here. It's pretty expensive."

"So this is the last time we're ever gonna see each other."

"Most likely."

"Did we settle it? I mean, between us?"

He thought about it, then said, "Yeah, maybe so. That's funny . . ."

"I wish I could be sure. Did I ever tell you I was sorry?"

He thought about that. He couldn't remember. "I don't know. It doesn't matter."

"Yes it does. And I am sorry. I always will be. Because I really did love you, Floyd. I still do. Do you understand that? It's just . . ."

"Yeah, I think I understand. Really, I'm doing pretty good, Kay. I'm not angry at you or anything.

This other stuff . . ." He shrugged. "We should have stayed partners."

"Maybe. It would have been better for you. I really messed you up, didn't I?"

"Nah. I was already messed up. You know that."

She studied him and then said, "What if I came up to the room with you, for a while? To say good-bye."

He gave a soft, embarrassed laugh and looked away. "You don't owe me anything like that, Kay. Anyway—"

"What if I wanted to? What if I was the one who wanted it? Would it make things worse for you or better?"

He turned to stare at her, and remembered the way he'd felt with her sometimes, a way he'd never felt any time else in his life—the thing he was always going to miss, no matter how much he wanted not to. "Yes," he said, unable to remember exactly what her question had been, not even sure what he meant.

She released the emergency brake and drove past the taxis and the uniformed doormen and the well-dressed guests clustered beneath the light, toward the dark rectangle of the ramp to the parking garage.

3

Apparently the short black, impatient woman had just been helping with the move. As far as he could tell, there was no one but the woman who looked like Jes Wellington living over there with her baby. It seemed obvious to him now that she wasn't who he'd thought she was. There was a great resemblance, but . . . She'd changed her hair since moving in. It had been straight and black, not very long, the way he remembered Jes; now it was shorter and curly and blond, and that made it easier to see the difference. He'd never have made that mistake the way she looked now.

And she really was an ideal neighbor, by his standards. He rarely saw her at all except when she was going in and out of the garage. He hadn't noticed any visitors. Not that he was watching all the time. That was Mrs. Neuenswander's job. And he'd never heard the baby cry at all. In fact, his main impression about the woman was that she was a good mother, very involved with her baby, which he liked. She obviously didn't go out to work, so she either had money or worked at home, as he did. Probably the latter. Nobody with so much money they didn't have to work was going to live here. He found that he liked feeling kindly toward a neighbor who didn't want anything to do with him. He felt like the good guy, instead of the misanthrope.

When the weather finally turned warm in the spring, after the usual Kansas false alarms, she began coming outside occasionally with the baby, to sit on the porch or on a blanket in the yard in front of it. No nude sunbathing, or sunbathing of any kind, really. Mostly she wore sweats and T-shirts, just like himself, and had obviously come out to get some fresh air, for herself and the baby. She wasn't exactly voluptuous, anyway. Tall as she was, he and she could have worn each other's clothes—or at least she could have worn his, and she seemed to like loose, oversized garments.

Their relationship didn't change, of course. They didn't even look each other in the eye when they happened to be out at the same time. He wasn't tempting fate, and she seemed truly oblivious to his existence. That might have bothered him a little, except that she treated everyone that way. One day when she was out with the baby, Mrs. Neuenswander pounced, smiling, chattering, making overtures to the baby. He didn't hear what the baby's mother said, but Mrs. Neuenswander returned quickly to her own apartment, not smiling. Zach began to think he could take tips from his newest neighbor.

That wasn't really why he took to watching her now and then, looking down through the horizontal blinds, poised to back away quickly if she started to look up. She never did, though. She either had no idea he was watching her, or didn't care. It wasn't really spying. He just enjoyed watching her with the baby, the way they interacted, which seemed a little odd but which pleased him in some peculiar way. It was the way she talked to the baby, and the way the baby watched her as she did. He couldn't hear anything she said, and wasn't interested in trying. Whatever it was, she spoke to her baby as if they were having a real adult-type conversation and she expected the baby to respond. And the baby seemed to be listening seriously and considering a response, just waiting for a chance to break in.

Zach's father had been a bomber pilot who'd disappeared in Vietnam several months after he'd been born. His older sisters remembered their father in varying degrees, of course, but he knew him only as photos on his mother's bedroom wall and his oldest sister's dresser. His mother never talked much about that time, and he'd never really thought about it much. Watching the woman across the way talking so seriously to her baby—and seeming so confident on her own, so self-sufficient—made him imagine that she was telling the baby all about the father who wasn't there, all the serious, private things that she herself wanted to remember but that you couldn't really say to a child old enough to understand them. He liked imagining that his own mother had told him such things once, that it might all still be in there somewhere.

He knew it was fantasy. His mother's situation had almost surely been very different from this woman's. Although of course he didn't know what her situation was. There were people today who'd find fault just with what he could see—the absence of a man, the peculiar closeness between the reclusive mother and her baby, what could easily look like an unhealthy obsession. There was a part of himself that was troubled by the obvious fact that the two were each other's whole world. But there was another part of himself that liked it. Envied it.

Fantasizing about his own past that way, he began really to think about his future for the first time. He guessed the baby's mother was about his own age, but watching her he felt much older. He could see himself, twenty or thirty years in the future, as if it were next week, sitting there in this same place, wearing ragged sweats, or no longer bothering to dress at all, drinking one Dr Pepper after another, eating chips out of the bag and tuna out of the can, sliding the mouse around, pecking at the keyboard, squinting at the screen. And content. How could that be? He didn't think it could, really. It was just that he couldn't really imagine anything else.

4

He took Kay's advice and made an appointment
with a regular doctor, but he didn't know if he'd
go or not. It was set for the week after he was supposed to see Loomis again, so he could tell Loomis
he had it, if the subject came up. If everything just
went back to normal, he might cancel it. He could
also tell Loomis he'd gone to Atlanta and talked to
Kay, and make it sound like he'd sorted things out.

He decided to spend the rest of his "vacation"
doing the things he'd been putting off at the two
houses he owned. At the place where he and Kay had
lived, where he still slept most of the time, he began
throwing out things from the marriage, rearranging
furniture, making it more his own place. At the big
old ranch-style house his mother had sold him for a
dollar when she was still enough in her right mind, he
finished some of the things he'd begun right after
she'd gone to the nursing home, then abandoned when
Kay left. There were black plastic bags sitting in the
garage, filled up and tied, ready for the junkyard or
the Salvation Army. There were all the small, broken
things his mother had let go during the last months
she'd lived there. The built-in dishwasher, for instance,
obviously hadn't been working for a long time, although he remembered seeing his mother put things
in it after meals Kay and he had eaten there. He supposed she'd taken everything out again after they were
gone, and washed them by hand. She'd had that kind
of crazy slyness. Had it all her life, really. It wasn't
her real problem, any more than Kay was his.

The main level—the living room and dining room—was mostly empty. He and Kay had taken the better pieces to the other house, sold some of the others along with their own. But the kitchen and bedrooms were pretty much as they'd been. Decisions would have to be made, but he wasn't ready for that yet. He only wanted to do the mindless things that filled time, like carrying bags of trash to the dump, fixing running toilets.

He began sleeping there more often, rather than drive all the way back across town. The utilities were still connected, but there was no phone and no TV cable. He sort of liked the absence of a telephone, and he didn't care about the TV. It occurred to him that nobody at the department—not even Jerry—even knew he owned this place.

He slept not in one of the bedrooms on the upper level, but in the little storage room next to the garage, on the lowest level, that had been converted to a sickroom when his father had been dying. Placed there to be put out easily, when the time came, like the bags of trash. His mother had said it was so that she could get him into the car, if necessary, if he had to go to the hospital, and maybe she believed that. Lassiter liked the other reason better. It made him sort of like the room.

There was no longer a bed—his mother had junked it almost as soon as Jake Lassiter's body no longer occupied it—so he wrestled one of the twin-size beds down from the guest room, walking the mattress and then box springs awkwardly along the hall and then down the two short half flights of stairs, across the landing at the middle, past the kitchen, and back up along the long hallway to the garage. He never even considered leaving it in the guest bedroom and sleeping in it there, surrounded by his mother's powdery-smelling frills and hangings. One of the things he liked about the downstairs room, with its concrete-block walls, was that there was still a faint antiseptic smell from the scrubbing his mother had given it after his

father's death. It was the one room in the house
washed completely clean of his parents. Besides the
bed, all he needed was a chair from the kitchen and
a card table to set things on—the extra change of
clothing and toiletries he brought from the other
place.

Then a few days before the meeting with Loomis—
which was by then feeling more like a dental appointment—he found a message from Loomis on the answering machine at the other house, asking him to
come in whenever he could.

He listened to it three times, trying to figure out
whether it was good or bad, whether Loomis needed
him for something, or had simply decided to get it
over with and ask for his badge.

It made him feel dizzy, almost as if he were having
one of his episodes, although he knew he wasn't. Probably just hyperventilating. He sat down in a chair and
leaned forward, cupping his nose and mouth with his
hands until the feeling went away, and then grabbed
the phone before he could think about it anymore,
and dialed Loomis's office number.

"Hey, thanks for calling right back, Floyd," Loomis
said. "I'm sorry to interrupt your vacation, but I need
your help with something. Any chance you could come
in sometime today, so we could talk about it? If you
can't . . ."

"No—no," Lassiter stammered. "I mean, sure I can.
I'll come in right now."

"Great."

He felt buoyed, hopeful—and also afraid of the feeling. He did something he hadn't meant to do. He
called Jerry.

He'd told himself he didn't want to bother Jerry,
didn't want to foist his problems on him. But really
he was afraid of learning that Jerry was working with
a new partner. He was more afraid of that than he'd
ever been of Kay leaving him for another man.

Jerry sounded glad to hear from him, and even
thought he might know what it was about. "There was

an APB on the wire from L.A. . . . that Art Theft
Detail they have, that sends across the bulletins with
all the pictures . . . some hooker ripped off a bunch
of rich old Hollywood-type guys . . . jewelry and artwork and stuff like that."

Lassiter frowned. "Yeah? So what's that got to do
with Robbery/Homicide?"

"Nothing. No particular reason to think she's even
from around here, near as I can tell. I mean, as if
she'd come back here anyway. You know she's sitting
on a beach right now in Tahiti or the Caymans or
somewhere. But I guess they think she's from this part
of the country—Kansas, Iowa, something like that."

"I still don't get it."

"Yeah, well, there's some kind of pressure coming
down. Don't know from where, exactly. Somebody
important wants it checked out, seriously. Probably
somebody that knows one of these old farts. Anyway,
Loomis wound up with it."

"How come?"

"SID had it first, but near as I can tell, all they did
was take a look at the mug and decide they didn't
know her. They did order a copy of the video it came
from. Been showing it the last couple of weeks to
everybody in the law enforcement community. Most
of the lawyers and media, too, I think. Biggest thing
since they got hold of that one of the TV news lady
and her cameraman a few years ago. Better, too."

"Are they dubbing it, like they did that one, and
spreading it around?" Lassiter asked. "If she's from
around here, maybe somebody'll recognize her."

"Don't know about that. My guess is, the LAPD's
getting a lot of requests for copies from the departments in this area. You can tell the mug is a video
still, and . . . it's head-and-shoulders, but you can kind
of tell she's naked . . . and there's this white blur
behind her—looks airbrushed—that's gotta be part of
a naked guy sitting on a bed."

"So she was a porn actress?"

"A private one, I guess. Just her and the old gomer

who hired her, acting out his old junior high fantasies, you know?"

"The media's seeing it? I haven't seen a story."

"A select few."

"Like your girlfriend?"

"She's not . . ." Jerry made an exasperated sound. It was an old thing, but he always reacted that way, which Lassiter guessed meant that he wished it were true. "But, yeah, she saw it," Jerry said. "Not exactly news, I don't think, unless she turns out to be a local girl." He was silent for a moment. "So, anyway, the chief took it away from Special Investigations and dumped it on Loomis."

"Who happened to have a detective he wasn't using at the moment," Lassiter said.

"Yeah, that's about it, I guess. But you know, it could be an opportunity to show what a hell of a detective you are. Even without my able assistance. The thing is, nobody expects you to find her. You just go out and turn the town upside down and file a report that shows you looked under every rock, and she's not here. Something that makes the pressure go away, and Loomis loves you forever. And if you found her . . . Jesus. You'd probably get a movie deal. I'm beginning to think I'd like a shot at it myself."

Lassiter laughed. It was the first time he'd laughed in a long time. Jerry was one of the few people in the world who could always make him laugh. Kay had once been another. "It's my big break at last."

"Seriously, Floyd. It's a fat pitch. Knock it out of the fucking park and let's get back to work, okay?"

Lassiter felt dizzy with relief again. Let's get back to work. Loomis hadn't given him another partner yet.

"More I think about it," Jerry said, "it's right in your ballpark. All puzzle, no perp."

That was a small, familiar dig at his tendency to become more involved with the one than the other. The reason he needed someone like Kay or Jerry to remind him what they were doing and to keep him on the right path. Even that gave him a tug of pleasure.

"But what if that isn't what Loomis called me about?"
he asked.

"Well, then you're fucked, Floyd. What can I say?"

Loomis started by asking him how things were, and
Lassiter gave his little prepared speech. Got a doctor's
appointment, went to Atlanta and talked to Kay, starting to get on top of it, eager to get back to work. The
conversation with Jerry had buoyed him up enough
that he even thought it sounded convincing.

"Glad it's working out," Loomis said. "I thought it
would. These things are always tough. I know that
myself." He shook his head. "You want to know why
I called you." Lassiter had noticed the accordion
folder lying in front of Loomis, but hadn't been in
position to see what the label was. Loomis pushed it
across the desk toward him. "All in there," he said.

The name on the file was MUNDY, CELESTE. It wasn't
as thick as he'd thought. Most of the bulk came from
the videotape cassette wedged into the bottom.

"It's bullshit," Loomis said. "I'll tell you that right
out front. If you'd been working—" He shrugged. "I
don't know what I'd've done with it. Maybe worked
it myself. Thing is, it's got weight behind it. Chief gave
it to me himself, said it's got to go to a good detective
who takes it seriously."

The compliment warmed him, but Lassiter didn't
show it. He scanned the original LAPD bulletin, saw
nothing important that Jerry hadn't told him. Nothing
to suggest why they thought she was from around
here. They seemed to think there might be other victims who hadn't come forward, and they'd recovered
only about half the stolen goods, from fences in the
L.A. area.

"All I'm gonna ask you to do is what the chief
said," Loomis said. "Take it seriously." He paused.
"And then give me a report I can give to the chief
to shove up the ass of whoever thinks this is worth
our time."

Lassiter smiled, nodded. The woman in the glossy

version of the mug shot was facing the camera, but
not looking directly at it. Bare-shouldered, as Jerry
had said. She looked like she was headed past the
camera, maybe to adjust it. He pulled the video loose,
saw nothing written on it. "I heard about this," he
said.

Loomis made an annoyed sound. "I'm surprised you
haven't seen it. You're probably the only cop within
five counties who hasn't."

"I heard it was SID that had it. They get anything
at all?"

Loomis shook his head. "There's a list in there of
the hookers they said they showed the mug to. Maybe
they did."

"I'll start there," Lassiter said. "I'll try to find her."

"If you do, you can have my job, and I'll go on
vacation." He gave Lassiter a lopsided smile. "Take
as long as you need. You'll get the vacation time back.
And I know you'll do a good job, Floyd. I appreciate
you doing me this favor. I'll owe you."

Loomis looked at him, smiled faintly himself. "Better wait till I do it."

Loomis nodded but said, "That other stuff you
mentioned . . . I have a feeling everything's gonna
be fine."

For some reason, instead of reassuring Lassiter, that
gave him a hollow, frightened feeling, in the pit of his
stomach. Because Loomis had no idea what his real
problems were. He'd lived with them a long time—
some as long as he could remember—and had kept
them from intruding until that moment when they'd
exploded out of him, here in this same office. How
lucky it had been, when he thought about it, that his
wife had left him so recently, providing that ready-
made explanation.

He put the folder under his arm, stood up. "You
want me to work it out of the office, like normal?
That might be . . ."

"A little awkward. I know. Nah, it's up to you. You
want to, that's fine. You want to work it on your own,

just check in when you need something, that's fine, too. It's not like there's any urgency about it. If she's around here at all, she's probably been here since October."

"October?" He hadn't paid attention to the dates in the material he'd glanced at.

"Yeah. That's when she split L.A. Far as they know, anyway. Last time anyone saw her, that they know of." He gave a grunt of humorless laughter. "It's a little stale. Oh, by the way, there might be a P.I. or two show up, working for the insurance companies. They've only found about half the stuff, and some of it's pretty valuable. I'll let you know if any of 'em check in here."

He decided to use his mother's house as his office for the investigation. There wasn't any telephone, so nobody could reach him there—but he liked that. It would be him and the case—him and the woman he was looking for.

His mother's house fit very well, now that he was the only one in it. It was screened off from the rest of Wichita, one of three big old ranch-style houses around a roughly circular lane, widely separated from one another inside a thick ring of cedars. There were two open places in the trees, like tunnels leading in, and neither was where it would be easily noticed from the outside if you weren't looking for it. The oddest thing was that the three houses faced outward, into the cedars. The front door of Lassiter's mother's house was unusable, and the concrete porch had been removed long ago, leaving the door hanging high on the wall with the nearest branches scratching it. The circular lane that provided access to the houses was really a kind of alley, running around behind them, visited daily by the mail carrier and weekly by a city garbage truck. The mailboxes were out there now, but the garages still faced the other way, toward the original front, and new driveways had been built from turnaround circles in front of each garage, running back along the side of the building to the sand lane.

It had all been a mystery when his family had first moved here, but later, when he'd come back to Wichita to join the P.D., it had taken him half an hour at the courthouse to solve it. The original three families had all been related to one another, and the three houses had been far outside the city, with a road running around the front, the enclosed rear area providing a kind of courtyard, for gatherings and for the playground equipment, some of which could still be found, rusted, inside the wild growth at the center of the circle. When the expanding city had begun to reach them, they'd put in the nearly impenetrable ring of trees, built the driveway extensions, sealed themselves off—and then finally abandoned the place altogether, vanishing from the county's records like the cliff dwellers from Southwestern canyons, as the grid of ordinary streets had enveloped them. Lassiter thought there might be people living in those shabby little houses—old themselves now—who had no idea there was anything inside these trees but more trees. That's how it looked from the outside.

At any rate, it was ideal for his purposes. The house was mostly empty, but he didn't need much. He brought the VCR over from the other house, to look at the video from L.A., hooking it to the little TV from his mother's bedroom on the upper level, moving that and its wooden stand down to his basement room. There was no cable—not even rabbit ears—and even the local stations were only grainy patches of moving gray smears. But he didn't care about that. He only wanted to see the video.

And as it turned out he didn't watch much of that—only enough to feel reasonably fairly sure he'd recognize Celeste Mundy if he saw her. He'd never been much for porn anyway, and mixed with violence, as this one was, it interested him even less. It was helpful, because you always got a better idea of what someone really looked like seeing them in motion than you did from a static mug shot. It would have been more helpful, for his purposes, if she'd kept her clothes on longer. People didn't look the same naked.

He could tell that his marriage had changed things, though. There'd been a time when he'd really been indifferent to such videos—when he'd still been in that gray, neutral, safe place where he'd lived, inside himself, for so long, before Kay had drawn him out.

He didn't feel quite that way now, after spending those few years sleeping beside a woman. It wasn't that the video filled him with lust. It made him feel edgy and apprehensive, almost panicky, as if something terrible that he couldn't name were about to happen.

That might have been partly because of the video's quality. Or rather Celeste Mundy's. Not that she was beautiful or voluptuous—far from it. But she was completely convincing. He could see that the man was acting, mouthing lines he'd memorized. But when she spoke he became less sure that it was a scripted fake. It made for an odd, kaleidoscopic sense of the real and the phony intertwined, so that it became more and more difficult to tell which was which, to be sure he knew what he was seeing. No doubt that also had something to do with the uneasiness that grew in him as he watched it, finally forcing him to turn it off and go back to studying the material Loomis had given him.

He could see why the insurance companies were still after her. At a conservative estimate, the stuff she'd taken would have netted her more than a couple hundred thousand, even with the deep discount—like 90 percent sometimes—that most fences required. There was between one and two million dollars in stolen goods—mostly jewelry and artwork—out there somewhere. Maybe not much, all told, by Beverly Hills standards—but enough to make it worth the insurers' while to get it back. It also meant she'd probably had enough to go anywhere she wanted. The odds she'd picked Wichita were pretty slim.

He started with the prostitutes. He was mildly familiar with that world, not so much from the brief period he'd spent in Special Investigations in the sixties—that had been mostly narcotics work—but from questioning prostitutes in connection with armed robberies and homicides. Mostly, of course, he was familiar with the streetwalkers, and the brothel in the northeast part of town that was only a small step up. Those were the women who tended to pick up the most useful information—criminals who'd just made a big score often celebrated by patronizing them, and a surprising number of them seemed to think there was some sort of hooker confidentiality. Or maybe they just forgot there was anyone there listening. And the women they dealt with were also the ones with the most to gain by having a cop for a friend.

He knew little about the high-class circles of the call girls, especially those who worked the big hotels—still less the rarefied atmosphere in which Celeste Mundy had worked. That was a different world. There were few pimps. Many of the women were self-employed entrepreneurs—some with entirely legitimate lives as housewives, students and businesswomen. They didn't socialize much with one another, nor were they interested in talking to a cop (unless it was one they were paying off, which you heard about now and then). Like any other entrepreneurs they hooked into a distribution and merchandising network—if not an actual out-call service, then bellhops, taxi drivers, hotel clerks . . . That was just a part of their overhead.

The odds of any of the streetwalkers knowing anything about Celeste Mundy were pretty slim, but no smaller than the odds that she was even in Wichita, and he had to start somewhere, at least retrace some of the ground SID had covered. And you never knew. Someone could hook him up to someone else, who could hook him up to someone else, who could hook him up to someone else . . .

Diamond wasn't on the SID list, but she was the one Lassiter knew best, so he started with her. She'd been around awhile—a long time for a streetwalker; she looked about forty-five or fifty to him, so he guessed she was in her thirties—and she'd been a good informant in the past. She really seemed to think of it as a kind of civic duty, not just a way of scoring points. She also claimed really to enjoy her job, for the most part, which she saw as giving pleasure to unhappy men most women wouldn't have anything to do with.

When he'd driven back and forth three times without spotting her, he decided she must not be on duty this evening. The women were rarely away from their spots more than fifteen minutes. Most of their business was conducted in the alley right behind the storefronts. But then he spotted her coming out of one of the little courtyard motels, looking pleased with herself.

Catching a customer who'd rent a room for an hour instead of just driving around to the alley was a choice plum down here. The customer was usually still gone in fifteen minutes or so—no more than half an hour—leaving the prostitute with thirty or forty minutes of solitude with a hot shower, a bathroom and a TV set. Some of the motel owners included other little perks—free snacks and soft drinks mostly—to attract their business.

She dipped, grasping the car window frame with both hands, her head on a level with his, and smiled at him. When he offered her the photo, she took it readily and studied it.

He expected her to shake her head and hand it back. To his astonishment, she frowned and said, "Yeah, I think I know this one. Haven't seen her in . . . Jesus, ten years? Has it been that long? She was . . . well, I *think* she was this *kid*." She was silent, thinking. "Yeah. Damn. Ten years." She was silent again, her gaze turning inward, then sighed and smiled at Lassiter. "Why you lookin' for her now?" She handed the photo back.

He took it and studied the photo for a second himself, as if she'd noticed something in it he hadn't.

"How sure are you?"

"Oh . . ." She reached a hand in and he gave her picture again. "I wouldn't swear on a Bible or anything," she said, handing it back once more. "But it sure does look like her. Ten years later, I mean. She was right out of high school then."

"High school. You mean here? Which one?"

She shook her head. "Not a Wichita school. Some little town." She frowned. "I don't remember how I know that. I might be thinking of somebody else, but that's what came into my mind." She shrugged.

"You don't remember *which* little town? Goddard? Derby?"

She shook her head. "I don't really remember any of that part for sure. It's been ten years . . . if it's who I'm thinking about, and I didn't really know her very long. I don't even remember talkin' to her. We worked a party together once. That was—"

"You remember who set it up?"

"Well, it was a frat party, up by the university. They had this vacant house on . . . I don't know . . . one of those streets up there. You know, the ones named after colleges. Yale and Harvard and like that."

"You remember which frat?"

"Nah. Only reason I remember it as well as I do is 'cause we all got busted."

"Busted? She did, too?"

"Sure. We all did. Except she was a juvenile. Her and this other girl. I'm pretty sure that's the last time I ever saw her."

"Who was the other juvenile?"

"Don't know. That was the only time I *ever* saw her. I don't think she was a pro." Diamond frowned. "That part was kind of bad, now that I think about it. She didn't really want to do it—I mean, after she got there. She was a sister, and there was this one brother, some kind of basketball player, I think, and I remember I thought she must be with him, and I said to him right away, I said, 'Man, you better get that little girl out of here.' But he just laughed." Diamond made a wry face, shook her head. "I don't know. I'd forgotten all about that part. I didn't like that." She sighed. "But then the cops came in. And I never seen her again, either."

He waited to see if she'd remember something else, then asked, "You remember her name?"

She laughed. "Lassiter, baby, you kiddin'? Probably wasn't her real one anyway, whatever it was."

"Who else was at the party . . . I mean, who's still around?"

She was silent for a long time, her smile gradually fading, then shook her head. "None of 'em. None that's still around. Just me."

"You know where any of them are?"

She gave him a humorless smile. "A couple of 'em. But you ain't gonna be able to talk to 'em."

He understood what she meant. He thanked her and drove to the City Building, where he buttonholed Lieutenant Corcoran in the Special Investigations Division. Corcoran had been in the division back then, but he didn't remember the bust. There'd been a lot of them. Lassiter could see he didn't want to have anything to do with the case, but he also felt guilty about palming it off on Loomis. He talked Corcoran into going downstairs with him, and over to the courthouse basement, to look through the old arrest reports.

After a couple of hours of sifting through the cardboard file boxes, they came up with several similar busts in the right time frame, but only two that had involved two juveniles, one black and one white. Corcoran knew one of the white girls, who was still around.

They took the remaining report upstairs to see what they could find out about the two girls in it. Neither name appeared in the database, which meant little. They hadn't necessarily given the arresting officers their correct names. Also, any juvenile records were

probably sealed—expunged by now, if they hadn't
been busted for anything else in Sedgwick County
since then.

The black girl had identified herself as Margo
Walker and given an address in a middle-class black
neighborhood north of the university. A check of the
city cross-reference directory showed that there had
indeed been a Walker family living at that address at
that time, with a daughter named Margo. Which
meant she'd given a real name, at least, even if it
wasn't *her* real name. The white girl had called herself
Jocelyn Peete, and had given an address a block or
two north of Central, downtown, which Lassiter
guessed was one of the flophouses in that area, patron-
ized mostly by transients. Even if she really had been
staying in one of those, after ten years that would be
a dead end. One interesting thing—although probably
equally useless, except that it seemed to Lassiter to
match the impression he had of Celeste Mundy's in-
ventiveness—was that she'd volunteered to the arresting officer that she came from New Mexico and
was part Navajo. She'd claimed she'd arrived in Wichita the day before, for the first time ever, and hadn't
understood what kind of party she was being invited to.

The Margo Walker whose name the young black
prostitute had given ten years before was now Margo
Gilkey, wife of Dr. Elwood Gilkey, an ear, nose and
throat specialist. She herself was a phlebotomist at one
of the clinics across the street from Wesley Medical
Center on Hillside. The Gilkeys had a five-year-old
daughter, and their address was considerably more up-
scale than that of her parents.

Lassiter drove to the clinic, thinking about how to
inform Mrs. Gilkey that her name had appeared in an
arrest report for prostitution from ten years before.
She might know about it, but he guessed she didn't.
He hoped she'd have some idea of who the real girl was.

But as soon as he identified himself and began talking about the frat party, her face turned suddenly a

much lighter shade of brown, and she gripped the edge of the receptionist's counter as if she were about to faint.

"Maybe there's somewhere we can sit down and talk," he said.

She took a moment to regain her composure, stealing little glances at the other women around her, all of whom gave a good imitation of indifference. Then, not speaking, she motioned him past the end of the counter and led him to an examination room, where she locked the door and sat down, putting her head on her knees.

He gave her a minute or two, then said, "It's not you I'm looking for, Mrs. Gilkey. It's someone else. I thought you might be able to help me."

She looked up at him, then sat up straight. She cleared her throat. "I've been waiting for this a long time," she said. "But I guess I'd gotten to thinking it wasn't really going to happen." She gave a long sigh. "My father knows about it, of course, but my husband doesn't. Not that it would be a problem, since nothing really happened . . . but I've just never . . . it's not the kind of thing . . ."

"I understand. It's the other girl I'm interested in. The other juvenile. She said she was half Indian and gave her name as Jocelyn Peete. Do you remember her?"

She stared at him for a moment, then began shaking her head slowly, then nodded instead and said, "Of course I remember her, but I don't know anything about her. I mean, I don't *really* remember her. I probably wouldn't recognize her if I saw her."

He fished out the photo and offered it to her. She hesitated, then took it, glanced at it and handed it back. It surprised him, because it was what people did when they did recognize someone but didn't want to say so. "No," she said.

"No, that isn't her? Or no, you don't remember?"

She hesitated again, even though it wasn't a question she should have had to think about. "No," she said. "I don't remember."

He didn't take the photo from her. "I know this is extremely unpleasant for you," he said. "But maybe if you take a little longer look at the photo, something will come back. I don't want to take any more of your time than I have to."

She nodded, pressed her lips together tightly, and looked at the photo again. She shook her head and handed it back to him. "I'm sorry. It just doesn't . . ." She shrugged. "I suppose it could be her. But it's ten years. And she's white, you know."

He nodded and took the photo. Cross-racial IDs were always suspect—which meant that Diamond's was, too. "I just don't remember her well enough to say," Margo Gilkey said. "I was thinking about other things."

"Right. I understand. She gave her name as Jocelyn Peete. Does that ring a bell?"

She shook her head. "I'm sorry."

The funny thing, he thought, was that the name seemed to ring a distant bell in his own mind. Not that he thought he knew her, but . . . something about the name itself, from a long time ago.

He stood and handed her one of his cards. "If you happen to remember anything—"

She took it and stared at it, then said, "If you catch her, it will all come out, won't it?"

"Not necessarily. If this Jocelyn Peete is the woman we're looking for, she's wanted in a different state for something entirely different. She's probably not even around here. And the girl you met may not even be the same woman. One of the other women who was at the frat party thought she might be. But it's not a solid ID. Just a lead I'm following. I don't see any reason any of this old stuff—"

"It was supposed to be kind of a joke," she said.

He waited, feeling the same kind of apprehension he'd felt watching the videotape.

"My boyfriend was on the WSU basketball team.

You'd probably recognize his name." She glanced at Lassiter, but he didn't say anything. She shrugged. "He wasn't charged with anything. None of them were. The men. Just . . . But it doesn't really matter, because nothing really happened. The police came."

"That's good," he said.

"It was supposed to be the first time this fraternity had rushed a black student," she said. "I don't even know if that's true or not. I mean, I don't know if they were really rushing him, or if they just invited him to this party. He told me he wanted to get into the fraternity, but he didn't want to go to this party and be with these other girls." She shook her head. "I believed him. I was just a stupid little high school girl. But I was going with this big-shot college guy, so I thought I knew it all. I thought I was something."

"You can't be blamed," Lassiter said.

She shrugged irritably. "Of course, it wasn't really like that. I think it was like . . . like maybe he was supposed to *supply* a girl, you know? Maybe they really were rushing him, and that was part of it. I don't know. I just know that once we got there, everything changed. He went off with this white girl." She was silent for a moment. "They had all these mattresses everywhere. That was all. Not even a chair. Just mattresses in these empty rooms in this big old house. There were . . . I don't even know if there were as many as half a dozen girls. Maybe not that many. And there were . . . I don't know how many guys there were. A lot of them."

She grew silent. Lassiter felt an old, hard thing forming in his gut, part fear, part anger, part . . . what? Some kind of wanting, for nothing at all. For nothingness. Just to let go. "But nothing happened," he said, knowing it was a lie. "Because the police came."

She nodded, not looking at him.

"It was all just a mistake," Lassiter said.

"They were all white," she said. "And they kept smiling. They smiled all the time."

He cleared his throat and reached inside his jacket for the arrest report in his inside pocket, folded in thirds like a letter. He handed it to her.

She looked at it and then at him. "What?"

"The record was sealed, and it's been expunged by now," he said. "This is the arrest report. It's the only document remaining. You want it?"

She looked at him, as if afraid of some trick, then took it from him. "Thank you, Detective . . . I'm sorry, I . . ." Suddenly, there were tears in her eyes.

"Lassiter," he said. "It's nothing. Nobody needs it. It never happened."

She nodded, blinking. "It's like a dream to me," she said. "That's how I think about it sometimes, like just something I dreamed, you know? A long time ago."

"Yeah." He did know. "The past is only what you remember," he said. "It doesn't really exist anymore. It's just in your head, like a dream."

"That's right." She folded the already folded paper in half, not having looked at it. "I'm sorry I can't help you find her."

He shrugged. "Like I said, she's probably not around here anyway."

The things Jocelyn Peete had told the arresting officer didn't help any. The address was indeed the kind of place he'd thought it was, called the Charlton Arms, but there wasn't anyone there, or anyone associated with it, who'd been around ten years before—and if there had been, they wouldn't have remembered her. Given their clientele, they made it their business not to remember anyone from the day before.

So he spent a day looking for public officials who might have seen her back then—cops, jailers, attorneys, judges, bailiffs. Some were dead or had moved away. One, the court clerk at the time, was in the same nursing home as his mother, and in the same condition. He found only a couple of people who were still around, and the first one he talked to, the former assistant D.A. who'd filed charges against the adult prostitutes—now a partner in a private law firm— didn't even remember it.

Millie Desmond, the former Social and Rehabilitation Services caseworker who'd handled most cases involving juvenile prostitutes back then, was a bankruptcy attorney in her sixties with an office overlooking the river and Riverside Park, adjacent to the Murdock Street bridge. She'd gone back to get her law degree when she was in her fifties. She remembered both girls, but mainly Margo.

"That poor little girl," she said sadly, shaking her head. Then her expression hardened. "That asshole boyfriend of hers should have had his balls cut off."

"No argument there," Lassiter said. "But she told me nothing really happened." His and Millie's eyes met for a second, and neither of them had to say what they both knew.

She looked away with a shrug. "Why not? I told her parents the medical treatment was just routine stuff. Exams required by the law. Even though nothing had happened. I guess they believed me. They wanted to." She looked at the photo of Celeste Mundy.

"The other one . . . this *could* be her. I wouldn't swear to it, but . . . yeah. There's something in the eyes. She was a tough little customer, I'll tell you that. And confident. Damn near arrogant. She made it very clear that she had her own agenda and didn't need any help, which I guess was true. Anyway, I had other things—"

"Why was it true?"

"She got herself sprung soon after going to the Youth Detention Center. Some cop—"

"Cop?"

"Not Wichita P.D. From—umm, wait a minute . . ." She was silent, thinking. "Sand Creek," she said. "A cop from Sand Creek. He came over and talked to the judge, and next thing you know, she was out of here. Never saw her or even heard of her again, until now. I think the cop was given custody. Something like that. He might have been a relative."

"You remember his name?"

She shook her head, then stopped and said, "Something Hispanic, I think. But there are a lot of Hispanics in Sand Creek. Maybe that's why I think that."

"What about her name?"

"Jocelyn Peete actually sounds right. Or it doesn't sound wrong, anyway." She laughed.

"She told the arresting officer she was half Navajo," Lassiter said.

"Hmm. I don't remember that. But it sort of makes sense. It's an Indian name. I don't know about Navajo, necessarily . . ."

That was it. The Potawatomi reservation. Mayetta had been full of Peetes. Why had it taken him so long to remember that? He had a vivid memory, suddenly, of one of the strange graves at the Potawatomi cemetery—the mounds of rocks with thatches of twigs and brush, but with the same flowers, the same veterans flags and plaques that you'd see anywhere. He could see one of those names on the placards they'd had, just below the smiling photo of the man himself: Jonny Peete.

"I don't remember anything else," Millie Desmond said. "Sorry."

Something in her tone caught his attention, and he saw she was looking at him with a kind of concern. How long had he stood there in silence, remembering that Potawatomi grave? Or had he spoken aloud?

"No," Lassiter said. "Thanks for your time."

The downtown library had a copy of the current Sand Creek phone book, but he was let down to find that there weren't any Peetes in it. He'd been counting on finding some. He went back out and sat in his car in the library parking lot, thinking which way to go next. It was obvious. Hector Briseno. But the thought of calling Hector made his stomach tighten up. He didn't even know why, exactly. He'd done nothing wrong back then. He'd gotten a citation. It was Hector who'd been eased out, sent home to Sand Creek with a deal that gave him his full pension in exchange for leaving without a fight. But Lassiter had always felt like he'd done the wrong thing, like what had happened to Hector was his fault. It didn't make rational sense—he couldn't have let him die, couldn't have done anything differently; he'd been over that a million times in his head—but none of that mattered. He still felt guilty about the whole thing.

As far as he knew, Hector might not even be alive anymore. He'd have to be pretty old by now. Probably retired, which meant he'd be calling him at home.

This Jocelyn Peete—whether it was her real name or not—might not even be the woman he was supposed to be looking for. Everything was tissue thin. With every line he followed, he expected the whole thing to dissolve completely, leave him with no leads at all.

But he'd become curious about Jocelyn Peete, in her own right. She sounded interesting. She sounded like she sure *could* be Celeste Mundy, in terms of audacity. He might as well see what he could find out about her. What else did he have to do?

At first Hector sounded pleased to hear from him, which made him feel relieved, as if he'd expected, without knowing it, to be blamed and reviled. But then something changed. He thought it was when Jocelyn Peete's name came up.

"Well," Briseno said, "there was a girl named Peete who lived here a long time ago. More than ten years, I'd say. But her name wasn't Jocelyn. It was Maria. And she's dead. Long dead. More than ten years, for sure. She's the only Peete I ever heard of in Sand Creek, and she was an orphan."

Lassiter told him what Millie Desmond had said, about the Hispanic cop.

Hector grunted. "Well, you know, Floyd, there's a whole bunch of us Mexicans over here. That's Sand Creek. Mexicans, Methodists and Mennonites, in equal thirds. And not too many of the Mennonites get to be cops. So . . ."

Hector's voice on the phone, his way of talking, made Lassiter feel a little like a rookie again—and he liked the feeling. It seemed strange to him now that he'd been reluctant to call.

"How come you're lookin' for this girl, all these years later?" Hector asked.

Like a rookie reporting to a superior, Lassiter laid it all out for him, leaving out only the parts about himself and Kay and his "vacation."

"Bullshit," Hector said when he finished. "That's a bullshit case. You guys got nothin' better than that to do over there nowadays?"

"There's some kind of weight behind it," Lassiter said. "I'm really doing Loomis a favor."

"Ah. I wondered. Same old shit. Well, fortunately, I'm gonna be out of it in a couple years. They're makin' me retire."

"You're still working?" As soon as he said it, Lassiter regretted the surprise in his voice.

Briseno laughed. "Hard to believe, ain't it? Somebody so old'd still be so dumb. Truth is, I don't know what the hell else I'd do. Sit out at the truck stop with the other old farts, I guess, drinking one cup of coffee all day long and flirting with the waitress. That's all I can think of. Tell you what. I'll see if I can dig up a roster from back then, maybe figure out who this mysterious Mexican cop could have been. If I come up with something, I'll let you know. You sure it was P.D.? Not the sheriff?"

"No, I'm not."

"I'll take a look at their rosters, too, then."

"I appreciate it, Hector. I really do."

"Nada. Gives the old fart something to do. And it's a little more interesting than any real work I got to do. I'll give you a call."

"Great."

"Maybe you better fax me a copy of the stuff you got from L.A. The mug shot and all. Not the video. Probably give me a heart attack."

"Will do. Thanks again." He drove to the City Building and used the fax in the property room. He also put one of the glossies he'd had made into a manila envelope and mailed it.

5

Saturday

There was a moment, while the sun was coming up, when Jes could imagine her hometown as some other place entirely, some town she'd never been to, before the edges of the roofs and the treetops became quite clear. It was something she enjoyed, the way she'd enjoyed lying on her back on the living room carpet as a child, looking at the ceiling and trying to imagine that it was the floor, that she was looking down at it, the furniture hanging down all around her.

She remembered Jo awakening her that first time, a finger to her lips. There'd been no back fence then. They'd gone through the opening in the hedge, jumped the gully. Jo had jumped it at the widest place, daring Jes to follow her—and when Jes had, she'd suddenly looked frightened and rushed to catch her when she landed. Probably that had been another time, but they were all conflated in her memory. And the old coaching tower, the cold metal rungs and the splintered wooden platform. Lying on their stomachs in the dark, waiting to watch Sand Creek emerge, turn into this alien place, and then into itself.

That tower had been shorter than this one, but in her memory it was much higher. They'd been far up above everything, able to see over all roofs, all the way to the countryside beyond the farthest edge of town, the place where the rest of the world began. The tower was taller now, and so was she—and she'd been out there in that larger world, the one Jo had vanished into—but she could no longer see that far. She could barely see past the roofs of the single-story houses between her and the taller buildings downtown.

Headlights moved on the curving streets among the bigger, newer houses directly across from the school, and she looked that way, watching the first car find its way out to the street, stop for nothing, and then turn. That had all been open fields and gullies when she'd first climbed the tower. All that was left of that was the strip of weedy land and the gully between here and her house.

She couldn't have said how many people were in the car. When she could, it would be time to go. Unless a light came on first, in one of the rooms at this end of the school. Then she'd climb down and go home, maintain the pretense that no one could see her, that no one knew about her early morning visits to the tower. Probably they all did. Which was only fair, since she knew as much or more about most of them, and even passed it on to others sometimes, for money. She was a kind of spy now. But they didn't seem to mind. Or at least they didn't say so if they did. That was how it worked.

She wondered if they all knew she wasn't really writing a book, which was what she'd told everybody, at the newspaper and here, when she'd quit. At the time she hadn't been lying, or hadn't thought she was.

It still seemed like a good idea for a book—the connection between the orphan trains and the diaries of pioneer women, both of which had been products of that odd, confused period between the Civil War and the Depression, when the cities back East had swollen from the immigrations that had begun with the Irish famine, while the open land of the West had been cut gradually into farms and towns and finally states by the people fleeing all that to have their own lives and homes.

The superfluous children of the East had been welcome, and not only because the farms needed workers.

If there was a single thread that ran through the pioneer diaries of the farm wives, it was the lost children, the ones never born, the ones too weak to live long.

Jes still thought it was a good idea for a book. She'd even done some research, made some notes, written some chapter drafts. But all that had been before she'd quit the newspaper. Since then the only time she'd really thought about it had been when someone asked her why she'd quit, what she was doing now, besides making a living. *Writing a book.* But it was a lie now. There were always other things ahead of it. Always a couple of magazine articles working, or correspondence that had to be kept current, or files that had to be organized, or housework . . . or anything.

It was stupid. She'd spent her whole life becoming a writer, and now here she was—even successful at it, making more than enough money for herself and Susie. People saw her articles in the magazines, on the racks at the supermarket, and whether they read them or not, when they saw her they said, *Hey, Jes! Saw your article! Way to go!* She was a kind of celebrity in her hometown, which turned her weirdness into "eccentricity."

And she was a phony, a failure before she was thirty. Already an old maid living inside her closed doors with her dog. She'd done what she'd set out to do . . . and now what? Maybe Jo's choice had been better, after all. She'd just done what she thought she needed to do, for better or worse, as always. At some point Jes had stopped following her up the tower, wanting her own identity, thinking she could do better. Maybe if they'd left together . . .

Maybe maybe maybe. She stood and stretched, feeling stiff and old, which she knew was just a variety of self-pity. She was still in pretty good shape. She could still bat clean-up, maybe not on a state championship high school team, but on a team of women her own age. She was probably in better shape than any of her old teammates, several of whom were wives living in those houses where the weeds and gullies had once been. She *would* write a book. She was a writer, for christsake. Just do it. It didn't have to be *the* book, just *a* book.

She laughed silently at the familiar pep talk, which, in her mind, she always heard in Jo's voice. Susie had come to the foot of the tower and was looking up, wagging her tail, as eager to go home as she'd been to come. Even a little impatient, because she knew they were running late. Dogs always knew the time. They loved their food and they loved their people, but what they really loved was their routine. Some people were like that, too. Especially women. They were her core readership, probably. What a phony she was, all the way around.

She went down quickly, jumping the last three or four feet, making Susie yip with excitement.

"Mama's a phony," she said. "But you don't care, do you?" She stood there, thinking about why dogs liked people so much. Not just because they gave them food and shelter and all that. Because they were entertaining, she thought. *We must be so fucking entertaining.* She saw that Susie was looking worried, confused, and she bent to rub the dog's head. "Sorry, kiddo. Everything's okay."

She straightened and pulled the chain leash from where it hung on one of the crossbars, hooked it to Susie's collar, wrapped it twice around her fist, and braced herself for the dog's inevitable first lunge.

That over, they moved with relative order toward the gate. Susie went a little slower than she wanted to, Jes a little faster. Susie could have dictated the pace—according to Dr. Scott, the vet, she was the biggest, or rather the heaviest, dog he'd ever treated. Some of it was fat, but not much really. She was still practically a pup, only three. In her own mind—and sometimes in Jes's—she *was* still a puppy. But she weighed more than Jes and was still growing.

Hector had brought Susie to her in a cardboard box not long after she'd stopped letting anyone into her house—even Hector. He'd said he'd have to take her

to the pound if he couldn't find someone to take her,
acted like she was doing him a favor by taking the
fluffy little dog with the huge feet off his hands. He'd
claimed some rent skipper had left her behind, but
he'd also somehow known that she was half malamute,
half Doberman, and that her name was Susie. Jes had
decided to call her Tala, which, according to her
mother, was an Indian word for she-wolf. But it had
taken only a day or so for her to realize that the dog's
true name was Susie, after all. Jes doubted she'd be
much help against an intruder. The best to hope for
would be that her look, and maybe the low growl she
sometimes gave, would cause a burglar to soil himself
and flee before she herself turned tail for the basement. Jes could make her flee for cover down there,
just by speaking harshly to her. She had no idea there
were even scarier people in the world.

"You should have known the rest of the Wellingtons," Jes said aloud, causing the dog to look back at
her. "I'm the wuss of the family."

They came to the gully, and she let Susie lead her
to the place where it was narrowest, and they crossed
together. Inside the back gate, she turned Susie loose
and went through the other gate and up the steps to
the side door and into the kitchen.

The light on the answering machine was blinking.
The little surge of hope she felt annoyed her. It was
stupid to think Jo would call. She didn't call on real
anniversaries; why would she call on one you had to
be crazy even to calculate in the first place? Jes had
worked out, long ago, that this was the day on which
they'd become a day older than their mother had lived
to be. She didn't know why exactly. But she'd written
the date on the calendar every year, to remember it,
and had somehow gotten it into her head that Jo knew
about it, too, and would call.

When they'd been kids, they'd believed that they
knew each other's thoughts, that they even thought
the same things sometimes, when they weren't together. But they'd stopped thinking that way even be-

fore Jo left. Sometime after their mother had died and
before their father had. That was about as specific as
she wanted to be about that. It was an anniversary
she didn't want to calculate, even if she could—the
date when she and her sister had stopped being twins.

The last time Jo had called, three years before, it
had been a few days after their mother's birthday,
and probably that had been why she'd called, although
neither of them had mentioned it. Jes had had the
impression Jo was in California. She didn't know why,
exactly; Jo hadn't said. Maybe just because that was
where she'd sometimes talked about going, where Jes
always sort of thought of her as being. Except when
she thought of her being in New Mexico. They'd both
talked about going there when they were little. To
look for their "real" family, their mythical brother,
who was supposed to rescue them but was taking his
time about it.

Jo had been drunk or stoned or something when
she'd called. Not quite intelligible. And Jes hadn't
really wanted to talk to her. It had been a bad time
for that, a time when she was still thinking that all
she needed to do was sever all connection with her
family, think of herself as having no family, and create
her own life, which would have nothing to do with the
past. And everything would be okay.

She didn't think she'd sounded angry or hostile on
the phone—just unresponsive. Indifferent, maybe a little impatient. She shook her head. There was no way
to sugarcoat it. She hadn't wanted anything to do with
her sister, and Jo had gotten the message and hung up.

But this call wasn't her. No message on the answering machine, and the caller ID showed a Wichita number and the name STAIRCASE E. Some kind of business.
Siding or aluminum blinds or something like that.

She went into the kitchen to make coffee. Standing
at the sink, looking out the window at the backyard
and the high school grounds beyond the gully, the
coaching tower, she considered that, even though
she'd decided she couldn't just pretend the past had

never happened, shut it all out the way she shut out the present, it was nevertheless true that Susie was her only real family now, and the only one she was likely to have, and that that really was okay. She'd like to hear from Jo, but if not . . .

She could live with it. Most people didn't even realize what a fine thing that was—just to be in a situation you could live with.

6

Millie Desmond called to tell him she'd asked around a little among her old SRS contacts, and that one of them—a woman who'd been a juvenile offender back then and had also been at the Youth Detention Center when Jocelyn Peete was there—had told her she'd already known Jocelyn before that, because the two of them had lived at the Charlton Arms, a flophouse a block off north Broadway. The woman also claimed to have heard from somebody or other that Jocelyn was back in town again, and living at the Charlton Arms again.

"This woman is a junkie and three-fourths full of shit," Millie told him, "but I thought I'd better pass it on, just in case."

He checked it out, and found a guy who also looked full of shit to him—he claimed to be a traveling salesman but looked more like a janitor—who said he thought the photo of Celeste Mundy kind of looked like somebody he'd seen around there not too long ago. Of course, he didn't remember her name or anything else about her. Except that he thought she'd had a baby with her.

Lassiter figured the traveling salesman had either been sampling his own stock, or just liked spouting bullshit to cops—not an uncommon thing in these kinds of places—but he stopped to check with the apartment manager on his way out. He'd checked with him on his way in, at which time he'd claimed never to have met anyone who looked even remotely like Celeste Mundy in his entire life—but sometimes one person remembering something could suddenly improve somebody else's recall.

Of course, he made the traveling salesman's ID sound a whole lot more positive than it really was. Instead of looking baffled, the manager made a soft farting sound through his lips and allowed as how, well, yeah, now that he thought about it again, and looked a little closer at the photo, there *had* been a female guest of the establishment who somewhat resembled her. But he didn't remember any baby. He was sure about that. "We don't allow babies here," he said. "They cry."

He was even able, by examining his records, to come up with a name for the woman—but it was such an obvious phony, it seemed like a waste of time and effort to write it down. *Celia Staircase.* Right. And of course the manager had no idea where she'd gone from there.

But at least it was a name, which gave him something to do while waiting to see if Hector Briseno would come up with anything. It was no surprise that there was no Celia Staircase in any of the area phone directories, or that the name failed to pop up in any of the computer registries for hotels, motels, airlines, buses, or anything else during the preceding year.

But when he asked Southwestern Bell for unlisted numbers, they came up with a Staircase. Eddy, not Celia. That was so unexpected it felt almost like a major breakthrough.

He ran the name on some search engines on the Internet, and came up with a local Eddy Staircase whose address was in the old Riverside neighborhood, north of Riverside Park, inside the V where the Little Arkansas branched off from the big river. It wasn't that far from Friends University and Kansas Newman College, but it wasn't the kind of area where you'd expect to find apartment houses.

In his mail was a manila envelope with a Sand Creek P.D. logo in the corner, and inside was a mug shot—obviously a yearbook photo—of a smiling young girl, along with a folded sheet of paper on which was typed: "She did live here, after all. Left town about ten years ago. No cop yet. Interesting. Let me know what you find on your end. HB." There was no name on the photo, but it had to be Jocelyn Peete.

He could see the resemblance Diamond and Millie Desmond had seen. Apart from the differences in age and hairstyle and so on, the two looked a lot alike—but at the same time there was some difference he couldn't quite put his finger on that made him feel doubtful.

One difference he did see, but it was a confusing one. Both of his female witnesses had described Jocelyn Peete as tough and smart. A little arrogant, Millie Desmond had said. And those adjectives just didn't fit the girl in the yearbook photo. Despite the bright smile, her eyes looked uncertain, maybe even a bit frightened. On the other hand, Celeste Mundy's eyes fit the two women's descriptions to a T. Tough and smart. Arrogant? Hard to tell. Confident, certainly. But time rubbed a little of the bark off everybody, and more than a little if you were living on the edge.

But anyway, it hadn't been Celeste Mundy the two women were describing. It had been the high school girly they'd both met, Jocelyn Peete. And it was hard to see the girl they'd described as the girl in the photo Hector had sent him. There was something going on here that he knew he wasn't getting, something Kay or Jerry might have picked up on, but not him.

Which probably meant he should just stay away from it, unless he could see some way that it really connected to Celeste Mundy. He didn't need to invent problems for himself. Put it on hold, anyway, while he cleared up the loose end of Celia and Eddy Staircase, which most likely had nothing to do with any of the rest of it.

He drove to the City Building and used the fax machine near the property room to send an inquiry to the LAPD, asking if they had any information on a Jocelyn Peete, approximately twenty-eight to thirty years old, originally from Sand Creek, Kansas. He didn't connect it to the Celeste Mundy thing. He didn't want to get anyone there needlessly excited. This was his thing, not theirs.

It was nearly dark when he came back down to his car and headed for Riverside to call on Eddy Staircase.

The address turned out to be the rear apartment of one of a pair of old brown duplexes set perpendicular to the street, facing each other across a narrow lawn split by a cracked driveway. Lassiter drove past the place before realizing his address had to be there, and drove around the block to come back to it. All the other buildings were ordinary houses, mostly two-story, mostly a little shabby, but still single-family dwellings. The twinned duplexes should have looked out of place in the block, but they didn't really, because they were from the same period, back before the war. The world of Andy Hardy movies, hump-backed cars, white-suited milkmen, kids on bicycles.

Lassiter turned off his headlights and pulled up into the driveway that appeared to run all the way back to the alley, between facing double garages.

Three of the units, including the one where Eddy Staircase reputedly lived, looked deserted. The only one showing any lights was the front apartment to his right as he moved slowly up the drive. Turning into the alley behind the garages, he glanced back and up and saw that there were indeed lights on inside the row of the upper windows at the back—an orange glow, filtered by curtains, in the Eddy Staircase apartment, and a somewhat brighter gleam of light along the outer edges of what looked like metal horizontal blinds in the other.

He went a little past the side of the garage and pulled in. Getting out of his car, he was surprised by the pleasant touch of the breeze, after the heat of the day. It had a soft, moist odor that made him think of coming rain, although he supposed it was just the faint smell of the river. The duplexes wouldn't be a bad place to live, he thought, for a couple without children, or a single person, someone like himself.

Four doors faced out of the front wall of each duplex building, two per apartment. He stopped at the rear door, the one nearest the garages and the upper room where the light was on, and knocked. He was about to knock a second time when he heard footsteps coming down a stairway, somewhere not far behind the door where he stood.

There was a moment of silence long enough to make him look to see if there was a peephole in the door. There wasn't, but he still had the prickly feeling of being studied, because it inevitably reminded him of the moment before going through a door to arrest someone, not knowing what might be waiting. A soft click from inside made him start and take an unconscious step to one side of the little concrete porch. But it hadn't been a metallic sound, hadn't really sounded like a gun. It came a second time, then twice in rapid succession, and he understood what it was. The person on the other side of the door was flicking the light switch, trying to turn on the porch light.

Then the door opened, with no light behind it but the glow from above, pouring down the stairs that faced the door, a few feet inside, and he saw the naked form of a young woman silhouetted against that light.

He gave another kind of start, almost took another step, this time backward, completely off the porch, but managed not to. There'd been a brief smell of straw and manure in his nostrils, and he'd been sure that he was looking at that other silhouette, somehow, impossibly, transported all those miles and all those years, from the screened-in porch at the farm.

But it was gone as quickly as it came, and of course that wasn't who was behind this screen, nor was she really naked.

"Guess it's burnt out," she said, looking up at the small glass globe attached to the wall above the door. "Is there even a bulb in there?" She opened the screen just far enough to lean forward to look up, then closed it again and shrugged. "Sorry."

She wore an oversize maroon T-shirt that reached nearly to her knees, and she was a tall woman, maybe even a fraction of an inch taller than himself. He couldn't make out her face very clearly, backlit as she was, but she had short, very curly blond hair—more like the girl in the yearbook photo than the woman in the video still. Remembering that, remembering the instant when he'd first seen her, he frowned. There didn't really appear to be enough light behind her to have penetrated the dark T-shirt that way. What he could see of her body now didn't even look quite like the image he'd seen. She was thin, almost boyish in shape. She wasn't one of those women who filled out a T-shirt well enough that you could guess whether or not she wore anything beneath it. It had been something in his head, at least in part.

"You're a cop," she said. It wasn't a question, and it didn't even have the sound of something she'd just figured out. It was a flat observation, said the same way she might have said, "It's dark out."

"Yes," he said. "Detective Floyd Lassiter. I was looking for—"

"You got a badge?"

He fished the plastic case out of his jacket pocket, flipped it open for her. She looked at it for a second, really looking at it, not just glancing, the way most people did. She didn't seem wary. She had more the demeanor of an attorney than of someone who'd been in trouble with the law.

"Thanks. Just a second." She turned away from the door, putting herself once more squarely between the light and him, and he saw again a female shape, more clearly outlined than he'd have expected, but it wasn't quite the one he'd seen before, and it didn't affect him the same way, although he turned his eyes automatically to the side. She flicked another switch and the lights brightened, revealing a small, bright, clean kitchen. Oddly, the greater light didn't seem to have the kind of effect the dimmer light had. But he could see her face more clearly, and for a second he was sure he knew her, so sure he almost spoke, but then he was just as sure he didn't. Again, it was like an echo of how his episodes usually began, but didn't have the same feel. Maybe, he thought, it was just regular déjà vu, the kind normal people had.

"Who were you looking for?" she asked.

Somehow, for some reason he couldn't have explained to himself, he knew she was Jocelyn Peete, the girl in the yearbook photo, the one Diamond and Millie Desmond had met. He wasn't at all sure she was Celeste Mundy. In fact, he more or less assumed she wasn't, although of course there was a strong resemblance. Especially in the eyes. There was that puzzle again, the eyes matching one woman, and everything else the other.

"Detective?"

He realized he'd stood a bit too long looking instead of talking. "Sorry. I was looking for someone named Eddy Staircase. According to the phone company—"

"Eddy's my brother. My name's Celia."

He hadn't really expected anyone to claim either name, particularly the latter, so for a second he didn't know what to say. "So, umm, this is your brother's place?" he said at last.

"No. It's mine. He doesn't live here." She paused, then said, "If you use your first initial in your phone listing, everyone knows you're a woman living alone."

He nodded. "But you don't have a listing."

She smiled. "You got it, didn't you? No harm in being too careful."

He nodded again. "So where is your brother?"

"I don't know. I haven't seen him since I was a baby. I don't actually have any memory of him."

Lassiter didn't say anything. It sounded a little crazy, but when people started talking about themselves, the best thing to do was shut up and let them talk.

"When we were babies, my sister and I were taken

away from our parents," Celia Staircase said. "We were adopted by another family. But our brother . . . I don't know. He was a lot older than us. Our adoptive parents never told us much. They didn't know much themselves. When we were little, my sister and me, we used to think Eddy was going to come and find us, you know? Rescue us." She smiled. "I mean, when we were unhappy. Our adoptive parents weren't really bad people. All kids get unhappy."

"Why were you taken away from your natural parents?"

"So they wouldn't kill one of us."

"Kill one of you?"

"They were reservation Navajo—real Navajo. Traditional. The Navajo believe that human twins are unnatural—any multiple human birth. Animals have litters. Humans have one child at a time. So when twins are born, they have to get rid of one of them." She shrugged. "Navajo don't have twins very often, but it happens. So other people—white people, mostly, but some other Navajo—try to prevent it. Try to get the babies away before anything happens. That's what they did with us."

"You were lucky."

"One of us was. But maybe they're right. Maybe one of us should have been killed."

Lassiter grunted. "Your sister?"

"No. Myself. But it must be hard, with a pair of babies, to tell which is the bad one."

"I'd think so," Lassiter said. "Do you have a baby?"

She looked surprised. "Me? No. Why do you ask?"

"You lived at the Charlton Arms before you moved here, right? Someone there said he thought he saw you with a baby."

A half smile curled one corner of her mouth; then she said, "Well, he was wrong. But I thought you were looking for my brother."

"Actually, I was looking for you. Eddy was the only Staircase that popped up with a phone number."

"So why were you looking for me?"

She hadn't changed her expression, but something had happened in those eyes that looked so much like Celeste Mundy's.

"I didn't start out looking for Celia Staircase," he told her. "The guy who thought you had a baby also thought you looked like the woman I was really looking for."

She laughed. "It gets more and more complicated."

"There *is* a strong resemblance."

"Really? But you don't sound very sure."

"No. I'm not."

There was another little silence and he replayed in his mind the last few lines they'd spoken. He had the elusive feeling that he'd missed something. Had she ever actually admitted being at the Charlton Arms? But there couldn't be two women using the name Celia Staircase.

He put his hand in his jacket pocket, let his fingertips rest on the edges of the two photos—the one of Celeste Mundy and the one Hector had sent him. Which one? Then he remembered something she'd said.

"Maybe it's your sister I'm looking for," he said. "Does she look a lot like you? Does she have a baby?"

"No. I mean . . . yes, she looks a lot like me. No, she doesn't have a baby." He could tell she didn't like this line of questioning. For the first time she looked a little rattled. "But she's never been around here," she said. "She still lives at home."

"Where's home?"

"New Mexico. Near Santa Fe."

New Mexico. He felt suddenly sure that this was the woman who'd been arrested ten years ago at the frat party . . . or her sister . . .

"So she stayed home and you left," he said. "How long ago?"

She didn't like that question, either, but she shrugged.

"About ten years. Since I graduated high school and went off to college."

"Where?"

"U of A. Arizona. Then I was in Houston for three years, getting my law degree, and then I worked with a firm there for a year, and then I went out on my own. Family law. Mostly divorces and child custody. Okay?" She was smiling, no longer rattled. *Arrogant*, Millie Desmond had said. He wasn't sure that was the word. But she was ten years older.

"So how'd you end up in Wichita?"

She sighed, shrugged. "I decided to take a year off, kind of a sabbatical. My kind of practice can be pretty stressful. I'm not even sure I want to go back to it. I'm not sure I want to practice law anymore. I probably will, but I like thinking maybe I won't." She smiled. "Wichita's a quiet place. I heard it was friendly."

"Is it?"

"Seems to be so far."

Lassiter glanced around, at the darkness between the two long buildings, the only light coming through the open door, and, more dimly, from a streetlight somewhere. The stars weren't clear, as they'd been recently. They were obscured by some kind of haze. High clouds maybe. The kind you couldn't always see by daylight.

"This is a pretty quiet neighborhood," he said.

"Yes, it is. I like it."

"So what do you do?"

"Do?"

"You're not in practice. What do you do all day?"

She smiled again. "Nothing much. Sleep, eat, read, listen to CDs, watch TV. Sometimes I just go out and drive around, listen to songs on the radio. I know that sounds pretty boring—and it is—but it's all I want right now."

Lassiter decided he liked her. No matter who she was, he liked her. He liked standing here on the porch in the dark, bantering with her, the night wind ruffling his hair and now and then the hem of the T-shirt she wore. But it wasn't anything sexual. Not even romantic. He didn't have a word for it, and yet it seemed oddly familiar, like something he'd felt before.

He could see in her eyes that he'd been standing too long without speaking, that she was beginning to wonder about him. "Is that a Navajo name?" he asked. "Staircase?"

"Yes. Or at least, it was my real parents' public name. So it's my public name. It's not my true name, of course. And it's not my legal name, either, for that matter. The one my adoptive parents gave me. The one I practice under. So I have three different names."

Another name. He knew she was waiting for him to ask what her legal name was, but he didn't. He knew it wasn't going to be Mundy. Instead he said, "I didn't know they had staircases."

"Who? Oh, the Navajos. No. But the Anasazi did."

"The who?"

"Anasazi. The old people. The cliff dwellers. Like at Canyon de Chelly, you know?"

He'd seen it on TV. "I thought they used ladders."

"Yes, mostly. But there are also places where they cut steps into the rock. 'Staircase' is one way of translating the Navajo word. It's a phrase, really . . . for those steps."

He thought he saw where this was going, and was relieved. "So your true name . . ."

"I can't tell you my true name. It's not that Navajo phrase, if that's what you mean. You can't tell anybody your true name. It would give them too much power over you."

"Nobody? What about somebody you trusted?"

"Doesn't matter. Because sooner or later they'll die and become ghosts. And ghosts are nobody's friends. You'd never want a ghost to know your true name, no matter whose ghost it was."

Lassiter wondered if any of this was true, or maybe some mix of truth and invention. Probably that. He didn't really care. He enjoyed hearing it, hearing her tell it. He felt good, in some way he hadn't in a long time, and in some way he couldn't describe. And he had an idea that she felt the same. There was something going on here that had nothing to do with him being a cop or her being whoever she was.

"So what name do you practice law under?"

Her eyes gleamed in the gathering darkness. "It's the one everyone knows me by, except here. Celia Briseno. That's who I am when I'm at home."

He was stunned. It was the last thing he'd expected. Had it been some kind of setup, some kind of punch line, a way of telling him she was that much ahead of him? He didn't know. But if she was Jocelyn Peete . . . then Hector must be the Hispanic cop himself, the one Millie Desmond remembered. Did that make sense? Or should it have been obvious?

"Is that the name of the woman you're looking for?" she asked with what seemed innocent curiosity.

He shook his head slowly, once again feeling the two photos with his fingertips, sliding them against one another, like shuffling cards, not knowing which would come up. He lifted out the smaller one, the yearbook photo Hector had sent him, and showed it to her.

"This is her, ten years ago. Her name is Jocelyn Peete."

He could tell by the way she looked at the photo that he'd caught her completely off guard. If she'd been expecting anything, it was the Celeste Mundy photo. But she hadn't been expecting this.

"Jocelyn Peete?" she repeated, wrinkling her forehead, looking like she'd never heard the name before. She was good. But he knew he'd startled her. She'd recognized the face.

She turned the photo over, looked at the back, looked at the front again, then handed it to him. "Looks like a high school yearbook photo," she said.

"It is. Sand Creek High School. Sand Creek's a little town about twenty-five miles north. I got the photo from a cop over there, a friend of mine. He might be a distant relative of yours. Or your adoptive parents, anyway. His name's Briseno. Hector Briseno."

Their eyes met for a second. One of those seconds when you and the perp both know it isn't working. But . . . was she the perp? That was what he didn't know.

He put the photo back in his pocket, feeling the edge of the larger one, grasping it for a moment but not wanting to bring it out. Not wanting to see her face when she saw it. Not wanting to see that *that* was the one she'd expected. She was good, but he didn't think she could hide that from him now. And it was what he was here to find out. He let go of the photo and took his hand out of his pocket.

"There are a lot of Brisenos in the world," she said.

He nodded. He couldn't think of anything else to say.

"Was there anything else?" She was watching him through the screen, and he had a feeling that she hoped there was, the same way he wished he could come up with something. But there wasn't anything he could think of, except Celeste Mundy.

"No. Thanks for your time."

"No problem."

He walked back to his car inside the widening, fading path of light her open door cast on the grass. Only when he stepped out of it did it disappear suddenly, the door closing at last, the world turning dark all around him.

7

Sunday

He decided to take Sunday off, to think about it. By the light of day, his conversation with Celia Staircase seemed a little crazy. He was no longer entirely sure he hadn't been having one of his episodes at the time—that continual feeling that she reminded him of someone else was a tip-off—except that he usually knew for sure afterward.

He was still convinced that Celia Staircase was Jocelyn Peete, which meant that Hector Briseno wasn't being straight with him. Something was going on that he didn't quite understand. Not necessarily criminal. He felt the old tug of curiosity about that, which was good, but he didn't want to be messing up other people's lives in what was really a make-believe investigation.

The real question for him was whether Celia/Jocelyn was also Celeste. That would make it a real investigation. He wasn't sure now it had been a good idea not to show her the other photo, to get her reaction to that. He'd gotten used to thinking of himself as not being any good at reading other people, had gotten in the habit of leaving that up to his partner. But now, dealing with this strange woman, he had to rely on his own intuition—and it felt oddly comfortable to him. There'd been a time in his life when reading one particular person had been virtually a matter of life and death to him. He'd been wrong a lot, but had gotten better. In his memory, that was virtually all he'd done back then. He knew, as a matter of fact, that he'd gone to school just like the other kids. He'd collected stamps, listened to the songs on the radio, played baseball, had friends of a sort. With an effort, he could remember some of that—actual moments. But it took no effort at all to smell the liquor on his father's breath, to feel the texture of the flannel shirts he'd worn, the gray oil- and manure-stained workpants. The smell of the old barn. All those things were still right there.

Things he thought he'd put far behind him, in another life that really had nothing to do with him now. And here they were again. Maybe it was because of the thing with Kay, or maybe it was the episodes, the blowup . . . but he didn't think so. He thought it was Celia Staircase. He didn't know how or why, but she'd brought this stuff back, put it right there, as real as yesterday.

And because of it, he didn't want her to be Celeste Mundy.

He realized that he was talking. Standing in the kitchen with his cup of coffee in his hand, saying it all out loud to himself, as if he were talking to Jerry, laying it out for him. Talking to himself. He really was fucking crazy.

He sighed and took a sip of coffee, found it cold. He poured another cup and carried it out to the front porch, sat down on the swing. He and Kay had lived in this house for four or five years, and this was maybe the third time he'd sat in this swing.

It was nice, though. Cool. More like spring than summer. There was a gray haze obscuring the sky, making it seem earlier in the day than it was, as if he hadn't slept late. What the hell. It was Sunday. You couldn't sleep late on Sunday.

It was quiet. No traffic along Topeka Avenue, which was one-way all the way from downtown to Pawnee, so that even this residential stretch served as a major thoroughfare, especially in the evening, when people got off work. That was why the house had been so cheap. Location.

But on a Sunday it was almost like a regular neighborhood. The street was just a little wider than normal.

This is how cops live, he thought. Even detectives, even on two salaries, they'd had to make that kind of compromise to get a house this nice. It was basically a working-class neighborhood—people who'd worked at Boeing for a hundred years and finally saved up enough to buy one of these old houses. Not something really nice. Not something over on the east side of town, or out in the new developments to the west. Not so new anymore, really. Just to him. He was becoming an old man. Fifty-four. He knew that wasn't really old. But it felt like seventy-three to him.

He realized that the telephone was ringing, in the kitchen at the back of the house. For all he knew, it had been ringing for a long time. He'd turned off the answering machine since he was there to answer. He wanted to ignore it, but he couldn't. Instead he got up and walked back there slowly. If they hung up before he got there, it wouldn't be his fault. They hadn't waited long enough.

But the phone was still ringing when he got to it. He squinted at the LCD display of the caller ID. No name, but the area code was 213. Los Angeles. Probably every cop in America—every homicide dick, anyway—knew two area codes. Los Angeles 213, New York 212.

He picked it up and said curtly, "Lassiter. Robbery/Homicide." Just the way he would at the division.

"Detective Lassiter. Sorry to bother you at home on a Sunday morning." It was a man, youngish-sounding. Lassiter had automatically written the caller ID number on the pad beside the phone. He glanced at the clock and wrote down the time.

"No problem," he said.

"Ah. Good. This is Detective Sanders Burton of the LAPD. You said Robbery/Homicide?"

"Yeah."

"I thought you'd be in burglary, or maybe vice or missing persons. But you're the one who sent this query, right?"

"Yeah. Do you have anything on her there?"

"No. This may be a mistake. Is she a murder suspect there?"

"No . . ." He hesitated, then said, "Jocelyn Peete is a missing person. We don't have a separate unit for that." Both statements were true.

"She's been missing ten years, and you're still looking for her?"

He remembered deciding not to mention in the query how long she'd been gone. Burton knew something about her. "Yeah. You got something on her?"

"Jocelyn Peete? No. I thought it might have something to do with this whore we're looking for, Celeste Mundy."

It was only a half question, and Lassiter remained silent. But he couldn't lie to a brother officer about a case that officer was working on.

"I thought you might be working on that case," Burton said.

"Yeah, I am," Lassiter said.

"But . . . so this girl isn't connected with that?"

Lassiter sighed. "I don't know yet, Detective. I've come across this missing woman, and I'm looking into that. It's, umm, a long shot, so I didn't want to . . ."

"Right. I get it. But what makes you think she might be connected?"

"A couple of people mentioned her name when I showed them the photo. But the IDs were very tentative. Ten years . . . you know. She was a kid."

"So you haven't actually got her there." Burton sounded disappointed.

He wanted to say no, but he said, "There is a woman here who could possibly be Jocelyn Peete, living under a different name."

The disappointment was replaced by excitement. "Have you gotten a look at her?"

"Yes. I interviewed her in connection with the

missing-person thing. I didn't mention your thing. She denied being Jocelyn Peete."

"Hmm. You . . . I have to ask, Floyd. You don't—"

"Think I spooked her? No. I think she bought my story. I'm not sure I don't buy hers."

"But if she is our girl . . . just a cop even coming around, about anything . . . But of course you had to take a look. You had to talk to her about the Peete thing. What did you think? Obviously, you're not convinced she's Mundy."

"No. But there is a resemblance. I'd say a better resemblance to Peete than to Mundy . . . but they all kind of look alike. That's why I sent the query."

"Right. Sure." Burton thought about it, then said, "Listen, Floyd. You got anything you can hold her on, maybe just get prints . . . ?"

"Why? You have Mundy's, to match 'em with? That wasn't in the bulletin."

"Just came up with 'em. Another client decided to come out of the closet, and his video camera turned up some latents. A woman's prints. And he says it can't be anybody but her. It's a real break, 'cause she was super careful about that kind of stuff. We're sending out an addendum to the bulletin tomorrow morning. So what about it?"

"Printing the woman here? No cause."

"Hmm. Damn."

Burton was silent. This was obviously a very big deal to him. Maybe a career maker.

"You in that Art Theft Detail?" Lassiter asked. He thought it was a little silly himself, more of a P.R. thing than anything else. But it was all movies and celebrities out there—that's what other cops had told him. Like everything was a movie, bigger than life.

"No, I'm in burglary and theft, normally," Burton said, as if admitting to something shameful. "But there's only two guys in Art Theft, and they got a lot to do, so I'm helping them out."

The big chance, Lassiter thought. He felt sympathy and contempt for Burton at the same time.

"I think I'm gonna come out there," Burton said.

"What? You mean to Wichita?"

"You mind?"

Lassiter gave an involuntary laugh. "No. It's your money. It's just . . ."

"The taxpayers' money, anyway," Burton said. "It's just . . . I think it's the quickest way to know—and I've seen all the tapes, with all the different hairstyles and so on, so maybe . . . It's just, if it is her, I'd like to get there before she skips again. Not that I think . . ."

"I understand. It's pretty thin, though."

"Frankly, Floyd, it's more than anybody else has got. You mind giving me a quick rundown on what she said? Maybe something'll ring a bell that I can check here before I leave."

"Well, I think I already said she denied being Jocelyn Peete. She's living under the name Celia Staircase, in a—"

"Say again."

"Celia Staircase. Regular 'staircase.'"

"Hell of a name to hide under."

"She says she's Indian, that it's a translation of some Indian name."

"Indians don't have staircases."

"I said that. It has to do with those cliff dwellings, you know? I guess they have stairs of some kind."

"Hmm. It's weird enough I can see why you might halfway buy it."

"It gets weirder. She says she's a lawyer, but not practicing. She won some kind of settlement in a lawsuit in the little town in New Mexico where she used to live, but because of it she didn't feel comfortable staying there, so she decided to move somewhere else. And she picked Wichita."

"She have family there or something?"

"Nope. The only family she mentioned was a brother back in New Mexico, named Eddy—that's the name she's using for her telephone number."

"Eddy Staircase."

"Uh-huh."

"I don't mean to be insulting, Floyd, but why Wichita?"

"I asked the same thing. She says somebody told her it was a friendly town."

"Is it?"

"Probably. I meet more of the unfriendly ones, in my line of work."

Burton laughed. "Does she look like an Indian?"

"Who doesn't?"

"Danny Glover? Paul Newman?"

"Paul Newman played an Indian in some movie."

"*Hombre.* But he was a white guy who'd been raised by the Indians. Apaches."

"Well, she looks more like an Indian than Paul Newman does. But so do I."

There was a short silence, and then Burton said, "I'll fly out tomorrow morning, early. I'll give you a call when I arrive. All right if I call there, or should I call the department?"

"Might as well call here. They'll just tell you I'm on vacation."

"Right. Want me to bring the other videotapes with me?"

"No. Not my thing."

"I'm glad to hear that, Floyd." He sounded like he really was—and also a little surprised. "I'm looking forward to seeing you."

Lassiter didn't say anything. He couldn't lie to a brother officer, and he'd begun to feel a little uneasy about Burton coming here to look at her. He didn't really *want* her to be Celeste Mundy.

When they'd hung up, he went back out to the porch, where it was even hotter now. But the chair was in the shade, and there was a wind blowing across the porch—not exactly a cool wind, but not hot, either. And there was a smell in it that he liked—a smell like rain coming, although there wasn't a cloud in the sky.

8

She went to the downtown library and used one of their computers to log onto the Internet through her Yahoo account, then used Alta Vista to search for anything on the Wichita Police Department. It turned out the City of Wichita site had a very attractive page devoted to the cops—but no information on individual detectives, not even a listing of names by division. It wasn't nearly as helpful as the big fancy LAPD Web site. Their Art Theft Detail posted all its bulletins, so it was fairly easy to follow their progress. The bulletin on her had included a mug shot that was obviously cropped from one of the videos, and she thought she knew which one. Sam Dunwich. In retrospect, she had probably made a mistake taking his wife's jewelry. Jo had thought about that, but had hoped his fear of his wife would work the other way, make him clam up and claim ignorance when the old bag discovered it and went on her inevitable rampage.

The L.A. bulletin also referred to "several victims befriended by the suspect, who later burglarized their residences, taking various items of art, jewelry, silver and porcelain." Befriended. Cops lived in a strange world of their own, spoke a language that was a mixture of unadorned reality and weird euphemisms. And what was this porcelain shit? Somebody was ripping off his insurance carrier. Probably they all were. Fine with her. Anything that might confuse the cops. The most important thing, from her point of view, was that the bulletin listed no known associates, and no areas known to be frequented by "the suspect." Also, the date when she was "last seen," according to the bulletin, was two weeks before the day she'd actually left. Unless they were being clever—which wasn't like the LAPD—there were at least three clients they hadn't heard from, including Bannerman. That fit with what she'd expected from him, that he'd use his own resources to look for her, not the cops. It was one time she didn't like finding out she was right.

She didn't know of any reason why the LAPD would alert the WPD in particular, and even if they did, there was little reason for the Wichita cops to spend much time and effort on it. She checked the bulletin again, found that it hadn't been updated since last time—almost two months now. Hard to see how the WPD could really be interested in her.

No matter how she looked at it, it seemed unlikely that the cop's visit the night before had anything to do with Celeste Mundy. He hadn't shown her the photo, for instance. But he'd shown her Jes's senior yearbook photo. How the hell could he have gotten hold of that, except from Hector? Or unless he'd already traced her to Sand Creek somehow. But then, if he was looking for Celeste Mundy, and he knew that much, why visit her at all? Why alert her? The closest he'd come to saying anything at all that might be about Celeste Mundy had been that pointed remark about some people being paid to be friendly. But that could just as easily be about the bust ten years ago at that frat party. And that's essentially what he'd said it was about. But how had he ended up with the wrong photo?

It had to be Hector. A message to her, delivered through this cop who even said he knew Hector. How much did Lassiter really know? Maybe nothing. Maybe he was no more than the messenger.

That it made such sense made her uneasy, though. In her experience, things didn't often work out that easily, that close to what you wanted to happen. You had to be suspicious of your own desires. First, you had to know what you wanted, which most people didn't, really. Then you had to be alert to the temptation to reconstruct the facts to fit that. That was the only way, in the end, to protect yourself from the tiger. Otherwise, you were sleepwalking down the path, having some dream of being safe, getting where you wanted to go, while the tiger zeroed in on you.

Her plan, all along, had been to stay in Wichita—have nothing to do with Jes or Hector or Sand Creek—until she was sure nobody had her scent, or that those looking for her had given up. She also had a plan for getting a message to Bannerman, to let him know that she was just going to hold on to the painting as insurance. That as long as he left her alone, didn't try to find her, he didn't have to worry about it for the rest of his life—but otherwise, if anyone but the L.A. cops came after her, he did. She didn't think he could hold back the L.A. cops, and she wasn't really all that worried about them. But she was waiting for them to give up before sending the old Nazi the message.

She'd already violated her own rules once, trying to call Jes the other morning. Fortunately, Jes hadn't answered, and she'd had the sense not to leave a message, although she'd taken off the block on the caller ID. Maybe that was how Hector had gotten on her trail. That was a question to which she still didn't have an answer. She'd thought about Margo, but Margo was too shit-scared to tell anybody anything. And how would she and Hector get together? He might be able to find her, if he already had some reason for thinking Jo was in Wichita—but that took her back to the original question. She could think of only two reasons. That he'd traced the phone number from Jes's caller ID and asked an old friend from the WPD to go visit the address, see who lived there, and if she looked like the woman in the high school photo, show it to her and mention Hector's name. The other was that he'd seen the LAPD bulletin himself, thought she might have come to Wichita, and asked Lassiter to look for her.

Either explanation was okay, and both seemed more likely than that the WPD would be looking for Celeste Mundy, and would find their way to Celia Staircase, with a photo of her sister in hand. But there was still that chance. There was a part of her saying, Look, you were visited by a cop who knew more about you than he should have. Get the hell out. Right now.

But if it was Hector, maybe she should get back to Sand Creek—get Eddy to Sand Creek—sooner than she'd thought. And maybe, if she listened to that other part of herself, and ran again, she'd never get either of them back there at all. They'd be living like this from now on. The whole point had been to get home, to the one place where Eddy might have a chance for a better life than she'd had, or than she could give him all by herself. If she blew it now . . .

And there was that other question: Who the hell was Lassiter? Did she know him? Had he been one of the cops ten years ago? Or had she met him sometime, through Hector, when she was little? There'd been that one little moment when she'd thought she knew him, or that he reminded her of someone she knew— something like that—and then it had gone away, and she hadn't been able to figure it out. Probably it didn't mean anything at all, but it kept popping up in her thoughts, as if it did. Maybe it was some association with Hector, from a long time ago, that only her unconscious remembered. But that was one of those things she wanted too much to believe. And her reading of Lassiter, as a man, was that there was something wrong with him, something going on down deep, that might make him dangerous. She didn't know what it was—only that he was the kind of man she'd have turned down if he'd come to her out in L.A., wanting to be a client.

She logged off, went back to her car, and drove to a row of pay phones in Riverside Park, near the small cages of birds and small animals, where the whole zoo had once been. As she'd expected, they were deserted, and when she called the WPD she got a young guy who was probably working dispatch and answering the phone at the same time, instead of the usual receptionist.

"I'm trying to get in touch with Detective Floyd Lassiter," she told him, making her voice sound anxious, a little frightened. "Does he work on weekends?"

"Well, ma'am, right now he's on vacation. I could—"

"Oh no! On vacation? When will he be back?"

"Well, I don't know, ma'am. What you might want to do is call Lieutenant Loomis tomorrow, in the Robbery/Homicide—"

"Homicide? I thought Detective Lassiter worked on drug cases. I don't understand."

During the brief silence, she pictured him beckoning to someone else, or making notes on a pad. His voice was a little different, a little more businesslike, when he spoke again. "No, ma'am. As long as I've been with the department, Detective Lassiter has been in Robbery/Homicide division. Now, do you have a problem that involves illegal drugs? Are you in some kind of danger? I could send a car to get you. If I could get your name and address—"

She hung up, got quickly back into her car. So, a homicide dick who was on vacation. Who had no good reason to be visiting her on a Saturday night, showing her a ten-year-old photo of her sister which he'd gotten from someone named Briseno, unless it was that man who'd sent him to talk to her, as a personal favor.

She wasn't sure enough to call him on her own phone, as she had Jes. That had been stupid, anyway. Crazy to think that Jes would have figured out what day it was, the way she had, or that she'd remember the name.

She turned west to Sim Park, then north a block to the long, curving road that ran back along the river, coming out again by the museums, across the loop of the little river from Riverside Park. Instead of using that phone again, however, she went south, crossing

the main branch, and found a phone at a convenience
store on Seneca. She dialed the Sand Creek P.D. and
then Hector's voice mail. She didn't expect him to be
there on a Sunday, but if he was, she'd just hang up.

But he didn't answer. She listened to his recorded
voice, waited for the beep, and said, "Hector, it's me.
I got your message."

9

The cobblestone clouds seemed to hang only inches above the roof of Lassiter's car, making a narrow world in which the wind moved in all directions at once, as if looking for a way out, flattening and whipping the weeds in the median, pushing his car first one way and then the other as he passed under the bridges. Coming out again into the open, he had to grip the wheel with both hands to keep the wind from sending his car across the median and into the oncoming headlights. It would have been easy just to relax his hands, let the car go where it wanted. But there were other people behind those lights.

He'd come away from the nursing home with the beginnings of a headache, the way he often did, but he was hoping the wind might blow it away, as it sometimes seemed to. He felt that if only he could lie down in the dark, with the window open beside the bed, and let the moist air blow in the smell of the rain, he'd be able to sleep. Not the way he had been, but really *sleep*. It seemed to him that he hadn't really slept for years, for longer than he could remember.

Thirteenth Street was coming up. He had to decide whether to get off there or not, to go on home, to Kay's house, where the room he slept in had windows. He didn't want to decide until he had to—didn't want to decide at all.

He felt a stab of pain on the left side of his head, back behind his eye. Then another, and then they were gone. Icepick headaches. He liked them because they made the regular headache recede for a while.

And because they had a name. Everyone knew what
they were. You could tell someone you had icepick
headaches and they knew what you were talking
about.

He leaned forward to peer up through the windshield at the clouds. This kind of weather—any quick
change in the barometric pressure—sometimes
brought on the seizures, and the icepick headaches
were often precursors to one. Not always. He didn't
really feel anything yet, though. Maybe he should just
go on home, try to get to sleep before anything
started.

He turned off onto the exit ramp at Thirteenth
Street. The street was full of cars. He'd forgotten
about the kids. Even on a Sunday night they were out,
with their windows open, moving slowly, calling to one
another, the ratchety, monotonous thump of the music
pounding from their radios. Here they were mostly
black. Beyond Broadway, nearer to North, they'd be
mostly white and Hispanic. And Vietnamese, he supposed. Half the stores on Broadway, between Thirteenth
and Twenty-first, had signs written in Vietnamese nowadays. Did Vietnamese kids cruise in their cars and
listen to the radio?

Now and then one of the black kids glanced at him
as he sat at the red light at the bottom of the exit
ramp. Mostly they were indifferent. A few grinned,
turned or leaned forward to say something to someone
else—an old white guy in an eight-year-old car, trying
to go somewhere on Thirteenth at this time of night.
Must be lost.

The wordless pulse of the music, always the same,
rode the wind into his own car, reminding him of
other nights, other music. Almost always, he had been
alone in his car—his parents' car—just as he was now.
Had he minded? He seemed to remember minding,
but he wasn't sure why. He liked being alone. What
he remembered, or thought he did, was that sense of
being free, being able to go wherever he wanted. How
had that gone away? Had he traded it for not being

alone? If so, he ought to have it back now. But then, where was it?

The light changed and he turned west. He crossed Topeka on a green light, not wanting to stop to turn left, to interrupt the flow of traffic. It didn't matter. He could still turn on Broadway. Or Main. There were lots of ways to get home from here, and he knew them all.

He didn't turn at Broadway. He didn't like Broadway—the lights, the storefronts. He preferred getting around town on streets like Topeka and Main, the one-way streets with mostly houses on either side. He hit a red light at Main. The traffic had thinned out quite a bit, and the kids he could see now all looked white. No Vietnamese. Most of the cars were coming toward him, turning south on Main, toward downtown, to cruise the main drag with the kids from East and West and the other schools. Just before the light turned green, he noticed that he wasn't in the left turn lane. Apparently, he'd decided. He'd narrowed down his choices to Celia or his mother's house.

This time he drove up the alley and parked in the blackness beside the tall wooden fence that enclosed the backyard of the house next to the duplexes. When he'd turned off his engine and his headlights, he sat for a while in the dark. The dark made the headache recede; light made it flare up. The only light he could see at the Staircase apartment was that dim one from the upper room. He hoped she hadn't replaced the porch light.

Out of the car, in the open between the two duplexes, he had to lean against a wind that was stronger and colder than he'd expected. He looked up at the clouds, saw that they were swirling, seeming to slide in different directions, past and through each other. No spiral patterns, though.

Lowering his eyes, he had a moment of vertigo, and the step he took was a stagger, the wind pushing him a little toward the street. But then the dizziness was gone, as brief as the icepick headaches. Had he had that before? Maybe it was just something ordinary and physical, an inner ear thing. He had a tendency now to think that anything unusual was a part of this stuff he had. Some of it was probably just age. Just weird little things that didn't mean anything.

He'd knocked once and was listening for the sound of her footsteps inside when the first few heavy drops began to fall. Not enough to bother him. And it was only water. He'd never really minded the rain. He remembered walking all the way home from school once in the rain, all the way from town to the farm, walking slowly because he was in no hurry to get home. *Only water.* He knocked again.

He could tell this time that she was coming down the stairs, her footsteps moving toward him. The stairway must be just beyond the kitchen, facing this door. She didn't even click the porch light switch this time, nor did she turn on the kitchen light. It was as if she knew who it was and that the light would hurt him. Her eyes, peering at him through the small opening she made, seemed larger than he remembered, and for a moment he wondered if this was the same woman, if he had not made some sort of mistake, if he had not dreamed that other woman . . . or was dreaming now.

But she spoke his name and opened the door wider. "Detective Lassiter." Her voice was hardly more than a whisper, but he imagined that he heard some sort of welcome in it. And she was smiling—a sardonic half smile. He knew what it meant—that she thought him a fool—but it pleased him anyway. He was used to it. Women always looked at him that way at some point, early on, the first or second or third time he met them. They knew he was different from other men, and that was how they first reacted. Later, they became motherly, protective. One had made the mistake of marrying him, confusing that feeling with the other thing. He hadn't known enough then to warn her. But it had all worked out in the end.

"You have some more questions?" she asked.

He shook his head. "No. I came to tell you what's going on. To tell you the truth."

She looked suspicious for the first time. Maybe now she wouldn't believe anything he said. That was what happened sometimes.

"It's Celeste Mundy I've been looking for," he said. "Not Jocelyn Peete. And there's a detective coming from L.A. tomorrow to take a look at you. If you don't know what any of that means, it doesn't matter. If you do—"

"Why are you telling me this?"

He looked away, then up at the sky again. It wasn't that simple to tell the simple truth. He looked back at her. "I can't explain it to you. It's personal." Seeing her reaction, he said, "Not that way. I don't want anything."

She didn't seem to have anything to say, and he guessed that was unusual. Lightning flashed directly overhead, illuminating the space between the duplexes for a moment, in black and white, the brief light making his headache pulse and also showing him the female shape of her, and the fluttering of the hem of whatever it was she was wearing—some kind of robe, he thought, not a T-shirt this time. That first stiff wind had become erratic and unpredictable, and it was filled with the smell of a coming storm. He wasn't sure he'd be doing this if it wasn't for that. The lightning flashed a second time, making her for a moment a white, headless shape, shot in negative. Too much like a corpse at the—

The icepick headache stabbed him again. Three times. Bang! Bang! Bang! He took a sideways step, making some sound he couldn't hear, then shook his head hard. *Why had that happened?*

"What's wrong?" Celia Staircase asked. "Are you all right?"

"Fine," he said automatically. What had they been talking about? He had no idea. He must be questioning her, but he didn't have his notepad out. There was nothing to give him a clue. It was raining, and it was dark. Early morning or late night? He was in a fix.

"Sorry," he said. "I just have a headache. What were we talking about?"

He could see by her reaction that that hadn't worked. He was pretty sure this had happened before, but surely not in this situation. He couldn't remember it happening at all. He didn't know what it was called or . . . anything. He didn't know a fucking thing. He didn't know what day it was. Maybe he wasn't working, since he didn't have his notepad out. But what could he be doing here? He was pretty sure he knew this woman, although he had no idea what her name was. Why was he standing on her porch in the rain, like a salesman, without any lights on?

"You were telling me about a detective who's coming here from Los Angeles to see me," she said, studying him. "You remember that?"

He didn't, but he tried. Something about the airport. "Is he flying in?"

"I don't think you said. Probably. Do you know where we are?"

"Sure. Wichita. I grew up here. I went to North High. The Redskins." He laughed, then frowned. "Sorry," he said. "Aren't you . . . are you an Indian?"

She smiled. "Yes, but don't worry about it."

"I'm a police officer now," he said.

"I know. Has this happened before?"

"Yeah, I think so." He closed his eyes. When he tried to reach for some things, in his mind, it was like there was a wall . . . or nothing there, a space he couldn't get to the other side of, a fallen bridge. He thought maybe he *could* get to the other side, get through the wall, if he made a hard enough push, but he also thought that would hurt. It scared him. He wasn't sure it wouldn't injure him in some permanent way. "I think it goes away," he said. "I think so."

But, Christ, what if it never did? What if, this time, it didn't?

"I need to sleep," he said. He looked up at the sky, was surprised by the swirling clouds, had a fleeting memory of lightning. He looked at her, embarrassed. "It's dark," he said. "Is it late at night?"

She didn't seem to think there was anything wrong with the question. "Yes. And it's raining and you're getting all wet." She stood looking at him for a moment, and then she reached to unhook the screen. "You'd better come inside." She held the door open for him.

He hesitated. He wasn't sure that was something he should do. She was wearing some kind of thin garment, maybe only a nightgown. And his partner wasn't here . . . He looked around at the other apartments, thinking Jerry might be talking to someone else, but they were all dark. Why wasn't Jerry here? He couldn't remember what they were doing, what the case was. Was he even working? If not, what was he doing here?

The woman leaned out far enough to touch his sleeve. "Come on, Detective. You're all wet. And there's something wrong with you."

He looked at her. *Detective.* He must be working. She reminded him of someone. He knew there was something wrong . . . something . . . one of those . . . he couldn't think of the word for it. Was this the same thing?

She gave a tug on his sleeve, and he said, "Oh. Sorry," and went in.

He was in a kitchen, without any lights on. Too dark to take notes. And he didn't have his pad out. He tried to find it, feeling his pockets, but couldn't remember where it was. He gave up and stood in the dark, wondering where he was, what was going on. He didn't feel like he was in danger. Just having one of those . . . whatever they were. He didn't know this kitchen. He could hear water dripping onto the floor, and there was water on his face, and a stream of water down the side of his neck. He wiped it, discovered that his hair was wet.

It got even darker and he heard a lock being closed and looked toward the sound, but could see only a whitish blur moving toward him.

10

Jes jerked awake, sat halfway up and looked at the door, the direction of her parents' bedroom. But the door wasn't there. There was only a confusing patch of darkness seeming to float in the gray of the bedroom. It lit up suddenly, lightning flashing outside, the screech of it seeming to leave an echo not of itself but of the cry she'd heard in her dream—Jo's cry.

She was sleeping in her parents' bedroom. It was hers now, had been for a long time. Her father, Rafe Wellington, had been dead for more than a dozen years, her mother, Maria, longer than that. Jo had been gone ten years, and neither of them had slept in that other bedroom since before that. Neither of them had even lived in this house for five of those years.

But obviously, she'd been dreaming about Jo again. She couldn't remember the dream itself, only that terrible cry of pain and fear and . . . something worse. In the dream, she'd thought that Jo was dead, that he'd finally killed her. She sat up, wanting to get the echo of that terrible, final tone of despair out of her mind. It had been like the sound an animal might make. Even worse than any of the sounds Jo had really made. If she'd made any sound that bad back then, surely Jes would have had to get up and do something, not just lie there with her pillow wrapped around her head, pretending to sleep.

Or maybe not. She had no real reason to think there was any limit to her own cowardice. She lay back down and closed her eyes, breathing deeply, noticing for the first time the calming sound of the rain outside the window. She tried to relax into the rhythmless beat of it, the slap and whisper, hoping it would wash away that awful dream sound and the self-knowledge it brought, but when the lightning flashed again, she jerked, her eyes opening, and gave a small cry of her own. The crash of thunder that came close behind it was so near, it seemed to rattle the window glass. When it was gone, she imagined she could still hear a strange high-pitched whining sound.

Then she laughed, understanding that it wasn't her imagination. She got up and went to the bedroom door. Susie rushed in, panting audibly, her nails rattling on the hardwood floor. She went to the bed, then came back to Jes, then went and sniffed the door Jes had closed again, then looked up at Jes in a kind of reproach. Do something about this, her eyes said. There was a half-mad gleam in her eyes that made even Jes a little nervous. *She looks the way I feel inside*, Jes thought.

She went to the dog and put both her hands on the big head, rubbing it, smoothing the fur of her neck. "Sorry, baby girl," she said. "Mama can't make the storm go away."

Susie stayed perfectly still, not exactly relaxing but not wanting to move while Jes was stroking her and making the meaningless sounds of comfort, not wanting her to stop. If she did stop, Jes knew, the dog would jerk back into motion and begin pacing the room as if the lightning had gotten inside her bones, setting her into aimless motion. Jes felt some of that itchy electricity herself.

She went to bed and sat down, bringing Susie along with her, and continued to soothe the big dog until she had gradually soothed herself, and there was nothing left of the bad dream. She'd been dreaming about Jo a lot lately. When they were kids, she'd have thought that meant something, that Jo was sending her some message. She hadn't believed in that "twin sense" for a long time, maybe since before Jo had left. Because they hadn't really been twins anymore, for a while before that, apart from looking alike. She'd felt that way about it, anyway, and she thought Jo had, too.

She gave Susie a dismissive pat and got up and went to the window to look out at the storm. It was still a ways until fall, but maybe there'd be a temporary break in the heat, at least. You couldn't count on it. Sometimes a storm like this just made everything muggier and more miserable. Through the window, through the rain, she could make out only the rough forms of the furniture on the deck to her right, and the yard itself was only a gray, shimmery plane, with a dark, uneven border that hinted at the fringe of bushes and trees enclosing it. As she watched, lightning struck a third time, revealing for an instant the shape of the school building over on the other side of the gully. And then it was gone and the sound of thunder seemed slower, more distant, and the rain sound itself was diminished. It was moving on. Susie nudged her thigh, and she dropped a hand automatically to the dog's head.

Could it be that Jo was really out there somewhere, close enough for her to sense? Once or twice lately she'd thought she glimpsed her sister, climbing into a car in a parking lot or turning down an aisle at the supermarket. Once or twice, in the mornings, she'd gone into the bathroom, not awake yet, and been momentarily surprised not to find Jo standing in front of the mirror, spending an eternity putting on her makeup, studying herself in the mirror. That face that everyone else thought was so like Jes's own but that to her was Jo's face, not at all the one she herself saw in the mirror.

Of course, it was absurd, even in the middle of the night, awakening from some nightmare in the middle of a thunderstorm—even if there was such a thing as twin sense—to think that Jo might come back to this area, just come back and live by herself, without letting Jes know. Or at least Hector. And Hector would tell Jes. Wouldn't he? She realized she wasn't sure.

But the thought that he might not, might even keep Jo's presence secret from Jes, to protect her, made her think better of him.

She looked down at Susie, who was nudging her thigh, wanting more petting, and then shook her head and said sternly, "Come on, you big baby. It's only a storm. You're going back to the basement, where you belong." But it was a fake, and Susie knew it. She made no move toward the door, only wagged her tail a little and looked back at Jes. "All right," Jes said. "But you stay on the rug. You don't get on the bed. You're not a puppy anymore." She tapped the big oval throw rug with her toe, pointed at it, and Susie lay down there obediently, her eyes still looking up. "Now stay," Jes added as she climbed back into bed. The dog had never actually been trained, but now and then she did what she was told.

Jes lay on her back, her eyes open, looking at the featureless gray of the ceiling, wondering if Hector knew where Jo was. It wasn't a new thought. She'd suspected for some time that Hector was even in touch with Jo, keeping track of her. Of course, neither of them had ever talked about anything like that. There were too many things she wasn't supposed to know, that she didn't want Hector to know she did—and maybe the same the other way around. It was like having a set of shared secrets you pretended to keep from each other. Not so much to spare the other person as because you yourself preferred to believe he didn't know. Hector was the nearest thing she and Jo had to a relative anymore, since Aunt Jimmie had died. And although she and Jo had lived with Aunt Jimmie for a couple of years after their father's death, they'd never had the same kind of connection with her that they'd had with Hector for as long as she could remember.

Feeling a little foolish, she closed her eyes and tried reaching out to Jo in her mind, the way they had when they were kids. She wasn't even sure she remembered how to do it. But it came back with surprising ease.

It was like reaching out for what she had only ever been able to describe, even to herself, as a kind of solid place in her mind—a bright, warm, solid thing that was her sister, inside her mind.

Once, in college, a little drunk, unhappy about something she didn't remember now, she'd reached out this way. But she'd been too drunk, or Jo had been too far away, or it was just a fantasy anyway—which was what she told her roommate, who came in and asked what she was doing. She remembered guiltily how she'd laughed about it, telling her roommate. Laughing at the little girls they'd once been, Jo and herself.

She opened her eyes suddenly and sat up. For just a second she'd felt something. But what she'd felt was terrible. She put her arms around herself, shivering, then put her hands to her cheeks and felt tears she hadn't known were there. She looked at the window again, as if she could see all the way through it to wherever Jo was.

She hadn't exactly felt Jo. That was what was terrible. She'd touched the place where Jo ought to be, and there'd been nothing there. Not the same thing as being at a distance, or being drunk, or anything like that. Those things seemed to make it impossible even to find her way to that place inside her mind, made it seem not to be there, to be only a fantasy. But this time it had been there, solid as ever. But no longer bright and no longer warm, because Jo was no longer in it.

Jo was gone. She was really gone. Gone forever.

11

"Open the motherfucking door, motherfucker! I'm gonna kick your old white ass."

Lassiter sat up and blinked at the man outside the window. It wasn't a dream. He turned his head to look out the front windshield—it hurt to do it—and there was the river and the apartments on the other side. He'd fallen asleep while driving and run off the road. Jesus.

Another hard thump. He saw now that there were two of them. The one in front was very angry, but the other was standing back, looking uncertain, his arms crossed as if he were cold.

"What's the matter?" Lassiter asked.

The man suddenly laughed. He bent his head down, leaning on the car with both hands, and shook his head from side to side, laughing. Then he looked around at the other guy and said, "He says, 'What's the *matter*?' Fucker tries to run over my ass and wants to know what's the matter. He's gonna wonder what's the matter . . ."

The other man said something. Lassiter couldn't make it out, but it sounded like he was trying to calm his friend down. Lassiter realized he was in no condition to deal with some kind of altercation, but he couldn't quite make it feel real. It was like everything outside the car was still a dream. He looked toward the passenger side and saw that his shoulder holster and weapon and his jacket and one of his shoes were set on the seat, all wadded up together. He realized that he had only socks on his feet, and that they were wet. He'd been out in the rain, without his shoes. What in the hell had he been doing? He had a vague memory of running into something and dropping one shoe . . . but he couldn't quite get it. And he wasn't sure it hadn't been in a dream . . .

The car was rocking back and forth, and he realized that the man outside was pushing on it, making it rock, as if trying to turn it over. Lassiter didn't think that was possible. He'd seen it done by crowds a couple of times. He sighed, feeling very tired, as if he might not have the physical strength to drive home. He had some bruises, too, probably from when the car had come to a stop. His chest, his jaw . . . And he was wet and cold. He felt the jacket, and it was drier than himself, just a little damp. He began untangling it from the holster.

"Whoa, shit!" someone yelled. The rocking subsided. "Gun, man! Fucker's got a gun. Haul ass!" The voice receded quickly, and they were gone so suddenly he wasn't entirely sure they hadn't been part of the dream. What had that all been about? Had he dreamed all that while driving the car? "Fucker's got a gun." They were gone and he was alone. How far had he driven?

This was different from anything before. There was a blank place back there somewhere, right before he'd fallen asleep.

He searched for the other side of it. He'd visited his mother. It hadn't been raining yet when he was driving back into town. He'd thought how nice it would be to go to the house on Topeka and sleep with the windows open, if it rained. Why hadn't he gone there? When had it started raining?

He knew he'd been thinking about stopping at the duplex where that woman, Celia Staircase, lived. He remembered standing on her back porch, with no light, talking to her through the screen, but this time it had started to rain. Had he really gone there? He thought he had. Christ! What had he said to her?

What had he been thinking about saying to her? It

took a moment to come. Burton, the L.A. cop. He
remembered now. He'd been irritated by the whole
thing, the way it was turning out. It was this kind of
practice thing, not a real case, and he wanted to get
back into Loomis's good graces—and he'd done a
good job, too. He'd actually found somebody who
could be the one they were looking for. Maybe even
was. He remembered thinking that. But . . . it was the
thing with Hector. He'd gotten interested in that, so
he'd sent the query, and next thing you know there's
this L.A. cop. He didn't need it to turn into a real
burglary case, working with outside cops. He needed
to get back to homicide. And besides, he liked her.
And she was something to Hector, probably. So fuck
L.A. That's what he'd been thinking.

No use worrying about it. If he had told her, and
she was Celeste Mundy, it would just mean she
wouldn't be there when Burton arrived. Fine with him.

He cataloged the aches and pains he'd picked up
when the car had stopped. Probably he'd run into
something he couldn't see from here. Hopefully not a
person. Or maybe he just hadn't had his foot on the
accelerator anymore and it had coasted to a stop. He
still had a tiny trace of the headache, but that was
nothing. It felt like he'd been in some kind of fight.
A bruiselike pain right in the middle of his chest.
Soreness in his arms and shoulders like the kind you
got from hitting the bag at the gym. Not really that
many bruises, actually, or at least not pains that felt
like bruises. He'd take a closer look at home. And
the hinges of his jaw ached. That seemed strange. He
opened and closed his mouth a couple of times,
wincing.

Maybe he'd had his teeth clenched tightly while he
was driving. Some part of him realizing he was in trouble. Or maybe, shit . . .

People with grand-mal seizures clenched their jaws,
didn't they?

Damn. Time to take everybody's advice and see a
doctor.

He had to turn the key twice to get the engine started again. At first he thought it might not and he'd have to walk—which almost seemed like an appealing idea. He just hoped to Christ he hadn't *done* anything.

He thought about that for a moment. A fistfight? It was hard to imagine. During the thing with Strickland he'd automatically backed away. He'd *never* crossed that line, and he didn't intend to. That was his father, not him.

He frowned, realizing this was going to bug him for a while. He put the car into reverse and began backing carefully toward the roadway.

PART TWO

12

Monday

The aches and pains gave Lassiter an odd kind of pleasure, reminding him of Saturday mornings after high school football games, a small kind of pain that had made him feel stronger, launched into his own life. Unafraid.

Riding that feeling, he bypassed the shower stall in the utility room and went up the carpeted stairs to the big tub in the bathroom connected to his mother's bedroom, the one room in the house he had left almost entirely untouched, apart from the few things she'd taken to the nursing home with her.

Sitting in the tub, soaking amid the soapy, powdery smells that were now a little stale, with a hint of mold and dust mixed in, he wondered about his own motives, as he had dozens of times before. Sometimes it had seemed to him that he hated to wipe out the last of the life his mother had lived during the years of his father's illness and, afterward, on her own. Sometimes he thought it was only some kind of fear, the same kind of ridiculous, superstitious fear that made him uneasy about putting some other book on top of a Bible, even though he'd never gone to church, never believed any of that stuff. But this morning it seemed clear to him. He'd been saving the dismantling of this bedroom, saving it the way he might the last portion of some food he loved. Putting off that final pleasure, knowing there'd be no more like that. It would all be gone. Not a crumb left.

Savoring in a different way the small, scattered pains in his body, speculating on the cause of each the way a pathologist would look at each bit of damage in a corpse—the bruises on his shoulders and chest mapping the steering wheel, the sharper pain in his knuckles the moment when his hands had flown from the wheel and struck the instrument panel—he came around tentatively to his first stab at reconstructing his scrambled memories of the night before.

It seemed to him that there was a bigger blank place than usual, which made sense. This one had been not just bigger but different. There were too many points of pain that couldn't be explained any other way, especially the muscle ache that was worst in his jaw, making him fight off each yawn, but not only in his jaw. At some point the night before, every muscle in his body had been clenched tight like a fist. And stayed clenched for long enough to leave this pain that was deeper than any of the bruises.

Odd images that felt like memories of forgotten dreams had begun to float up, too elusive to capture, which was always the way it was. Something very vague about a fistfight . . . and a woman . . . A fight *with* a woman . . . or to protect a woman? Probably the latter. He wished he remembered it, if that's what had happened in the dream.

His aches and bruises wouldn't really fit with a fight, though. And certainly not with a woman. No scratches, for one thing. Nothing to the face except the ache in his jaw. No groin pain. Women who didn't know how to fight mostly just pushed and slapped and scratched, or went for the ears or hair. Those who did know how went for the eyes, the throat, the solar plexus, the groin, the feet and shins and knees—whatever was most easily available, among the spots most likely to make a man forget his original plans. He'd helped teach those classes himself, usually playing the attacker, wearing more padding than any football player or hockey goalie. And still winding up with pain like this the next morning—but not exactly like this. If he'd been in a fight at all, he'd been punched, the way a man would punch, but hadn't really been hurt much by it. It hadn't been a fight. It had been a seizure.

As for what had really happened, apart from that—he remembered everything up to the moment he'd stood on Celia Staircase's porch, feeling the first drops of rain, listening for her footsteps. He thought she'd come to the door, but that was where it became scrambled and dreamlike, with too many parts missing or nonsensical to be sure. The next thing he was sure of was waking up in the car on the riverbank—and he was really sure of that only because he'd gotten a little clearer after that, on the drive home, and he'd felt sure *then* that's what had happened. He'd also thought that some black guy had been yelling at him through the window when he awakened, some guy angry about something. But then he'd disappeared. Didn't seem very likely.

If he had talked to Celia Staircase—or whatever her name was—what had he said? He knew what he'd intended to tell her. He shook his head, knowing now how far he'd already been into the seizure when he'd been driving back from the nursing home, thinking he was clear and normal.

He considered going back to the duplex to ask her what had happened. Yet how stupid would that be? Some residue of the seizure-dream had left him feeling that he could do that, that they were sort of friends. Something like that. Even when the dreams were crazy, they could leave you feeling real emotions like that. Even regular dreams were like that sometimes. No way he was going back over there and make even more of a fool of himself.

Then he remembered Burton. He'd talked to him—yesterday morning? Jesus. It seemed like days ago. But Burton had said he'd be there the next morning. Which was this morning. And he'd have to meet with him. Burton would probably want him to go with him to the duplex. He gave a grunt. That ought to be interesting, if he really had acted crazy the night before.

What the hell. The main thing now was to do what Kay had told him to do a hundred times—see a doctor. And for real, not just to pacify Loomis. It was strange how little the idea seemed to bother him now. He'd been thinking for a long time—a *long* time— that keeping his job was more important than anything else. Of course, he didn't want to lose his job, but . . .

Something had happened inside him. Maybe just because this one was so obviously something that had to be dealt with, that could make him a danger to other people. The thing in Loomis's office should have given him some hint of that. Strange. But last night he'd been driving around for a while in the rain, not knowing what in the hell he was doing. Maybe asleep, maybe inside some kind of fantasy, maybe just all clenched up behind the wheel, letting the car go where it wanted. He was lucky he hadn't smashed into something, lucky he hadn't run over anyone.

He sat up straight, then climbed out of the tub and went out through the bedroom and down the stairs to the bottom level, naked and dripping, and then all the way back along the lower hallway, past his own bedroom, to the door to the garage.

After a few minutes, he relaxed and let out a breath. If the car had struck anyone or anything, it hadn't been going fast enough to leave any indication on the car itself. Maybe that was what the black guy had been yelling about, if he'd been real. He stood there, thinking about calling dispatch to ask about hit-and-runs the night before, how to phrase the question. Then he began to feel cold and realized he was still wet and naked. All he could see through the little rows of windows in the two garage doors was the massed green of the cedars along the back, but the light told him it was still gray.

He went back inside, got a towel from the shelf beside the shower stall, and dabbed and rubbed himself as he went back up to his mother's bedroom to empty the tub. Back in his own bedroom, he dressed hastily, feeling a kind of urgency about getting over to the other house, seeing what messages he had and putting on some clean clothes, to deal with the L.A. detective.

As he drove beneath the gray sky, it struck him how clear and sharp everything seemed. It was like coming clear again after a seizure, but larger and more subtle, as if, without knowing it, he'd been in some vaguely dreamlike state for a long time, for years, a sort of nightmare in which he'd been slinking around, frightened and baffled. But this morning he'd awakened not into that dream but into the real world, and was himself again, no longer frightened that same way.

Burton's was the only message on the answering machine at the house on Topeka. He'd called less than an hour before—it wasn't ten yet—saying he had a room at the Airport Hilton, and would wait there awhile for Lassiter to call back. He said he hoped Lassiter would pick him up and take him by to meet Celia Staircase, but if he hadn't heard anything from him by lunchtime, he'd go ahead and take a taxi downtown.

What the hell. Lassiter waited for the tape to finish and then picked up the phone to call the hotel.

Burton reminded him a little of Danny Davidson, who was also a little guy who talked a lot, but was a pretty good detective. While Lassiter drove, Burton talked about his flight, his hotel room, the breakfast he'd had, and also now and then about the case. As they were taking the exit on Seneca, to go north to the Riverside area, Burton said, "I sure wish you'd let me get a word in edgewise, Floyd."

Lassiter gave an involuntary laugh, then winced and said, "I've got some kind of problem with my jaw. It hurts a little to talk."

"Hey, no problem. I can do the talking for both of us. You think it's gonna rain? I didn't bring a raincoat. Matter of fact, I don't own one."

Lassiter leaned forward a little, peered at the clouds. "It's hard to tell," he said. "It might snow."

Burton gave a laugh, then studied him and said, "Shit. Are you serious?"

Lassiter shook his head, but then shrugged. "Kansas is different."

"Hmm." That seemed to shut him up for a while. As they were nearing the first bridge, Burton said, "So, Floyd, if you don't mind telling me, how came you to be working this case when you're on vacation or suspension or whatever?"

Lassiter considered his response, then said, "It's kind of a test."

"Oh. I get it. 'Cause it's a bullshit case nobody cares about. Makes sense. Are they gonna be surprised, huh?"

Lassiter glanced at him. "You mean, if this is her. What are the odds?"

"Yeah, I know. I just have a feeling."

That was like Danny Davidson too. Hunches. But he'd learned to trust Jerry's hunches.

"Even if this isn't her, I'd say you've done a good job," Burton said.

"I had to."

"Right. I know. I think you must be good."

"For a place like Wichita? Yeah, I guess so. Anyway, there's some kind of weight behind it."

"Tell me about it. You think there's weight *here* . . . And by the way, I didn't mean just for a place like Wichita. There's good cops everywhere." He paused, then added, "And bad ones." Lassiter glanced at him, wondered what was behind that. It hadn't been just a breezy comment. But it was true enough.

Burton said, "I know it probably looks like I'm, you know, looking for the big bust. Trying to be a hero to the rich guys. Make my career. But, umm, I guess I want you to know, Floyd. We're kind of in the same boat. I need to . . . I need to do good on this, you know?"

Lassiter nodded, found himself thinking of Hector

Briseno. And of himself. Good cops and bad cops, and sometimes they were the same people. That was what made it hard.

"Actually, this isn't as thin as you think," Burton said. "Wichita makes a lot of sense, if you watched all the videos. There's patterns, you know? Little things. And she wrote the scripts. I was already kind of figuring her for this side of the Mississippi, the— the *flat* states, you know?"

"Plains states."

"Right. Plains states. And a middle-sized city not close to any other cities. Wichita fits." He considered something, then said, "I figure she comes from some little town right around Wichita, you know? Assuming this is her. Got in some kind of trouble there, moved to the city, got into the game . . . you know. Winds up in L.A."

Lassiter nodded. Burton was good. He wanted to ask what kind of trouble he'd gotten into, but he didn't. Burton would tell him eventually, if they worked together.

"It's really kind of tragic," Burton said. "She's a very talented lady. I don't mean . . . I mean *really* talented. The scripts are really well written. She's a good actress. Hell, she's a good *director*. I mean, all these kids come out there looking to make a fortune in the movies, and she really could have done it. But she's doing this stuff instead." He shook his head.

"Maybe she doesn't want to be famous," Lassiter said.

"Hmm. Yeah. Good point. Maybe so. Nowadays nobody can hide anything. I hadn't thought of that. You're probably right." He fell silent again looking out the passenger window toward the river beyond Riverside Park, then turning his face to the front again as Lassiter turned north onto Celia's street.

"She's good at this, too," Burton said. "She planned it all out pretty well. If this isn't her, she'll probably get away with it. The lady's a gol-durn criminal genius,

Floyd. That's one of the reasons I'd like to meet her. You don't meet too many of those."

You don't meet any of those, Lassiter thought. Career criminals were stupid, by and large. Too stupid to do anything else for a living. And then he thought, '*Gol-durn*'? They'd driven all this way, with him chattering most of the time, and that was the closest he'd come to profanity. That made Burton about as unusual a cop as Celeste Mundy was a burglar.

At Burton's request, feeling a little like a traitor, Lassiter went to the door by himself, while Burton sat in the car and watched. He'd parked at the curb out front, instead of going up the alley the way he had the two times he'd been here before. It was guilty behavior, but he figured he was entitled to a little. He suddenly had a very strong hunch that she wasn't here anymore.

He knocked on the front door this time, but the place felt empty to him. Funny how a building could feel that way. He knocked three times, without result. The third time, he thought for a second he heard something—not footsteps, but a kind of cry—but then decided it had been some bird, for it had seemed to come more from above than from inside. A prairie gull. It had sounded like that.

He turned away and saw Burton coming up the old driveway toward him. He shrugged, shook his head. He was relieved that she was gone, which he knew wasn't the way he ought to feel, but you couldn't help how you felt. He'd done his part. If you forgot about the night before, which he certainly had. Eventually they'd go in and make a latent match, and they'd know he'd found her. For what that was worth.

"You think she's faded?" Burton asked. For the first time Lassiter could see the effects of the early morning flight, the loss of sleep. He felt sorry for him.

Lassiter shrugged. "I guess I probably spooked her, after all."

"No blame, Floyd. You did your job. And maybe

she's just out for breakfast or something." He didn't sound as if he believed it.

Lassiter thought about saying that even if she'd skipped, she might not have gone very far. But he wasn't sure yet how much he wanted to bring up about Hector Briseno and all that. He'd have to think about it. Anyway, it wasn't really likely she'd return to Sand Creek, where more people knew her. "We can come back again, after you meet the lieutenant."

Burton nodded and turned back toward the car. Following, Lassiter noticed the For Rent sign in a corner of the big living room window of the apartment attached to Celia's. An unoccupied apartment, probably the last place anyone would think to look for her. Was she that bold a "criminal genius?" She might be.

"Hey there! You gentlemen!"

Lassiter turned his head, saw an elderly woman in a bathrobe standing on the porch of the apartment opposite the one for rent. He and Burton changed direction and walked toward her. "You're police officers, aren't you?" she asked when they were near.

"Yes, ma'am," Burton said.

"And you're after that girl over there."

"You think we ought to be?" Burton asked.

It struck Lassiter that Burton was breaching protocol by being the one to talk to her. But he didn't really mind. He was used to being the one who stood and listened, and put in an occasional question. And it was Burton's case.

"Well, of course I wouldn't know about that," the woman said. "But, umm, well, I'll just say it's a shame how young women behave these days, that's all. And with a baby."

Burton looked at Lassiter, who blinked and shrugged, equally surprised. He'd discounted what the guy at the Charlton Arms had said, had believed her denial. If there'd been a baby, after all—if she'd lied to him so easily about that—it changed everything, forced him to rethink what he could remember of what she'd told him. He felt disoriented and suddenly apprehensive again, as if, after a brief recess, he were slipping back into that world he thought he'd awakened from this morning.

"How she behaved," Burton said. "Mrs. . . .?"

"Neuenswander. The one time I tried to speak with her, just as a neighbor, you know? Welcoming her. She said something very . . . vile. Well. I'd never repeat it. But it wouldn't surprise me at all if—"

"You don't happen to know what her name was?"

"Well, no, I never—"

"Celia Staircase," a gravelly voice said. "Ain't that a doozy? Right there on the mailbox." An old man, shorter than the woman, wearing a stained gray work jacket that hung open, revealing his white sunken chest, came into view. Sewn on the jacket was an oval with the name TED. "Didn't you fellas see it?"

"Yes, sir—" Burton began, but he was interrupted by the woman.

"When were you ever close enough to see it?"

"I get out and walk," he said calmly, "and I ain't blind like some. I could read it from the driveway."

"I only asked—" Burton said.

"And you made sure to read it," the old woman said. "You took a good look every time you went past there. What else did you manage to see?"

"We think she used different names," Burton said.

"I managed to find out what her name was, anyhow," the old man said. "How come you to be out here flappin' your gums with these fellas about someone you didn't even know their name?"

"These gentlemen are police officers," the woman said primly.

The old man gave them a glance. "You here to take her away? I won't give you no trouble."

"No, sir. We just wanted—"

"You see any badges?" the old man asked his wife. "How do you know they're cops? You just start in blabbing everything you know, 'cause they say they're cops?"

"You're just so *hateful*."

Lassiter stepped forward to show the old man his badge case. The man gave him a look that suggested he took Lassiter a little more seriously than he did Burton. Or maybe that he'd seen him before.

"I'm Detective Lassiter, WPD. This is Detective Burton." If they asked to see Burton's badge, he'd tell them the other cop was from L.A., but there was no reason to introduce a new topic with these two.

"Can't be too careful around here," the old man said. "You could be robbers come to kill us and take our valuables." He gave a gruff laugh that turned into a cough. "'Course, they ain't none. Tornado got 'em all. Had to move in here, with stuff the Red Cross gave us. Like livin' in a hotel."

"What you know about that?" the old woman put in sullenly.

"Andover?" Lassiter asked.

"That's the fella. We was in Oklahoma, else we'd be dead. Folks on both sides got killed. Come back, couldn't even figure out which pile of trash was ours. Found one screwdriver, out of all my tools."

"Terrible," the old woman said. "My mother's china . . . but we're still alive, so we're lucky."

The old man gave a grunt that might have been assent.

"About Ms. Staircase . . ." Lassiter said.

"I knew you were a police office because I saw you talking to her one night," the old woman said. "I saw you show her your badge, and you were taking notes. That's how I knew."

"When was that?" Burton asked. "What night?"

It struck Lassiter as a curious question, but that was only because of his own circumstances. If he'd never gone back a second time, he'd have assumed Burton was checking the old lady's memory.

"Saturday. Night before last."

Burton looked at Lassiter, who nodded. Lassiter was pretty sure that if she'd seen him the night before, she'd say so, so apparently she hadn't.

"You notice any other visitors?" Burton asked.

The old woman thought about it, obviously wanting to supply something incriminating, but finally shook her head. "'Course, it's not like I keep track or anything."

The old man gave what Lassiter was sure was a laugh, but covered it by clearing his throat. "She ain't bein' blackmailed, is she?" he asked. "I might be able to give you a lead."

"He imagines things," Mrs. Neuenswander said. "He's very old. Ten years older than me."

"Ten years ain't much when you're one hundred and fifty," her husband said.

"If it's a stalker you're looking for—"

"No, ma'am," Burton said. "Can you tell us who lives in this other apartment, on the other end?"

"Oh, he's a very nice young man named Vincent. Zach Vincent. He keeps to himself and he has a beard, but he's always very polite. I think he works at home, the way they do now. Something to do with computers. I've noticed him carrying computer things in and out. We had a very nice chat when he first moved in."

"None since," the old man said. "One was enough for him."

"Do the two of them know each other?" Lassiter asked quickly. "Vincent and Celia Staircase?"

"Not that I ever saw," Mrs. Neuenswander said. "They both keep to themselves."

"So she works at home, too?" Burton asked.

"Well, I suppose she has some way of making a living." Lassiter could see how eager she was to speculate about that, except that Celia seldom went out and had no callers.

"I don't keep track of her comings and goings," she said.

"Only when you're awake, anyhow," her husband said.

"Well, I'm not awake at night," she said pointedly, not deigning to look at him.

"You boys don't want to pay no attention to her," he said amiably. "She's crazier'n hell."

There was a brief silence. Then Burton said, "Well, thanks for your time." He gave each of them a nod.

"You aimin' to talk to the fella next door?" the old man asked.

"Why?"

"'Cause he ain't there. Drove out Friday night and ain't come back yet."

"Now who keeps track?" his wife muttered.

"I ast him once if he'd like me to keep an eye on his place when he's away," the old man said. "And he said he would. So I do."

His wife regarded him suspiciously. This was obviously new to her.

"Well, thanks for telling us," Burton said.

"No trouble. You fellas take care."

"Nice people," Burton said to Lassiter as they walked back to the car. "Nice to see a marriage that's lasted so long."

Lassiter started to laugh, then saw that Burton was serious. *Gol-durn.* L.A. must be a different world indeed.

"If she hasn't skipped," Lassiter said, "maybe she will when she finds out we were asking the neighbors about her."

"You think Mrs. Neuenswander's gonna tell her?" After a pause he said, "I don't think she's coming back. I've got a strong, bad feeling." He turned around again and looked back at the duplex. "Think we could see into that garage?"

"I don't see any windows."

Burton stood as he was for a moment, studying it, then abruptly set off toward the garage at the opposite end of the long drive. Lassiter stood beside the car and watched.

Burton stopped in front of the garage and studied it. He looked up at the room that overlapped it and the apartment. He took a step to the side and peered down the narrow space between the two buildings, but apparently saw nothing that interested him. Finally, he got down on his hands and knees by the garage door, and lowered his head to try to see beneath it. He obviously wasn't able to see anything. He sat up on his knees for a moment, then bent down again, this time extending one arm to push upward on the door handle. Lassiter couldn't tell that it moved at all, but Burton spent a little longer looking this time, his arm straining against the handle. Finally he let go of it and climbed to his feet, brushing off his pants.

"The car's there," he said when he got back to where Lassiter was standing. "Maybe we're in luck."

Lassiter didn't say anything, not sure how he felt about that.

"Or maybe she left it and took a taxi to the airport," Burton said. "We could check cabbies and flights. You guys could, I mean."

"Sure."

"Wish we could get in there," Burton said.

"Don't see how."

Burton nodded, then said, "You didn't feel sure enough . . . ?"

"Nope."

Burton nodded, accepting it. He got in the car.

"Did she leave her car in L.A. when she split from there?" Lassiter asked as they were heading back south.

"Wish I knew. We don't even know where she was living there. We didn't know she had a baby."

"If she does."

"Yeah."

They came to Riverside Park, and Lassiter turned left toward the Murdock Street bridge and downtown.

"Maybe we ought to take a swing through the park," Burton said. "She might just be out for a walk."

Lassiter shrugged and turned back south along the road beside the river, past the place where he'd come to a stop the night before. He could see the wheel marks. The sight of them had a dreamlike quality, seemed to set off little explosions of partial, dreamlike memories, none solid or sensible enough to grasp.

When he got to the City Building and had turned Burton over to Loomis, he'd start looking up the names of neurologists in the phone book.

13

Tuesday Night

It was late afternoon on Tuesday before Zach got home, and he knew he wasn't going to get any more work done until he'd gotten some sleep. Two days shot. When he'd gone up to K.C. on Friday, he expected to be back by Sunday sometime, but the problems Darrell and his secretary were having with the accounting software had turned out to be more complicated than he'd expected. In fact, the problem hadn't really been with the software; it had been with Darrell and Jo Anne, his secretary. They seemed to think that if the software was set up correctly, it would somehow fix the cash-flow problems they were having because neither one of them knew how to run a business. He'd really spent most of his time using the software to explain basic accounting principles to them—hell, basic arithmetic. He still wasn't sure Darrell understood the difference between a majority and a plurality.

What was going on there had nothing to do with software. Or with accounting, really. There was obviously something going on between Darrell and Jo Anne, which pissed him off, because he liked Darrell's wife, Alicia, better than he liked his cousin. Last time he'd been up there, Jo Anne had told him all about the problems of being a single mother with a deadbeat ex-husband, never knowing if she'd be able to pay the utility bills. This time she was driving a Lexus and talking about how much fun she'd had accompanying

Darrell on business trips to places like Vail and Bar Harbor. As far as Zach could tell, Jo Anne's compensation hadn't increased any, but judging from the expense account information, it would be cheaper to buy a house in Bar Harbor than to spend a weekend in a hotel there. He had a strong hunch that what Darrell really wanted was a short course on how to use the software to cover up embezzling. Or maybe just to hide money from Alicia's divorce lawyer.

It had been raining while he was gone, but things weren't any cooler. It had been a mistake to turn the air conditioning off. Climbing the stairs from the garage to his office was like swimming up into warm water. He was sweating when he reached the top, and not from the exertion. He looked at the stuff piled on his desk—stuff he'd intended to do Monday—and sighed, then turned on the fan set on top of his big filing cabinet and opened a couple of windows. He didn't intend to do anything until he'd had some sleep, anyway, but it took forever for the cool air to work its way up the stairs to the office. Maybe the fan would push the sticky, hot air out and pull the cool air up faster while he slept.

As he was about to turn from the side window, he heard a baby's cry and looked back, surprised, at the duplex across the way. Had he ever heard that baby cry before? He didn't think so. And wasn't *that* sort of odd? There wasn't any second cry, and after a minute he was no longer sure that what he'd heard had been a baby. It could have been a cat out in the alley somewhere. It could have been some kind of bird. Maybe he hadn't even heard anything.

There was something about the other duplex—or maybe it was that cry—that made him feel uneasy. He had the odd conviction, looking at the front of the building, that it was now vacant, like the other half. But there wasn't anything he could see that was any different. Just something in his mind, from lack of sleep and the stress of the last couple of days.

He shook his head and headed down the stairs to turn on the air conditioner.

"No," Zach said, and for a second he thought he'd fallen, but he was in a bed. He must have had a nightmare. He raised his head and peered around in the darkness, disoriented. The clock on the wall said 11:14, but that didn't seem right. It felt like he'd slept a lot longer than that. Then he remembered and lay back on the pillow. He'd slept all the way through the afternoon and evening and it was night now. He closed his eyes again experimentally, to see whether he wanted to stay in bed or get up and do some work.

The cry came again. He sat up on one elbow, surprised, and listened for it to come again. When it did, it was clearly not a cat but a baby. The baby over there in the opposite duplex. The sound was miserable and forlorn. He was very sure he'd never heard the baby cry like *that* before, and he didn't like it.

He got up and went to the window, opened the blinds enough to peer out, but all he could see was the front of the other building. No lights anywhere. The cry came again, and he wondered how long he'd been hearing it, fitting it into his dream, before he'd awakened himself.

Something had to be wrong. No way would the woman over there let her baby cry like that without doing something about it. Nobody would. She wasn't there. That cry was the cry of a baby left alone for too long. Zach swallowed, knowing something had to be done, but not knowing right away what it was. How could she have gone out and left the baby alone so long? Had something happened to her?

The baby shrieked suddenly, making him jerk. That had been a cry of anger or pain, not despair. Not bothering to dress or turn on any lights, Zach made his way out to the living room and found his phone, dialed 911.

"Dispatch."

"Umm, yes. I want to report . . . well, there's a baby crying, and . . ."

"Is it your baby, sir? Are you the father?"

"No. It's in the apartment across from mine. It woke me up—"

"Did you wish to file a complaint?"

"No, no. That's not what I mean. I think there's something wrong with it. I think—"

"You think it's injured? Do you suspect abuse?"

"No. I just think it's been left alone. Its mother is . . . I think she's a good mother, from what I've seen. She'd do something."

"Do you know that she's not there, sir?"

"No, it's just the way it's crying."

"Does she normally leave the baby alone?"

"Not that I know of. I mean, no, I think she's a good mother. That's why—"

"The baby sounds to you like it's in some kind of distress, and it just keeps on crying."

"Right, exactly."

There was a short silence, during which Zach could hear other voices, speaking to one another as if from far away, numbers followed by bursts of static. "Do you have children, sir?" the dispatcher asked, returning.

"No. I'm not married."

"Well, sir, crying is normal for babies. When they're sick, or teething, or . . . lots of things. And sometimes there's nothing to do but let them go on crying."

"I know that," Zach said. "This is different. And this baby—"

"Have you tried contacting the mother yourself?"

That stoppd him. It sounded like an obvious thing. Why hadn't he? Because it was so late at night, because of the way she'd looked at him that time . . . but really it was because he was so sure there was something wrong. "No," he said. "I haven't. I don't really know her. I don't know her name."

"Well, sir, if you're concerned about the baby, maybe the first thing would be to go over and ask if you can help. As long as you're not going to start a fight or something. You don't sound angry."

"No."

"If you don't feel you can do that, we could send somebody . . . but then, if there really isn't anything wrong . . ."

"I get it. You're right. Sorry I bothered you."

"No bother, sir. You're right to be concerned. If you do find something that seems wrong, if there's no adult there, call us right back and we'll send somebody out."

"Thanks." Once he'd hung up, though, the prospect of going over there and knocking on her door, at eleven-thirty at night, didn't seem as easy or as reasonable.

Well, he had three choices. Ignore it and go back to bed. Call the cops again and insist that they come out, when it might be unnecessary—he knew what he'd think of someone who sent the cops to his door in the middle of the night when there wasn't any reason for it. Or he could go over there and knock and maybe make a fool of himself. But a well-meaning fool. As little as she already thought of him, it wouldn't make much difference. Hell, it might work the other way, although he didn't really think so. It would be important, like the dispatcher said, not to be angry, not to seem to be complaining. To be really concerned about the baby. Which he was.

He took a deep breath. Showing concern, expressing sympathy—that wasn't the kind of thing he was good at. Feeling it, yes. Showing it, no. That was part of the problem he always had with women. If someone had a problem, he wanted to help them solve it. But if it was something that couldn't be solved, just something they felt bad about . . . what could you do?

He went back to the bedroom and put on some sweatpants, then headed up the stairs to his office. He'd left the windows open and it was actually kind of cool up there—a pleasant nighttime surprise. A good time to work, anyway.

Sitting in his swivel chair, his hands behind his head, waiting for the system to boot up, he noticed the stack of phone books under the printer stand. The third one down was the cross-reference directory he'd paid a fortune for because it seemed like the kind of thing an independent businessman ought to have, but he had never actually needed it.

He leaned to work it out of the stack, then sat back and opened it in his lap. Probably it wasn't new enough, anyway. When had he bought it? He found his own address and the ones for the other three apartments—but the only listings were for himself and the Neuenswanders next door.

He turned to the screen, bending forward to click on the browser icon, then paused as the goddamn Norton Utilities box popped up. Yes, he knew the drive needed to be optimized. *Go away.* He clicked a little harder on the exit box, so sysdoc would know he was annoyed with it.

As he was moving the cursor toward the browser icon, the baby cried again.

It was worse up here with the windows open. He could tell it was right over there across from him, in that upper room that mirrored his office. But it was worse in a different way, too.

These were loud, angry, heartbroken sobs. He felt his own lower lip begin to quiver in sympathy, and shook his head hard. He waited, his teeth clenched, for her to come back and calm the kid down again.

But she didn't. Or at least, he didn't calm down. It just went on and on, way past the point where anyone, especially a mother, could have ignored it. Jack the Ripper couldn't have ignored it if he'd been over there, killing the kid's mother. That was a thought that didn't wind up as funny as it had started out.

Breathing a quick curse, he went quickly back down the stairs and grabbed the first T-shirt he saw. He was two steps from his front porch, in the grass, before it occurred to him that he was barefoot. *Fuck it.* He went straight toward the other door, ignoring the walkway, hopped up on the porch, yanked open the screen and knocked on the wooden door.

Belatedly, he imagined how he must look to Mrs. Neuenswander. Would she be on duty this late? Maybe not. The windows were all dark over there. He suppressed an angry impulse to wave, just in case.

There wasn't any sound inside the door he'd knocked on. The place felt empty to him. He felt more sure than before that there was no one in there but the baby. But that was the kind of pseudoscientific shit he didn't believe in. He rapped again, a little harder, a little louder. Maybe someone else would call the cops, to investigate *him*. That would be okay. But he straightened a little automatically, trying not to look sneaky, trying to look like he had proper business here, as if he came over here all the time at midnight.

He sighed, wondering what to do now. He noticed something white on the flat black mailbox, and stepped back up on the porch, leaning his head to see what it was. An index card with a name on it, apparently, but it was too dark and the hand lettering was too faint for him to make it out. The first name began with a C, he thought, but the rest was just a smear. He glanced around, looking for some source of light, but there wasn't any. He could rip it off and take it back to his apartment, maybe get the phone number . . . she'd never know . . .

The baby shrieked, making him jump and then move backward and look up again. The baby sounded thoroughly pissed off. He had an idea it knew he was down here . . . it had heard his knock if no one else had . . . and wanted to know what the fuck he was waiting for.

He looked at the other door, the one that went into the kitchen at the rear of the apartment. *If you're gonna be a bear, be a grizzly bear.* That's what his high school football coach had said a lot. Usually not to Zach. Mostly when he'd noticed Zach he'd just shaken his head and gone off to talk to someone else.

He looked at the door right in front of him, another

thought occurring to him. *If you're gonna be a burglar, be a grizzly burglar.* Didn't have the same ring. He went back and opened the screen and tried the knob. Locked. Of course. The baby suddenly grew silent again. The kid had fucking good ears.

On his way to the rear door, he stopped to try to peer past the curtains covering the big front window, but it was too dark even to tell if there was a gap or not. Just blackness. The wood-framed screen door at the rear wasn't quite shut; it stuck out a quarter of an inch. Probably just because of the recent rain, the moisture swelling the wood. Or maybe it was that way all the time. He pulled it open, started to reach for the knob of the inner door, then stopped himself. First things first. He lifted his hand to knock on the in-side door.

It swung inward as soon as he struck it. It hadn't even been completely closed, let alone locked. He didn't hear anything inside, not even the baby, and nothing but black was visible through the narrow opening. He spread his fingertips to push it open a bit more.

Silence. Definitely time to call the cops. I tried the back door and it wasn't even closed, and there didn't seem to be anybody there—except the baby.

The baby suddenly cried out again, nearly right above him, and he pushed on through the door and went carefully across the dark kitchen, one hand in front of him, feeling for where the knob of the door to the stairs ought to be. Then he was on the stairs, barely able to make out the edges by the little light that filtered from the open door of the baby's room, and the baby had grown silent again, knowing he was coming, and then he was in the room and they were looking at each other.

The baby was standing in its slatted bed, its hands gripping the rail, regarding him doubtfully, as if vaguely disappointed. Then the smell hit him, and he realized this wasn't going to be quite as simple as grabbing the kid and running, or whatever it was he'd had in mind. The baby's solemn eyes, in the dim light, reminded him of how it stared at its mother when she talked to it, out on the lawn. How could that woman not be here with it now if she was in the apartment at all? Impossible. The baby was giving little spasmodic sniffles that were part hiccup. Its legs were apart for balance, and its heavy diaper hung low enough that he could see it was a boy.

He didn't like the idea of turning on the light, but it had to be done. The baby gave a little gasp and blinked comically. For a second the little boy was on the verge of screaming again, Zach thought, but then he didn't, almost as if he'd restrained the impulse. This near, Zach was stupidly surprised to see, even in the half-light, how much the baby resembled his mother, except for the black hair.

Yellowish stains ran down the baby's legs. The mattress sheet, which had pulled loose and gotten wadded into a corner of the bed, was a collage of stains varying from yellow to a sort of reddish brown.

Zach moved toward the bed and the baby let go of the railing, tottering on his spread legs, and reached up to Zach, to be picked up. Nearly falling, he grabbed the rail again with one small hand, reached to Zach with the other, looking anxious and threatening more tears. Zach had to push back the urge to pick him up immediately, and instead reached over the railing to push the sodden diaper the rest of the way down with his fingertips. Then he put his hands under the baby's arms, and lifted him out of the diaper and over to the cleanest corner of the bed, waiting until he'd taken hold of the railing again to let go. The baby gave a little whine of disappointment, another hiccup, but then seemed to shut off anything more with an act of will. Zach didn't know a great deal about babies, but he felt pretty sure there was something different about this one.

"Hang on, kid," he said softly. He went to the dresser and pulled open drawers, trying to move quickly without getting in his own way. There was nothing but women's clothing in the top two drawers, which seemed curious to him. But the third drawer contained baby clothing, and the fourth a cache of towels, sheets, and what looked like regular, old-fashioned cloth diapers. He pulled out a towel and returned to the baby, using it to wipe away as much of the filth as he could.

Of course, it wasn't enough, just a dry towel. Some of it was crusted, and there were welts beneath it. The baby had obviously been here by himself, untended, for more than just a couple of hours. More like a couple of days. There was baby powder and mineral oil on top of the dresser, and a half-full box of disposable diapers inside the closet. He pulled one out, glad that he wouldn't have to salvage the safety pins from the original diaper. He needed something wet to clean the rest of the crud away. Didn't she have any of those things called wipes? If so, he didn't see them. He considered just wrapping the kid up in a towel, the way he was, and getting out of here.

That was probably the rational thing to do. On the other hand, the rational part of him was beginning to believe that there was no one else in the place. After all, he'd have found out by now if there were. All he needed was a damp washrag.

"Okay," he said. "Be right back." The baby looked at him as if it understood the words, and made no sound as he went out the door. Halfway down the stairs, however, he heard it begin crying again, angrily, accusingly. Zach set his jaw and stumbled a little, going down the rest of the way, made clumsy by the sound, then hurrying to the bathroom, halfway along the hall.

He'd never have opened the closed bedroom door in a million years if he'd known that's what it was. But the bathroom door opposite was also closed, and he forgot for a second that everything here was backward. He was halfway through the door before he realized his mistake, and when he did he wondered if maybe the smell in the room hadn't also caused him to turn this way.

She was lying crosswise on the bed, spread-eagled, facedown, her head turned toward the wall opposite him. She was naked, and he had the initial impression that her body was daubed here and there with dark paint. Then he understood what it was, and also that no one would sleep in that position, unless maybe they were stoned. And he didn't think she was. That wasn't paint, and that wasn't just B.O., either. She'd been lying here in this warm, muggy room for a while—probably about as long as the baby had been by itself upstairs.

He felt a surge of anger that overwhelmed the fear—a crazy desire to go through the rest of the apartment and find the son of a bitch . . .

But then sanity and fear returned. She hadn't been a weak woman. Whoever had done this to her could probably do the same to him, if he was still here. The important thing was to get the baby out.

Turning to leave, he noticed fleetingly that the whole room had been trashed, with clothing and broken things scattered on the floor, a chest of drawers overturned, the drawers spilling out, a spidery crack in the dresser mirror, like a car window hit by a rock. Or a forehead?

He didn't pause to take a better inventory, but he did make himself go into the bathroom, grab a washrag and moisten it, before going back up the stairs. The bathroom looked fine, as the kitchen had. As the baby's room did, for that matter, apart from the baby and his bed. It was like some kind of bomb had gone off only in that one room. Except it hadn't been a bomb.

He took the steps back up to the baby's room three at a time, no longer worrying about being quiet, his fear and sense of urgency growing. He wiped the baby off quickly, as well as he could, doused his hand in mineral oil and rubbed it everywhere he could, then wrapped another towel around the baby, took him in one arm, grabbed the mineral oil and the powder, and headed for the door, stopping only to grab the worn teddy bear that lay on the floor at one end of the bed. It looked old enough to be something the kid might need.

"Okay," he said aloud, a little breathless, "we're out of here."

14

Majors could see the TV vans parked together inside the fenced lot beyond the alley at the far end. The TV people were standing around exchanging wisecracks, waiting for the show to start, putting on a little show of their own for the residents of the big apartment building who'd wandered down to see what was going on. Everyone seemed to be staying on the other side of the alley, anyway, and the people at this end were keeping to the other side of the street, well outside the tape. The way the two duplexes were built, with only the two avenues in, it was an easy scene to control. The only person he could see inside the tape so far, besides the criminalists, was a uniformed cop listening politely to an elderly woman on the porch of the street-side apartment of the building opposite the vic's. The rear apartment would be where the guy who'd found the body lived, and there'd be an officer with him, too, to make sure he stayed put and couldn't talk to anyone but cops. The fourth apartment had a For Rent sign in the window.

The two uniforms who'd responded first—the only ones to go in so far besides the neighbor—were waiting for him on the sidewalk, just outside the tape, along with a middle-aged woman.

"Ms. Metcalf?" he asked.

"Yes?" Her eyes darted nervously from him to the people across the street, to Burton behind him, and back to him. She'd gotten past the initial shock and was beginning to worry about what effect this all might have on her business. "I, umm, it's Mrs.," she said.

"Mrs. Metcalf. I'm Detective Jerry Majors of the Wichita Police Department," he said, offering his hand, which she shook. "This is Detective Burton." He'd decided not to say who Burton was unless someone asked. He could use another pair of eyes, since he didn't have Floyd's, but he didn't need any jurisdictional problems. On the way, he'd asked dispatch to get hold of Floyd, but that wasn't easy these days. Either he wasn't spending much time at home or he just wasn't answering his phone.

"You're the owner?" he asked the woman.

"No. Just the manager."

"That's fine." He handed her the papers, and she looked at them blankly. "That's a search warrant," Majors explained. "It allows us to search the entire premises of the apartment where the body was found."

The woman frowned at him. "I gave them permission."

"Yes, ma'am, and we appreciate that. We still have to do it by the book . . . you know. In case there's some problem in court later. Lawyers."

She nodded. "Do I need to sign something?"

"No, ma'am. Just read it. I'd also like you to stay around for a while, if you don't mind. In case we have some questions."

"Yes, I'll stay. I want to help."

"That's great. Thanks a lot. By the way, the other apartment there . . . it's vacant, right?"

"Well, yes. But it's rented . . . by the young woman . . ."

"She took both apartments? Is there a connecting door?"

"Oh, no. That wouldn't . . . I don't think she was using it for anything. I mean, I don't really know . . ."

"I'll need to get the warrant amended to cover that address, too," Majors said. "In the meantime, would you mind if we had a quick look around?"

"No. Not at all. I don't think there's anything—"

"Would you happen to have the key?"

"Oh, yes, of course." She fumbled in her purse, came up with a ring of fifteen or twenty keys, found the one she wanted and worked it off the ring.

"Thanks very much," Majors said. "I know this is very disturbing. We'll try to keep you no longer than necessary. Detective Burton . . ."

"Got it," Burton said. "No need for you to stand, Mrs. Metcalf. Why don't you have a seat while we talk?" He steered her deftly to one of the patrol cars at the curb, talking all the way, opened the rear door for her to sit down, and then stood in the open door, chatting for a moment more before he pulled out his notebook. Majors saw her smile for the first time. Majors thought he himself was pretty good at schmoozing, getting people to relax during questioning—at least he was a lot better at it than his partner—but this guy was way ahead of him.

He turned to the two uniformed officers who were waiting to give him their report. He listened in silence, letting them tell all about it. This was an unusual event for them, a big deal, and it was worth giving them a little time, a little attention. You never knew when you'd need them. And now and then you could even learn something from them beyond the facts. When he'd been in uniform, detectives who didn't really listen had always pissed him off.

He didn't learn anything out of the ordinary this time, but they'd done a good job, by the book. It didn't sound as though they'd contaminated the scene any more than they'd had to, in order to make sure the vic was beyond help and that there was no one else inside. He congratulated them on a good job, accepted their notes, looked at them to make sure they were in proper form and readable, then put them in his clipboard, under his own notebook. He thanked them again and sent the younger one off to question the people across the street.

He gave the older one the key to the vacant apart-

ment. "I know you know how to do a walk-through,"
he said. "I just want you to know my ten rules. The
first five are 'Don't touch anything.' The other five are
'Write everything down.' The one little thing you notice but don't write down will be the first thing the
defense attorney asks you about when you get on the
stand. Right?"

"Got it."

"Good. And don't turn on any lights. Use your
flashlight. If you see something you think is important,
come back out the same way you went in, and find
me. If you can't find me, find Lieutenant Kreider. If
the lab guys don't take it away from you, go back and
finish the walk-through. Then go through a second
time, with the lights on, same rules. Make a second
set of notes, even if it's exactly the same as the first.
When you're done, bring your notes to me or Lieutenant Kreider."

He turned away, walked over to the car where Burton was questioning the apartment manager, and drew
him away. "You mind questioning the neighbor," he
asked in a low voice, "after you get done with her?"

"Mind?" Burton muttered back. "Hell, I was afraid
you were gonna ask me to walk through with you.
I've seen five corpses and I don't hope to see any
more. There's a reason I'm in burglary."

Majors smiled. It had been a long time since he'd
been young and stupid enough to feel contemptuous
of such an attitude. If he could do his job without it,
he'd be glad if he never saw another corpse. "I'm sure
you'll want to see her face at some point," he said.
"After all, she's probably your perp."

"A coroner's mug shot'll be fine."

Majors nodded. He pulled the notes he'd just gotten
from the uniforms out of his clipboard. "These are
the patrol guys' notes. His name's Vincent."

"First or last?"

"Oh . . . last. It's in there."

Burton glanced at the notes. "Zachary," he said.
"Nice old biblical name." He put the notes in a jacket

pocket. "I like to ask my own questions first," he said. "If you don't mind."

"Not at all. And I appreciate your help . . . Sandy."

Burton smiled, shrugged. "What else have I got to do?" He headed back to the woman sitting inside the police car, who was sipping some coffee someone had given her.

He went to the uniform standing on the porch of Vincent's apartment, to point out Burton and tell him who he was. The door to the apartment was open, and through the screen behind the cop, Majors could see a lanky, bearded man, not too old, maybe thirty, in a T-shirt and sweatpants, plus unlaced sneakers, walking back and forth, holding a baby to his shoulder, bouncing it up and down. As he looked, the baby gave a burp, and the man said, "Atta boy. Knew you had it in you."

"How come he's still got the baby?" he asked the cop.

"One of the EMTs checked the kid out. Said he was okay, just a little dehydrated. He didn't want to go with them, put up a fuss, so they said he might as well stay here till the caseworker shows up."

"Ah." The baby didn't want to leave Vincent. But Vincent had told the uniforms he didn't even know the vic's name. Which had sounded to Majors like protesting a little too much. And he'd been vague about why he decided to go into the apartment by himself instead of just calling the cops. So maybe it would be easy. He took another glance at the man with the baby, then looked away again. That didn't feel right.

The coroner's van swung into the area between the two garages, out of the alley, did a Y-turn, and backed up toward the porch of the murder apartment. When it stopped, the driver climbed out to open the rear doors while Sally Crow hopped down from the passenger side, with her "big black bag." Everyone called it that because she herself was so tiny.

Majors moved quickly to intercept her, let her know

he was the one working it. He liked to talk to the AME at the scene, right after she came out. It wasn't SOP—in fact, it was kind of against the rules; the detective was supposed to wait for the report—but some of them indulged him, including Sally. She understood why he did it.

She'd stopped to talk to Kreider, to get a layout of the place. Majors moved into her line of sight and gave a little wave. She looked at him and rolled her eyes when she saw who it was.

Annie Babicki was standing on the far side of the alley, behind the yellow tape. She'd been waiting for him to notice her, and she raised one eyebrow in a question. He shrugged, nodded toward Kreider, meaning it was up to him.

"Hey, Jerry."

He turned to see Sally standing beside him, smiling brightly. "How bad you guys screw up the scene?" she asked.

"Not too bad. 'Course we took the spectators through for a tour, and some of them took souvenirs, but other than that . . ."

She laughed. "So where's Floyd? Still inside?"

Majors shook his head, trying to answer casually. "He's on vacation."

"I heard that." The way she said it, he knew she'd heard all about the blow-up in Loomis's office, too.

"He'll be back pretty quick," Majors said. "In fact, I got a call in to him right now. He met the vic."

"No kidding? Hey, I hope he is back soon, Jerry. See you in a bit."

She went inside, through the back door. The driver of her van had unfolded the gurney in back of it and was over chatting with Kreider's people. There wasn't going to be anything for anyone but the technical people to do for a while. Majors headed for the alley to talk to Annie. A young photographer was with her, a guy he didn't recognize. He was looking past Majors, scanning the scene carefully, looking for a shot.

"How come Kreider's here?" Annie asked.

"Good evening to you, too, Annie." He glanced behind him, shrugged. "Who knows why Kreider does anything?"

"I know there's no point in asking what happened—"

"Don't know yet."

"The dispatch call we heard was to check out a report of a female adult, possibly injured. Since Sally just went in, I assume she's dead."

"Yeah, that's what I figure, too."

Annie shook her head. "There was also some mention of a baby."

"Was there?" He turned to look toward Vincent's apartment. "There's a baby over there."

"So who lives there?"

"A citizen named Zachary Vincent. Good old biblical name."

She gave him a funny look. "Zach Vincent?"

"You know him?"

"Well, yeah. Not well. I mean, if it's the same guy. Tall, bearded—"

"That's the one. How do you know him?"

"He's a computer geek. When they put in the new system at the paper a couple of years ago, they hired him to teach us all how to use it. He was pretty good. I almost understood some of it. We had to go to regular classes for a week, an hour every day, just like in college. Kind of fun."

"So what do you think?"

She pursed her lips, said, "Well . . ." then shook her head. "Hard to believe. He's a little strange, but just like computer guys are, you know? Sort of . . . disconnected. And he tries to act like he's kind of a grouch, sort of cynical, you know? But inside . . ." She shook her head.

"He's over there walking the baby and burping him right now," Majors said.

Annie smiled. "That's easier to believe than him killing someone."

"That's kind of what I thought. But then, a lot of people thought Ted Bundy was a hell of a guy."

"Is Zach really—?"

"No." He said it a little more curtly than he intended. Also a little more definitely. "No more than anybody else at this point, I mean. Who knows? Right now he's just the only person we know about who has any connection to the victim at all. And he claims he didn't even know her. Didn't know her name. Living right across from her. You believe that?"

"Sure. He's a computer geek."

Majors smiled, shook his head.

"So what about him getting the baby?" Annie asked. "Is he a hero or just a goof?"

"Not sure yet. Maybe both."

"Can I talk to him?"

"If he wanders outside the tape."

"Which I'm guessing that cop on the porch isn't gonna let him do."

"Whenever Kreider's people and the AME get done, you can go talk to him."

Annie sighed.

"How's Sam?" Majors asked.

"Glad to be back on dayside . . . Hey, there's Floyd. So he's working?"

Majors turned to look. Lassiter was standing out on the sidewalk, gawking at the scene like any spectator. Annie must know he wasn't working. His clothes looked rumpled and he looked unshaven, but that might only be the light. What bothered Majors was that he looked confused, looked like some drunk who'd happened along and couldn't figure out what was going on. And Floyd didn't drink.

"There was a rumor he'd been suspended," Annie said in a low voice. "Don't know why."

Majors was silent. He hated lying to Annie. But then he said, "No, he's just taken a little time off, what with Kay and everything . . . Excuse me."

But before he took a step, someone barked, "Hey, Detective! When do *I* get in there? I'm on deadline."

The photographer. Majors turned slightly to look at him, feeling an odd sort of pleasure. The man's abrasive voice was like a splash of cold water that brought him back to himself. "And you are . . .?" he asked softly. In the corner of his eye he saw Annie purse her lips and look away, recognizing that tone.

The photographer didn't notice anything. He smiled. "Rod Olander. *Mid American*."

Majors weighed his options. This guy was going to be a royal pain in the ass. He'd have to be broken in. But there was no point in penalizing Annie, and Majors had more important business at the moment.

"Soon as the coroner and forensics are finished," he said. "That's the drill." He couldn't resist adding, "Just follow Ms. Babicki's lead. She knows how it works."

"Yeah, thanks," the photographer said with undisguised insolence as he turned away. Jesus. Who'd hired that guy? He must be really good.

Floyd had started up the driveway that ran between the two buildings, and Majors stepped quickly to cut him off before he'd gotten past the front apartments. Floyd apparently saw him, for he stopped, although he wasn't looking at Majors. He didn't seem to be looking at anything in particular.

"You got my message," Majors said.

"Yeah." Floyd looked off to the side, toward Vincent's apartment. "Burton's working it with you," he said. "That's good."

Majors glanced back, saw that the L.A. cop and Vincent were standing on the porch. Vincent was still holding the baby, which looked like it had gone to sleep against his shoulder.

"He came along and I asked him to question the neighbor for me," Majors said. "The baby's fine, by the way." It occurred to him that this could be what was bothering Floyd. He had a thing about kids.

"That's good," Lassiter said. But he was looking at the other apartment now.

"Floyd?" Majors waited for his partner to look at

him. "Listen, there wasn't really any need to bring you out here. Why don't you go on home and get some sleep? Come see me tomorrow."

Floyd gave a little smile. "No hurry, huh? Just 'cause you've already lost the first forty-eight." His eyes wandered away, toward Burton and Vincent. "We should have gone in," he said.

"What?"

"When Burton and I were here yesterday. If we had—"

"You didn't have a warrant. How could you? You didn't have cause." Majors saw what it was. Maybe she'd still been alive. "You couldn't," he said.

"No." Lassiter was silent for a moment, then said, "Well, at least Burton will know for sure now."

Majors nodded, then lowered his voiced and asked, "So what about Burton? What do you think?"

Lassiter shrugged. "Burglary guy. Good cop."

"Why'd he come out here? I mean, to Kansas. How'd that happen? You sent some query?"

Floyd looked at him as if he didn't know what he was talking about, then nodded. "Yeah, I guess. I guess it was just the only thing they'd gotten, you know? Lot of pressure . . ." His voice dwindled away, and his eyes drifted away, toward the back door of the apartment. After a moment of silence, not looking at Majors, he asked, "How bad, Jerry? Is it bad? What did . . . what happened to her?"

He'd really liked her. Majors could see that. And that made Majors think a little more of her, want to find her killer that much more. The killer had hurt Floyd a little by killing her. But he said, "I don't know yet, Floyd. I'm waiting for Sally Crow to come out." He studied Lassiter's face. "You know," he said, "you can't blame yourself. You didn't do anything wrong. You just did your job. And you couldn't have prevented this. You didn't have any way of knowing this was going to happen."

Floyd looked at him, gave a little smile, nodded.

"I will need to talk to you," Majors said. "Right

now you're the only person I've got who I know talked to her. Why don't you . . . go home and get some sleep or something? We'll talk in the morning." He made himself laugh. "Truth is, you look like hell, Floyd. Don't smell so great, either."

Floyd gave a perfunctory smile, obviously unoffended but also uninterested in bantering that way. "You're right," he said. "I'll . . . I'll come up to the division in the morning. Okay?"

"Sure. Great."

Floyd nodded, seemed about to say something else, but then just said, "Okay," and turned and walked away, toward the street.

Majors watched him until he'd passed the tape and disappeared into the darkness and the crowd. He felt suddenly apprehensive, felt an urge to go after him, as if he might never see him again if he didn't. He shook his head sharply, snapping himself out of it, and turned back to his job.

Burton and Vincent were standing on Vincent's porch, talking while Burton took notes. The baby appeared to be asleep against Vincent's shoulder. Sally Crow was still inside. The techs were still working. The news photographer, Olander, had disappeared, so he walked back over to talk to Annie.

"Sorry Floyd's having trouble," she said. "This probably doesn't help any."

"No." He looked at her, his mind blank, unable to remember what she was supposed to know and what she wasn't. "Uhh, can we talk off the record?" he asked.

She gave him a curious look. "Sure." How many years had it been since he'd spoken that way to her? He'd insulted her, but she didn't give any sign of it.

"I'm sorry," he said. "It's—"

"I understand, Jerry."

"See, Floyd was working this case. I mean, he was on a case that involved the vic, and he'd spoken with her."

"You mean, before he decided to take some time off?"

Majors sighed, shook his head. "Loomis asked him to take some time off. He was having some problems. But then this case came along—the other case, not the murder—and Loomis asked him to kind of look into it, as a favor. It wasn't a homicide."

Annie waited, not saying anything.

"It wasn't supposed to be *real*," Majors said. "I mean, we were just doing a favor for L.A., and there wasn't even any reason to think she was here."

"But Floyd found her."

Majors laughed. "Yeah." He shook his head. "Of course. Floyd found her."

"Why was L.A. looking for her?"

He was silent, thinking about it. *Fuck it.* "She's supposed to have committed some burglaries out there. In Beverly Hills or someplace like that. Rich people. We don't even really know this is her, for sure. Floyd thought she might be, I guess. Listen, Annie. I don't care if you put that stuff in the paper. Maybe Loomis will, I don't know. I don't see a problem." He told her about Celeste Mundy, what he knew about that case. "I can't give you the name she was using here. I mean, assuming this is her."

"I know. So, that guy talking to Zach Vincent . . ."

Majors glanced that way, nodded. "Yeah. LAPD. I don't think I want to give you his name. Better get it from Loomis."

She nodded, making some more notes. "It's a good story," she said. "The L.A. stuff, and Floyd finding her—if it's her, I mean."

"It's a bullshit case, though. Who cares about a bunch of rich old gomers getting some trinkets stolen by a call girl?"

"Nice attitude for a cop."

"A homicide cop."

"I assume you don't want me to quote you on it being a bullshit case, and the old gomers and all that."

He smiled. "The chief probably wouldn't like it."

He dug in his jacket pocket. "I've got a mug shot of her, Celeste Mundy. I can't give it to you yet, but this is her." He handed it to her.

She looked at it, did a double take. "*This* is Celeste Mundy?"

"Yeah. Why?"

Annie looked like someone trying to figure out what the joke was. "Well, she looks a hell of a lot like someone I know. But that would be impossible . . . I mean . . ."

"Who?"

"No. It's impossible. This is some kind of weird fluke."

"Who?"

The way Annie looked at him, he thought she was going to stonewall him, but she said, "Her name is Jes Wellington. She lives in Sand Creek. She worked on the *Mid American*, in the metro department, and then she worked as our Sand Creek bureau chief. Sand Creek's her hometown. And then she quit to freelance, a couple of years ago. She writes for women's magazines . . . but serious stuff. Spousal abuse, that kind of thing. I'm very sure she hasn't been out in California." She stopped, looked past him for a moment. "Zach would know Jes," she said. "She was there when he was teaching that class. I mean, she took the class."

Majors took the photo back. "You're saying he would have recognized this woman as Jes—what was it? Wellington?"

"If she looked like that, I'd say he would. This is weird. Because it can't be Jes. I mean, Jes can't be Celeste Mundy. But . . . Christ. Could *this* be Jes? The dead woman? But Zach said he didn't know her." She looked toward Vincent's apartment, and something in her expression made Majors look around, too.

Burton had disappeared. Vincent was standing in the grass in front of the porch. A woman Majors didn't recognize, but who he assumed was from SRS, was reaching out to take the baby. It didn't look like he was going to give the baby to her.

Then he thrust his arms forward, almost as if he *wanted* to be rid of the infant. And as he did so, the baby twisted in his hands and reached back toward him, gave him a single soft cry of surprise. A light flashed, and then another. Majors saw the photographer moving in a slow half circle nearby. Another flash. Then he saw the SRS woman walking away stiffly, self-consciously, holding the baby against her. The baby wasn't making any sound, but it was squirming, fighting her. Vincent looked stricken. He looked very much like a man watching someone take his own child away.

Then he seemed to remember where he was and looked around. Majors looked away, to avoid his eyes, as did Annie. When he glanced back, Vincent was gone and the door was closed.

"Does he look like a man who didn't even know the name of that baby's mother?" Majors asked.

Annie didn't say anything.

Sally Crow had come back out. She was standing talking to Kreider, stripping off her rubber gloves.

"Time to go to work," he said.

He could tell by the set of Sally's jaw how bad it was, and it made his stomach begin to churn a little in anticipation. It was hard to make Sally look that bothered.

Before he could reach her, he was intercepted by the patrolman he'd sent to walk through the other apartment, who handed him two notepads, both of which appeared to be filled.

"Anything I should know?" Majors asked, stifling his annoyance at the interruption.

"No, Detective. Just a vacant apartment, I'd say."

"Okay. Thanks."

Sally had brought a faint smell of death with her from the apartment, something that helped him begin to settle down. It might not even be from this scene. It got into the hollow places inside the hair, into the skin. The longer a forensic pathologist worked with bodies, the harder it was to get rid of. Sally would go home tonight and shampoo with lemon juice, which was what they all did. The women, anyway.

Kreider had gone into the apartment after his people. "I can't give you much yet about time and cause," Sally said. "Based on rigor and lividity, size of the corpse, room temperature, blah blah blah . . ." She drew in a breath, paused as if counting to ten, and spoke again. "I'd guess twenty-four to forty-eight hours, probably closer to forty-eight. Maybe even a little longer. There are several different possible causes, and I won't know which one actually did it until I get her on the table."

"What does it look most like?"

"Off the record. First impressions, I'd say she was either beaten to death or strangled—hands, I'd say, from behind. Someone very strong, either way. Or maybe more than one. Everything's so smashed up . . . Kreider's people will have to help you on that. But there's a lot of bruising, probably a lot of subdermal damage, and I don't think the hyoid's intact."

"Sexual assault?"

"I don't think so. But if it's what it looks like, I wouldn't be surprised if Kreider's people find semen somewhere. Maybe not even on her."

"Lust killing."

"Something like that. I didn't notice a single object in that room that wasn't broken. It was like a bomb exploded in there. Except it was a human being that exploded."

He didn't like the way that made him think of Floyd's flare-up in Loomis's office. But Floyd had moved away. He'd hurt nothing but a telephone.

"There are a few little odd things," Sally said. "But there always are."

"Like what?"

"Keep in mind that this means nothing until I can do a full P.M., okay?"

"I always do."

"And that's the only reason I'm talking to you at all right now. Okay. Defensive wounds. No broken fingernails. She had short fingernails, anyway. But there's blood under them."

He shrugged. "So she scratched him."

"I don't know. I'm not sure it isn't her blood."

"Huh?"

"Like I said. Odd. And I don't know for sure yet. Also, most of her fingers appear to be broken. But not the way you'd expect with a woman. They're more like the breaks you get in a man's hand, from punching. And maybe that's right. She was a strong woman, in good condition. I'd guess she was an athlete."

She grew silent, but she didn't seem in a hurry to leave, the way she usually was. Usually, when an AME was willing to talk to him like this—which was against the rules—they were obviously doing him a favor and were eager to be on their way. It was different this time.

"There's something else you want to tell me?" he asked.

She thought about it, then said, "She didn't die easy, Jerry. It might have just been the fight that trashed the room, the way she defended herself. She knew her baby was upstairs." Sally sighed. "I really want you to get this guy, Jerry. I really do."

"I will."

She nodded, not as if she believed him, but as if she knew he meant it. "I gotta go."

Burton was waiting for him near the apartment door.

"What about Vincent?" Majors asked. "You like him?"

Burton shook his head. "Nah. Anyway, if his alibi checks, he's in the clear." He paused, then said, "He could be hiding something else, though."

"You mean his real relationship with the vic?"

"Yeah. And with *my* vics' stolen property."

"You want to try for a warrant?"

"Probably not. He invited me to come in and look

anywhere I wanted. He's probably a smart enough guy to play reverse psychology that way, but my guess is there's nothing there. If he's got any of it, it's already somewhere else." He frowned, hesitating the way Sally had.

"What?" Majors asked.

"Umm, is Floyd Lassiter a pretty good friend of yours?"

"He's my partner."

"Oh." Burton was silent for a moment, then shrugged. "So what now?"

"No. What were you going to say about Floyd?"

Burton sighed. "I don't know him at all. He's your partner. I just, you know . . ."

Majors stifled the surge of anger he felt. It was too much, anyway—it showed how deep his own doubts were. There was no reason to be mad at Burton. "I understand where you're coming from," he said. "But Floyd's been having a lot of personal problems lately. His wife ran off with an ATF guy—"

"Shit. Didn't know that. Forget it."

Majors was tempted to let it go at that, but he knew he couldn't. "Was there something besides the way he looked tonight?"

Burton hesitated. "You sure you . . ."

"I'm sure."

"Probably nothing anyway. Just one of those . . . It's just, I had the feeling Floyd wasn't all that happy about me calling him. I mean, kind of like he hadn't really intended for us to connect Celia Staircase to *our* girl, you know? I mean, I had to ask him straight out, was he the one investigating our case in Wichita, and was that how he came up with this woman?" Burton shrugged. "But he answered me straight, so . . ." He shrugged again.

They moved to one side as Sally's helper emerged from the apartment door, pulling the gurney behind him, with one of Kreider's guys at the other end, the two men pausing to lift it carefully down from the porch without jostling the black-bagged body.

"I think he liked her is all," Burton said. "That's the feeling I get. Sometimes, you know . . ."

"Yeah, I know." He watched the two techs load the gurney into the back of the van. The driver went around to the front, and Kreider's guy hopped in behind the body and closed the door. The van pulled away, moving slowly until the way to the alley was cleared, then accelerating a little and disappearing into the darkness, the way Floyd had.

Majors shook himself. He realized he'd just cut Burton off, spoken more curtly than the L.A. cop deserved. "You want to go with me on the walk-through?" he asked, looking at him.

"Me? I'm a burglary guy."

"You're a dick, right? Two pairs of eyes are better than one."

"Sure, if you want me to. Lead on."

Majors hesitated for a second, not knowing why, then stepped onto the porch and went in.

15

Wednesday

It was an arresting photo, by a photographer she'd never heard of. Good enough to make her read the story, which was the kind she usually avoided—the brutal murder of a woman living alone, or in this case with an infant. This story, and the photo, made her uneasy in a particular way, because of the man in the photo, whom she knew, and who had also made her uneasy when he'd taught that computer class on the new system at the *Mid American.*

As far as she knew, there wasn't anything wrong with him. He seemed to be a perfectly nice guy, well intentioned but with a little of that social ineptness and obtuseness that always seemed to accompany computer expertise. He'd made her uneasy because he was one of those tall, slender, soft-spoken men like Jay—those men who always reminded her of her father. She'd thought he was interested in her, focusing on her, but that was a part of it. She always thought that, with men who seemed to match that template in her mind, even when they seemed totally oblivious to her.

The computer class had been right around the time Jay died—right after it, she thought, and a waste of time, because she'd already decided to quit, but hadn't wanted to tell Fred yet. So she'd been especially susceptible to those old vibes right then.

Still, she couldn't keep from looking at the photo. Her eyes kept straying back to it, to the expression on the face of the baby, the way its small arms stretched out—and the mystery of Zach Vincent's expression behind his beard. That was one of the things that made her uneasy, she supposed. The beard made him harder to read, although, in fact, he was one of those men who was easy to read, who seemed to be hiding nothing. The photo was like one of those Renaissance paintings, angels reaching out toward robed humans, their hands not quite touching.

She knew the woman, too, the SRS caseworker. She'd interviewed Laurie Cox once for an add to a story someone else was doing on changes in infrastructure and social services. Laurie Cox had obviously thought that the privatization of foster care and adoptions in Kansas was an unmitigated disaster, but had been afraid to say so for attribution.

Susie barked, out in the backyard, and Jes glanced at the windows on the other side of the kitchen table. Hector's old Crown Vic was pulling into the driveway. She watched as it came to a stop, and the door opened and he began pushing himself up and out, his hands braced on the door and the car frame. As if his legs were no longer strong enough by themselves. She felt a chill of apprehension. Hector was the strongest person she'd ever known, but even he was running down, becoming as old as his years. He'd be gone soon, one more ghost—even Jo felt like a ghost to her now, a thought that reminded her of that strange dream, brought back the chill of it. When Hector was gone, it really would be just her and Susie.

Strange to think that he was the same age as her father. She watched him walk along the walk toward the porch, noting that Susie's gruff barks had turned to something more like pleading whines because she'd caught his scent. Hector was really the only other person in Susie's world, too. Jes got up to open the door before he rang.

He lifted his head and saw her, but didn't smile. "Morning, Jes," he said.

Something was wrong. Something bad. She felt an

impulse to go out to meet him, but she didn't. She stayed behind the screen as she'd trained herself to do, as he expected her to do.

He stopped on the other side of it and looked off toward the south, as if he saw something in the sky there.

"What is it, Hector?"

He glanced at her, then away again. "Why'n't you get dressed and come on out so we can talk?"

She was wearing her old raggedy bathrobe over her pajamas—fully covered—but Hector came from a different generation, and "dressed" meant something different to him.

She nodded. "I'll meet you out back. Susie won't shut up unless we go back there."

He gave a grunt of assent and turned away. Closing the door, she thought how much more sense it would make simply to invite him in, the way any normal person would. But he understood.

She felt her apprehension increasing while she changed clothes, putting on jeans and a sweatshirt, slipping on some moccasins. She couldn't get it out of her head that whatever it was had to do with the story in the paper, but that was only because she'd already been troubled by that, thinking about Zach Vincent. And of course it was a woman her own age, someone who could have been Jo—and if someone had died, who else could it be that Hector would be coming here to tell her about, looking the way he was? But this woman had had a baby, and Jo was far away somewhere.

She went out briskly and sat down in the wooden Adirondack chair on the deck beside the one he was sitting in. "Just tell me," she said.

He looked at her for a second, then shrugged and said, "It's Jo. She's dead."

Even though she'd just been thinking about it, she couldn't believe it. Her first thought was, That's ridiculous. Jo couldn't really *die*. And if she did, wouldn't

Jes know? But then she remembered the dream again, and realized that she did. It was true.

She found that she couldn't say anything. She just had no idea what words to speak.

"You saw that story in the paper?" Hector asked. "The one with the photo of the baby and the—"

"*Christ!* Are you saying that was *Jo*?" It was if something had shifted, the ground had moved beneath her, and she was suddenly in some world that was not quite the same as where she'd been. Her sister was a murdered woman in a story she'd read in the newspaper. Over there in that city where she'd lived and worked. Annie Babicki had written the story. Zach Vincent . . . she shook her head, feeling overwhelmed for a moment by confusion. Something wrong there— Jo and Zach Vincent. She closed her eyes, then opened them wide. *The baby.* It was Jo's baby. Had something snapped? Could you go crazy, just like that?

"She was living under the name Celia Staircase," Hector said. "She'd been in Wichita since late last year sometime. She was hiding out, 'cause the LAPD was looking for her for some burglaries. They knew her as Celeste Mundy. I checked their Web site, where they have a photo of Celeste Mundy, and it was definitely Jo. And now they've confirmed that the murdered woman is Celeste Mundy."

Jes stared at him, not taking in any of it. She went back over it in her mind, to see if any of it made any sense to her. One thing stood out to her: *in Wichita since late last year.*

She gasped. "She called me!"

"What?"

"While I was out with Susie, just . . ." She shook her head, finding she'd lost track of what day it was. "Day before yesterday, I think. Or maybe . . . I don't know."

"Did she leave a message?"

"No. But it was that name you said. Staircase. On the caller ID. E . . . what was the first name?"

"Celia."

Jes frowned. "No. This was E. Staircase." Then she got it, and said, "Oh shit" under her breath. "Eddy," she said aloud. "She was using Eddy Staircase." She found herself smiling idiotically, felt suddenly on the brink of giggling hysteria. *Just like Jo. My God, that's Jo all over. My God . . .*

She swallowed, shuddering, holding herself together. Hector was looking at her, but he hadn't asked the obvious question.

"It's an old thing from when we were kids," Jes said.

"Maybe it's the baby's name."

Oh yeah. The baby. Christ. She knew that her whole life was changing, all of a sudden, and that it was too complicated to try to think about.

"She called me, too," Hector said. "Left a message I didn't understand."

"What?"

"That she got *my* message."

"But you didn't—"

"No. I didn't think I did. I mean, I didn't know she was in Wichita. But I guess . . . maybe I did. Send her a message, I mean."

"I don't know what you're talking about. I'm not tracking."

He sighed. "No reason you should. A few days ago, I got a call from a guy I used to know in the WPD, Floyd Lassiter. Homicide detective. He was looking for Celeste Mundy, and he was asking about Jocelyn Peete. That's when I looked up the photo on the LAPD Web site, so then I knew Lassiter was on the right track."

"Peete." She shook her head, tempted to smile again. Peete had been their mother's maiden name.

"It was the name she gave when she was busted," Hector said.

The giddy feeling evaporated all at once, leaving her feeling chilled, as if she were catching something, had a fever. "I didn't know that. So what did you tell this cop, Lassiter, when he called you?"

"I told him the only woman I'd ever known in Sand Creek named Peete was a woman named Maria, a long time ago, and that she was dead. That's true. I told him I'd look into it and get back to him if I found anything."

"Did you?"

"Lassiter is too good to stonewall," Hector said. "Look how far he'd already gotten."

"Okay. So what did you do?"

Hector sighed. "I sent him a high school yearbook photo, with the name Jocelyn Peete written on the back."

She waited for the rest, but there wasn't any. "That's it?" she asked.

"Yeah." He paused, then said, "It was a senior yearbook photo."

It took a moment for that to sink in. "But Jo wasn't . . ." Then she got it. "You sent him *my* yearbook photo?"

He shrugged, like *What's the difference?* None, she supposed. Especially since Jo was dead. She felt astonished all over again. *Jo dead.*

"Anyhow," Hector said, "I guess Lassiter found her, living under this Staircase name, and he talked to her. I think that's what she meant when she called me."

"What?"

"I think maybe, for some reason or other, she got the idea that that was a message from me. Lassiter's visit. I don't know. Maybe if he showed her the photo I sent him. And told her where he got it. Something like that."

"This Lassiter wasn't mentioned in the *Mid American* story."

"No. In fact, it turns out he isn't really working. He's been on some kind of suspension or something."

"Why?"

"Don't know. Loomis—L. J. Loomis, the homicide

lieutenant over there—he didn't tell me and I didn't want to ask. He said Lassiter really was working on the Celeste Mundy thing, though, as a kind of favor to him."

"Isn't that strange?"

"Oh, I don't know. An L.A. case. Why waste the time of somebody who's on duty? What I can't figure is why homicide was working it."

"So you talked to this Loomis?"

"This morning, for a few minutes. I tried to reach Lassiter, but I couldn't. I didn't tell Loomis much of anything. Except, me asking if the dead woman was Celeste Mundy—had to tell him something. He asked me if I'd come over and talk to the detective on the case, and I said I would. That's where I'm heading when I leave here."

"So what are you going to tell him?"

"I've been thinking about that, and I think I'm going to tell him the truth. I wanted to see what you thought."

She remained silent. One of the problems was that she wasn't entirely sure what he meant by that. There were things she didn't think he knew, and things he didn't think she knew—although she did, so maybe he did, too. It sometimes seemed to her that they were conspiring to keep the secret that there weren't really any secrets.

"The whole truth?" she asked.

"As much of it as he needs to know. I plan to give him the basics, and answer any questions he asks. If he doesn't ask a particular question . . ." Hector shrugged.

She nodded. "That's fine. I'll trust your judgment. I don't know that it makes any difference now."

He studied her for a moment, then said, "I want to try to keep them from bothering you."

She shrugged. "Well, thanks. But I don't know that—"

"Celeste Mundy stole some valuable things from some important people," Hector said. "They'll be

looking for them. The cops, the insurance companies . . .
maybe other people."

"Oh. I see. Who more likely than her twin sister."
But that seemed remote to her, unimportant. There
were other things that bothered her more, things she
was just beginning to think of. The funeral. The obit.
And then there was the house and stock trust, the
things Jo had an interest in. She'd be the only heir,
but . . . .

No. She wouldn't. The baby. What did that mean?
What if the father showed up? What if he was
adopted? She felt suddenly overwhelmed.

"I'll need to see about the baby," she said. "Where
is he now?"

"I expect he'll be at the Children's Home," Hector
said, "over by Wesley. They'll be trying to find next
of kin."

Next of kin. It occurred to her that in Hector's
world, there'd be no question about what to do with
the baby. She'd automatically take him in. Maybe
Hector assumed that's what she'd do.

"You got a lawyer?" he asked.

"What for?"

"In case any of these people give you trouble. The
ones looking for the stolen stuff."

"Oh. Yeah. Bill Potts."

"No. A *criminal* lawyer. If people think you have
this stuff, that's a crime."

"Shit. I don't know. You know them. Who . . . ?"

"Manny Machado."

"You *hate* Manny Machado."

"That's why."

"I don't know. I went to high school with Manny.
You have to tell your lawyer everything."

"He's not your shrink. Did you kill Jo? *Are* you
holding any of the stolen goods?"

"No."

"Then you got nothing to tell him that's a problem."

She nodded, not quite sure that was true. But the
idea of her even needing a criminal lawyer was so

bizarre that it was crazy to be debating it this way. She was feeling irritated, impinged upon. Her twin sister was dead, and she was pissed off that her life was going to be disrupted. What an asshole.

"If I did have any the stuff, you've just warned me to hide it," she said.

"Yeah, I know. You can stash it at my place if you want."

For just a second she thought he was serious, and then she laughed. Hector didn't smile. He never smiled at his own jokes.

He stood up, gripping the arms of the chair the way he had the car frame. Susie, who'd been dozing contentedly at his feet, having gotten a surfeit of attention while Jes was dressing, sprang to life and scrambled awkwardly to her feet, her tail flapping. Hector, on his feet, put a hand on the dog's head and ruffled her fur.

"Storm coming," he said. "Over toward Wichita. Take care if you're going over."

He must think she was going right over to see the baby. Or maybe he was saying she ought to. "You too," she said.

She watched him go out the gate and then disappear past the corner of the house, along the driveway. Susie gave a kind of yelp, then came close to Jes, looking apologetic for the display of emotion, her head down.

"It's okay," Jes said. "We couldn't help loving him, either." The big dog looked up at her, its tail wagging.

"How'd you like to have a little brother?" Jes asked at last.

Susie's tail wagged harder.

Jes gave a grunt of laughter and shook her head. "Easy for you to say."

16

"Floyd is the only thing I know of that connects Briseno to this," Loomis said. "You have any other ideas?"

"He knew about Celeste Mundy? He had the name?"

"Yeah. He asked me if the vic had turned out to be her. And then before I could ask him anything, he said he was coming over to talk to you."

"Me by name?" Majors asked.

Loomis thought about that. "No. Whoever was working the case."

"When's he coming?"

"Sometime this morning. I told Dorothy to let me know as soon as he shows up. But I thought we'd better talk first."

Majors nodded.

"The Celeste Mundy case is on our Web site," Burton said. "I mean, if he happened to look at that . . ." His voice faded away, and neither of the other men said anything. "Not very likely, I guess. He used to work here?"

"Long time ago," Loomis said. "Before my time. Lassiter might be the only one left who—"

"There's Dooley," Majors said.

"Yeah. That's right." Loomis said to Burton, "He worked undercover here, as a narc. You know, the sixties . . ."

"And he and Floyd worked together?"

"Not as partners. On some drug cases. Floyd was in Special Investigations when he first came in." He glanced at Majors and their eyes met. Neither wanted to mention the specific connection between Floyd and Briseno.

"Have you talked to Floyd since last night?" Loomis asked.

Majors shook his head. He assumed Floyd was sleeping in—he'd looked like he needed it. He hoped that was why he hadn't heard from him yet, anyway. He didn't want to call or go looking for Floyd himself, as long as he had an excuse not to. That was the good thing about Briseno coming. He could wait a little longer before beginning to wonder where Floyd was.

"He hasn't filed any report yet," Loomis said. "So we don't know who he's talked to. Maybe Briseno. Or maybe somebody who would have told Briseno."

"It's probably something like that," Burton said.

Ever since their brief exchange about Floyd the night before, the L.A. cop had been bending over backward to give Floyd the benefit of the doubt, but for some reason that irritated Majors more than if he'd done the opposite. It was like he was being humored. He also didn't like the fact that Burton had already been here in Loomis's office when he'd arrived for this meeting.

Burton said, "Maybe Floyd had some reason to think she came from—what is it? Sand Creek?"

That jogged Majors's memory. "I showed Annie Babicki the photo of Celeste Mundy last night," he said, "and she said she looked just like a woman from Sand Creek. Another reporter who used to work on the paper here."

Loomis gave him a curious look. "I didn't put it in my notes at the time," Majors said guiltily. "We were just chatting . . ." He gave a helpless shrug, feeling stupid. He knew what Loomis was going to say before he said it.

"You think you should be on this case, Jerry?"

It wasn't quite as strong as he'd expected. At least Loomis was asking his opinion. Majors nodded.

"I can handle it." Then, although he wasn't sure it

wasn't a mistake, he couldn't keep from saying, "You know, the only reason we're thinking about Floyd at all is because we haven't got anybody else who even knew her." Vincent's alibi was solid. He was the one guy in Wichita Majors was sure *didn't* kill her.

"Well, actually we do," Burton said. "I mean, *we* do."

"Right," Loomis said. "I was going to ask you if your guys out there could look into that possibility."

"Most likely none of those guys would've done it in person," Burton said.

"But they'd have the connections to hire somebody," Loomis said. "Some of them, anyway."

"Some of them. Definitely. You realize, though, we don't necessarily know who all her clients were. Just the ones that came forward. And this guy, if that's what it is, he obviously wasn't interested in calling the cops."

Majors nodded. He felt out of it—off to one side and a half step behind. All the best suspects were out in California, on Burton's turf. The only one he had was Floyd. And what if it *was* Floyd? Did he really want to be the one . . .?

"Jerry?"

Majors jerked, realized he'd missed something. "Sorry. What?"

"I said, besides maybe Briseno, you got any leads into her life, other possible connections?"

Majors shook his head. "Mrs. Neuenswander would love to give us anything she could, and she's got zip. I still have a little trouble believing that Vincent didn't even know her name. Even though we know he didn't do it . . ." He shrugged. "The problem is, even if he did, where does that take us? To Annie Babicki? Hell of a choice, Floyd or Annie."

Loomis gave a half smile. "He must have clients. I don't know what to tell you. You just have to pull whatever strings you've got." He frowned. "Seriously, Jerry. If it starts going in that kind of direction, you hand it off to me, okay? That's an order. That's why

I get paid the big bucks." He didn't smile. "Your job is find somebody else."

"Whoever really killed her," Majors said.

"Exactly."

"No problem."

Loomis laughed. He looked at Burton. "And you'll check out the other angle for us?"

"You got it."

Loomis nodded. "Maybe Briseno will wrap the whole thing up for us." He picked up the casebook lying on his desk. "Anything interesting in here?"

"Yeah," Majors said. "There's the wounds under the fingernails. All the blood there turned out to be hers. That looks like some kind of torture, which would fit with some guy trying to get back whatever she took. But then everything else looks like somebody in a blind rage—"

"Not quite blind," Loomis said.

Majors looked at him blankly, then got it. "You mean how thorough it was."

"Right. You ever see a scene like that, where every single thing was broken or . . . thrown down or whatever? In a funny way, it's almost methodical, like somebody being careful not to miss anything."

"Like a search disguised as an explosion," Burton said. He looked interested in the idea.

Majors was interested, too. It was an idea that pointed away from Floyd. He felt stupid for not having picked up on that. *That's my problem*, he thought. Floyd was the brains of the partnership. Working with him, he'd gotten out of the habit of paying that kind of attention.

"Or maybe two guys," Burton said. "One after the other, you know? Whoever it was that slept on the sofa, maybe, and then . . ." He shrugged.

Majors didn't like that idea as well, but it was something that had to be considered. A trail of rainwater spots and stains, plus some sheets that had been stuffed into the dryer but not actually washed or dried, told a story of someone who'd come in out of the rain, and evidently rested on the living room sofa for a time. Then somebody had stuffed the pillow back into the hall closet and put the rain-damp sheet in the dryer. That part didn't fit Floyd. Why would he be sleeping on her sofa? He had his own house.

And there was no real DNA evidence, apart from the vic herself. No sign of sexuality activity—not even semen elsewhere in the room, as might be expected in a lust murder. The only clear latents they'd found, apart from hers, were Vincent's, and they were all consistent with the story he told of getting the baby.

The most interesting thing that had been found was nearly $100,000 in cash, stashed in a plastic bag in the bottom of the Diaper Genie in the baby's room. If somebody had conducted a search, they obviously hadn't found that. And there wasn't any evidence of any search, anyway, apart from the odd thoroughness of the destruction in the bedroom. The other rooms were all undisturbed, except for Vincent's entry and that of the mysterious visitor who'd come in out of the rain. Otherwise, forensics couldn't say with confidence that anyone else had been in the apartment. If the killer wasn't Vincent, and wasn't the guest on the sofa, they knew absolutely nothing about him. Or them.

"When I call my department," Burton said, "you want me to get a current list of what's still missing?"

"I've got a list a P.I. gave me," Loomis said. "Only four things, though." He scanned his cluttered desk, then came up with a creased single sheet of paper and handed it to Burton. It looked to Majors like a sheet of bad photocopies.

"Yeah, this is some of it," Burton said, frowning. "A local P.I.?"

"No. A guy from L.A. who checked in here this morning. Very proper. Claimed he didn't carry a gun. First P.I. I ever saw—"

"Not Tim Haffner?" Burton said.

"Yeah, that's the name."

Majors had moved closer to Burton to get a look

at the page, which was divided into quarters, each with a photograph of an item and some descriptive text beneath. There was an antique diamond brooch and a necklace that appeared to go with it, plus what looked like a painting of some mountain or desert scene, although it was a little too murky to be sure, and a block of four old airmail stamps showing a prop plane flying upside down.

"You know him?" Loomis said.

Burton grinned. "Yeah. Kind of funny they'd send him. How'd he get here so fast?"

"He said he was in St. Louis, on some other case, and he got a call from his office, telling him to hop a plane and fly over here, and a fax of this stuff. He seemed okay."

"Oh yeah. Haffner's fine. He'll be no problem."

"He really doesn't carry a piece?"

"True. Doesn't like guns. He's not really a P.I."

"He had a license."

"Oh yeah. Sure. I mean, he isn't *really* a P.I. Like not carrying. His family owns part of the agency—it's a big agency, mostly insurance work like this. Recovery of fenced goods, that kind of thing. So . . ." He shrugged. "Tim has some kind of worthless college degree, like, I don't know, French poetry or something. So he's a detective." Burton smiled. "I think he works mostly divorce cases. I've heard that he sometimes provides, umm, special services for some of the female clients. The young, attractive ones."

Loomis grunted. "He did strike me more like a salesman than a P.I."

"I doubt he'll be here long," Burton said. "They probably already have a real detective on the way, to replace him. One with a real big heavy hunk of metal."

Loomis nodded and dropped the sheet on his desk. "If you notice somebody like that around, let me know."

"Definitely."

Loomis looked at Majors. "Might as well go on back

to your office. I'll tell Dorothy to call you directly when Briseno shows up. Let me know after, will you, if he gives us anything?"

"Sure."

Going back along the hallway, Majors glanced out one of the narrow windows and saw, to his surprise, that it was raining, and so dark it might have been evening. It made him feel uncomfortable, as if it must mean something. It made him miss Floyd even more.

17

The parking garage was gone, but otherwise the City Building wasn't really that much different. The first drops began to fall while he was walking from the new parking lot, a block away. He held the file folder a little closer to his body, to shield it, but didn't duck his head or walk any faster while people ran past him, both ways, with briefcases and newspapers over their heads. It was only water.

He wasn't really sure whether the lobby was different or not. It had been too long, and he'd never paid much attention to that kind of thing in the first place. The elevators were in the same place, anyway. It didn't occur to him to look at the building directory until he was getting out on the floor where homicide had been thirty years ago. But it was still there.

There was a waiting room now, and a receptionist wearing one of those little telephone headsets and peering at a computer screen. You couldn't see the detectives wandering around between their overflowing desks, looking irritated or baffled or bored or self-important, typing reports with two fingers, scratching their butts and their balls and fiddling with their shoulder holsters. For the first time in thirty years he realized he'd missed the camaraderie. Maybe that was why he hadn't been back here in all that time. He'd been in Wichita often enough, worked with guys from the WPD. But he'd stayed away from the building without quite realizing it.

For some reason he also didn't quite understand, he didn't tell the receptionist who he was, only gave her his name and told her he'd like to see Detective Majors. She told him Majors was in a meeting, and asked him to have a seat.

The only other people in the waiting room were sitting right across from him, an old man with his head bandaged and a very pregnant young girl, maybe still in her teens. The old man's bandage covered his right eye and ear and ran around to the back of his head. Could be a gunshot wound, through and through, small-caliber, in the eye and out some seam or soft spot. He had a magazine in his lap, but he wasn't looking at it. He kept his one eye fixed on the door behind the receptionist. He looked to Hector like he'd been waiting a long time—a lot longer than he wanted to, anyway. The girl had a magazine, too, and she looked like she could sit there and read it forever.

The door from the outside hallway opened, and two young guys came in, dressed casual, like golfers. They exchanged greetings with the receptionist and went right on in. Working undercover at the country club? When he'd been their age, he'd worked mostly undercover, but it hadn't been at any country club, and he hadn't dressed anything like that.

He felt the receptionist's eyes on him and looked back at her out of the corner of his eye. She was studying him, looking troubled, and he understood what it was. Loomis had told her there was a detective from Sand Creek coming in, told her to let him know when he arrived. But Loomis hadn't told her the name, and Hector hadn't identified himself, and he'd asked for Majors, not Loomis. But he looked like a cop to her, so she wasn't sure.

He pushed himself up, leaving the folder on the chair, and walked back to the desk. "I just realized I should have told you it was Lieutenant Loomis I talked to," he told her. "Not Detective Majors."

"You're the detective from Sand Creek?"

"Yes, ma'am."

"Oh, dear." She punched a couple of buttons on her phone.

"Should have said so," Hector murmured, but she was already talking to the person at the other end.

"Detective Majors will be right out," she said, a little stiffly.

"Thanks. Sorry." He turned back toward his chair and saw the old man glaring at him resentfully through his one good eye. *Sorry to you, too, Gramps.*

He'd picked up the folder but hadn't sat down when the door opened behind him. He turned to see a man of about forty enter the room, wearing a black knit shirt, jeans and a dark sports jacket. The man scanned the room, glanced at the receptionist, who nodded at Hector, and then approached with his hand out.

"Detective Briseno? I'm Jerry Majors. Sorry if we've kept you waiting."

"No," Hector said, shaking his hand. "I just got here."

"Good. Come on in."

Instead of the big open room full of desks and men and talk and clacking typewriter keys he'd been imagining, inside was a maze of cubicles through which Majors led him, past glimpses of computer screens and snatches of murmured conversations. It could have been any office. At the far end they walked past one of the tall, narrow windows. To Hector's surprise, it looked like night outside, but it didn't appear to be raining.

Majors's cubicle was against the outer wall but had no window.

"How long since you were up here?" Majors asked, steering him to a chair and sliding quickly into his own seat behind the gray metal desk.

"Long time," Hector said. "Before they had these wall things. Detectives still wore suits."

Majors blinked, then laughed. "Today's dress-down day," he said. "Supposed to be good for morale. We do it once a month." He shrugged. "Lieutenant Loomis didn't tell me exactly what—"

"I didn't tell him." Hector put the folder on the

desk and opened it. He offered the photo that lay on top to Majors. "This your vic?"

Majors looked at the photo, at the open folder, at Briseno, and then reached forward to take the photo. He looked at it, looked at the blank back, then studied the face again for a moment. "I'd say so," he said. "Quite a bit younger. Can I get a copy of this?"

"You can have it. I'm leaving the folder here. Glad to be rid of it." He paused for Majors to say something, and when he didn't, he said, "She was twelve years younger then, in that photo. Seventeen. Her parents were dead. Her mother died when she was nine and her father when she was fifteen. She lived with her father's cousin, an old widow lady, for a couple of years and then quit high school and moved out, came over here. A few months later, she got busted at some kind of college fraternity party, for prostitution. But she was still a juvenile, and in those days it made a difference. Soon as they let her go, she disappeared. Hasn't been back since, far as I know. Till now."

Majors frowned at the thick file folder. "So what's in there?"

"Mostly . . . mostly it's about her mother and father, and how they died."

"Wrongful deaths, I take it?"

"Yeah. They both went to inquest and were ruled accidents. No homicide investigation."

Majors grunted. "What kinds of accidents?"

Hector sighed in spite of himself. "Maria fell off a counter in the kitchen and hit her head on a corner. Rafe dropped his shotgun on the floor and it went off, blew off his head."

"Really?"

"No."

There was a short silence. Hector decided he'd reached the point where Majors would have to ask questions. He wouldn't volunteer anything else.

"Okay," Majors said. "I'm guessing he was an abuser. Unintentional homicide and suicide."

"He killed her," Hector said, "and I'm sure he

didn't mean to. He loved her. He was a nice guy when
he was sober." He shrugged. It was a common enough
story.

He expected Majors to ask why Rafe Wellington
hadn't been charged, but instead he said, "And then,
six years later? He shoots himself?"

"No." Hector closed his mouth and met Majors's
eyes.

Majors returned his stare for a moment, then looked
away. "Someone killed him. Because of what he'd
done."

He knew that Majors understood the game now,
that he had to ask the right questions. Hector was
impressed by how easily he seemed to accept it. "I
imagine that was part of it," Hector said.

Majors nodded. "She was abused, too, but she had
to wait until she was big enough." He looked at Hector. "You knew what had probably happened, but you
decided not to investigate."

"Close." He paused, knowing that this was where
he was crossing the line for good. "I helped her get
away with it. I cleaned up the scene and gave her an
alibi. And I didn't investigate it."

Majors looked thoughtful, then nodded. "You
haven't told me her name," he said.

"Jocelyn Wellington. Jo for short."

Majors looked at him as if surprised. "She didn't
go by Jes, too, did she? Did she ever work for the
newspaper here?"

Hector didn't change his expression, but he felt a
sudden weight in his gut. This was all wasted. They
already knew about Jes. But he only said, "No."

Majors grunted. "Our vic's photo hasn't been released to the media. How'd you know it was her?
Have you been in touch with her since she came
back?"

"No. I wish I had. She did try to call me. Left a
message on my voice mail."

"When was that?"

"Sunday."

"What was it?"

"She said, 'I got your message.' "

"Which meant?"

Hector shook his head. "Don't know. I've got an idea, but—"

"What is it?"

"A few days before that I'd gotten a call from Floyd Lassiter—Detective Lassiter. He said he was investigating this California thing, this fugitive named Celeste Mundy." He saw Majors frown, and thought he was going to say something, but he didn't. "He called me about Jo's juvenile pros arrest. He'd found out about it somehow, and also connected it to the woman he was looking for. I don't know how. Didn't really surprise me. Lassiter was always a hell of a detective. Very smart.

"Anyhow," Hector went on, "he had the name she'd given when she was arrested—Jocelyn Peete. Her mother's maiden name was Peete. He also knew she'd come from Sand Creek, so he was calling me to see if I knew her."

"He didn't know that."

"No. Didn't seem to. I told him at first that I didn't. But then I took a look at the LAPD Web site, and their photo of Celeste Mundy was obviously Jo. So I sent him a high school yearbook photo, with Jocelyn Peete written on the back. What I'm thinking is, maybe Lassiter showed her the photo or mentioned my name or something, and she took it for some kind of message from me." He shrugged. "That's all I can come up with. Doesn't make much difference now."

"You never know," Majors said distantly. "When did you hear from Lassiter again?"

"Never did. Jo's phone call came from a booth in Riverside Park, so I knew she was in Wichita. I was still trying to decide whether or not to look for her myself when she got killed." It occurred to him for the first time that he might make a pretty good suspect himself. He even had a motive—keeping her from revealing what he'd done a dozen years ago. He tried to figure out how he felt about that, but couldn't. It would be a kind of joke, maybe even fitting.

"Is this the photo you sent him?" Majors asked.

Hector shook his head. He fished the other one out of his pocket and handed it to Majors, who held the two of them side by side in front of him and nodded.

"Twins, right?" He waved the smaller photo in the air. "This is who you're protecting."

Hector was impressed. "Not very well, obviously," he said. "Most people can't tell them apart."

Majors looked at them again. "I'm not sure I can, either. It's just . . . it seemed like there had to be two of them. And there's something . . ." He studied the photos for a few seconds more, then shrugged and put them down.

"I'm just trying to keep Jes out of it," Hector said. "She doesn't have anything to do with it. She didn't know Jo was back until she saw the paper. She's got enough problems."

"I assume she was abused, too. Was she in on the father's killing?"

"No. She thinks it was an accident, like the coroner's jury ruled. Finding out it wasn't . . . that's one of the things I'd like to protect her from. What difference does it make now?"

Majors sighed, shook his head. "I can't answer that." He glanced at the folder and then at Hector. "How did you think this was going to help me?" he asked.

"By eliminating stuff there's no reason to waste time on. None of it has anything to do with what happened to Jo."

"How can you be sure of that?"

Hector thought about it. "I don't know. But I am. There's only the two of us left. Jes and me. And neither of us had anything to do with it." He shrugged.

Majors studied him for a moment longer, then looked away as if giving it up. He looked suddenly tired. Hector supposed he hadn't had much sleep. They'd lost a lot of time off the top.

"You knew Floyd," Majors said, "when you worked over here."

"Yeah."

"There was something that happened ."

"That doesn't have anything to do with it, either. That's ancient history."

Majors nodded. "I just . . . I wondered if you'd mind telling me what actually happened. You hear different things, and Floyd never talks about it. Floyd's my partner, by the way."

It was Hector's turn to study Majors. Something odd was going on here. Could *Lassiter* be a suspect? Surely, if he was, Loomis wouldn't have his partner working the case. If Loomis *knew* he was a suspect. If that was the way it was, Hector didn't envy Majors.

"I don't mind telling you," he said, putting just a bit of emphasis on the last word. "We were both working undercover, but from different directions. Narco. It was the sixties—not as bad as now, but it seemed bad enough at the time. I was working regular narco, made up to look like a biker. Mustache and all, you know. The Mexican bandito look. Lassiter had been brought down from . . . someplace . . ."

"Fort Riley," Majors said.

"Fort Riley. Yeah. That was a big drug town then, 'cause of the army base and the war and all. I think Lassiter had been in the Riley County S.O. Anyway, he had a good rep, and nobody in Wichita knew him. There was this special unit, involving the city and the feds and, I don't know . . . everybody. And they brought in guys like Lassiter, that even the local cops didn't know. So we didn't know each other when the whole thing started.

"He'd gotten way inside this gang. I say 'gang,' but it was nothing like now. But, anyway, he was on the inside, and I was supposed to be with this biker gang that wanted to score a bunch of dope to resell. The idea was to ask for enough stuff so they'd have to bring in somebody from higher up. We thought the

K.C. mob had a finger in—which was true—and we hoped maybe they'd send somebody, you know?

"So, we get right up to the exchange. We got the fucking money, they got the fucking dope. All we have to do is trade suitcases. It's me and this real-life biker, some guy we had by the balls so he had to play. And there's three of them—including Lassiter, but I didn't know he was a cop—and this guy in a suit I was hoping was syndicate. The real biker—I think that was a mistake. I think it was him being scared shitless that the guy in the suit picked up on. I mean, he's a real big guy, mean and dumb, half stoned most of the time, and we're buying a bunch of dope. What's he got to be scared about?

"Anyhow, we get right up to the swap, and the guy in the suit says, 'Wait a minute.' He goes up to the biker and looks him in the eye for a long time, not saying anything . . . you know. And I can see the guy's about to blow, so I act impatient and I say something like, 'Hey, what the fuck? Let's do it.' And the suit turns to me and looks at me the same way, and then he says, 'What's this shit? This guy's a fuckin' narc.' "

Hector laughed, making Majors frown. "It seems funny now," Hector said. " 'Cause this big, bad biker, when the guy in the suit says that, he barfs all over him. Projectile vomiting, you know? Everybody gets hit. And then the guy's on his knees, yelling about how we made him do it and blah blah blah. He was crying, I swear to God." He shook his head.

"So, anyhow, I'm fucked. They take my piece and they drive us out in the country, to this big farm pond where bodies got dumped sometimes. And they've got me hogtied on the ground, and the biker's supposed to shoot me with my own piece, to prove he's on the level, and I'm yelling at him that they're gonna kill him anyway, and he's confused, but I can see he's gonna do it." He stopped, suddenly having a vivid memory of that moment. He'd believed he was about to die. Believed it. Something had happened then. Something had changed that had never changed back.

It was because of that that he hadn't cared much about getting bounced from the WPD later.

He remembered the cows. He was lying on his side in the warm mud, his wrists and ankles tied together behind his back . . . and he was looking out across the brown water of the pond, and there was a pasture on the other side . . . and there were those three cows over there, just eating grass and being cows. Not caring. Not knowing they were ever going to die. He remembered thinking that it wasn't fair, that it was some kind of cruel joke, that this was the last thing he was ever going to see, and it was these cows he was looking at, thinking how much better it would be to be them, as if it were his own fault, as if he'd made some wrong choice—but at the same time, another part of him thinking, *This isn't too bad. The last thing to see. This is okay.*

"But Floyd stopped it," Majors said.

Hector blinked at him, realizing he'd gotten lost in his own thoughts, drifted away. He had no idea how long he'd been sitting there, spaced out. Apparently he really was getting old.

"Yeah." He didn't know to describe what it felt like to be waiting for the gunshot, and to hear the loud voices that sounded so far away, and then gunshots—but not *the* gunshot—and not understanding, seeing the cows jerk and begin to trot away, over the crest of the slope, and not being sure whether this was death or not, thinking it wasn't all that bad so far, that maybe he didn't have to be so scared, after all, and then . . .

"I didn't really see exactly what went down," he told Majors. "It was all behind me. All I know is the biker and one of the other guys got killed. Lassiter told me who he was and untied me, and gave me my piece back and, umm, and then he went to get help . . ." and the guy who was still alive but gut shot had been rolled up in a ball, moaning, sounding kind of like a cow, thinking he was dying, and then suddenly smelling the cow shit and then realizing that wasn't what it was, and thinking it was the guy on the ground, which it was, but it was also him . . .

"Anyway, it came out okay," Majors said. He looked now like he was sorry he'd brought it up.

"Yeah," he said. "It was a long time ago. And it was kind of confusing at the time."

"I didn't know Floyd killed two of them," Majors said. "Fact is, I never knew he'd killed anybody."

"He had to. It was righteous." He'd have said so, at the time and now, even if he'd seen Lassiter execute each of them in order. But he hadn't had to lie.

"Sure. I never would have thought—"

"He got a citation," Hector said.

Majors nodded. "I know. I never got the impression he was especially proud of it, though."

Hector shrugged. "The thing you have to understand, I never really knew Lassiter that well. I guess it seems funny. But that kind of thing, I don't know. It doesn't make you best buddies. And then I left the department—"

"You were the scapegoat, is how I've heard it. The whole operation was blown up, and the big guy got away with the money and the dope both. And somebody had to take the blame, and Floyd was the hero . . ."

"No. I just had a chance to work in my hometown, and I decided to take it. That's all." He'd been saying that so long, it felt true to him. Maybe it was.

Walking him to the elevators, Majors said, "These girls are important to you."

Hector nodded, and then had to think how to explain it. "Rafe Wellington was my best friend," he said. "We went to grade school together."

He watched Majors's face but couldn't tell whether he got it or not. Majors hadn't asked him what he'd tried to do about the abuse, whether he'd tried to do anything at all.

He didn't now. When they were at the elevators,

Majors said, "There's something I'd like to ask you. You say you didn't know Floyd well, but . . ."

One of the doors opened. It was empty, so Hector put out a hand and held it open.

"I'd suspect you or Loomis or myself before I'd suspect Floyd Lassiter of something like this," he said.

He saw the relief on Majors's face and hoped it was deserved. The revelations had made Majors trust him about other things, and that bothered him because he knew he wasn't that trustworthy.

They shook hands, and he stepped into the elevator and let the door close. Going down, he heard a distant rumbling that seemed to be coming up from the bowels of the building. But at the bottom, in the lobby, he saw the big windows running with water, and the darkness beyond illuminated now and then by lightning inside the lid of cloud that sat over the city, grumbling to itself like some living thing. People were still going in and out, making quick dashes with newspapers and briefcases held over their heads. But most were waiting in the lobby that seemed only partly lit in the strange darkness. The air had grown thick, almost palpable, and warm, as if the air conditioning were turned off.

"It's supposed to sound like a railroad train," a woman standing near him said. "You listen for a railroad train." He thought she might be talking to him, but she didn't appear to be speaking to anyone in particular. Some of those around her gave slight nods, but no one looked at her. No one looked anywhere except at the windows and the storm beyond. Their eyes were bright and expectant, devoid of fear.

Hector remembered climbing up on a roof, when he was a teenager, to see a tornado a couple of miles away. He had thought sometimes that it was the same kind of impulse that had drawn him to police work. Not so much curiosity or a desire to protect others from bad things as an odd conviction that the nearer he got to the bad things, the better view he had, the

safer he himself was. Maybe everyone felt that way.
The ones who'd gathered here, anyway.

But in police work you mostly saw only the results
of the bad things, after they'd passed. Otherwise, they
could be right there beside you—like Rafe Wellington—and you wouldn't know what they were,
wouldn't be able to do anything to make anyone safe.

You could be out there standing square beneath
those dark clouds, right at the center of it all, thinking
you were in charge, and over there, just beyond what
you could see, there'd be that trailing edge, dropping
its little orphan funnels of wind and cloud, many so
tiny they died in the wind of the rest, others eating
their siblings and growing larger, like gods in old
legends.

You could think you were seeing it all, but you
never saw any of that until somewhere, in someplace
you couldn't see, in some way you hadn't expected,
that gathering darkness would pounce suddenly on the
earth and strike it like a fist, destroying whoever was
there.

18

The funeral home hadn't been happy about doing things so quickly, or about her refusal to come in and pick out a casket herself, or about the very minimal information she gave them for the local obit. But they agreed and said they'd send a hearse to Wichita to get the body. They'd call first, to make sure the body would be released to them, and call her if there was any problem. She waited a half hour, which she spent looking for the documents on the house and the stock trust, before remembering they were in a safe deposit box at the bank. Then she spent another fifteen minutes finding the key. The funeral home never called, so she decided to go on. She could check her messages from a phone at the newspaper. The doorbell rang just as she was picking up her purse in the dining room. She looked through the window there and saw a shiny red car, new-looking, sitting in the drive.

The *Intelligenser*. She'd assumed they wouldn't be happy with the obit supplied by the funeral home, but she'd expected them to call her, not just show up on her porch. Maybe they'd assumed she'd try to duck them.

The doorbell rang again. Her car was blocked in the driveway, and the reporter could see it was there. She sighed and went to the door.

The man standing there wasn't quite what she expected. He was tall, tanned, not bad-looking, with blond hair that looked sun-bleached. He looked like an aging surfer. And he wore a somber expression so obviously fake she nearly laughed. Too old to be a summer intern, but you never knew who was going to turn up working for a paper like the *Intelligenser*. He did have a notepad in his hand.

"Ms. Jesamyn Wellington?" he asked, his voice full of phony sympathy. She wondered if he was from the funeral home. But they wouldn't send someone dressed in faded jeans and a maroon sports shirt.

"Yes? I was just on my way out."

"Ah. I don't want to keep you. I just have a couple of questions."

"All right. Make it fast."

He took a half step forward, then stopped when he realized she wasn't going to let him in. He gave a little smile. "I'm sorry about this," he said. "You know how it is."

She liked the smile. It was one of those that was sort of boyish and sort of roguish at the same time. It was the transparent smile of a man used to getting his way with women. The kind of man who didn't frighten her at all.

"What do you need to know?"

He blinked, smiled more broadly, then seemed to remember something and dug in one of his back pockets, came up with a card case, extracted a card and held it out to her. "Always forget to do this," he said. He noticed she wasn't opening the screen and held the card up for her to read.

It identified him as Timothy Haffner, a licensed private investigator from the Bloomberg Detective Agency in Los Angeles.

That was quick. "You have a license?"

"Sure. It's no good here, though." He put the card case back and brought out a thin expensive-looking wallet, opening it and holding it up for her to read the card inside the plastic window. It looked authentic. But then, how would she know?

"Have you checked in at the police department?"

"In Wichita." He put the wallet away again. "I went by the station here, but they said I'd have to speak to a Detective . . . Briseno? And he wasn't in. Anyway, legally I'm just a private individual talking to another private individual, if she's willing to talk to me. Kind of like a reporter."

"You've done a little investigating already."

"That's my job. Listen, I know this is a bad time, and it's very sudden and all that. And you're on your way somewhere. But I'd really appreciate it if you'd just take a few minutes—"

"Who are you representing?"

"My agency represents an insurance company."

"So you're looking for the stolen goods."

He winced. "You know about that. Yeah, some of 'em."

"Really, I don't know anything at all. I just heard about it all for the first time a couple of hours ago. I didn't even know my sister was in the area."

"So she wasn't in touch with you?"

"Not for about ten years."

He blinked. "No kidding."

"What did happen exactly, Mr. Haffner? All I know is she's supposed to have stolen some things out there."

He looked uncomfortable. He pursed his lips, looked off to the side, sighed and looked at her again. "Any chance we could sit down?"

She hesitated a second, then shrugged. "Sure. There's a chair right there." She pointed through the screen at the Adirondack chair. As he looked at it, she slipped out through the screen onto the porch.

He spun with impressive quickness, then smiled when he saw her perching herself on the porch railing, her back against the corner post.

"Have a seat, Mr. Haffner."

"Tim. Thanks." He sat down, giving her an appraising look as he did so. She felt as if they were about to compete in some contest and were sizing each other up. She knew what kind of contest it was, and that it had little to do with her sister or anything that had happened in California. She didn't mind. It was something she hadn't done for a long time, something she even kind of missed.

Jo had always been better at reading men than she was, but Haffner was easy. He was one of those who was always on the lookout for it—and who, she guessed, judging from his easy air and that killer smile, usually got it.

He was still looking uncomfortable. "So you don't know about the videotapes," he said, obviously hoping she did.

She shook her head. "What videotapes?"

He sighed again, then began telling her about them, not pulling any punches. She liked that about him, and she wasn't particularly shocked. In a way, it was more or less what she'd assumed Jo was doing—in the same ballpark anyway—and she wasn't surprised she'd found a way of doing it that put her in control and made good money.

She didn't say anything when he was finished. What could you say, really? He looked off toward the south, where lightning was flashing occasionally inside a dark mass of cloud, and she heard a distant rumble.

"It was just starting to rain when I left," Haffner said. "But then it stopped all of a sudden when I was on the highway. It was strange . . . like suddenly driving into a different world . . ." He gave a little laugh and shook his head.

"That's Kansas," Jes said. "One year at the K.U. relays, when I was a student up there, I remember watching the steeplechase—five thousand meters, I think. When it began and when it ended, it was bright sunshine, hardly a cloud in the sky. But in between, during the race, there was rain, high winds, hail and even a little snow. The temperature dropped by ten or fifteen degrees and then went back up again. The runners were mostly from places like Kenya and New Zealand. They must have thought they'd come to another planet."

Haffner laughed. "I do have to admit the weather

worries me a little. You know. *Wizard of Oz* and all that."

She smiled. "You're staying in Wichita?"

"Yeah, at the Airport Hilton. By the way, is there anything to *do* over there?"

She laughed. "Well, there's movies. Restaurants." She thought about it. "Do you bowl?"

He laughed. "Afraid not. Maybe I'll learn." He gave her a sudden direct look and a dose of that smile she'd seen before that struck her like a kind of mild electrical shock, a warm current running out from her face and down her body. This boy was *good*. "Maybe there's more to do over here," he said.

She laughed again, then thought: *Your sister's been murdered. Her funeral's tomorrow. You have to figure out what to do about her baby. And here you are flirting with this guy you don't even know. What kind of slut are you, anyway?* She sighed, sobering, and said, "No. Even less, I'm afraid."

As she expected, it didn't crush him. "Oh well, guess it's room service and pay-per-view. What more does a guy need?" He gave her another quick look, just checking, then gave it up.

"You do have some questions to ask, right?" she said.

He smiled ruefully. "Right." He paged through his notepad, as if looking for something, although it didn't look to her like there was anything written on most of the pages. Finally, he looked up and said, "You know, really, unless you've got the stuff—or you can tell me somebody who might—I'm not sure I do have any questions."

She stared at him. "Can I see that license again?"

He smiled. "My father and my uncles own the agency. I don't usually get this kind of case. I just happened to be closest. I was in St. Louis, and they called me while I was eating breakfast this morning, so I hopped on a plane. They'll be sending a real investigator as soon as they can."

"Why were you in St. Louis?"

"Working a divorce. That's mostly what I do. I'm hell on divorces."

"I'll bet you are."

He pursed his lips, accepting the shot. "I've never actually caused one, that I know of." Then he said seriously, "This is kind of an opportunity for me. I know that sounds terrible. But if I could do anything at all, before the other guy gets here, I don't know . . . Maybe Dad and Uncle Ray would think, well, maybe the kid's not a complete moron. Maybe we should let him try something more challenging, like a repossession or some skip tracing." He gave her a crooked smile.

She studied him for a moment. "Yes, I know what you mean."

"So if you have any suggestions . . ."

She gave a soft laugh, shook her head. "You either are really terrible at this, or extremely good. I don't have any suggestions, though. You obviously know more about Jo and what she's been doing than I do."

"You didn't even know about the baby?"

"No."

"Hmm." He looked off at the sky to the south, seemed to notice how much darker it had gotten. "I better get going," he said. "I've taken up more of your time than I meant to. It's been nice meeting you, Jes." He held out his hand tentatively, obviously prepared to draw it back if she didn't shake it.

She did. "You too, Tim. Good luck with your investigation."

He smiled, then said, "Oh . . . I forgot." He dug in his shirt pocket, coming up with a crumpled sheet of paper folded in quarters. "They faxed me this. I'm supposed to show it to everybody." He offered it to her.

She took it from him, began unfolding it. "What is it?"

"The stuff I'm looking for. There's only four things. And two of them really go together."

The first thing that caught her eye was the photo of

a block of four old airmail stamps showing an old plane flying upside down. She did a double take.

"You're telling me Jo swiped a block of inverted Jennies?"

"A block of what?" Haffner took a step nearer, to see the sheet.

She pointed out the stamps to him. "The inverted airplane was called the Curtiss Jenny. That's probably the most famous American stamp ever. I mean, for collectors. I can't imagine what it's worth now, especially a block of four. It's amazing that one of your clients had this. I would have thought they were all in the Smithsonian by now."

"One of our client's clients," Haffner said absently, taking the sheet back and looking at it with new interest. "I take it you're a stamp collector."

"Not really. For a little while, when I was a kid. Jo stuck with it, was kind of serious about it for a while." In her mind, she could see Jo at the desk in the old bedroom—the tweezers, the magnifying glass, the little black dish and the bottle of carbon tetrachloride for bringing out watermarks. And the big orange Scott catalog she'd saved up to buy. Jes had loaned her two dollars, and had never gotten it back, but hadn't minded. It was an image that filled her with joy, as did the thought of Jo having those rare stamps they'd seen only in the orange catalog.

"She didn't take those to sell," Jes said. "She took them for herself."

"You think so? They didn't find them in her apartment."

"I don't care. They're somewhere around. There's a safe deposit box, or an airplane locker, something. Somewhere. Hey, if you could find those—"

"She probably didn't really take them," Haffner said.

She looked at him in surprise. "What? What do you mean?"

"Well, you aren't going to write about this, are you? I mean, this is off the record?"

She nodded, frowning.

"Well, what the insurance companies think is that some of this stuff might not really have been stolen. You see? Just reported stolen. This is all stuff that was reported late, when the cops began turning up more of her customers. Once they were involved, they all had something to report, you know?"

"Insurance fraud."

"Always a possibility with these kind of guys and this kind of stuff. I mean, it's kind of hard to believe they wouldn't even report it stolen."

"Yeah." Jes felt deflated. She'd liked the idea—liked the vision it evoked, of that year when they were twelve, still just little twin girls, doing the things little girls did. Best not to think of that year anyway, probably.

"Do they know they were all customers?" she asked. "Did they all have videos?"

"No. That's another thing. I think the cops only have two or three videos, and there were . . . well, there were a lot of these guys. Probably not all of 'em, you know, are telling the truth. They all said they destroyed the videos. Which makes sense, I guess. If I'm that old and that rich and . . . respected, or whatever—the youngest is, like, sixty-eight—I guess that's the first thing I'd do when the cops got involved."

"How many?"

"Christ." He was silent, then said, "I really don't know, Jes. I mean . . ."

"How many?"

"The number I heard was eighteen. But you know, could be high, could be low."

"Eighteen. And she got stuff like this? She must have had a lot of money on her."

"Cops found about a hundred thou, is what I heard. In the Diaper Genie."

Jes gave a soft laugh.

"Eighteen seems high to me," Haffner said. "I mean, how many guys could get that rich and that old, and be that stupid?"

"Stupid?"

"Well, they all trusted her. Let her get so far inside their security, and believe me, these guys have all got world-class security. And what if she kept copies of the tapes?"

"Blackmail?"

"Makes sense. I mean, nobody's said so. But don't you think that would make a good motive?"

Jes looked at him. "You think of that yourself?"

He smiled, obviously pleased. "Trouble is, I'm not after the killer. I'm just trying to find this stuff." He folded the paper and put it back in his pocket. Jes hadn't really seen the other things—jewelry, she thought—but she didn't care. "I'm sure the cops have thought of it," Haffner said. "I better get out of here—for real this time. Sorry we had to meet under these kind of circumstances."

"Me too. Good luck. Again."

He laughed. "And good-bye again."

Back inside, after he'd driven away, Jes found Susie sitting on her haunches, looking oddly disapproving.

"Okay," Jes said, "I know. Here I am, hiding in my house, not even letting Hector in, and then along comes this good-looking, smooth-talking private eye from California, and I'm out there on the porch flirting like a brazen hussy. I didn't *do* anything, did I? Face it, Suze. We're not as wonderful as you think we are. Be glad you're a dog."

19

The yellow tape was gone, but there was still a key box on the front door. Lassiter fished the key ring out of his pocket and opened the box with one hand, keeping the casebook shielded from the rain. He unlocked the door, put the key back in its box and went in, closing the door behind him.

It was dark in the living room, thanks to the storm, but he didn't turn on any lights. He waited for his eyes to adjust, hoping to see something familiar, but as far as he knew, he'd never been here before. He thought he remembered the kitchen and the hallway. Those bits might be from a dream, but he didn't think so. That was the way things came back, on the edges. He also thought he remembered the bedroom door, and a naked woman walking through it, closing it behind her. But that could be Celia Staircase or the other one, the one in the video. He had trouble coming up with that name, but didn't fight it.

The living room looked like that of a single mother of limited means. Just a woman with a baby, struggling to get along on her paycheck. Except that there was no paycheck. She'd been disciplined about using the money hidden in the Diaper Genie, but that didn't surprise him. The woman he remembered would be.

The furniture had come from some big discount store. A suite, but not an expensive one. The few wall hangings—drawings of birds and cute little children, a French poster of a woman with a parasol—were the kinds of thing you'd find at Kmart or Target. There was an armchair, a sofa—he thought he recognized

something about the sofa, but then it vanished, and
he ignored it. Sofas all looked alike. The coffee table,
the two lamp tables with matching lamps, the TV
stand, the TV with the VCR built into the base and
the rabbit ears on top meant nothing to him except
that she hadn't even gotten cable. The woman he'd
met—the childless lawyer from New Mexico, living on
a legal settlement—made no sense in this living room.

He flicked on a lamp, on the lowest setting, just
enough additional light to confirm that the room was
unfamiliar to him. He'd share his observations and
impressions with Jerry, if they were working the case
together instead of apart. That was what he felt guilty
about—withholding such information from Jerry, the
information he needed to do his job. He couldn't feel
guilty about things he couldn't even remember. He
was sorry she was dead—genuinely sorry, because she
had been interesting and smart, and he'd liked her,
and now he'd never be able to know her, to answer
the interesting riddles she'd presented to him.

But the bigger problem was not knowing that he'd
killed her. Not *knowing*. The night before, realizing
he wasn't going to sleep, he'd turned on Kay's laptop
and begun trying to write his statement, but he hadn't
been able to finish even the first sentence. Because he
didn't know. He wouldn't have arrested a purse
snatcher without knowing more about it than he did
about this. What that meant was that he couldn't confess, because he couldn't honestly allocute. They'd
have to catch him. They'd have to prove it.

He'd thought that ought to be easy, though. He'd
expected Jerry—or maybe Loomis—to show up at
Kay's house. That was more or less why he'd gone
there. A little before daylight, he'd gone up to the
City Building and slipped into forensics to take a look
at Kreider's preliminary casebook. What it had mainly
told him was that they didn't have enough from the
scene to convict him or anyone else.

His only chance for redemption was not in confess-
ing, leaving it up to the others, but in making sure

himself that the one who'd done it would be convicted.
That was what he was good at.

He sighed, going back to the porch again, in his
mind. And from there, he was almost sure, to the
kitchen, and from there maybe—no, surely—to the
hallway. And from there . . . what?

He had an idea that he had walked along the hallway in the dark, past all the doors. But it was too
much like a dream, and it led here, to this room he
didn't recognize. And it was mixed up with other
things that had to be dreamlike. A white, ghostly
woman who backed into the dark, beckoning him,
then floating off into the dark when he approached . . .

He thought briefly about the other end of the gap,
the pounding on the windshield, the river there in
front of him, through the rain, and the pain he still
felt, mostly in the hinges of his jaw. No change there,
and he didn't think there would be. Sometimes that
was the way it worked. What you could get back had
to come from the other end.

He turned off the lamp, feeling that it was all probably a waste of time. Coming here. Doing anything at
all. He stood still in the dark, looking at nothing, a
part of him wanting to think, to reason, but shut out
by the other part that knew how futile that was.

He opened his eyes, not remembering that he'd
closed them, and brought his wristwatch near his face.
No time lost. He went on through the living room into
the hallway.

It didn't seem any more familiar, which disappointed him. Of course, a hallway was just pretty
much a hallway, especially when there was nothing
hung on the walls, when the wallpaper was some light
beige color—probably that off-white color they called
eggshell. If it reminded him of anything, it was of the
hallway in the farmhouse, that led to his bedroom,
with that other door he had to go past . . .

He went down the hallway to the kitchen, to start
over again there and come back the way he must have
come that night.

The kitchen was familiar. Of course, he'd seen it from outside the screen door a couple of times, but this was different. He'd come in here. He'd stood here and looked around at the appliances. He remembered that, and it was a real memory. He'd had rainwater in his hair, on his clothing. He'd been confused at the time, well into a seizure, but he remembered it now. He'd been here.

Knowing that, he suddenly remembered what had happened in between. She'd realized there was something wrong with him, and she'd unlocked the screen and told him to come in. And so he'd come into the kitchen and stood there, confused, not knowing what to do. He suddenly remembered clearly the sound of water dripping onto the floor. He looked down and saw them—the whitish oblongs where the techs had brought up some of them, however they did that. So that was all real.

Then what? Here he was standing in her kitchen, dripping water on her floor . . . Briefly he had an image in his mind of his jacket spread on some low table, his shoulder holster on top of it. But there wasn't anything like that here, and the image was gone so quickly it bore no real weight of meaning or reality.

He went back to the hallway and looked at it from that direction, but it still didn't look particularly familiar. Any more than it ought to anyway, since he'd just walked the length of it. He stood looking at it then shook his head and turned and opened the door that led up the stairs to the baby's room. He was pretty sure he'd never been up there at all, so it would be something to look at fresh, and make a fresh place to come back to the hallway from.

The baby's room had been worked, of course. The whole apartment had. But given the fact that the baby had been left behind, the money in the Diaper Genie undisturbed, no sign of a search—the likelihood that the killer had never gone up there—it probably hadn't been worked quite as thoroughly as some of the other areas.

He hadn't really looked at the portion of the case-book covering this room, so he opened it now. What caught his eye was a list of titles—not books but videos. Movies. He glanced around but didn't see any anywhere. Maybe the techs had bagged them and taken them away for some reason. Maybe just to watch. From the titles, they all appeared to be ordinary commercial videos. *Gone With the Wind, Home Alone 2, What About Bob?* So why weren't they down there, where the VCR was?

He checked the map of the room, looking for the reference number of the videos. The closet. There were two doors that looked like closet doors, but the one on the outer wall actually opened on the stairs leading down to the garage.

The closet was one of those deep ones with two racks, one along each side. But in this case there was only a clothes rack, and the other wall had been fitted with shelves, presumably for shoes and hatboxes and so on. The videotapes were on the top shelf, the titles showing on the spines of their jackets.

He reached to pull one down, not bothering to put on a pair of the thin disposable gloves, as he would have at a fresh crime scene, because they'd already been dusted. But as soon as he had one of them in his hands, he thought, *Were they?* He turned it around to look at the black plastic spine, and saw a tiny triangle of the gray powder.

It would have been an easy way to frame himself. But he wouldn't have expected Kreider and his guys to screw up in any obvious way like that.

He wondered why the videos were still here, though, given Celeste Mundy's history. But probably the tech who'd dusted and mapped them and listed the titles hadn't known anything about Celeste Mundy, or that this woman might be her, at that moment. Also, they all appeared to be real prerecorded movie videos, with the proper jackets and labels and the little square write-protect holes that prevented them from being recorded over. Some of them were still in shrink-wrap, with PREVIOUSLY OWNED stickers attached. Tapes from a bin in some video store.

Going through the ones that had been opened, he found another with a little spot of fingerprint powder in almost exactly the same place as the first one. The stuff was almost impossible to get rid of. But why the same place? Maybe because of the way the tech had dusted them. But something about the two little spots of dust bothered him, and he couldn't figure out at first what it was. He put the two cases side by side and studied them. One was roughly triangular, the other more like a half circle. But then he saw it—they both had one perfectly straight edge, and there was nothing on the case itself that would have caused that. But he didn't know what it meant, if anything at all. He put them down and examined each of the others more closely. All turned out to have some powder residue in that same area—and on three of them, he could see, faintly, that same straight edge, on the unbroken surface of plastic.

He imagined the tech placing something like a sheet of paper there, before applying the dust, a kind of stencil . . . but why? It made no sense.

He went back to the first one and turned it over, looking for anything else that was unusual about the dusting pattern. Because he was looking for signs of dust, he almost didn't notice the thing that explained it. The spot of powder lined up with the write-protect notch on the edge of the case. The straight edges didn't quite match, though. He looked at the others and found the same thing. Each spot was on the same place on the side of the case, right next to the indentation in the plastic on the edge of the tape.

Then he got it. He touched one of the spots with a fingertip, to feel the tackiness, the residue of adhesive to which the powder had clung. Adhesive tape. If you covered the write-protect notch with something like adhesive tape, you could record over what was already there.

Why would she keep copies of the videotapes she'd

made for her clients—and disguised like this? Blackmail was the obvious answer, which suggested a motive for the murder. Jerry needed these tapes . . .

Then he remembered that he already knew who the killer was. She might have been blackmailing former clients, but that had nothing to do with the murder. These tapes would be only a false trail for Jerry to follow, if he discovered what they really were—and eventually he would. Based on what was in the casebook, Jerry would get nowhere. And he'd come back and look at everything again, more closely. Maybe he wouldn't notice the fingerprint powder, or maybe he would. But he'd view the tapes eventually, just because they were the last things he hadn't looked at himself.

Lassiter went out into the baby's room and looked in the bottom drawer of the little dresser, where he'd seen a stack of brown grocery-style paper bags. He put the tapes in, hesitating over the ones that were still in shrink-wrap before tossing them in, too. Jerry would notice eventually that the tapes had disappeared, and that would be a problem, but less of a problem than getting off on the wild goose chase of looking for a blackmail victim. Leaving the four unused tapes sitting there by themselves would only call attention to the missing ones.

He rolled the top of the sack tight, to make a handle, and went back downstairs.

The hallway at the foot of the stairs still didn't look especially familiar, even from this direction. He was pretty sure he wasn't going to find the kind of thing he'd come to find. But the tapes made him feel that he'd done something positive, anyway—spared Jerry some lost time and effort. It was better than coming away completely empty-handed.

Back in the living room, he paused and considered the TV with the built-in VCR, then set the sack down on the coffee table and bent over to study the controls. But he didn't really want to hang around and look at the tapes here. Not here. He didn't want to look at them at all, although he'd have to confirm what he believed. It would gnaw at him until he did.

He turned from the TV to retrieve the sack, and saw, for a second, what he'd nearly remembered in the kitchen. His wet jacket and holster lying on a low, flat surface—this coffee table.

A second later, he wasn't so sure, but didn't it make sense? Or did it? He looked around the room, looked down at the sofa, seeing it from this side for the first time, and he had another flash of dreamlike memory, accompanied by a slight wave of nausea.

The sofa . . . there was something . . .

He turned his back on it and then sat down, feeling unsteady, to leaf through the casebook. Rain-stained sheets in the dryer. A pillow in the front hall closet. And yes, the sofa. A makeshift bed for someone who'd come in out of the rain.

20

Annie Babicki wasn't there, of course. She was at the City Building. Jes couldn't tell whether the rest of them knew or not. There were so many she didn't even know, who glanced at her in curiosity, then went back to what they were doing. Ed Rossiter gave her a smile and a wave from behind his terminal across the big room in Sports, and Sally Davies looked up as she went past the rim, distracted from the proof sheet she was marking up, frowning, then breaking into that big crooked smile of hers and saying. "Hey, Jes! How the hell are you?"

She stopped to chat. Sally's tomboyish good humor had always reminded her a little of her sister, and she liked remembering that. It was obvious Sally had no idea what had happened. Of course, Sally didn't even know she had a sister. Nobody here did.

"It's good to see you again," she said to Sally, who'd paused for a response, and Jes saw her face fall a little, heard how impersonal her words had been. She smiled. "It really is," she said. "I have to go talk to Cubbage about something."

Sally smiled sympathetically. "Catch you later, girl."

Jes had forgotten what an all-purpose excuse going to see the metro editor had always been. Most people in the newsroom didn't like him much. The common take on Fred Cubbage was that he was a myopic jerk, but a great editor. Part of that was just newspaper mythology—the city editor was supposed to be a jerk. During her summer internship at the *Mid American*, she'd had the distinct impression that Cubbage considered her a hopeless incompetent, and she'd been surprised later when they'd offered her the job—even more surprised when she'd learned it was Cubbage who ranked the reporting interns. He hadn't acted any differently toward her when she'd taken the job. She'd wondered once if he had something against her, and had wanted her to be hired so that he could torment her. He'd pressed on her exactly the kinds of stories she didn't want, the ones she was afraid of. And when she'd written the stories, she'd waited at her desk for him to come out of his office door and shout, "Wellington! Get in here!" In his office, he'd bombarded her with all the questions she didn't have the answers to because she'd neglected to ask them. But after a while she'd realized she wasn't afraid of those assignments anymore—of any kind of story.

Stuart Merow, the newsroom's computer guru—"systems editor" was his official title—was standing behind one of the clerks, a kid Jes didn't know, watching what she was doing on her terminal, diagnosing some problem. As Jes went past, he glanced her way, did a double take and said, "Hi, Jes. How you doing?" The way he looked at her and the way he said it told her he knew. But he was one of Annie's closest friends in the newsroom.

She shrugged it off. It wasn't a secret, after all. It was just that she was so used to secrets. "I'm okay, Stuart," she said. "How are things going for you?"

"Same old, same old." He indicated the clerk with his eyes, then rolled them upward.

She smiled and went on. Belatedly, she remembered his connection to Zach Vincent. She knew she had some questions about that, even though she wasn't exactly sure what they were. She'd try to catch him on her way out.

She stood outside Fred's door until he glanced up and noticed her. He showed no surprise, only waved to her to come in, as if he'd been expecting her. Then he turned back to what he was doing while she sat down and waited. He stared gloomily at his monitor for a long time, then gave a loud sigh, evidently giving up, and punched the Save button, blanking the screen.

He swiveled back to face her. "I'm sorry about your sister," he said.

It was so unexpected, she didn't know how to respond. *Thanks* didn't seem quite right. So she only nodded and got down to business—something Cubbage had taught her. "What kind of coverage are you planning?"

He pursed his lips. "We've got a couple of things in the files on your parents. The inquests, I mean. That's part of the story, I think."

"Yes."

"I'm not quite sure how to handle *you*," he said. "I mean, as far as the story's concerned. You used to work here. It's always a pain in the ass when one of your own becomes a part of a story. We're not supposed to look like we're taking advantage, you know? Getting an edge on TV and the rest. Although I don't see why not. They do that kind of thing all the time." He sighed. "There's also the problem of how big to play it. Is the fact you used to work here part of the story? I mean, worth more than just a mention?" He looked at her.

"I don't see how, really."

He gave her a look of disappointment. "You don't. Well, how about the fact that the guy who found the body also used to work here, and that the murder victim looks exactly like you, which means the SOB *had* to recognize her?"

She'd thought about that, but not in the context of a newspaper story. "It's complicated," she said.

He gave her a sardonic smile. "No shit. Straight out, Jes. If Annie Babicki interviews you and asks you what you knew about all this—Vincent and your sister and the L.A. stuff and all that—are you gonna tell us the truth?"

She nodded. "That's easy. 'Cause I don't know anything about any of it. I didn't know she was in Wichita until this morning."

He gave her a sharp glance. "From our story? We didn't have the name or a photo."

"From a cop friend." She left it at that, and Cubbage accepted it.

She saw him relax a little, and realized he'd been afraid it was going to be a different kind of problem. "So, I guess there'd be no real point in asking you to write a sidebar yourself . . ."

He left it hanging, but she didn't respond. "Nah. Dumb idea. I mean, we could *do* that . . ." He paused.

"But it would be wrong," she said automatically. It was an old newsroom thing, something from the Watergate tapes. The old guys found it funny for some reason. She'd been in grade school then. "So what are you gonna do?"

"Hell, what business is it of yours? You're the subject."

For a second she wasn't sure whether he was serious or not. Then she gave a soft laugh. That was Fred's idea of a joke. Not many people got them, but he didn't seem to care.

"What do you think about the idea of Annie interviewing you?" he asked.

"Like I said . . ."

"Background on the family?"

She had to think about that, and he remained silent, letting her. "There are things I don't want to talk about," she said.

"Sure. In every family. Nobody necessarily expects you to know why your sister went off and . . . I mean, if you do know, and you're willing to say, great . . ."

"Nope."

"Okay." He hesitated, and she knew he was thinking about asking, *Nope to which one?* But instead he said, "Just the neutral facts, then. The chronology. And then she took off and I didn't see her again for twenty years or whatever. Like that. Plus how you feel about it, of course."

She gave a laugh at the way he slipped that last in.

"I don't know how I feel about it yet," she said. "I'm still working on it."

"Well, hurry up. Annie's gonna be back here in about half an hour."

She laughed again. "It isn't going to happen that quickly, Fred. You know that."

"It does on TV." He gave her one of his tiny, rare smiles. The smile showed her, as it always had, how much of his demeanor came from shyness, and made her feel sad—something she'd never say to him.

"You don't mind talking to Annie?" he asked.

She shook her head. "I like talking to Annie."

"Morton!" Cubbage screamed, making Jes jump. Some things you never got used to. The fifty-year-old "copyboy" materialized at the door. You saw him all over the building, but somehow he always seemed to be right around when Cubbage yelled for him.

"Get hold of Babicki and tell her to get her ass back to the newsroom. Half hour tops. She'll be at the P.D. or the S.O."

Jes smiled. "I thought she was coming back anyway."

He said, "And I thought you were an only child."

She saw that he was actually hurt, and the knowledge stunned her. It was somehow breathtaking. She'd hurt Cubbage. Down inside.

"Fred . . ."

"Well . . ." He waved a hand. "I can see why you wouldn't want people to know. I mean, nothing against your sister . . ."

"Every family has secrets, like you said."

He nodded. But she knew it didn't make it all right. He'd expected to be different, to be someone she wouldn't lie to. Hector had felt the same way about being excluded from her house along with everybody else, she knew, although he'd done a better job of concealing it. Thank God Cubbage had never tried to visit her since Jay's death.

Neither of them seemed to have anything to say. It was normal for Hector to be silent, but with Fred it made her nervous. "That was a great photo," she said. "Who's this Olander?"

Cubbage gave a sour look. "Pain in the ass. Came out here from some little horseshit weekly in California. Probably all the dailies got sick of him. But he is a great photographer. No question about that. You ever notice how often people who are really good at things are also major league assholes?" Not waiting for an answer, he said, "Probably won't be here long." He frowned, thinking about that, then looked at her. "How about you? You're doing okay with the freelancing? Selling stuff?"

"To magazines you probably don't read. Yeah, I'm doing okay, Fred. There's just me and the dog to feed. Of course, she's a *real big* dog."

"What about the baby?"

She stared at him, feeling blindsided. She'd always heard that Fred was a hell of a reporter in his day, but that he alienated too many people he'd interviewed. Kind of like Olander.

"That's something else I haven't got worked out in my mind yet," she said. "I'm going over to the Children's Home to see him when I leave here."

He nodded. "I was just gonna say, if you need a real job again . . ."

"I won't."

". . . don't bother trying here," he finished.

"If you really can hire someone, and you need someone, for God's sake don't hold the spot for me . . . if that's what you're doing . . ."

"It's not. But you want me to stop asking?"

She thought about it, shook her head. "Never."

"Good."

Feeding Eddy his supper, Zach filled him in on the problems he was having with the Myerson Realty software. The anonymous author was wildly disorganized, of course, but every now and then he'd come up with some ingenious and elegant algorithms. Zach was trying to preserve those parts of the program, where appropriate. What really bothered him was that a couple of them would work well in other programs, better than what he'd written, and it felt like stealing to use them.

"I'd like to at least be able to give him credit in the source code documentation, you know? So at least any other programmers who look at it would know it's his. I mean, there's no *law.* It belongs to the realtor, really . . . but that's not the point . . ."

Eddy listened soberly, with apparent interest, while his jaw worked rhythmically on the strained carrots and applesauce, as if he were mulling a response he'd make as soon as he'd finished eating. Zach stopped talking and grinned involuntarily. Eddy's lips turned up in response, a stream of orange slime running from one corner of his mouth onto his chin. Zach laughed and grabbed a paper towel from the roll to wipe him off. Eddy gave a soft sound of pleasure that might also have been a laugh. Did babies his age laugh? Jesus. What he didn't know about babies. But it didn't seem to matter. He couldn't quite get a handle on the effect this little guy seemed to have on him—just by liking him, was all he could figure out. The kid liked him. And he didn't have to. Plenty of people could take care of him now.

But Laurie Cox, the social worker who'd taken Eddy from him the that night, had practically begged him to come see the kid, to let her put his name on Eddy's visitors list. Actually, it turned out he *was* Eddy's visitors list. He was the only one on it who wasn't a cop or a social worker. Laurie Cox turned out to be very nice by daylight, and he felt a little ashamed of how he'd thought of her that night—the faceless, uncaring bureaucrat. She thought it was important for Eddy to have some contact with someone he knew. He'd explained to her that the baby didn't really *know* him . . .

She'd responded by handing Eddy to him and saying, "Tell him that."

Zach had the impression Eddy's situation was complicated by the fact that he *hadn't* been abused or neglected, as far as anyone could tell. Which apparently pretty much meant that any blood relative could claim him—and they'd found an aunt over in Sand Creek, his mother's sister. As Zach understood it, Eddy was essentially like a lost kid picked up by the cops. He wasn't a ward of the court or the state, and there was no basis for making him one as long as he had family with no known history of abuse or neglect.

The aunt was coming in today to see Eddy for the first time, and she could just take him away with her if she wanted. This could be the last time he'd see the kid. He thought about that, and found that what irked him was that he'd never be able to tell Eddy about the way he and his mother had looked together. He'd seen them; the aunt hadn't.

But it was none of his business. And Eddy was too young to remember any of this anyway. He wouldn't remember his mother *or* Zach. That's what the nurse who took care of the infants had said. It seemed impossible, but Zach guessed it was true. He'd been about Eddy's age when his father died. As far as he knew, they'd never seen each other. But there were photos from the funeral, his mother and the three girls like stair steps in a row, Zach in his mother's arms. And he didn't remember that.

Since he'd grown silent, Eddy had become more involved with his food, and was now spitting it out instead of swallowing it. That seemed like a reasonably efficient way of communicating that he didn't want any more. Zach ripped some more paper towels from the roll and scrubbed Eddy's face, just hard enough and long enough this time to annoy him a little, although he didn't bear a grudge. As soon as the scrubbing stopped, he was happy again, extending his arms upward.

Zach picked him up and carried him to the rocker. He sat down with the baby against his shoulder, the way the nurse had shown him, and began patting and rubbing his back gently. It seemed a little foolish to him, and Eddy began squirming, trying to arch his neck and look around . . . but then he gave an astonishingly loud belch.

"Hey, it works!" Zach said.

Eddy wasn't impressed. He laid his head down, the wiry little body turning all soft and boneless against Zach, seeming almost to melt into him.

Zach sat rocking slightly, filled with a kind of wonder that the baby could go to sleep that suddenly. That trustingly. This must be some secret that men like him weren't supposed to know, that only mothers knew. He could sit right here forever and rock.

He closed his eyes, noticing for the first time he was humming tunelessly, subvocally, wondering how the vibration of his voice in the bones of his shoulder and chest felt to the sleeping baby, guessing it felt reassuring. And his heartbeat . . . If he was very still within himself he could feel Eddy's heart beating softly and slowly—or was it his own? And the faint rhythm of his breathing, the tiny body expanding almost imperceptibly with an indrawn breath, relaxing again, more deeply than before . . .

"Mr. Vincent?"

He opened his eyes with a jerk, not sure for a moment where he was. The nurse was bending over him, lifting the baby up and away, one small fist pulling at his T-shirt for a second before letting go.

"Jesus," he said. "I'm sorry. I didn't think I'd . . ." He shook his head, looked at the clock. It had been only a few minutes at most, not the long time it seemed.

"It happens all the time," the nurse whispered. "You wouldn't have dropped him."

He started to ask how she could know that, then decided he preferred just believing that she did know. He watched her put Eddy down in the baby bed and put a thin blanket over him. Eddy squirmed, his forehead wrinkling, seemed about to fuss, then let out a breath and relaxed again, not awakening.

The nurse touched Zach's arm. "His aunt is here. She's out front. She wanted to meet you."

He hesitated, feeling trapped. Of course she did. But he didn't know how he felt about the aunt. He wanted her to take Eddy home with her, wanted him to be somewhere he belonged, not living in some foster home. But he didn't want her to take Eddy away from him just yet. He felt caught at a disadvantage, made groggy by a few minutes' dozing. Why now?

He followed the nurse as far as the end of the hall, where she turned and went back toward the nursery, leaving him on his own. The receptionist had disappeared also. It was like they were being left alone together, like some romantic couple. The only other person in the waiting room was a tall, thin woman, easily recognizable, even from behind, as a sister of Celia Staircase. She was looking at the photos on the wall, but then she turned and smiled at him.

He thought, *Wait a minute.*

"Hi, Zach."

The aunt. "You're Jes," he said stupidly. "You're twins."

She smiled crookedly. "My sister and I were twins. How are you these days?"

"I'm, uhh . . ." He couldn't think what to say. *Fine,* he thought. *I'm fine.* But it didn't come out. Instead he said, "You know . . . when she first moved in . . ."

"You called Stuart Merow because you thought she was me."

He was silent for a second, working it out. It wasn't hard, but his mind seemed half paralyzed. "You talked to him."

"I was just up there."

He nodded, feeling a step behind. "She didn't recognize me," he said, then winced. "I mean, of course she didn't recognize me. I meant . . ."

"I know what you mean, Zach. It's an old story to me."

Yes, he supposed it would be. "I started to say something to her," he said, "'cause I thought it was you. But then she gave me this look . . . it was obvious she didn't know me. She just thought I was some guy, you know."

"She knew you knew me," Jes said. "I'll bet she changed her appearance after that."

"Yeah, that's right. I don't exactly know how. Her hair, I guess, and maybe . . . I don't know, makeup?"

"She was good at that. Not looking just like me."

He nodded. "She still looked like you, but not, you know . . ."

"Not exactly like me, so it could have just been an unusual resemblance."

"Right. Exactly. That's what I thought." He thought back over it. He had the nagging feeling that he ought to have figured it out anyway, that he must have missed some obvious clue. But what could have been more obvious than her face?

"Do you have to be somewhere?" Jes asked. "Or could we talk for a minute?"

"I'm in no hurry. My boss lets me set my own schedule."

"That's great. Where are you working now?"

He gave a wry smile. "At home. Dumb joke."

She smiled and sat down. He did, too.

"I'm glad I ran into you here," she said. "I wanted to have a chance to thank you."

He sighed. "It was stupid, what I did. Eddy would have been okay either way. I mean, if I'd just called the cops."

She studied him for a moment, and then seemed to let it go, which was a relief. He was tired of trying to explain why he *hadn't* just called the cops, and feeling like he was lying. Even his own mother didn't believe him. He could tell.

"I really didn't know her," he said. "I didn't even know her name—I mean, the name she was using. Nobody believes that."

"I do. The last thing Jo would have done would be to get chummy with her neighbors. I'm sure the police believe that, too. She was hiding out, after all. And she knew that you knew me."

"Jo. That was . . . ?"

"Jocelyn was her name. We called her Jo."

"So Jes is short for . . ."

"Jesamyn." She spelled it, watching him.

"Great names. Jocelyn and Jesamyn." He felt at a loss. "Was she younger or older?" Then he realized what he'd asked. "Jesus . . ."

"No, it's actually a good question. She was my big sister, by nearly five minutes. And we were sort of that way. Big sister, little sister. You know? Do you have brothers?"

He shook his head. "Three older sisters. Really older sisters. No twins."

"Ah, the baby boy. So you were spoiled."

"Spoiled? It was hell."

She laughed. He liked her laugh. He'd been the only one who could make his mother laugh, even when she was sad or angry. That had sort of been his job. Making Mom laugh, especially when she was sad.

"We always wanted a brother," Jes said. "Not a baby brother, though. We wanted an older brother."

"Tough thing to manage. I would have liked a brother, too. Just to have another guy around."

"What about your . . ."

"My father died in Vietnam. He was a pilot."

"Oh. I'm sorry."

Zach shrugged. "I never knew him. I was less than a year old. Probably for the best. I expect I would have been a big disappointment to him."

"Why?"

He laughed, although it was an ancient joke, and not even exactly a joke. "Well, you know, the computer geek. He was pretty much the macho stud himself, I guess. The right stuff and all that."

"Is your mother disappointed in you?"

He shook his head. "Only that I haven't produced any grandkids yet, and don't look likely to. I think she's kind of hoping that I'm Eddy's father. Which I'm not, by the way."

"I believe you. If your mother's satisfied with you the way you are, I doubt your father would have been very disappointed. Anyway, if he'd lived, you wouldn't be the same person."

"That's true. I'd probably be exactly the kind of asshole I don't like."

She laughed. "Hard to imagine."

He felt his mouth wanting to form a grin of pleasure, and he looked away, pursed his lips.

"So what's gonna happen with Eddy?" he asked.

"Well, I think I pretty much have to take him." She made a sound of exasperation and shook her head. "That sounds terrible. I have to take him. But it isn't anything I expected. Like yourself. What if you *were* Eddy's father?"

He'd thought about that, but he didn't say so. "It'd be tough. I know what you mean."

"He may be getting a raw deal," she said. "But he does own half the house, for what that's worth. And he'll get the whole trust fund eventually. Jo and I never used any of it."

"Sounds like a great deal to me," Zach said.

"Except for not having a real family."

He wasn't sure how she meant that, so he didn't say anything.

"I'm stalling," Jes said. "I'm afraid of going back there."

"Why? Afraid of what? He's perfectly harmless, except for the diapers. Those can be pretty . . ."

"I'm afraid he won't like me," she said. "Or that I won't like him. I'm also afraid he'll think I'm Jo."

He thought about that. He had the feeling she was hoping he'd say something reassuring.

"I wouldn't worry about that, anyway," he said. "Thinking you're Jo. Maybe just right at first, when he first sees you, but . . . you aren't the same person. He'll know that."

"You think so?"

"Of course."

"But you didn't even know her, right?"

"Touché. But I saw her with him. I got kind of an impression of her personality, you know. And I . . . I don't really think you were much alike. I mean, I think—"

"Why not? How would you say we're different?"

He could see that this was a serious question—maybe more serious a question than he ought to be trying to answer.

"I didn't really . . ."

"I know. But what did you mean by that? I'm just curious."

She wasn't just curious. But he had to come up with a good answer. He couldn't think of anything better than the truth.

"The main impression I had of her was a sort of . . . *ferocity*," he said. "Kind of like, you know, the mama bear. The lioness with her cubs. I felt pretty sure she'd do anything . . ." He stopped. Maybe she had.

Jes was nodding, looking sad. "That sounds right," she said. "And I'm not like that. You're right about that, too."

"That doesn't necessarily mean . . ." He hesitated. *Doesn't necessarily mean you'd make a bad mother,* he'd been about to say. It was true, but it felt too presumptuous. It crossed some line.

But she was looking at him, waiting. "Doesn't necessarily mean what?" she asked.

"That there's anything wrong," he said. "Just being different . . . it doesn't mean one's good and the other's bad. There are all kinds of ways of . . ."

He saw that she was nodding, looking away toward the hall that led back to the nursery. He felt as if he'd just blown some opportunity, but he didn't know why or how.

"I should get on with it," she said. "I'm just stalling."

"Listen," he said, "you're going to like Eddy and he's going to like you. I don't have any doubt about

that. I really don't." Somewhat to his surprise, that
was true. It even brought a momentary twinge of jeal-
ousy, which he stifled immediately. "The thing is,
you're the closest thing to his mother he's ever going
to find."

Jes looked at him. "That's true, isn't it?" Her eyes
slid away, though, as if she were doubtful. The she
shrugged. "I'd better get to it. I'm sorry to keep you
here like this."

"No problem." He started to turn away, then
stopped. "Umm, are you going to be taking him with
you right now, today?"

"No. I've got too many things. There's the
funeral . . ."

"Oh, right. Of course. Better to get all that stuff
out of the way first."

"And I have to make a place for him," she said.
Then she looked at him. "Will you keep visiting him
while he's here?"

"Sure. That's why I asked."

She nodded. "I appreciate it. And I know Eddy
does."

He shrugged, feeling uncomfortable, unable to think
of any response that didn't seem either self-serving or
idiotic. He didn't even know how to say good-bye. He
just gave her a little silent wave and turned toward
the door.

21

Someone was knocking. He sat up groggily, surprised to find himself on the sofa, confused by the knocking, which was coming from the wrong direction, not the front door.

"Floyd? You in there?"

For a chilling second he thought it was his father. And he realized he wasn't at home. He didn't know where he was.

"Floyd? This is Hector Briseno. I'd like to talk to you."

Hector. He stood up, his eyes beginning to make out the dark forms of the furniture, beginning to remember. Celia's place.

That sudden memory of why he was there made him gasp. He'd killed her. In real life, not in some dream. Killed her.

He went to the front door and stood there, unsure what to do. But he had nothing to fear from Hector. He had no *right* to fear Hector. He didn't understand that . . . it was a strange thing to think, a kind of dream thought. But it was true. He opened the door.

Hector was walking away, up the driveway toward the garages. It was misty, not really rain, and thick clouds were covering everything, hanging low, with lightning flashing inside them here and there, no thunder. Lassiter realized he had no idea what time of day it was, how long he'd slept.

Hector was coming back. "Thought you must be in there," he said, reaching the porch. "Since your car's in the alley. How you doin', Floyd?"

The part of his mind that handled conversation didn't seem to be working yet, and he had no idea how to answer anyway. He shook his head, to clear the cobwebs, and said, "Not bad. How are you?"

"Oh, not so good, really. Gettin' old. You know." He looked away, studied the sky, then said, "Your vic here was a girl I knew. Someone I cared about. You probably figured that out. I just wanted to see where she lived. Any chance . . . ?"

"Yeah, sure," he said, and stood aside so that Hector could enter the apartment. He followed him in and flicked a switch, turning on the overhead light.

The old man stood there in silence, looking it over. In that garish light, it once again looked unfamiliar to Lassiter. And sterile.

Hector gave a sigh, shook his head. "She never lived here," he said. "I mean, it wasn't Jo who—"

"Jo?"

Hector turned and looked at him. "Jocelyn. We called her Jo. There's nothing here that looks like her."

"That was her real name?" Lassiter asked. "Jocelyn Peete?"

Hector gave a soft laugh, shook his head. "Jocelyn Wellington. Peete was her mother's maiden name. Probably the only thing she could think of when she got busted the first time and they asked her name. When I said she didn't live here—"

"I know," Lassiter said. "She was hiding. This was a front." Wellington. Another name. He wasn't sure he could remember all of them. Celia was the woman he knew, the woman he remembered. Jocelyn Wellington was a stranger. But apparently this room had suited neither of them, except as a mask.

"The bedroom's down the hall," he said, "and the kitchen's at the—"

"Nah." Hector gave a tight shake of his head. "I don't want to see it. I didn't come here to investigate. I don't know why I . . . I guess I just wanted to get out of the rain."

It was one of those questions he didn't quite know he was going to ask until he did. "She didn't have a sister, did she?"

Hector looked at him. After an odd little pause he said, "Yeah. There's a sister. Jes Wellington. Jes and Jo." He looked around the room. "I think I'd like some fresh air." He headed for the front door.

Behind where he'd been standing, blocking the view, Lassiter saw the sack of videotapes on the coffee table. He'd forgotten all about them. He followed Hector back out onto the front porch, where he stood looking out into the rain, which was falling a little harder now.

"That's where that Vincent guy lives," Hector said, nodding toward the apartment opposite.

"Yeah."

"You think . . ."

"No."

Hector turned and looked at him. "I was gonna ask if you thought maybe he knew her a little better than he claims he does. I know he's not a suspect."

He did? "I don't know," Lassiter said. "Maybe." He was confused, not even sure what question he was answering. *Maybe what?*

"I was up to the division," Hector said. "Talked to a guy named Majors. Seems like a pretty good dick to me."

"My partner," Lassiter said, agreeing.

"Yeah, that's what he said. I expect you guys are a pretty good team."

We were. Lassiter shrugged.

"Well," Hector said, and then was silent again. "Guess I better go home and get out of the rain."

His white hair was plastered flat on his head, and slow streams of water ran down from it, down the side of his neck, past his ear, and across one cheek, beneath his eye. In that moment he looked incredibly old to Lassiter, older than anyone he'd ever seen. And tired. Tired of life. *I'm tired, too,* Lassiter thought, *and I'm sorry.* He was on the verge of saying it—*I'm sorry*—and then realized he meant to apologize for the thing that had happened all those years ago. But it made no sense to feel sorry for saving a man's life. It wasn't that he was sorry for, of course. It was . . . just being there, seeing the older cop's weakness and humiliation. His diminishment. *Having* to save him. And of course he was sorry about the girl.

"Take care driving back," he said.

Hector nodded, stepping off the porch, then hesitated and said, "I oughta tell you. I told Majors all about that . . ."

"Sure," Lassiter said. "Of course you did."

"I hope I didn't get you in any trouble."

"None I wasn't already in." Again, he wasn't quite sure what they were talking about; it seemed like it could be a number of things. But what they were saying was true for all of them.

Hector turned away again. "So long, Floyd."

"You know, I met her," Lassiter blurted. "I talked to her."

Hector turned around again.

"I liked her," Lassiter said.

"Yeah." Hector didn't seem surprised.

"I wanted to help her," Lassiter said. There was something he needed to get across to the old man, but he had to be careful. "I never wanted her to die. I wanted her to . . ." He shook his head. "I just wanted her to be okay."

Hector frowned, then said, "Listen, Floyd, I don't know what all happened, but it wasn't you finding her that killed her, if that's what's bothering you. It was the son of a bitch who did it. You shouldn't ever feel guilty about doing what you're supposed to do."

Lassiter looked back at him in silence, feeling a great darkness spreading out inside him. This was how it was going to be now. How could he possibly live that way?

Then headlights burst from the alley, and he jerked, thinking paradoxically, *No! I'm not ready!*

The car made a tight circular turn, much like the

way he turned himself, getting into his mother's garage, the headlights sweeping across himself and Hector, and then stopped in front of the closed door of the nearer garage bay. Vincent, the guy who'd found her, got out and looked at them across the top of the car for a second, then ducked his head and went quickly to open the garage door.

The two men stood in silence, watching him drive in and pull the door down again.

"Well," Hector said then, "I guess I'll go home and dry off and have something to eat, and get some sleep. That's a pretty good time when you're as old as me." He didn't laugh.

"I think I'll do the same," Lassiter said. *I just have to figure out where home is today.*

"Funeral's Friday morning," Hector said offhandedly. "Sand Creek Cemetery. Unless it rains too much, of course."

"Friday." Lassiter had no idea when Friday was. *Tomorrow? The next day?*

He watched the old man walk off and disappear into the dark mouth of the alley. Then he went back and got the sack of videotapes, locked the place up and headed for his own car.

22

All her life she'd been used to people mistaking her for Jo. She'd said something like that to Zach Vincent. But it had been different with the baby. Worlds different.

She and the nurse had stood over his bed, murmuring, not wanting to awaken him, but then he'd opened his eyes, blinking, fussing a little, and she'd taken a step backward. The nurse had started to reach down to pick him up, and Jes had seen the tiny eyes suddenly fix on her, and she'd felt a cold stab of fear. He'd given a sharp cry, full of anger and fear and reproach, startling the nurse, and had crawled and climbed his way up along the wooden bars of the bed, reaching out to her, demanding her, complaining to her.

There hadn't been any choice, of course. The nurse had stood aside, frowning a little, as Jes had picked him up. He'd given another little cry and then grown silent, clutching her, seeming to want to burrow inside her body and hide there. She'd kissed the top of his head, a spontaneous act, but hadn't known what to say, what kind of sound to make. She'd realized the nurse was no longer frowning but smiling, but had kept from meeting her eyes. He'd pulled back, arched to get a better look at her. He'd noticed some difference. But then he'd relaxed against her again. Maybe denying what his instincts told him, the way an adult would, choosing to believe what he wanted to believe.

Somehow, it had stopped mattering to her. And any doubts she'd had about whether to take him at all or not had been settled. Eddy was her baby. She didn't know if it was good to feel that way, as strongly and suddenly as she did, but that was the way it was.

Afterward, out front, she and the nurse had worked out the logistics. She decided to come over right after the funeral. He already had most of the things she'd need, all but the few things the police were keeping for the investigation, like the Diaper Genie. And the Children's Home would lend or give her the rest. There was no good reason to wait, and she didn't want to. Part of her was a little afraid that if she waited, she might lose this certainty.

She first noticed how strange the world looked when she was on the Canal Route, driving past the sprawl of railroad switching yards and stockyards and grain elevators at Wichita's northern edge. The air was filled with an orange light that might have been the reflected glow from some unseen dying sun. Its real source was the plume of flame atop the tallest refinery stack, an eternal flame she'd never really noticed before. Now, beneath the lid of cloud, and in the gathering dark of night, it was the central feature of the world, seeming larger and taller than it could possibly be. The refinery itself was an immense, glittering fairy castle, the dull girders changed to mirrored steel.

The flame seemed to fill her with inexplicable excitement, a sense of mirrored power within herself. *The way Jo would have seen it,* she thought. *I can see the world both ways now.* It felt like an inheritance, a gift entrusted to her on behalf of the baby that somehow belonged to both of them. Granted to her because she understood that.

She'd been thinking it was stupid of Jo—an example of her usual impulsive shortsightedness—having a baby at all, especially in that zombie world she'd been living in. How could that flame that had lived inside her not have been quenched out there, in that kind of life?

But now she understood. The baby had been Jo's way of finding her way back, relighting herself. And she'd brought him to Jes. She'd meant to bring him all the way home, hadn't expected to die. But she'd known the kind of world she lived in, and had made sure to get him near enough.

It was time now to be clear and hard, though, the way Jo could be. That was the gift she'd need, and the one she was less sure of. She passed beneath the cloverleaf bridges that connected to the bypass, and then past the big truck stops and the rest, and into the dark countryside, where the farm ponds glowed with a diminishing reflection of that orange light, as the darkness finally overwhelmed it.

And then it was gone, nothing but darkness and darker shapes out there in the darkness. And then the rain began.

The first huge drops slapped the windshield, one or two at a time, unhurried, to splatter on the glass and then be smeared sideways by the wind, never making enough of themselves to require the wipers. She rolled up her window, not completely closing it, not wanting to shut out completely the cool air and the rain smell. A couple of miles ahead of her, gray against the black, a sheet of harder rain hung down like a veil between her and home, like some barrier she had to penetrate to get back there. That too would have been the way Jo would have seen it. She glanced in her rearview mirror, at the blackness between herself and that orange light suffused with power that she could no longer see. Between her and Eddy.

Then suddenly, startlingly, she was out of the rain entirely, driving on pavement that looked impossibly dry, although the oncoming cars on the other side of the median all glistened behind their lights in the dark, their wipers flashing.

This is the real world, she was starting to think when she drove just as suddenly into the sheet of steady rain that had been nearer than she thought. A spray of cold water splashed her face, even through the slit of the window, and she fumbled for the switch to close it, and turned the wipers up to full speed.

Even then it wasn't easy to see, and she leaned

used as a de facto bureau. There'd been two or three reporters and photographers in Sand Creek every day, and she'd had the room to put up the ones who needed to stay overnight. A brief tradition had developed of whoever was there gathering for supper at her place—usually just pizza or some other kind of carryout.

Jay had been a humor columnist for the *Mid American*. He was pretty good. Everybody liked him. He was old enough to know that he was never going to be more than a local columnist, but it didn't seem to bother him. He was a nice guy, quiet and polite and funny. They'd sent him over toward the end of the two weeks, to do some comic reflections on the phenomenon of small-town centennials, and he'd stayed for three days, sleeping in the guest bedroom that had been hers and Jo's a long time ago. It had been very nice having him there, eating breakfast with him before she headed for Wichita, having him there again in the evening.

She'd discovered, to her surprise, that he drank. He brought his own bottle and began with a small drink right after supper, but then kept the bottle and glass nearby, whether they were talking or watching TV, and had usually stayed up and finished it off after she'd gone to bed. She'd seen the empties every morning in the trash. But he'd never really acted drunk—only slurred his words just a bit sometimes, or laughed a bit too hard at something.

Then, the last night he'd stayed there, she'd awakened to find him climbing into bed with her, naked. She'd moved over a little, to make room for him.

That was a moment she'd thought about a lot since—about what had been in the minds of both of them. Later that night, after he'd gone back to his own bedroom, neither of them having spoken a word, she'd decided he'd been drunk, forgotten where he was, thought she was his wife . . . something like that. And maybe that was right, but it didn't explain anything after that. As for herself, she hadn't been fully awake. She hadn't really known who he was until he was moving inside her, the alcohol smell in her nostrils, and then . . . And then she'd just kept quiet and closed her eyes, and reopened them only when he was gone.

She'd lain there thinking about it for a little while, deciding it was a sort of accident—him drunk and not knowing where he was, herself half asleep. It didn't really mean anything. It wasn't really that important. Her main concern had been how he'd feel when he realized what he'd done. She'd more or less expected to wake up in the morning and find him gone, too embarrassed to face her.

But he'd been there at breakfast just as usual. Nothing had been different at all. She'd decided he must not even remember, or must think it had been a dream. It had seemed dreamlike to her by then. She'd been relieved. That was the best way.

Then, a couple of weeks later, Jay had shown up at her door at suppertime. He'd come in, not waiting for an invitation. He'd told her he was coming back from an assignment—a long drive from somewhere out in western Kansas—and had been feeling sleepy at the wheel, so he'd decided to stop there for a while. He'd asked for coffee.

The story had seemed a little odd, since it was only another twenty-five miles to his home. But he'd been his usual self. He'd only wanted coffee, and she'd had to talk him into eating something. Chatting with him over the meal, she'd felt more sure than ever that he didn't even remember what had happened that night.

After eating, he'd had another cup of coffee. It had been ten o'clock by then, so they'd gone to the rec room to watch the TV news. When the sports segment began, he'd gotten up and turned it off, then turned off the lamp, and sat down beside her on the sofa, putting one arm behind her head and kissing her, leaning her backward. She hadn't seen him drink anything, and the alcohol had been fainter on his breath, but still there. She'd helped him remove her clothing and then had removed his while he ran his hands over her body, neither of them saying anything, and then had lain back on the sofa and closed her eyes.

When she was sure he'd left, she'd gotten up and put her clothes back on and carried the coffee cup to the kitchen. She remembered rinsing the supper dishes and leaving them in the sink, taking off her clothes again and showering, then going to bed. She didn't remember what she'd thought.

The truth was, she'd never really thought about it, tried to figure it out, until he'd had his heart attack a few weeks later, mowing the lawn, and at the funeral she'd gone through the line with everybody else to say something to his widow, and looking at her face-to-face, she'd suddenly become aware of what had been happening during those weeks. Once a week, more or less, maybe ten times altogether. It had been like waking up suddenly. Realizing that what you'd thought was a dream wasn't. And not knowing what to make of it or what to do about it. It had felt like time lost from her life, even while she'd been living. When she'd gotten home from the funeral, she'd locked all her doors and sat by herself in the dining room with the shades drawn, wondering seriously if she was going crazy, if she ought to commit herself. In the end, she'd decided not to let anyone into her house anymore. Not even Hector. Not even other women. It had to be everyone or it wouldn't work.

She had no idea what Jay had been thinking all that time, how he'd been framing it. He'd had his fantasy, too, she supposed. They'd helped one another to dream each other's forbidden dream, and had been careful never to talk about it—or even think about it too carefully—to avoid chasing the dream away. Neither had known what the other's dream was, but it didn't matter.

But she couldn't let it happen again, because she knew it was a dream that would destroy her in the end, if she let it become real again. And it wasn't something she was ever going to talk to anyone about, even to escape that, so the only alternative was to shut them all out. Especially the ones who wanted to help. Because they were the ones who'd make her speak at last, if they could, make her confess that the dream Jay Gillespie had made real for her, for a while, was the dream of her father coming back to her.

23

Instead of making the tight U-turn into the garage, Lassiter sat in his car at the end of the long driveway, watching the way the misty rain seemed to drift and gather like snow, in his headlights, against the backdrop of cedars.

He liked thinking of the cedars in snow. There'd been snow the day he'd realized that those trees were a sanctuary, that his father wasn't going to pursue him there.

He'd thought at first it was because they were so closely clustered, difficult to pass through even for someone his size at the time. But that wouldn't have stopped his father when he was drunk. It had been a mystery, until he'd realized it wasn't the woods his father feared but the other side of them—those streets where the normal people lived.

That had been the moment Lassiter began moving toward his own life, toward the daylight. Some time later—the periods of time were vague in his memory now—he'd begun driving, had been able to take the car out into that other world, alone but safe. The night had belonged to him then. Not to his father.

Going inside, he put the sack of tapes down on the floor and hung his jacket and then his holster over the back of the kitchen chair that held the TV set. He pulled his shirt from his trousers and sat down on the bed to remove his shoes.

There'd been a place in the cedars, an open place he'd found. His place. Maybe the only place that had ever been truly his place. A kind of home. There'd been a flat slab of concrete tilting out of the earth, making a place to sit or lie. He'd decided it was a part of the original driveway, before the trees cut off the house from the street in front of it. And there'd been a space underneath it, to hide his things. There might be something there still, for all he knew. As soon as he'd been able to drive, he'd left the place behind without a thought.

He leaned back on his arms, looking around at the room where he lived now. He and the ghost of his father. He'd been thinking for a long time that he didn't feel the presence of that ghost, but the truth was, he was comfortable with it. It was always right there, too, like everything else he'd pretended to bury along with the dog, pretended to leave behind.

There was nothing physical left of his father here. His mother had had the meager furnishings—the bed, the flimsy lamp table, that was all Lassiter could remember—hauled to the landfill as soon as the old man's body was out the door. She'd kept only the "visitor's chair," the armchair she'd sat in for hours at a time, watching the old man die. She'd had it steamcleaned and fumigated, as she'd had the room itself washed and disinfected, like a killer getting rid of all the evidence.

The nurse who had come by regularly, during the old man's last convalescence, had wondered aloud once, when Lassiter was there, about the cold, cheerless room, when there must be other, warmer bedrooms in the house above. Lassiter's father had turnd his head on the pillow to look at Lassiter's mother. She'd smiled pleasantly at the nurse and said, "This will be so much more convenient, later on."

The doctor had ordered Lassiter's mother to give her husband a single shot of whiskey every day. It would make him feel better, the doctor said, and couldn't hurt him. His mother hadn't protested. Every day, there'd come a point when the old man had begun calling for his whiskey—calling for her to bring it. "Del! Del! Del! Del!" He'd chanted the name until his strength ran out and he fell asleep. Maybe he'd known by then it was what he had to do to get it.

Once he was asleep, she'd taken the bottle from under the sink and dutifully filled a glass and taken it to his room, where she put it down on the little lamp table at the head of the bed, just within his reach. Then she sat down in the stuffed chair and waited.

If he didn't awaken right away, she called out his name sharply, and when he opened his eyes to peer at her blearily, she said, "There's your whiskey." She watched him stretch for it, rolling onto his side, struggling to raise his head, his eyes closed in pain and concentration.

And now and then, and nearly always toward the end, he'd jostled the little table, or struck the glass itself with his fingers and knocked it over, sometimes sending it clanging and bouncing on the lineolum floor.

When that happened, Lassiter's mother would stand, wipe up the whiskey with the towel she brought, and carry the glass away. "One glass," she'd say. "That's what the doctor said." The old man rarely complained. He only lay back in the bed and wept.

Lassiter hadn't exactly enjoyed the little scene, but he had stifled whatever pity he was tempted to feel—usually by thinking of the dog. That was easier and less complicated than thinking of himself.

The dog hadn't been a pet. He didn't even remember its name. It hadn't even been his dog. It had been another creature of his father's. They'd been like allies in a prison camp, on the same side but usually too afraid to offer any real help to each other. Both had been ready to give the other up to save himself.

Or so Lassiter had thought. He still wasn't sure why the dog had snapped at his father the way it had. He thought sometimes that it had just gone crazy at that moment, or lost track of itself, acted instinctively and then realized with horror what it had done. Like himself at Celia Staircase's apartment.

It had happened on the slippery path beside the

barn, a beaten place in the snow that had turned nearly to ice. He himself had been the target when the whole thing began. Lassiter was sure of that, although he didn't remember the details, only the moment when the dog had growled and then given a sort of yip and snapped at his father's boot, not even touching the leather. It seemed to Lassiter that there'd been a moment of stasis, one of those moments when you ask yourself if you really saw what you thought you saw. Perhaps all three of them had been equally astonished.

And then his father had pivoted on one foot and kicked with the other. Kicked hard enough to lift the dog off the ground and send it smashing into the wall of the barn, and to send himself toppling, losing his balance on the ice. Hard enough that Lassiter, in his unreliable memory, could see the pain clearly in its eyes.

Falling had made his father angrier, of course, and he had regained his feet and pursued the dog, kicking it as it tried to slink away along the side of the barn. Lassiter had never been able to decide whether it had already been too hurt to run, or simply too frightened. In the end, at a relatively dry place where he could get some traction, Lassiter's father had methodically kicked the dog to death. Had kept kicking it for a while after it was dead. Lassiter again remembered its eyes—his memories of the moment were mostly of the dog's eyes—its paralyzing fear, and the pain, and then a kind of distant look, perhaps an understanding that this was death, and then nothing. Watching, keeping quiet, being glad it wasn't him, Lassiter had seen the moment of the dog's death in its eyes.

He also remembered exactly what his father had said, when he'd finally calmed down or simply gotten tired of kicking, and had stepped back to take a look at his handiwork, then shake his head in disgust and look at his son.

"That was your fault," Jake Lassiter said. "You killed my dog."

His punishment was having to bury it, having to scoop its frozen body into a sack, trying now not to look at the dead eyes, the curl of the lower lip, exposing the teeth, making it look fiercer than it ever had in life, and then having to dig the grave all by himself in the frozen ground in an open spot in the woods, back behind the barn, while his father stood and watched, finishing another bottle and tossing it into the grave on top of the dog as Lassiter began shoveling the frozen clods on top of it.

And then the barn, of course. Not punishment, but just because his father was in the mood now, and drunk enough . . .

He didn't want to get off on that tangent. He stood, tried to see what he wanted to do now, where he wanted to go. But there wasn't anything. There was nowhere to go from here. He sat down again.

He looked at the sack on the floor, looked at it for a long time. And then he reached for it, slid it toward him, peered inside.

The one he pulled out, according to the jacket, was a movie called *Modern Problems,* with Chevy Chase. He didn't think he'd ever seen it. He turned on the little TV, then slid the tape into the VCR it sat on top of, on the kitchen chair.

Everything was perfectly normal for a while. The FBI warning, the previews of other movies that had come out long ago, back when this one had. The credits . . .

When it changed at last, flickering and hissing loudly, the colors on the screen melting into swatches of black and gray before running together again, he saw a middle-aged man, a man who might be a little older than himself, sitting on a bed.

Immediately, there was a knock on some door that couldn't be seen, and the man looked toward the camera and said, "Come in," and then Celia appeared, the back of her, approaching the bed from behind the camera. He was a little surprised to see that she wore the warm-weather costume of a streetwalker—the tube top and microskirt and spiked heels. They looked . . . silly. An obvious masquerade, like a guy dressed up in a gorilla outfit.

"Aren't you Margaret Simmons?" the man asked, obviously saying something he'd rehearsed.

"My name's Flora," Celia said indifferently. She crossed her arms to pull the tube top up.

"No, wait," the man said. "Turn around."

"What?"

"Turn around." The man moved a finger in the air in a circular motion.

Rolling her eyes, she did so.

"You're Margaret Simmons," the man said. "Don't you recognize me? I'm Cindy Stubbs's father." He smiled dopily, the way anyone might, meeting someone unexpectedly on the street.

Celia stared back at him, unsmiling, then shrugged and said, "Yeah, okay. So you're Mr. Stubbs. I'll have 'em send someone else." She pulled the tube top straight and turned to go.

"No, no," the man said. "Wait. There's no need for that." He paused for a second, and Lassiter was sure it was because he was trying to remember the next line.

"What's the difference?" he said. "My money's just like everyone else's, right? It's just business, right?"

She shook her head. "I don't want to. I'll get you someone else."

He stood up suddenly and grabbed her arm. "I want to," he said. "And the customer's always right, right?"

It was obvious she could have pulled away from him easily. She was a good three inches taller than him and had at least twenty years on him, and was in better shape. But she acted like she couldn't.

"Please let me go, Mr. Stubbs. It wouldn't be right. I mean, Cindy was a friend of mine. I don't want to do her dad."

"Tough." He gave a yank on her arm, and she flew past him onto the bed. A nice athletic move, Lassiter thought, for the yank Stubbs had given wouldn't have budged her. This tape was better than the other he'd seen, because it was funnier. This guy was pathetic.

He stood over her, as if he now had control of her, and she looked back at him wide-eyed, as if she thought so, too. "You're a whore, right?" he said.

"Please, Mr.—"

"You're a whore, right?"

"I'm a working girl."

"You're a whore. Say it."

She closed her mouth sullenly, then shrugged insolently and said, "Yeah. I'm a whore. What are you?"

"I'm the guy paying for you," he said. "And you were always a little whore, weren't you?"

"I was not! I was . . ."

Lassiter turned the TV off. He'd sort of enjoyed it when she was clearly the one in charge. But he didn't want to see the rest of it.

He took off the rest of his clothes, turned off the light and lay down on the bed. In the silence he could hear the rain outside, which must be falling harder now, but which, muffled, sounded as soft as snow falling on branches.

He'd spent years waiting to be old enough and big enough and strong enough to give his father what he deserved, but the liquor had beaten him to it, shrinking the son of a bitch to a withered, shaky old man he didn't recognize and couldn't help feeling pity for, and then killing him. The accounting he'd hoped for was like something unfinished that he kept thinking he'd take care of eventually. Now and then he still had dreams—glorious, joyful dreams—about being face-to-face with his father, the way he'd once been, but being himself the way he was now, even in his fifties, knowing exactly how to take care of some drunken . . .

It was kind of a joke. Foolish now. But he didn't mind indulging it now and then, as long as nothing was really going to come of it. He'd worried about it a little, his first few years as a cop, almost expecting something like that explosion in Loomis's office to happen. But it hadn't. He'd always stayed in control,

the way he'd learned to do as a kid. And then when
it had happened, it had surprised him. And it hadn't
made any sense, coming out that way, among friends,
directed at a woman. It made no sense at all.

24

Zach stood at the sink, eating his cereal, and watched the cop unlock the yellow box with a key from his pocket, and then unlock the apartment door with the key before putting it back in the lockbox. Zach had thought the box held some sort of phone, like the old call boxes. But this was better—a simple, neat algorithm. It didn't even try to get around the weak point in any security system—the human being—which you could never really do. You had to trust the user to put the key back, and hope that nobody stole it from him. Trust and hope were always the irreducible variables that couldn't be eliminated or controlled, if you were writing code for people. Programmers, as a rule, hated that, and kept trying to write the perfect code. *Philosopher's code.*

He smiled at his own phrase, then sighed and rinsed the bowl and left it and the spoon in the sink. He poured out the cold coffee remaining in his cup, and went to the coffeemaker on the counter to get more. There was one cup left. Christ. He hadn't even gotten up the stairs yet. How could he have drunk a whole pot just fooling around down here? He made a new pot and guided himself resolutely up the stairs to his office.

Waiting for the system to come up, he stood at the window and looked across at the other apartment, at Eddy's bedroom window. It was funny to think of all the times he'd looked over there this same way, not even thinking about the two inside, thinking about something else entirely. Not knowing them, even their names.

And now he missed them. Soon the police would take the yellow box off the door, and then the apartment would stand empty for a while, and then someone would move in, and they'd be completely gone. He'd be back to his regular life. The only thing keeping him from being back in it now was himself. A week ago, he'd been perfectly happy—well, content, anyway. All he'd wanted from the world outside was for it to leave him alone to do his work.

He wasn't content now. He kept wanting to call someone, to find out what was going on. But he didn't know who he'd call, exactly, or what he'd ask. It wasn't really any of his business. He'd keep going in to see Eddy and feed him, as long as they told him to, and then . . . he supposed at some point they'd tell him not to anymore. Or he'd show up there and Eddy would be gone. And he'd be back in his regular life again.

Someone knocked on the door downstairs, and Zach got up quickly, glad of the interruption, then frowned going down the stairs, thinking about his own reaction. *Glad of the interruption?*

It was the cop.

"Mr. Vincent? I'm Detective Majors. I'm in charge of the murder investigation. I don't think we've met before."

"I saw you here the other night." Zach stepped back. "Want to come in?"

"Thanks."

They sat, and Zach waited for Majors to speak. He had the feeling Majors was waiting for him to say something—he'd brought an odd tension into the room with him—but if so Zach outlasted him.

"I should have been here sooner," Majors said at last. "We've been . . . we started out behind, since the body wasn't discovered immediately." He hesitated, then said, "You're not a suspect, by the way, if you have any concerns about that."

Zach didn't know if he did or not. He hadn't really thought about it.

Perhaps Majors could tell that, for he just shrugged and tugged a couple of small notepads from his jacket pocket. He peered at them like a man whose eyesight was just beginning to deteriorate a little, then put one back and flipped the other open and peered at it, turned a couple of pages.

"Okay," he said. He looked at Zach. "These are Detective Burton's notes, from when he interviewed you."

Zach nodded. "You want to go over them and see if my story has changed," he said.

Majors frowned. "No, like I said—"

"Sorry. Too much TV." Actually, he hardly ever watched TV.

"I want to see if maybe you might remember something you didn't that night," Majors said. "Sometimes things come back to people when they've had a day or two to think about it. It can be kind of confusing at the scene."

Zack started to shake his head, then remembered something. "A small thing," he said. "I doubt if—"

"What?"

"Just that when she moved in over there, there was another woman helping her. A black woman."

Majors seemed interested. "Can you describe her any better?"

"They were both bundled up," Zach said, shaking his head. "It was cold. She was shorter than . . . Jocelyn Wellington. That's about—"

"How tall, would you say?"

"I don't know. I'm not good at that kind of thing. I thought she was very short . . . but then, Jocelyn was tall, so it might have been . . ."

"Any idea of age?"

Zach thought about it. "I had the idea at the time that they were about the same age—about my age, around thirty—but I don't know why."

"They had a rental truck?"

"Right. A Ryder, one of the little ones. But a real truck, you know? Not a van."

Majors nodded, scribbled on his pad. "So I guess

you've read the morning paper," he said, not looking up.

"No, I don't subscribe. I look at the Web site sometimes."

Majors grunted, flipping a couple of pages as if not really paying attention to their conversation. Zach guessed it was the other way around. What had he said? Then he got it.

"Oh," he said. "I ran into Jes Wellington at the Children's Home. She told me her sister's name was Jocelyn. That's how I know that."

Majors looked at him and nodded. "So, I assume Detective Burton hasn't been back to talk to you since then," Majors said.

Zach shook his head. "Nobody has. Well, there was some insurance guy, but no cops. I've seen you and the other guy go in and out over there, is all."

"You mean Burton?"

"No. The *other* guy. He was here that night, I saw you talking to him. Burton told me his name but I forgot. I guess he was the cop who'd talked to her, something like that. Burton asked me if I'd seen him, but I hadn't. Not till then."

"Detective Lassiter? Is that the name?"

"Right. Yeah. Lassiter."

"And Burton wanted to know if you'd seen Lassiter over there, but you hadn't."

Zach nodded, but it wasn't quite a question. It was more like one of those things you repeated to yourself, to try to make something make sense. *And then you pushed that button and the file disappeared.* A funny question to ask in this case, he thought. Evidently the cops weren't keeping in touch with each other very well. No wonder they were having trouble.

Majors was flipping through the notepad. Zach had the impression he was looking for Burton's notes about that particular question and not finding it. He gave a little frown but shrugged.

"So that night was the only time you saw Lassiter," he said.

"Until last night. He was over there when I came back from the Children's Home, from visiting Eddy."

Majors hesitated just long enough to make it obvious that this was news to him. But he made a soft sound of assent and nodded, as if it weren't.

"There was another cop with him," Zach said. "I think he was a cop. I'd never seen him before. A big old guy with white hair."

Majors gave him a sharp look. "Hispanic?"

Zach blinked, a little taken aback. "I don't know. It was dark, you know. The storm."

"Right."

"I just saw them for a second or two," Zach said. "I was turning in from the alley to my garage, and the, umm, you know, the headlights . . . they were in the headlights for a second. They were just standing in front of the porch, talking. They looked at me, and I went on into the garage and closed the door, and came up the inside stairs. I looked out my office window, but the old guy was gone by then, and, umm . . ."

"Lassiter."

"Lassiter. He was closing the door, locking up that yellow box. I think he'd just stepped inside to get something. And then he left. That's all."

"To get what? Was he carrying something?"

Zach was feeling more and more uncomfortable. It no longer sounded quite like some lack of communication between the cops. It sounded like something he didn't want to be in the middle of. Still, he had to answer.

"He had a paper sack, you know . . . a grocery bag."

Majors was silent. Zach wondered if he knew how he looked—like a man whose worst fear has just been confirmed. He also looked incredibly tired. Probably he hadn't been getting much sleep. Zach suddenly decided that if there was something going on between the cops, and he ever had to choose sides, he'd go with Majors.

"Could you tell anything about what might have been in the bag?" Majors asked. He was no longer making any pretense that these were just routine follow-up questions.

Zach thought about it. "Not really. Something squarish, I'd say. Like books. If that's any help. It was only maybe half filled. The top was rolled up like a handle." He hesitated. "But this is just . . . I mean, I only saw him for a couple of seconds, like I said, and it was dark. I could be wrong. It could have just been shadows or something, you know?"

Majors gave him a little look that made him feel like a kid trying to con an adult. He looked away.

"You mentioned an insurance guy," Majors said. "Would that be Tim Haffner? From L.A.?"

"Yeah, that's right." Zach glanced around. "I've got his card here somewhere."

"Never mind. I know who he is. He's looking for the things she stole out in California."

"Yeah, that's what he said. He showed me a Xerox of some things. I hadn't seen any of them, of course. I don't know if he believed me or not. He kept sort of glancing around in here, you know? I said he could search the place if he wanted to, but he didn't. I told Burton the same thing, and he didn't, either."

"Yeah, I know. When somebody says something like that, it means they're either incredibly stupid or the stuff you're looking for isn't there. You don't appear to be incredibly stupid."

"But what if I knew that's how you think about it?"

Majors smiled. "Why take that kind of risk when all you have to do is keep quiet? No offense, but you don't strike me as the kind of guy who likes to live dangerously for the hell of it."

Zach gave a half smile. "That obvious, huh?"

"It's not an insult. Believe me." He was silent for a moment, then stuck out his hand. "Thanks for your help."

What help? Zach thought, shaking his hand. People kept thanking him for things he didn't feel he deserved any thanks for.

25

They'd all been recorded over. He didn't watch all of every tape, only enough to be sure, to get a good look at each old man. They all appeared well off, judging from the furnishings that could be seen, and most of them were older than Lassiter.

He'd been right to take them. Even if they never misled Jerry, if everything was over before it came to that, which seemed likely, these weren't things the family would want. Whoever wound up with her belongings. The sister.

He shrugged and began putting the tapes back into the sack, trying to think if there was any reason not to destroy them. Some of them might be ones the LAPD didn't already have—guys they didn't know about. Did he care about that? No.

He nearly tossed the four unopened ones in with the rest and went looking for a plastic trash bag. But at the last moment he decided he ought to be thorough. He'd watched some of all the other tapes, making sure they were what he thought they were.

He peeled the shrink-wrap off one, took the cartridge out and slid it into the VCR. The machine kicked it right back out. He tried again and got the same result. Not even a working tape. He put it aside and opened another. The VCR wanted nothing to do with it, either.

He couldn't think of any reason she'd have put the shrink-wrap on the tapes themselves because they were defective. He began to get an inkling of an idea, and he wasn't entirely surprised when he lifted the plastic flap along the edge of one of them and found that there was no tape at all, only the black plastic and the tiny metal rollers.

He hadn't really noticed it before, but both cassettes were the kind without the round windows on the side—no way to see the tape inside. He opened the other two. They were the same.

Lassiter found himself smiling, pleased not by his discovery but by Celia's ingenuity. He was sure that the whole purpose of the other tapes was simply to hide these, to make them look like unused extras to anyone who solved the first puzzle. A mask over a mask. Nothing to do with blackmail at all. He continued smiling, thinking of telling her he'd figured it out . . . and then remembered again that he couldn't.

He went to the storeroom and found a Phillips-head screwdriver with a small enough tip among his father's tools. Removing the tiny screws from the tape cassettes, he found inside each one a neat brown paper package—paper from a grocery sack. The first one he opened contained what looked like a metal cigarette case covered with black suede. It was very nice but it was only another container, not the real prize. Inside it, wrapped in tissue and inside their own case of clear, hard plastic, were four old postage stamps. A block of old 24-cent airmail stamps depicting a propeller-driven biplane flying upside down. Printed upside down, rather. He'd seen photos of these stamps, seen articles about them. He thought he remembered reading that only a single sheet had escaped the Post Office before the rest had been destroyed, and that that sheet had been broken up, dispersed. A single stamp was worth a fortune. A block of four like this, still attached . . .

The other three packages contained two pieces of massive jewelry, which didn't interest him—Burton and his rich men could have those cold, glittery things—and a tiny painting of some ancient siege.

Not a print, a real painting. He could see the raised ridges of the tiny, meticulous brushstrokes. It was a wonder, more so than the stamps because done by intention and by a single human being. One group of tiny warriors held the top of a rocky desert plateau, and another group encamped at the base—Romans?—appeared to be building a massive ramp of dirt and rock to reach the top. Some of the tiny figures on top looked like women and children.

There was a story in it he wanted to know. Celia could have told him, of course. Probably Jerry could, or Kay. Probably it was something everybody knew about, some famous, important thing. And it had wound up in his custody. These things, the painting and the stamps in particular, were his responsibility now.

He rewrapped everything carefully, put it all back together, everything but the shrink-wrap, and then put the four cases into the grocery sack with the others, turning them the other way so he'd be sure which ones they were.

Because he'd gotten winter into his mind, he was surprised by the warmth outside. It had stopped raining and there was a moist heat rising out of the ground, even in the dark. He was pretty sure it was night now, not just the dark of the storm clouds. It felt like night.

It was easy to find the place where he'd once passed through the thin shell of green to the interior of the cedars—but nothing else was easy.

The "path" was still visible, but it was more like a tunnel—or a gauntlet running between the stiff, naked branches standing straight out from the trunks on all sides. Maybe exposure hadn't been his father's only reason for not pursuing him here. It seemed a lot more forbidding than it had to him as a child.

You couldn't move quickly, couldn't really just crash through, the way he'd imagined his father doing. Because the crooked daggers of wood came at you from all directions. He had to move with one arm protecting his eyes. If the angle was right, a branch would snap off easily. If not, it could break the skin.

Twice he nearly impaled himself—once in the chest, once in the lower abdomen—moving to avoid one branch and running into another.

It was surprisingly exhausting, and he wasn't entirely sure he'd recognize the clearing, or that it would even still be there. Briefly, he tried crawling, but it didn't work any better and he couldn't see as well. When he did finally stumble into the clearing, which he recognized by the upthrust piece of concrete to one side, he was breathing heavily and his neck and arms were crisscrossed with scratches, some slight but some oozing blood. There were more scratches on his torso, he knew, beneath the shirt, and even a couple of places on his thighs that felt like they might be bleeding.

The clearing wasn't as large as he remembered it—not really a clearing at all, just a wide place between the trunks—but it provided a welcome respite from the jabbing fingers of wood. He widened it a bit more by breaking off more branches, and then sat down experimentally on the slanted concrete stone. It too seemed smaller, of course, but he could sit with reasonable comfort.

After resting a moment to get his breath, he felt beneath the rock on which he sat, putting his hand into the opening before thinking there might be small creatures living there now that wouldn't welcome his intrusion. But if so, they fled instead of attacking. The hole was empty, which surprised and disappointed him a little. Apparently he'd removed whatever he'd last hidden there, after all.

He rearranged the tape cassettes inside the sack and then rolled the paper tightly into a shape that would fit the hole, then pushed it in and made a little mound of twigs and dead needles—the carpeting of the little wood—to cover the opening.

That was done. They were safe for the time being, until he could figure out what to do with them. And so was he. This was the first place where he'd ever felt completely safe, once he'd realized his father wouldn't

follow him here. That—the knowledge that he really
was safe—had been the beginning of the rest of his
life. A completely different life, he'd thought, having
nothing to do with the first one. But it didn't really
work that way.

For a second he almost made some connection that
had to do with the problem of the things hidden beneath the rock. The dog . . . something about the dog.
Another hole in the ground, inside another small
wood. Another hiding place. If he'd had these things
when he'd buried the dog, he could have thrown them
in along with it, the way he'd imagined he was throwing in . . . what? His fear? No. His caring. His feeling.
He hadn't really, of course. It had still been there. It
had burst out in Loomis's office. But maybe now he
really had killed it. It would be buried with Celia
instead . . .

He gave a start. Of course. The tapes and the things
she'd taken belonged to her, and they could go with
her. It was a custom to put small things inside the
open casket, at the graveside . . . It couldn't be everything. That would be too much. But the stamps and
the painting. Those were the main things. He could
think of some way to bundle them, make them look
like something else . . .

Friday, Hector had said. He realized suddenly that
he didn't know what day it was. This might be Friday.
She might already be buried.

What was the last day he was sure of? He remembered Sunday, because that was when he'd visited his
mother . . . and when he'd visited Celia. That had
been such a long time ago. Surely the Friday of the
funeral had come and gone.

But it had been only yesterday, hadn't it, when he'd
talked to Hector, when Hector had said it was on
Friday? Wouldn't he have said it was tomorrow if this
was the day?

He needed to find a newspaper. It would tell him
the day, and maybe even have an obit in it, or something about the services.

He pushed himself up awkwardly, feeling as stiff and sore as he had when he'd come back to himself in the car, by the river, and began making his way painfully back the way he'd come, through the cedars.

26

"You're sure somebody hasn't just 'borrowed' them from property to watch them?" Loomis asked.

"They were never logged in. They were dusted at the scene, but the only latents were small ones, not a man's prints. So the tech didn't think there was any reason to bag them. And it turned out all the prints were the vic's." Majors shrugged, not quite looking at Loomis.

"We all saw the casebook," Loomis said. "We all knew what she'd been doing for a living. We all could have made the connection. None of us did."

"Floyd did." Angry as he felt, Majors couldn't help also feeling a touch of pride. Of course Floyd did.

"What makes you so sure it's Floyd?"

"Vincent saw him. Coming out with a sack. That's the only reason I looked around—to see if anything was gone."

"It's a solid ID?"

Majors nodded. "Vincent saw him when he talked to her and then again at the crime scene."

"Floyd was at the crime scene?"

Majors gave a tight nod. "I sent him home. He looked like hell. He said he'd come in the next morning." He paused, feeling Loomis's eyes on him. "The truth is, he looked guilty," Majors said angrily. "I knew it. I just didn't want to know it."

Loomis grunted. "I'm just trying to figure out whether you're pissed off at Floyd or yourself. Both, I guess."

Majors looked away counting a quick ten. "You haven't heard everything," he said.

"Okay. Tell me."

"Briseno was there, too . . . at the apartment, when Vincent saw Floyd come out with the sack. The two of them were standing out in front, talking, when Vincent was coming back from somewhere in his car. The same afternoon Briseno was up here. Pretty much right afterward. He went straight from here to there, and he meets up with Floyd. Vincent sees them talking. He puts his car in the garage and goes upstairs, and when he looks out again, Briseno is gone and Floyd's coming out with something in a sack."

"How does Vincent know Hector?" Loomis asked.

Majors gave an impatient shrug. "He doesn't. He said Floyd was talking to an old white-haired man who looked to him like a cop. He thought they were two cops, talking about the case. Sounds like Briseno to me, unless you know of . . ."

"Go on."

"Okay. Vincent also remembers now that he saw Jocelyn move in. She had a small rental truck, a Ryder—a truck, not a van—and there was this black woman helping her. It's cold and they're bundled up, so Vincent doesn't get a real good look, but he's sure she's black, and he thinks she's about the same age as Jocelyn. Also, they don't appear to have any baby with them."

"What about the other neighbors?"

"They were gone at the time. So, I check the Ryder places until I come up with a black woman about thirty who rented a small truck that same morning, for a local move. Her name is Margo Gilkey, and she lives up north of WSU . . . on the nice side of Hillside. Her husband's a doctor and she's a med tech. She works at one of those clinics across from Wesley. So I go to see her."

"Is she connected to Jocelyn Wellington, or Sand Creek, or—"

"Not that I know of. She's a Wichita native, from a good family. No sheet." He shrugged.

"So what'd she say?"

"That she wasn't going to talk to me unless I had a warrant and her attorney was there."

"She was expecting you?"

"She was expecting somebody. She seemed more pissed off than scared, I'd say. She did say one other thing. When I tried to tell her she wasn't in any trouble and she didn't need an attorney, she said, 'Yeah, right. That's what the other cop said.'"

"She didn't describe this other cop? Or ID him from a photo or anything like that?"

Majors shook his head.

"So you don't really know who he was—do you know it's a male cop? Anything? Or when he talked to her? Or that it had anything to do with Jocelyn Wellington? That she doesn't have some other kind of legal problem entirely?"

Majors frowned. He didn't. The questions were obvious ones, and he hadn't even posed them to himself.

"Is that what you've got?" Loomis asked.

"Well, no . . . there's, umm . . ." But he was distracted, his mind running back over the day—following the path from Vincent to the other apartment, the empty closet, and then to property and to Kreider's office, and then three Ryder places until he got the hit on Margo Gilkey, and then . . . In his memory, he'd been running from one bad thing to a worse one, a weight of blackness growing inside him . . .

"Jerry?"

He jerked. "Sorry. What . . . ?"

"You said there was something else."

"Oh, yeah." He shook his head to clear it. "When I was coming out of the clinic, I noticed that the building next door had a day-care center in it, so . . ." He shrugged. "Turned out the people there know Margo real well. She brings her own kid there. And one of them remembered there was this one time when she brought in a white male infant one morning and left

him there for a few hours, and then came back and
got him. She said he was the son of an outpatient who
had to have some procedure she hadn't expected."

"Sounds plausible."

"Yeah, sure. But the date in their records was the
same day the truck was rented, when Jocelyn moved
in. And the only information Margo gave them about
the kid was that his mother's name was Johnson.
They're supposed to get more, but I guess they have
emergencies like this now and then, and they don't
charge anything." He shrugged. "Anyway, I went back
to the clinic and checked on female patients named
Johnson who'd had procedures that day. There were
only two, and both were too old to have a baby."

"You never know nowadays," Loomis said. "Anyway, could have been the kid's grandmother."

"Baby-sitting him while she goes to the clinic?"

"Who knows? Or maybe she has custody of him."
Loomis made a note on the open pad on his desk.
"It's something to check out, to be sure." He was
silent for a moment, looking at the pad. "I'm not sure
there's enough yet for a material-witness warrant," he
said. "But I can probably get her lawyer to tell her to
talk to me."

"So you're taking the case," Majors said.

Loomis looked up. "The case? No. I'm taking
Floyd. Something's going on with him, and I want to
know what it is, exactly, before I.A. gets into it. I want
to ask Margo Gilkey about this cop who talked to her,
see if it was Floyd or not. You've still got the murder
case, and you still need to see if there's a connection
between her and your vic."

"You don't think the two things are pretty much
the same thing?"

Loomis shrugged. "If so, we'll find out. If you get
anything more about Floyd, you should let me know.
If I get anything that points another direction in the
murder, I'll let you know. Deal?"

Majors looked away, feeling Loomis's gaze again,

then said, "You sure that's the way to do it, Lieutenant? If Floyd was a civilian—"

"Then I *would* take you off the case," Loomis said. Majors was startled. "Huh?"

"You're locked on to one suspect, and you don't have as good a case as you think you do. It's the kind of thing that usually happens with relatives of the vic. The cop doesn't like one of them, for some reason, and it's easier than really investigating, and relatives always have some motive."

"This isn't like that," Majors said.

"I know. That's why I'm leaving you on the case. This isn't about the murder. It's about you and Floyd. You're scared and you're pissed off and you're a good cop, so you're overcompensating to keep from protecting your partner. It speaks well for you, but it's getting in the way of what you're supposed to be doing." He sighed. "Jerry, everybody knows you work best when you get mad about the murder. But you're not mad about the murder. You're mad at your partner. And yourself. You've forgotten all about Jocelyn Wellington."

Majors felt as if he'd been slapped. It was true. He remembered the image he'd formed—a faceless, sadistic monster, a thing he'd known he had to find and destroy. And that wasn't Floyd. There'd never be any way he could make that match Floyd. Part of what he'd been frightened by, he realized, was the possibility that he might be so far wrong.

"But what about the tapes?" he asked. "Why would Floyd take the tapes?" That was the part he was sure of, and he knew Loomis was, too.

"Jerry," Loomis said. He shook his head. "You know Floyd better than I do. Think about it. He's working on this Celeste Mundy thing. It's not even a real case in his mind, just . . . practice. Pretend. He doesn't expect to find her. And then he does. And remember, it's not a homicide case. She didn't kill anybody. She's this young woman with a baby, and these old rich men have been paying her to make porn videos, and she swiped some of their trinkets and took her baby and headed home. Granted, she's a felon. We'd arrest her. We'd extradite her. Floyd sent the LAPD a memo alerting them that he'd found her. But how does Floyd Lassiter *feel* about it? Who does he see as the victim—Jocelyn Wellington or her Hollywood clients? He does his job, but then she's killed, and the way she's killed . . ."

"I did think about that," Majors said. "That night at the scene, the way Floyd looked. I thought maybe he looked guilty because he thought he'd helped the killer find her." He was silent for a moment. "But why not just tell *me* about the tapes? I mean, I'm his partner."

"Not on this. This was always just his case. I think Floyd feels like he's the one who has to finish it."

Majors nodded. It all made sense to him, and it was a great relief. "He might finish it," he said. "We've got nobody better."

Loomis gave a half smile, but didn't dispute it. "The second I'm absolutely sure I'm right about this," he said, "you and Floyd will be working together again, on this case. But I have to know I'm right."

Majors nodded, feeling a little light-headed. He had the feeling—a familiar one, unfortunately—that everybody else was already a step ahead of him. Loomis. Floyd. Probably the killer.

"I take it you haven't seen Floyd since the crime scene," Loomis said.

That brought him back to reality, brought a little of the darkness back. "He was supposed to come in the next morning, but he didn't. I've left messages on his machine. I've gone by his house probably half a dozen times. His car's gone. I really don't think he's been at home, but I don't have any idea where he *would* be, except just driving around in his car."

"He'd want to play the videos," Loomis said. "What friend would he go to?"

Majors shook his head. "Me," he said. "Can't think of anyone else. Or maybe Kay. But she's in Atlanta."

"Assuming he hasn't left town, you must have *some* idea how I could find him. You're his partner."

"You'd think I would, wouldn't you? Besides Kay, the only other person I can think of outside the department is Briseno."

Loomis nodded. "That could have been what they were talking about. I'm sure Hector would do him a favor like that if he asked. What about relatives?"

"His mother's in a nursing home with Alzheimer's."

"Does she have a VCR?"

Majors smiled in spite of himself. "You think he's gonna take these tapes, thinking what they might be, you think he's gonna sit down and start watching them with his mother? Even if she's got Alzheimer's?"

Loomis gave a rueful smile. "Scratch that. People outside of law enforcement?"

Majors shook his head. "Not that I know of."

"Jesus. Nobody at all?"

"Well, there's, you know, informants, parolees . . ."

"Christ almighty." Loomis shook his head. "There's got to be somebody."

Majors shrugged and nodded.

"Have we got it straight between us?" Loomis asked.

Majors recognized his cue and stood up. "I think so."

"Any questions?"

Majors hesitated and then said, "Where does Burton fit in this mix? Is he still working his side of the street?"

"Why don't you let me worry about Burton?" Loomis said. "That's my job. You do your job and catch Jocelyn Wellington's killer."

27

Friday

After they'd gotten the metal framework positioned to their satisfaction, the two gravediggers spent some time tidying up, searching for small clods of dirt in the grass around the grave and tossing them into the pile of dirt a few feet away. Then they lowered the back flap of the canopy, hiding the dirt from the rows of empty folding chairs beneath the canopy, went scooting away on the little backhoe, zigzagging around the graves on some familiar path, the younger one hanging on to the back with one hand, the shovel over his shoulder, his long blond hair whipping.

Lassiter watched them reach the far corner and disappear behind a screen of trees that he supposed hid the shop and equipment sheds. He started his car and drove slowly along the curving gravel road to where he could see the two headstones also set just behind the canvas flap. That would be the parents. His eyes were no longer quite good enough to read the inscriptions from that distance, but he didn't have to. He'd only wanted to know where the grave was.

He still wasn't sure what he was going to do. The small wooden box he'd taken from his mother's bedroom, that now held the rare stamps and the little painting, sat beside him on the seat, and he put his hand on it for a moment, then looked off through the open passenger window at the expanse of the cemetery and the interstate beyond. The clouds were beginning to clear. It would be clear and dry for the funeral, a nice day. The breeze that came into the car, into his face as he looked that way, carried the sound of diesel engines rumbling in the big parking lot at the truck stop on the other side of the interstate, and even a hint of the aroma of diesel fuel and manure from some cattle truck.

It was the odor of the barn, of the back stall, but it didn't bother him. That smell was like an old scar one noticed now and then, and felt nothing about, without an effort to remember how it had been gotten. He decided to drive over to the truck stop and have some coffee and decide whether to come back or not once the graveside ceremonies had begun.

He was still tired. He'd slept, but not well. Coming in from the cedars the night before, he'd found the empty sleeve of the last tape he'd looked at, set right there on top of the TV, in plain sight, the tape itself still in the VCR.

He'd decided to watch it, for reasons that were no longer quite so clear or sensible in his memory as they'd seemed at the time. It had been a mistake, of course. Not that he couldn't be aroused, like any other man, feel that anger . . . Except that his anger, once begun, once let loose, threatened always to grow and widen, to encompass everyone and everything—his mother, Kay, Jerry, everyone—until there was no one in the world he wouldn't have destroyed.

He'd sat for a long time, wanting to think but unable to, his mind echoing with his own cries and complaints, years of them, all still in there. So tiresome. He'd felt so tired of himself. Standing up finally, to take off his clothes and go to the shower, he'd been stupidly surprised by the scratches and bruises on his body. He also discovered that he'd ejaculated at some point, watching the video, without even knowing it. That seemed appropriate to him. His body had nothing to do with him. It was a burden he had to carry, for reasons he didn't understand. Standing in the shower, washing it, he felt a weary contempt. How long was he going to have to drag this thing around?

What had it ever brought him but pain and disappointment? The few good things lasted for a moment and then went away, and then the body got old and began to run down, and the good things were gone forever, while all the worst things stayed.

He glimpsed movement, turned his head, and saw a car pulling into the cemetery. It looked vaguely familiar, but most cars did, anyway. It wasn't Jerry's, anyway, and he didn't see any procession behind it. He started his engine again and headed for the back exit and the truck stop.

There was a car parked right behind the canopy when he pulled in, and then it suddenly started up and moved away, vanished through some exit he couldn't see. It was as if he'd startled the car into flight. *Maybe that's the killer,* Zach thought. He imagined himself speeding up, tearing through these narrow, curving roads to follow the car, get the license number. A hero again. Right. An idiot again was more like it.

The hearse pulled in behind him, and he turned onto a side branch, to be out of the way. But then he made himself shut off the engine right there and get out to stand beside his car as the others passed. He'd intended to go to the service at the mortuary but hadn't. Then he'd driven a block ahead of the procession instead of joining it. At some point he had to stop acting guilty. He supposed that Jes would be in the limousine behind the hearse. All alone? He hated that image. Faces glanced at him from the other cars, and he tried not to look away guiltily, imagining the questions they were asking one another. *Who's that guy? A cop, you think? No, cops don't have scraggly beards. Gee, maybe it's the killer!*

The last two faces, in the last two cars, were familiar ones. Majors didn't look at him, but Burton did, leaning a little to wave, smiling, like he was having a good time. Probably he was. Probably this wasn't real to him, just sort of a movie. A picturesque funeral out in the sticks.

His own anger surprised him. But it wasn't Burton he was mad at. The L.A. cop just made an easy target. He didn't know who it was, exactly, or what. It didn't even really have anything to do with the funeral, the murder of Jocelyn Wellington. Coming here triggered it somehow—it had been building up since he'd started getting dressed, putting his suit on.

The hearse had pulled onto the grass not far from the metal contraption on top of the open grave. Six guys in black suits had materialized out of nowhere—or maybe out of the limousine—and were pulling the casket, very slowly and carefully, out of the back of the hearse. Pallbearers were always excessively careful, and he could understand why. Pallbearers always made him nervous, kind of like figure skaters and divers. You got to thinking it must never really happen, and then wham! Greg Louganis smacks his head on the board. The best diver in the world. Just a little reminder not to get too comfortable.

He looked toward the people finding seats in the rows of folding chairs. Obviously, there weren't going to be enough. That was good because it gave him an excuse to stand at the back without anybody wondering why he wasn't sitting down. He was also glad that so many people were here. Unconsciously, he'd been expecting one of those small, dismal funerals with three or four mourners under a gray sky. But obviously a lot of people in Sand Creek still cared enough about Jocelyn to come to her funeral. So Eddy had a place to go to, after all.

He crossed the road and found a position a few yards from the rear corner of the canopy. He saw Jes for the first time. She'd just gotten out of the limousine and was turning back, bending a little, offering a hand to someone inside. She wore a long black dress of some soft material that fluttered a little in the wind, and she was using her other hand to hold her tiny black hat against the breeze. Whoever was inside refused her offer, and she straightened and turned back again. She was slim and tall and . . . beautiful.

Christ! He'd known he was attracted to her, but when had she gotten to be beautiful? It was like her sister turning into someone who didn't look anything like her, just by doing something with her hair and her makeup. Maybe they were supernatural—witches, something like that. He was in trouble.

The person who'd declined her help in getting out of the limousine turned out to be the tall, white-haired man he'd seen talking to Lassiter. So, not a cop but a relative. An uncle or something, since the parents were both dead, according to the obit. That was good. She wasn't completely alone.

Nobody else got out. The old man closed the door, and the two of them headed toward the front of the seats. Looking that way, Zach saw that the entire front row was empty. The family row. Not such a great thing to have a whole row like that when there wasn't much family. He watched Jes take a seat toward the middle, but the old man wasn't with her. He was standing right next to Zach, extending his hand.

Zach gave a little start, shook the hand automatically. It was about twice as big as his own, and strong. His face looked vaguely Hispanic, or maybe Indian. Majors must have known who he was.

"You're Zach Vincent," the old man said. It wasn't a question.

Zach nodded, not quite knowing what to say.

"I'm Hector Briseno," the old man said. "I wanted to thank you."

"Oh." Of course. He gave another little nod. He was really getting tired of being thanked and praised. But when he tried to fend it off with words, it only sounded like false modesty. "I should have called the police," he said.

"Yeah," Briseno said. "That's true. But it came out okay."

Zach was just starting to think that he liked this old man, that there was something about him—when a hand clapped his shoulder. He found himself looking once again into Detective Burton's smiling face.

"Hey, Zach," he said. Then he offered his hand to the old man. "Detective Briseno?"

Okay. Detective. He'd been right. At first, Zach thought the old man wasn't going to take the offered hand, but then he gave it a perfunctory shake. "I'm Hector Briseno," he said. "I'm here as a friend of the family."

"Sure. I don't mean to intrude. I just thought I'd take the opportunity to introduce my—"

"I know who you are," Briseno said.

Burton waited, but Briseno didn't add anything.

"Well," the L.A. detective said at last. "That's great. Umm, I was hoping maybe we could get together—"

"Not now."

"No. Of course not. That's not what I . . . I was hoping maybe . . . tomorrow? I know it's Saturday—"

"I work till three on Saturdays," Briseno said. "If nothin' comes up, I'll be in my office."

"You don't . . . I don't need an appointment?"

Briseno shook his head.

Zach couldn't figure out whether Burton rubbed him the wrong way, or this was just his normal manner.

"Well, okay . . . great," Burton said. "I'll probably just drop by tomorrow. Just, you know, want to touch base. Well . . ." Burton laughed. "Listen, I'll stop bothering you guys. Detective Briseno, nice to meet you. See you tomorrow."

They both stood and watched him as he hurried off. Zach turned his head and looked for Majors, spotted him standing on the far side, his hands behind his back, looking at them. Zach nodded and Majors nodded back.

Zach was trying to think of something to say when Briseno said, "Why'n't you come sit with Jes and me? They're gettin' ready to start."

"But that's the family row, isn't it?"

"I'm not family."

Zach was nonplussed. "I'm not sure Jes—"

"She'll be okay. All those empty chairs make her uncomfortable. We'll say you're representin' the baby. Not that anybody's gonna ask."

Zach scanned the crowd, saw a couple of faces that had been watching them turn quickly back toward the front. "I don't know about that," he said. "I'm a stranger."

"They all know who you are. They seen your picture in the paper."

That silenced him. He wasn't sure he liked that idea any better, but it left him without objections. People glanced up at him as he followed Briseno along the ends of the rows toward the front, and he saw that Briseno was right. The expressions were curious, not suspicious. One old man on the end of a row smiled broadly at him and nodded.

Zach nodded back.

Tom Haney had started tapping his watch and giving her little looks, but she didn't know why. The family was here. Was she supposed to give him some kind of signal? She gave a little shrug, but he just looked away, as if he hadn't been looking at her at all. She sighed, irritated without knowing quite why. She wanted to get this over with as much as Haney did. If it was Hector he was waiting for, then he ought to be tapping his watch at him, not her. She assumed Hector had gone to talk to the Wichita cops, but she sure as hell wasn't going to turn around and crane her neck to look for him—look into all those faces she could feel staring at the back of her head. *There she is. The last one. The sole survivor.*

Then he was back beside her, easing himself carefully onto the flimsy metal chair. There was someone with him. He'd brought one of the *cops* up here?

But it was Zach Vincent. For a second she felt at a loss. It was one of those utterly mysterious things Hector did every now and then. She saw the logic in it—

the connection with Eddy, the only survivor who wasn't here. Actually, she was glad Zach was sitting here. She should have thought of it herself.

He gave her a little nod, a half smile, and she realized she was staring at him. She turned her face to the front. *Let's get this show on the road.*

Apparently it had been Hector they were waiting for. The young minister who'd been standing back beside the casket, looking content to wait there forever, stepped to the lectern and unhurriedly arranged his Bible and his notes.

She thought maybe he'd be okay. She liked his manner. At first she hadn't wanted a minister at all. But Haney had asked her who'd give the eulogy, or did she intend to put her sister in the ground without any words at the graveside at all? It was easier to cave to convention than to make some pointless big deal out of it. She'd turned all that stuff over to Haney, and it hadn't gone badly so far. The brief service at the funeral home chapel hadn't been too bad, and she'd been behind a screen, where nobody could see her.

"Jocelyn Wellington was twenty-eight years old," the young minister began. "She was the daughter of Rafael and Maria Wellington, of Sand Creek. She was born here in Sand Creek and lived her first eighteen years here.

"Jocelyn—or Jo, the name by which those close to her knew her—was a popular girl, a pretty and energetic girl, well liked by her classmates and her teachers and all who knew her. She was an athlete, winning high school letters in tennis and swimming, and playing on the school's basketball team. And she was also a very intelligent girl, a member of the Sand Creek High School gifted education program."

Jes waited nervously for him to say something about what a waste it was, but he didn't, and she relaxed a little, felt some of her irritation drain away. She was pretty sure he wasn't going to try to turn Jo into a "religious girl," along with all the rest. Jes had been to funerals at which people who'd been proud of being skeptical and irreligious their whole lives had been "converted" by their eulogists into crypto-Christians. But she was beginning to think she could trust this guy.

Most of what he was saying could have come from the *Intelligenser* obit—or from nearly anybody in the crowd after reading the obit, which was full of things like "Along with her twin sister, Jes, Jocelyn was a member of . . ." and so on. It reminded her why she and Jo had agreed not to go out for each other's favorite sport, despite the arguments of coaches and other students. But the minister seemed to agree that Jo ought to have her own eulogy.

She relaxed a little more. She hadn't even realized how tense she was. The next troublesome point would be when he got to the survivors, but none of it seemed quite as important as it had that morning.

The *Intelligenser* hadn't even mentioned Eddy's existence—something she planned to remember for a long time—but the question of survivors was really a technical one in her mind, a matter of newspaper style.

If you named someone in an obit, you had to say where he or she lived. If with the deceased, you said, "at home" or "of the home." Otherwise, you named the city or town. In this case, that was tricky. The clerk putting together the normal obit info to go with Annie's story had called her to talk about the problem. There was the question of what "the home" was. If the apartment, then it should be "a sister, Jesamyn, of Sand Creek." But then what about Eddy? *Of the home? Of Wichita? Of the Wichita Children's Home?*

The semester she'd interned, Jes had spent a couple of weeks writing obits, when the regular obit writer was on vacation, and the inflexible rules of style had bothered her, as they did most beginning reporters, when they got out and worked on a real newspaper. She'd interned in Topeka, and the paper there had actually been pretty generous. They'd allowed the names of grandparents to be included, along with those of parents and siblings and the current spouse, as well as the number of children and grandchildren.

But that was it. If someone's only known relative was a cousin or an aunt or a nephew, and the two had lived their entire lives together, it didn't matter. Lacking any of the approved kinship categories, the style was "No survivors."

That was the thing that had bothered Jes, even in cases where there were no known relatives at all. She'd argued it very seriously with one of the copy editors one night. "There are always *some* survivors," she'd said. "It's not like the whole world has died."

Ruminating, she almost missed the part of the eulogy she'd been waiting for. ". . . her twin sister, Jesamyn, and her infant son, Edward," she heard the minister say.

Yeah. That was fine. She mainly hadn't wanted the name Staircase used, although it was Eddy's real, honest-to-God, birth-certificate name. It wasn't because she didn't like it—quite the contrary; she thought of it as his true name, in the way Susie had turned out to be the dog's true name. It was because of that that it shouldn't be his public name.

The minister was reading from a small book she hadn't noticed, not the Bible. " 'Whither shall I go then from Thy Spirit? Or whither shall I go then from Thy presence? If I climb up into the heaven, Thou art there. If I go down to hell, Thou art there also. If I take the wings of the morning and remain in the uttermost parts of the sea, even there also shall Thy hand lead me, and Thy right hand shall hold me.' "

She didn't quite understand what it meant. Maybe it was only the graceful language that made the tears try to burst suddenly into the corners of her eyes. She blinked twice, managed to hold them back. Hector, in his mysterious way, pushed a handkerchief into her hand. She refused it the way he'd refused her hand, getting out of the car, but on second thought, she grabbed his hand and held onto it, never looking at him. She doubted he'd ever looked at her. He'd just known she might need a handkerchief right then.

When it was over, she let out a breath and released his hand.

"Not too bad for a Protestant," Hector said in her ear, and she gave a sharp, involuntary laugh that came very near to hysterics, requiring another act of will to cut it off.

"Keep that up and they'll need a second coffin," she muttered back to him. But she felt a lot better, a lot more herself.

Haney was there, holding a white plastic bag. A line of people was forming behind him. She looked up at the mortician, baffled by the bag.

"You're gonna have to stand up now," Hector said.

"Your memory book," Haney explained. "And a few copies of the program, plus some copies of the newspaper notices. A few other things."

She nodded, taking the bag from him, and stood up, holding it in front of her, a kind of shield. But she could get through this. This was the last thing.

She stood quietly as they came up one by one, patting her shoulder, giving her quick embraces, quick little kisses on the cheek, murmured condolences that she mostly didn't hear, but responded to with murmurs of her own, sounds of thanks. She'd been afraid of having to rebuff offers to visit her, bring her food, that kind of thing. But no one offered. She knew it wasn't because of Jo—it was because they all knew she'd refuse. It pleased her, but at the same time, in some irrational way, it didn't. It made her feel lonely, even knowing that she'd chosen the loneliness.

It should have been obvious to him from what he'd read in the casebook, but it had never even occurred to him that the casket would be closed. Of course it was. He felt like an idiot standing there, holding the little wooden box in his hands, even as far away as he was, between two of the cars parked along the road. He should have gone to the funeral home in the first place and given it to the sister.

But he'd have had to tell her not to look inside—

which was stupid—or explain the contents. And who knew how she'd react to that? She might just give them to Jerry. Or Hector. Maybe Hector would be the best person to give them to. He couldn't decide. He'd been too fixed on putting them in the coffin.

He didn't have to figure it out right now, today. He'd have a little time. Jerry knew he was there, but he wasn't doing anything about it, just watching the crowd. Burton was on the other side, so apparently he was working the case with Jerry. Well, it made sense. It was stupid to feel bad about it, like you were seeing your girlfriend with another guy or something. Burton would be going back to California, after all. And it wasn't very likely he'd ever work with Jerry again himself.

He couldn't hear what the minister was saying from here, but he was pleased that so many people had turned out for Celia. *Jocelyn.* He kept doing that. He could see Hector's white hair, up at the front, a little higher than everyone around him. There was a woman on one side of him—that would be the sister—and someone else on the other side, some other relative not mentioned in the obit.

He took a step backward, clear of the cars, preparing to return to his own car, which he'd left on the street, as soon as the service was over. As he took another short step, there was a sudden rustling movement nearby, and he saw a bird fluttering in the grass only a few feet away. He frowned, watching it flutter in a ragged circle, as if one of its wings were broken. Had one of the cars run over it somehow?

Lassiter was suddenly stymied. It was the kind of problem he couldn't walk away from. He had to solve it. But how, in the middle of everything else? Try to capture it without hurting it further, try to find a vet? Or maybe somebody in the crowd of mourners . . .

Then he saw the depression in the soft earth and understood. As if realizing it, the bird began fluttering more urgently, circling away from the nest, trying to draw him that way.

"I won't bother them," he said softly to her. But of course it didn't reassure her. He backed slowly away, along the row of parked cars, until finally he crossed some invisible line and she became suddenly unhurt and lifted a foot or so into the air, on two good wings, to swoop back to the nest.

A car door opened, and he looked up to see that the mourners were dispersing. He ought to be gone.

He looked toward the casket and saw Hector standing beside the sister, who remained seated. The third person had disappeared. She appeared to be speaking to a man who was handing her something. A line was forming behind him.

As Lassiter started to turn away, she stood up.

Of course it wasn't Celia. It was the twin sister. He'd worked so long on the case, but he'd never really found out much about the real woman—*Jocelyn*—only about Celia, who had a brother somewhere back in New Mexico, and a twin sister. He hadn't believed that story, but he believed in that woman. *Twins*. He liked thinking it all might be true—it was a story he liked better than the story Burton told . . . or the ones on the videotapes. . . .

He watched her a moment more, and then turned and headed for his car. He didn't know why seeing the sister should excite him this way. It felt like a break in a case, suddenly seeing the right path, knowing you were on the verge of the solution.

He needed sleep, that was it. He needed to get his head clear again. Because she *wasn't* Celia. She was a different person entirely, and really had nothing to do with anything.

Still . . .

You heard things about twins. Just superstitions . . .

He needed sleep.

But sliding behind the wheel, fumbling with the keys, he didn't feel sleepy at all. He was full of energy and some kind of inexplicable optimism.

28

"So why *did* you go in?" she asked.

Zach sighed. She was looking out through his kitchen door at the rear door of the apartment opposite. She wanted to know about that night, of course, and he'd been describing it the way he had two or three times already, to the cops, to Annie Babicki. He almost had it memorized.

"I should have just come back here and called the cops," he said automatically. But then—maybe because of the way Eddy squirmed in his arms, as if in protest—he added, "It was because of the crying. I mean—the *way* he started crying right then, when the door came open, and I could hear better." *You had to be there,* he thought.

She took a drink from the can of Dr Pepper he'd given her and nodded.

"You couldn't walk away from it," she said.

He was silent for a moment. "That's exactly right."

She turned back from the screen, took a final drink, tilting the can high, then looking around for the trash and tossing it in.

"Want to see upstairs?" he asked. When she'd arrived, she'd stood outside, looking at the other apartment, and when she'd come in at last she'd handed him the baby, then asked if his place was the same as the other, inside.

He'd given her a quick tour of the downstairs. He'd thought she might not want to look inside the bedroom, but she'd stood at the open door looking in for a long time, as if she could see her sister's body there.

Of course, his bedroom didn't look anything like the other one had. He'd been on the verge of saying, *Hers was neater,* but stopped himself in time. Actually, he'd straightened it up a little, just in case, and was glad he had. But he also knew she wasn't really looking at what was there.

She looked at him distantly, as if not having caught what he'd asked, then shook her head. "I've bothered you enough. I just wanted to—"

"No," he said. "It's no bother. The only reason I went in the bedroom . . . I was coming back down the stairs. I meant to go to the bathroom to find a wet rag." He stopped, seeing that she was listening politely, looking like a reporter. She wasn't interested in that. "It was Eddy's room," he said lamely, nodding toward the stairs.

"I know. I'm glad you did it."

"It was stupid."

She smiled. "We had that conversation already."

They were both silent. Eddy rested lightly against his shoulder, not fidgeting, seeming content.

"Have you had anything to eat today?" he asked.

She looked at him blankly, then shook her head. "Too busy. Too much . . ."

"Yeah. I was just thinking about having something to eat myself." He glanced at the icebox, trying to remember if there was actually any food in there. He didn't think so. "There's this little café over on Thirteenth," he said. "Over on the other side of the parks. I like to—"

"I should be getting back," she said.

He nodded, thinking this was when he should hand Eddy back to her. But he didn't, and she didn't reach for him. "It's about time for him to eat, too," he said. "But I don't have anything."

"I do. In the car. They gave me a bunch of stuff. Jo's stuff, mostly. Do you want to—?" She stopped. "Oh. Sorry. You just said—"

"I could feed him at the café," he said. "It's a nice walk. Not very far. And the food's good. I mean the grown-up food. And they've got high chairs." He hesitated, suddenly feeling self-conscious. "But you probably want to get him home."

She shrugged. "If he needs to eat . . ." After a pause she said, "It's such a nice day. I thought it would rain, but it didn't."

He nodded. "It's really not far. I could carry him. No trouble at all."

She looked at him for the first time. "I've got a stroller." She said it as if it were the solution to some difficult problem they'd been discussing.

A block up, along the river boulevard, was the big old turn-of-the-century home everyone called "Crumm Castle," which had sat empty on the corner for years while the owners and the city, which wanted to preserve it, haggled over the price. Now it was a bed-and-breakfast, with fresh paint and trim. They talked about it and then, crossing the bridge, about the derelict park on the other side—Oak Park, whose rest rooms had been known as a nighttime meeting place for gays, the site of frequent police busts, now and then of some respectable citizen who claimed he'd only stopped to use the facilities on his way home from a party or from the swing shift at Boeing. Perhaps tired of such controversies, the city had chained off the entrance roads and let the park grow wild— officially an "urban wilderness area." Anyone could walk past the chains, of course, but the official pretense was that there wasn't any problem there anymore.

On the other side of the river they grew silent, following the curve of the river branch through North Riverside Park, the smallest and oldest of the several parks in the U-shaped peninsula made by the river branch. It hadn't been a hot day, and it was even getting a little cool. Zach wondered if they ought to have brought a small blanket for Eddy. If they stayed long at the café, it could be dark by the time they walked back.

"This was Hector's idea," Jes said suddenly. "I didn't even think about it. I would have just gone and gotten him and . . ." She shrugged.

"You had a lot of other things to think about. Anyway, it's no big deal. I'm just somebody who happened to be there. I mean, I've got no . . ." He shook his head, looking out at the river.

"You're important to Eddy," she said. "You deserve at least to know how things are."

He waited, but she was silent long enough that he wondered if he was supposed to know already what she meant, if there was something he'd missed.

"I'm kind of a recluse," she said. "I live alone with my dog. Nobody comes into my house. I mean, nobody. Not even Hector. Not even other women." She was silent again for a second, then added, "I'm not going to try to explain it to you."

"You don't have to . . ."

"It was hard to decide to take Eddy in. I know that sounds . . ."

"I understand. I mean, I'm kind of a recluse myself. I—"

"I just wanted you to know that it isn't that I don't want you to see him anymore. Maybe there's some way . . . over here . . ."

"Sure," he said, trying to sound more casual than he felt. His relief surprised him. "Whatever you want to do is fine. I'll be glad—"

"I saw you."

"What?"

"I saw you with him. When I was there. I saw you feeding him, and talking to him. You talked to him like—like you thought he was going to answer."

"Sometimes I think he's getting ready to," Zach said. He pursed his lips and then said, "That's how his mother talked to him. I'd see them outside sometimes, you know. Sitting on the porch, something like that. She'd talk to him like that, seriously, and he'd watch her. He looked like he understood."

"Yes." After a silence, she asked, "What were you talking to him about?"

He laughed. "A program I'm having trouble with. I thought he might have some ideas. Maybe he does. Unfortunately, he can't talk yet to tell me."

"I wonder what she talked to him about," Jes said.

He bridled, thinking she was testing him, like the cops, then realized she was just talking out loud. "I don't know," he said. "About her own problems, I guess. Sounds like she had plenty."

When she didn't say anything, he asked, "Does that name mean anything to you? Celia Staircase? It seems so—"

"It's from when we were kids. An old Indian story. Kind of like a fairy tale."

He looked at her, but she didn't look back.

"I guess it's an old Indian story," she said. "Our mother was part Indian . . . She said she was. We didn't really know. But she told us these stories . . ." She shrugged.

"What was this one about?"

She didn't answer right away. "It was about two little girls—twins, I guess. We always assumed they were twins like us. They had a brother who was a lot older, who sort of ran away from home when they were little, and then . . . they got in some trouble and he came back and rescued them. Their names were Celia and Delia Staircase, and his name was Eddy. I don't know where the names came from. My mother probably made them up. She might have made up the whole story, just for us."

"That was the older brother you wished you had," Zach said.

"Yeah."

He thought about that—about Jo giving her baby that name. And according to Laurie Cox, it was his real name, the one on his birth certificate. And she'd lived under it herself—under such an odd name when she was hiding, trying not to attract attention. Maybe she'd thought it would have some protective power. Magic.

She looked at him suddenly, caught him looking, but smiled. The way he'd expected her sister to smile that first day he'd seen her.

"This is a very nice walk," she said. "I'm getting hungry. How far is it?"

He laughed. "Not far. Three or four blocks."

She nodded, looking ahead, then leaned forward to look at Eddy's face.

"He's asleep," she said.

"He'll wake up for the food. He likes to eat."

"That's good. 'Cause I've got a hell of a lot of food. With that and the other stuff, I was lucky I had room in the car for *him*. And there's still the stuff from the apartment." She shook her head. "He's got a lot of baggage for such a little guy."

Zach nodded, wondering if she'd put it just that way on purpose. She *was* a writer, after all.

29

"Turn here," Diamond said.

He turned the way she was pointing without really thinking about it. He wasn't even sure where they were. He'd told her he needed to talk to her about something, and that he'd pay her to listen to him while they drove—and he'd meant all that, but they'd been driving a long time now and he hadn't said anything at all. He'd nearly forgotten she was there.

She was pissed off. He'd heard it in her voice, and he could see it in her profile when he glanced at her. He was supposed to be conciliatory, to apologize . . . but for what? He was paying for her time, for christsake. Why did she care if he was talking or not? Wouldn't she rather be here than . . . ?

He clamped his jaw, firmly cutting off the anger before it could build any further. What difference did it make to him, after all, how she felt about it? She wasn't a friend. Not really. She'd just been the only one he'd been able to think of that he could tell it to without making things even more complicated. He'd typed it all up on Kay's computer, at his mother's house, before realizing he had no way of printing it out. So he'd put it on a disk, to take it somewhere. Not to the office, of course. One of those photocopying places that had computers. But once he'd gotten in the car, he'd known it wasn't enough, because he hadn't really *explained* it. He'd thought if he could tell it to someone—someone who'd listen and believe him and make an effort to understand . . .

But he hadn't been able to think of anyone. The obvious one was Jerry, but that was too complicated. Same thing with the sister, although that was an idea that he couldn't quite let go of, because he kept thinking of it as talking to Celia herself, which was who he really wanted to talk to, because he suspected she was the only one who'd have a chance of understanding it—which was crazy, of course, but it was all crazy. It was like a snake chasing its tail, over and over again, in his mind. But not a neat circle, a slithering, crooked shape that never held still—

"*Stop!*" Diamond's hand gripped his arm. He hit the brake, realizing he'd been about to drive through a stop sign he hadn't seen in the dark. Twelfth and Bitting. It took a moment for a map to form in his mind, to make sense. He was used to seeing this intersection from Bitting, not from Twelfth. Immediately to their right was a little bridge crossing the smaller branch of the river. On the other side of that, after only a couple of blocks, Bitting ended at Thirteenth Street, by that little neighborhood park just across the river from North High.

She was peering toward the park, to their left, and as he glanced at her, she pointed again, and said, "Pull in right there."

It was the entrance to the park drive, which was chained off a few yards farther in. As he turned into it, his headlights illuminated a half dozen black plastic garbage bags slumping against the sagging chain, a couple of old tires stacked to one side. It seemed fitting.

He expected her to be surprised by the chain, but she wasn't. "This is good," she said. "Turn off your lights."

It should have been obvious to him, but it surprised him when she slid closer to him and began feeling for his zipper. He jerked back and put out his arm to block her.

"That's not what I—"

"Yes, it is," she said. "You just don't know it. Leave it to me."

"I wanted to talk."

"So talk."

But of course he couldn't. Nor could he seem to prevent what she was doing, even though it really wasn't something he wanted. Even the feel of it was distant, disconnected from him, as if it were someone else's body. How easy it was to slip into that again, after all these years. Just go off into your mind and wait for it to be over. Like riding a bicycle. You never forgot.

He looked out the window at the dark trees. Like the little woods behind the barn. And the cedars behind his mother's house. Strange. Had he ever really been in control of anything in his life, or had he always just been bouncing along passively, absorbing whatever happened to him? Going to college . . . but then quitting to be a cop . . . then getting married to his partner . . . Had he ever really chosen any of it himself? What had he ever done because he wanted to do it, except hide?

"You're going to have to help a *little*," Diamond said impatiently.

Help? How? It didn't make any sense. There was movement in the rearview mirror and he glanced at it, saw a young couple, the woman pushing a stroller, the bearded man holding a sleeping baby. They were both tall and thin. The woman leaned to look past her husband at the car parked in the dark entrance with its motor on and its lights off, and Lassiter thought for one crazy second that it was Celia. She wasn't really dead at all, just out walking her baby, with . . . who? That mysterious brother? Her eyes even seemed to meet his for a second, as if she could see his in the mirror. But then the man said something, and she straightened up, and he heard them both laugh, and then they were gone. Lassiter knew what they thought, of course. This was Oak Park. He didn't mind. He thought it was funny, too.

Diamond raised her head again and sighed. "You really aren't interested, are you?"

He looked down at her, not understanding the question for a second, then shook his head. She sat up, and he rearranged himself, zipped up.

"Well," she said. "I tried."

"I know. Thanks."

She laughed, leaned forward to look at him, just the way the woman in the mirror had, and shook her head. "Lassiter, baby, I think you're seriously fucked up some way. Is that right?"

"Yes."

She nodded. "Well, we know one thing I can't do for you. So, you said you wanted to talk. That's cool. You can talk to me. You can tell me anything. I won't snitch. I promise. Cross my heart."

He looked at her, wondering if that was the truth, thinking of the confessions she'd heard and passed on to him. Did she always say that to them? *Cross my heart.*

But it didn't matter her. The point of telling her—of telling someone—was so she could relate it to the others afterward.

"I want to go somewhere else to talk," he said.

"Someplace you're more comfortable."

He nodded.

"Then let's go."

Being a victim doesn't make you the good guy. That got into his head somehow, like a song, and wouldn't go away. It was something he'd said once, to some perp who'd been complaining about how he'd been mistreated, what a hard life he'd had, something like that. Lassiter didn't remember the details, only that it had made him mad, and he'd said that, and the guy had looked at him like he had no idea what in the hell he was talking about.

"Is this where you live?" Diamond asked. She was obviously impressed by the place—not just the house but the tree-hidden neighborhood—and that made him feel vaguely ashamed. He shook his head.

"It's my mother's house."

"Your *mother*?"

"She doesn't live here any more. She's in a nursing home. She has Alzheimer's."

"Oh, I'm sorry, Lassiter."

He shrugged. "I guess we'll have to use the kitchen," he said. "It's the only room with two chairs."

"Can I look around a little?"

"Sure."

She seemed fascinated by the large empty rooms, and of course by the forest shutting off the nominal front of the house. "Nobody can ever see you here," she said wistfully, staring into the dark branches pressing against the big living room window. "It's all hidden and private."

He followed her up the short flight of carpeted stairs to the upper level, enjoying her interest in the house. He should have anticipated her reaction to his mother's bedroom.

"There's a shower in there," she said, coming out of the bathroom, as if she'd never imagined any such thing as a bedroom with its own bathroom, containing a shower. It struck Lassiter how much it was like the motel rooms on south Broadway, only bigger and fancier. More like the rooms in Celeste's videos. She could easily have shot one here. His being here with Diamond was like the beginning of one of them. But they weren't the right people for it. There was nowhere for the script to go from here.

"We could talk here," Diamond said. She spoke timidly, as if expecting to be rejected. He glanced around at the room, shrugged.

"Sure, if you want."

She smiled. "You mind if I take a shower first?" Her expression grew quickly serious. "I'll be quick."

He shrugged again. "I don't mind. There are towels in the cabinet next to the sink."

She kicked off her heels and began stripping her clothes off.

"I'll go outside," Lassiter said. He turned toward the bedroom door.

"Oh, don't be silly. Sit down."

He hesitated, then sat on the little chair at his mother's dresser, not looking at her. He saw he'd been wrong. There was another chair in the room, a reading chair with a gooseneck lamp behind it. He realized he had no idea what his mother had used that chair for, if she'd ever sat in it at all. There weren't any books in the room. She hadn't been a reader, even when she still could have been. Then he remembered the little TV, which he'd taken down to his basement room. That's what the chair had been for.

The water in the shower began running and then the sliding door closed. Diamond's few articles of clothing—a short skirt, a top and a pair of black panties—were stacked neatly on the corner of the bed nearest the bathroom. He felt another surge of guilt and shame. He didn't even know where Diamond lived, where she'd come from. What if he just went ahead and gave her the house? Would that be simpler than a will? He wasn't sure. He imagined just handing her the keys, telling her it was hers, leaving her here with it. He'd have to give her the car, too, but that was okay. He could walk.

He glanced up as she came out of the bathroom, scrubbing at one ear with the towel she carried. He looked away again automatically, then decided to look at her after all. She didn't mind. And he wasn't looking at her that way. He was looking at her the way he'd looked at so many other female bodies—at crime scenes, in the coroner's lab, in slides at trial. Her brown skin glistened a little, but there were a few whitish places—an appendix scar, a streak along her rib cage, beneath her left breast, that might also have been from an operation, and a puckered place on her side, right next to her other breast, that looked to him like a burn scar. Too big to be a cigarette.

"Like what you see?"

She was smiling at him.

"What's that scar?" He nodded toward her right side.

She looked down, raised her arm to look at it. "That?" She was silent a moment, and then said, "Don't remember. Long time ago, when I was a kid. Some accident, I guess."

Another liar, like Margo Gilkey and Celia Staircase and . . . all the others. Maybe that was how they recognized one another. By the lies.

"You mind if I lie down while we talk?" she asked. "It's just so good to get off my feet. I'm thinkin' about not charging you." Her expression changed. " 'Course, I can't really afford—"

"I know. Time is money. Sure. Lie down if you want. Just try not to fall asleep while I'm talking." He realized for the first time that he really was going to tell her about it. He hadn't known until that moment that there was any doubt of that in his mind—but there had been. Now there wasn't.

"Don't worry," she said. She lay down and turned on her side, her head propped on her elbow, ready to listen.

"Maybe you ought to put your clothes back on,"

She glanced at the pile of clothing at the foot of the bed. "My uniform? Not until I have to."

He nodded, understanding. "You want a robe or something? I think there's a—"

"No, I'm fine. And anytime you feel like joining me . . ."

He looked away, was silent for a moment, then said, "You remember that woman I was looking for? The one you thought might have been . . ."

"The one who got murdered in her apartment. Sure. That's really something. Who you think killed her?"

He looked at her, pursed his lips, decided there was no other way. "I killed her."

She kept looking at him, not saying anything, but he saw the change in her eyes.

"I didn't mean to. I mean, I didn't *want* to. I don't even remember it. I wish to Christ it hadn't . . ." He shook his head. "I liked her," he said. "I don't know what happened, exactly. I had some kind of . . . see, I have these . . . episodes . . . seizures, I guess. But nothing like that ever . . ." He stopped, because it wasn't true that nothing like that had ever happened before. There'd been the thing in Loomis's office. He shook his head.

"Why are you . . . why are you telling me?" Her voice came out in a whisper, and he realized she was frightened. Of course she was.

"You don't have to be afraid of me," he said. "I just needed to tell someone, you know? I mean, to *say* it. To try to explain it. I don't really know if I can. I wrote a statement in a computer downstairs. I was going to . . . Never mind. I couldn't explain it that way, but I thought maybe if I *told* someone."

"Why me?"

He thought about that. "I couldn't think of anyone else. That's sort of pathetic, isn't it? No offense, but . . ."

She sat up slowly, keeping her eyes on him, and wrapped her arms around her knees. "So what you gonna do?"

"Well, like I said, I wrote out the statement . . . I'm not going to get away with it. I mean, I don't *want* to get away with it. I'm a cop, after all." He laughed suddenly, thinking that was funny. Why hadn't he noticed how funny that was before? Maybe saying it out loud. Things sounded different when you said them out loud, to someone else. That was why—

She bolted, sliding off the side of the bed, staying in a kind of crouch as she grabbed her clothing. The skirt and top fell to the floor at the foot of the bed. Clutching the black panties, she ran out the bedroom door, staying low as if afraid of being shot.

It surprised him so much, he sat just looking at the door, listening to her steps fade quickly away down the long hallway. Then he frowned and patted his pants pocket. The car keys were there. She wasn't really going anywhere. Except maybe to one of the neighbors' houses. He thought about how that would look—a naked black streetwalker fleeing a cop's house—then realized how stupid it was to care about something like that, under the circumstances.

He didn't even know if either of them would take her in. She was his responsibility.

He stood and gathered up her clothing and shoes, and went out to the hallway. He took a look in each of the rooms as he passed, but he was pretty sure she'd head for the garage.

When he got there, he found the door from the house to the garage standing half open. The door of his car was also open. She'd looked for keys, hadn't found any. Suddenly concerned in a different way, he looked in the rear seat, but the shotgun was still there. He glanced around the garage but couldn't tell whether anything that might serve as a weapon was missing. Just to make sure, he stooped and looked under the car, checked out a couple of other places where she could be hiding, then went on out through the door that led to the backyard and stood at the edge of the concrete circle, trying to imagine how she'd have seen it, where she'd have gone from here.

The trees might have looked like a safe way to go, although they'd be almost literally impenetrable for a naked woman, unless she happened to find one of the paths. And even those wouldn't be easy.

"Diamond?" He called her name three times, a little louder each time, but there was no reply. "I'm sorry for scaring you. You really don't have to be afraid of me. I won't hurt you. I just wanted to tell you about it. Really. I've got your clothes and shoes here. Why don't you come put them on, and I'll take you back to Broadway? Or wherever you want to go. And I'll still pay you."

He put the clothing down on the concrete, where she might be able to see it, if she was near enough. Then, as an afterthought, he fished out his car keys, held them high with one hand and jangled them, then tossed them on top of the clothing. "I'll go back inside," he called out. "You can come and take the car. I swear I'm not going to hurt you. I like you. You know I do."

"You said you liked her."

The voice came from farther back in the trees than he would have expected. Maybe she'd found a path. But then there was a sound of dry branches snapping and a small cry like a sob. She was pushing her way through.

He remembered a time when he'd tried that, not long after they'd moved here. He'd been about twelve or thirteen, and fully clothed. He'd given up after a few hard-won feet, and every exposed part of his skin, plus much of the skin of his torso and legs, had been scratched and bruised for days afterward. Of course, he hadn't had the incentive of his father following him. Maybe if that had been the case, he wouldn't have stopped. Instead he'd explored enough to discover a couple of paths before the necessity had arisen.

He walked to the beginning of one of them—the same one that led to the rock beneath which the tape cartridges and their contents were hidden. He hadn't included that in his statement because he wasn't sure he cared about the stuff being recovered, and he hadn't wanted to get sidetracked on trying to work that out.

The sound of Diamond's movement had stopped, so he called out again: "You can't get all the way through, Diamond. You'll just hurt yourself more. And there's no need for it. There's a path over here, where I am. Head for my voice. I'll move closer."

There was no response, no sound of movement. Maybe she'd collapsed or fainted or something. Maybe she was seriously hurt. Some of the branches nearest the trunks were hard and thick enough to pierce flesh.

A greater silence fell suddenly, and he realized he'd been hearing the wind blowing somewhere overhead, and that it had stopped. He glanced at the sky but could see only black. "I think there's a storm coming," he called out. But there was still no sound.

He raised an arm to protect his eyes and moved into the tunnel of the path, trying to listen for further sounds of her movement, beyond the sounds of his own. Every few seconds he stopped suddenly to listen, but there was nothing. When he judged he was about as far in as she was, he stopped and called out, "Diamond! Where are you? Are you hurt? This is foolish. I swear to God I won't hurt you. I just want to help you and take you where you want to go, that's all. Please believe me. I'm not a killer. Whatever happened, it was some kind of crazy thing . . ." He stopped, not sure where he was going with that, then added, "I've got your clothes here with me."

There was another silence, and he was thinking about pushing straight into the trees himself, trying to find her. But then he heard the crackling begin again, punctuated by loud snaps and occasional gasps of pain. She was near enough that he could hear her crying, a low, steady sobbing that tore at his heart.

She wasn't going to come to him, and she wasn't going to turn around. There wasn't much point in that, anyway, because she was about halfway through. That seemed incredible to him. But surely she must be exhausted by now. Eventually she'd come to a place where she couldn't move on. Maybe she already had. She'd be trapped on all sides, held prisoner by the hard fingers of the trees, coming at her from all directions. She'd panic. And injure herself if she hadn't already. She might lose an eye, impale herself.

"I can get you out of here," he called. "I know the paths. I can—"

He heard her start moving again, more slowly. And not toward him or the house, but not straight out, as she had before. She seemed to be moving slantwise, and then he understood that she was trying to find his own path, somewhere ahead of him. He decided that was good. The main thing was to get her out of here now, even if it was on the other side. He stayed where he was, so as not to seem to be trying to cut her off, and there were little silences as she stopped to listen. He didn't say anything. He thought about moving the other way, back toward the house, but decided it would be better to make no sound at all.

Then he heard her moving more easily, more quickly, and knew she'd found the path. He began moving again himself, as quietly as possible, not trying to gain on her. Now he only wanted to be sure she got out. Presumably she'd be able to find help in one of the houses out there beyond the trees. It was a neighborhood of young married people with children, mostly, not a dangerous area.

He began to glimpse the glow of the streetlights beyond, and gradually became aware of the shapeless dark form between himself and the light. He was a little closer than he'd thought—close enough that he should be able to hear her crying again. Apparently she'd stopped. He stopped to let her regain her lead. Then he saw the form ahead of him move suddenly more quickly, as if propelled forward, and realized she'd reached the street. He began moving a little faster himself. He wasn't really trying to catch her. He just wanted to see that she was all right, that she found help.

And then there were headlights—a car passing by— and they stopped. He moved forward warily, nearing the curb himself. He stopped as soon as he could make out what was going on.

She was standing by the car, her arms folded over her breasts, wearing the black panties, from which a torn flap hung down on the side he could see. The driver's door was standing open, but he didn't spot the driver immediately. Then the trunk lid popped open, and he saw the man leaning into the trunk, coming out with what looked like a blanket. He closed the trunk and moved to the woman, who began chattering incoherently, pointing toward the trees.

"You're safe now," the man said, and Lassiter rec-

ognized the voice. He drew a little farther back into
the trees. What was he doing here?

Burton draped the blanket around her and then
held the rear door open for her to get in. Closing the
door, he raised one arm, holding what Lassiter realized only belatedly was a battery-powered spot. The
light came on suddenly, just as Lassiter began to retreat, and swept the trees. If it had been aimed directly
at him, he'd have been exposed. But he was able to
pull back, drop to his stomach, and as the light passed
over he rolled automatically to one side, freeing his
holster. But he didn't reach for it. He wasn't going to
shoot anyone. He hadn't had to shoot anyone since
that day by the farm pond, all those years ago, and
he wasn't going to start again now. Burton didn't even
have his own weapon out. It was that fact, somehow,
that made Lassiter sure the L.A. cop knew exactly
where he was, and that it was him the woman had
fled from. But that he didn't expect Lassiter to shoot
at him.

He could stand up right now and walk out of the
trees, into that light—and it would all be over. He
knew it was what he ought to do.

But he wasn't ready. Maybe if it had been Jerry out
there, or Loomis or . . . Hector. *Hector.* That felt right.
It wasn't what had happened between them . . . or not
just that, anyway. It was that Hector had known her.

Burton's light went off, startling him, and he heard
the car door close. He squinted, saw Burton's profile
at the wheel, talking into something, a mike or cell
phone. Then the car pulled away.

Lassiter lay there for a moment, feeling almost too
tired to get up, but then made himself rise and begin
fighting his way back along the path, half crouching.
Burton might be waiting for him. More likely, though,
he'd wait for Jerry or Loomis—whoever he'd called.

For the first time he began to feel anxious. Now
that he knew what to do, he might be prevented. And
the anxiety made him try to rush, try to push through.
He had to pause and get control of it before it turned

into panic. When he finally made his way back to the edge of the concrete turnaround, it was empty and dark—nothing was any different.

He couldn't spot Burton's car anywhere along the interior road, but he kept his headlights off and drove slowly away from the entry Burton would most likely use, going halfway around the circle and out the other way. On the other side of the trees, he stopped, alert for movement. But there was nothing ahead, nothing in his mirror. Just the ordinary dark. He drove on slowly, to the nearest street that led to a bridge over the river, not turning on his headlights until he was at the stop sign. He was pretty sure no one was following him.

West of the river, he turned north on Amidon, the wide road that would take him to the bypass, and then to the interstate, and then to Sand Creek. He drove slowly, watching his mirror, but the road was dark and empty behind him, and at the entrance ramp he accelerated into the darkness ahead.

PART THREE

30

The sky over the city was blue and clear, but Majors could see that wasn't going to last. There was a hell of a storm coming in from the northwest. When he turned on the car radio, he wasn't surprised to hear them talking about it already. There'd been twisters on the ground to the west of Sand Creek, and the local stations were sending their spotters out.

Somehow because of that, he wasn't surprised to find Loomis already at the office. The lieutenant came out of his office as soon as Majors reached his cubicle, as if he'd been waiting for him.

"Anything new?" Loomis asked, stopping at the cubicle entrance as Majors sat down.

Obviously there was, Majors thought. It would have taken someone who knew him to notice, but Loomis was about as agitated as Majors had ever seen him.

Majors shook his head. "Mostly, we're still just trying to identify all the burglary vics. It's like pulling teeth getting those names out of the LAPD, now that she's dead. The fucking Art Theft Detail won't even return my calls. Davidson—"

"Wait," Loomis said. He disappeared for a moment, came back with a page torn from a spiral notepad. He handed it to Majors. "Got these last night from a guy I know out there. Almost forgot."

Majors scanned the three names, saw none he recognized, and put the sheet down, wondering what Loomis had called his friend about. He doubted it

was just to get these names he'd so quickly forgotten
about. "Thanks."

"What about Davidson?"

"Davidson? Oh, he's working it from the insurance
side. Trying to run down big payouts that fit the time
and location. Last I knew, Binkley was waiting for a
call-back from his FBI guy. You know, any contractors
who might have been in the area." He shrugged. *Jerking off.* He knew it and Loomis knew it.

He waited for Loomis to say whatever it was he
had to say.

"Any idea how to get hold of Burton?" Loomis
asked.

"I know his room number at the Airport Hilton."
That was it?

"Yeah, I've got that. I thought maybe . . . well . . ."
He looked off toward the row of narrow windows that
Majors could no longer see since they'd brought in the
cubicle dividers. "Gonna be a big storm, looks like."

Majors didn't say anything until Loomis looked at
him.

"If I hear from him, I'll tell him you're looking
for him," he said then. "Want me to tell him what
it's about?"

Loomis appeared to consider it, then shook his
head. "Just tell him I'd like to see him when he gets
a chance."

"I doubt I'll hear from him," Majors said. "Unless
he finds some of the stuff. Maybe that P.I.—"

"Yeah, that's a thought. He's at the same hotel.
Thanks."

Majors sat for a moment, staring at nothing, thinking. Something between Loomis and Burton. Something that Loomis didn't want to tell him about, but
that agitated him enough to ask his help in running
Burton down. Something he wanted to talk to Burton
about *right now.* And the L.A. cop was already out
and around. Still working on California time, probably.

Maybe Loomis had a lead on the stolen goods, but

then why not tell Majors? Or maybe it wasn't even a work thing. Maybe the guy Loomis had talked to in L.A., the one who'd given him the three names he'd forgotten to bring with him when he came out to greet Majors, had told him . . . what? Burton's mother had died, something like that. Something personal. Maybe the guy in L.A. had called Loomis, not the other way around.

That made sense. It was an easy way of disposing of it, deciding not to worry about it. And Loomis didn't want to say anything because it was personal. And he was agitated because it was bad news. Nobody liked to deliver bad news. Loomis had thought about passing it off to Majors, but hadn't.

He was thinking the way Floyd would think, and it all made sense. But he didn't believe it. And he didn't like it.

The night before, he'd had one of those dreams in which he was late for something—way late. And far from where he was supposed to be. He didn't remember the details, only that he hadn't been getting anywhere, which was always how it was in dreams like that.

It didn't take a psychiatrist to interpret that dream. He was treading water. He might as well still be dreaming. He sighed and looked again at the sheet of paper Loomis had left, the three new names. Obviously, it wasn't a dream. Only a nightmare.

31

*There was a gunshot and he jerked and tried to roll
away, but there was something in his way,* and he
twisted and fought to get to his feet, awakening as he
did, coming back to himself finally, half on and half
off the backseat of his car. There was a strange flickering light outside the window, fading, and then another crash of thunder, another lightning strike, and
he saw the wire fence beyond the ditch, everything
reversed, like the negative of a photo, and the field
beyond that, the wheat flattened here and there as if
some giant had passed through, and he heard for the
first time the loud drumming of rain against the car's
roof and windows.

He sat up and drew a deep breath. Where was he?
He peered out the window, looking for something in
the darkness, in what he remembered of the landscape
he'd glimpsed during the lightning flash, to give him
a clue.

He turned cold inside, sat up straight. *Had it happened again?* The sister . . . he'd been going to Sand
Creek. He swallowed, shivered, tried to probe for the
same kinds of pains—the stiffness, the bruises. He
wrapped his arms around himself and realized he
didn't have his holster on, didn't know where his
weapon was.

After a frantic few seconds, he found it folded
neatly on top of his jacket on the passenger seat in
front, and the sight of it reminded him of Diamond's
small mound of clothing, and it all came back. Not an

episode, just the grogginess of first awakening and finding himself in the car, in a strange place.

He didn't think it was night, just the storm. A big one. He could feel the car rock a little when the wind gusted. Somewhere out in the country, outside Sand Creek.

It had been raining already when he'd driven past her house, but not like this. Just sprinkles. And the house had been dark, the windows black, but there'd been a car in the drive. He'd gone twice around the block, then stopped at the curb some distance away, his lights out, from where he could see both doors, the big front porch and the little concrete side porch. He'd known then that nothing in the world could make him walk up to either of those doors, in the night and the rain, to stand on either porch and listen for the footsteps and watch the inner door open and look through the screen into those eyes.

He hadn't driven away so much as fled. To find someplace to hide and wait for daylight. Lost himself in the turns of country roads he'd never driven before but that had felt familiar and comforting in some crazy way . . .

He let out a ragged breath. And now it was day, but still dark.

There was another crash of lightning, very close and loud, but what made him cry out was the sudden sense of dark shapes moving just outside the window, trying to get at him—until he saw that they were the limbs of roadside trees, pressing the window on that side the way the cedars pressed against the front windows of his mother's house. He'd parked halfway in the broad, flat ditch, against the trees.

He needed to move. The ground beneath his car's wheels would be getting soft. He looked at his watch. Eight-thirty. How long had he slept? He had no idea. He'd picked up Diamond more than twelve hours ago, and he remembered everything since then, but he didn't know how long any of it had taken. It was possible he'd slept only three or four hours. He felt that way.

He slid to the other door and pushed it open, bracing against the rain and wind, nearly falling onto the road as he pulled himself out. It was a narrow, two-rutted dirt road, and the ruts were running with water, as were both ditches.

The rain was surprisingly warm. He found himself just wanting to stand in it, to close his eyes and let it wash over him, as if it could wash away everything he needed to get rid of, leave him fresh and clean. He imagined tearing off his clothes—the fresh clothing he'd put on before going to find Diamond, as if it were a date—and leaving them in a heap there on the road. Not even getting back into the car, leaving them and the gun, walking off into the rain, along the humped road. It almost seemed possible, a real way out. Except that the storm would end eventually, and daylight would come.

Still, he stood where he was, his eyes closed, not caring how wet he got. Why care about anything like that? Or about anything? Why think? There was nothing he wanted to think about. Nothing. You couldn't really blank your mind, not think, but he tried it anyway, as he had so many times before in his life. What came—something always came—was a taste of the dream . . . or of some dream . . . or maybe not a dream. Something good, something about Christmas. He could smell Christmas—that sharp pine smell, not the cedars but the pines of the farm, and that crisp snow smell. Downtown lights and snow falling—not Wichita but some smaller place . . . Holton? He didn't know. He'd been there, but it had been long ago, before he'd paid attention to things like the names of towns. He just knew there'd been the lights and the snow and that Christmas smell all around . . . and something in a store window . . . a manger scene maybe, or Santa's workshop, with the elves all doing the same thing over and over, the wrapped presents coming out of somewhere, moving and falling beneath a tree, and then back again, around again, the little hammers rising and falling . . .

And people all along the window, peering in, their breath making white clouds in the air, fogging the big window here and there, and children sitting up high on the shoulders of their parents . . . everybody laughing and happy. He'd been up there too, able to see because he was sitting . . .

On his father's shoulders. The memory made him open his eyes. *That* father. The one he never thought about, never let himself think about. The one who'd made him a wooden sled for Christmas and taken him sledding on some big hill near the farm—just that once, he thought—the two of them sledding together, the man hunched up on the little sled, one arm tight around the boy who clung to his neck, shrieking . . . and then the boy racing ahead of the man back up the hill, eager to go again . . . and thinking, without thinking at all, that they'd do it again, that there'd be other Christmases like that, other times . . .

He didn't know what had happened. There'd been obvious things—the drink, the failing farm . . . whatever it was that had happened between the man and woman . . . something so bad it was unfixable . . . the long, ugly war between them, in which the dog and himself were really only incidental casualties. What was the phrase? Collateral damage? Something like that. But none of it was enough. It was a puzzle missing too many pieces. He'd known that for most of his life, and had sworn off trying to put it together, so long ago he couldn't even remember when he'd done that—sworn off thinking about it, remembering it . . .

He turned around, feeling suddenly afraid, as if the unwanted memories might be coming up the road behind him, slipping up on him. And then he looked across the top of the car at the trees, and then the other way, at the field spreading away into a haze of more fields.

He screamed at it all. No words, just a shrill, ragged, rain-strangled scream that he himself could hardly hear above the wind and the rain and the rolling of

thunder, and that turned into a sob, a convulsion that
made him stagger, fall back against the side of the car,
roll around and pound on its roof with his fists, and
then put his head in his hands and cry the way he'd
cried in Loomis's office . . . but glad of it this time,
wanting it, wanting to vomit it all out, let it be washed
away by the twin rivers that ran along the road . . .

But eventually he ran down. Because that was what
happened. You screamed and cried, but in the end, if
you were still alive, it was all still there.

He got back into the car and slid beneath the wheel.
He was soaked, and he'd soon begin to feel chilled,
but there was nothing to be done about that except
start the car and turn on the heater. Immediately, the
windows began to fog, and he switched it to defrost,
then sat and waited for that to take effect.

Okay. It was a practical problem now, a matter of
logistics. He wanted to tell Celia's sister what had happened. He wanted to give her the stuff Celia had
stolen.

Anything else? He couldn't think of anything. Kay,
Jerry, Loomis—they'd all have to understand it as best
they could, from what Celia's sister told them afterward. And from his statement. Which they might already have, since they knew about his mother's house
now. That was a problem, because the tapes and the
other stuff were still under that concrete slab in the
cedars. But it was his kind of problem. He'd deal with
it when the time came. They wouldn't necessarily be
staking it out. The most obvious way was to take the
sister there, telling her about it as they drove, then
give her the stuff, then turn her loose . . . he'd give
her his car. He nodded to himself. The only real problem would be getting the stuff from the cedars. But
there'd be a way.

What about Hector? Anything he needed to do
there? He couldn't think what. Celia's sister could tell
him what she wanted him to know. She knew him
better than Lassiter did.

His mother. He considered for a second going by

the nursing home to shoot her. But it really wasn't
worth the trouble. He'd never realized until now how
much he hated her, but it wasn't something that surprised him, or that even seemed to matter a great deal.

The windows were clearing enough to drive, and
the car was getting warmer, although he could feel
some shivers coming on. He thought the rain had let
up a little, and the wind had died. In fact, it seemed
very quiet now.

He shivered, convulsed a little, suppressed it . . .
and then felt the first stab, the icepick headache. He
sighed. *Just go away*, he thought at it. *Either kill me
or just fucking go away.* He wasn't going to put up
with that anymore.

He put the car in gear and let it move forward
under its own power, accelerating a little when he
thought he felt it grip, but making it lurch and swing
sideways a little, one rear wheel spinning in the mud,
sinking a little. He lifted his foot, let the car rock back,
tried it again. No dice. But the other rear tire was
biting gravel on the road surface. He gunned it and
swung the wheel hard against the expected skid. For
a second he thought he'd made a bad mistake—the
whole rear end was going to swing into the ditch. But
then it grabbed and fishtailed forward, up out of the
flat ditch and onto the road, water and mud splashing
up as high as the windows on both sides.

He slowed then, relaxed and patient. Eventually
he'd come to another road, which would lead him to
another, and eventually there'd be a sign that told him
where he was, and he'd know how to get back to
Sand Creek.

It would be awkward, getting her to go with him.
He might have to arrest her. Use the cuffs. But then
she'd be all right and he'd explain it all. *Jocelyn*, he
thought. But then he remembered that was wrong.
That was Celia. Her sister's name was something
else . . . similar . . . He couldn't quite come up with
it, but that didn't really matter. The last name was the
important one. *Wellington. Ms. Wellington. Hello, Ms.*

Wellington. I'm Detective Lassiter. I have some information for you about your sister's death, and I'd like you to come with me . . .

Maybe it would be easy.

32

Phone and power lines were down all over the county, plus three pileups they knew about—not counting the one on the interstate that the HiPo was working. That was the only 10-48 so far; no injuries in the others. None of it was anything for a city police detective to worry about, normally, but manpower was short in city and county both, so Hector was in the dispatch room, ready to help, when the radio report came in of the twister that hit the Portwell farm, out on the Cassiday road. That was about as much as he could make out. Even cell phones had become useless because of the storm, and radio traffic was starting to break up badly.

"I'm out of bodies," the sheriff's dispatcher said, looking at Millie. She swiveled and looked at Hector.

"Got it." He took a last drink from his coffee cup and headed out the door.

Burton, the L.A. cop, was coming along the hall from the parking lot, his hair plastered flat on his head.

"Glad you're here," Hector said. "We can use you. Dispatch is—"

"I really need to speak with you, Detective," Burton said. "It's important."

Hector didn't stop to think it over. "Then you'll have to ride with me," he said. He went past Burton to the big equipment closet and yanked it open. He pulled out one of the yellow slickers and tossed it to Burton, who barely caught it, then looked at it as if it were some strange piece of evidence.

"Up to you," Hector said, putting one on himself. "Grab a hat if you're coming."

He headed on toward the door to the parking lot, not knowing whether Burton was following or not— and not caring a great deal. The other man caught up with him in the vestibule, struggling with the slicker as he followed Hector back out into the rain.

It had let up some, and the wind had died—not a good sign. "Just so you'll know," he said to Burton. "A car's about the worst possible place to be during a tornado."

Burton didn't reply, only went around to the other side, yanked once at the door handle, then waited for Hector to slide in and unlock it.

"I have to find Floyd Lassiter," Burton said. "I'm helping out Lieutenant Loomis."

"You think he's over here?" Hector had a dark hunch about what was coming. How much of this shit was there still to get through?

"He kidnapped a woman last night," Burton said. "A streetwalker. Then he skipped."

"Took her with him?"

"No. I—I was trying to keep an eye on him, so I was around, but I didn't know she was in any danger, see?" He sighed. "Lassiter got away while I was—"

"And you think he came here? To see me?"

"I understand you owe him."

Hector glanced at the other man, who was looking straight ahead, then nodded and turned his own eyes back to the front. "Yeah. I do. I owe him my life, as a matter of fact," Hector said. "He hasn't contacted me, but if he did . . . yeah, I might help him. I'd want to hear his story."

"His story includes Jocelyn Wellington."

Hector looked at Burton again, surprised . . . but also not entirely surprised. This time Burton was looking back at him, his expression solemn. But wasn't there also a kind of light in his eyes, like a kid enjoying the effect of what he'd said? Hadn't there been exactly that same light in Jo's eyes, standing over her father's body?

"You know that for sure?" he asked.

"Personally? No. Loomis thinks so, though."

Hector nodded. That more or less confirmed it in his mind. He came to the stop sign at the Cassiday road, ready to turn out into the country, away from town. For a second he couldn't quite remember where he was going. The Portwell farm. A tornado. He found an image of Lassiter in his mind—Lassiter standing outside the apartment where she'd lived. Why had he been there? It hadn't been his case.

"What does Loomis think?" he asked. "Was Floyd protecting her, taking payoffs . . . ?"

"Not like that. Or, not just like that. Something else, like, you know, some kind of sexual obsession. Like the videos, only real. That's what Loomis thinks."

Sexual obsession, Hector thought. Was that different from love? Old as he was, he still didn't know. Love. Could someone who'd lived Jo's life even be capable of love? Or Floyd, for that matter . . .

He was supposed to be on his way to a tornado scene, where there might be injuries, and he was sitting here at this stop sign, with no cross traffic, thinking about . . . He shook his head and pulled out, turning left, away from town.

"The thing is," Burton said. "The sister."

Hector stopped, halfway into the intersection, and looked at him. "What?"

"I mean they're just alike."

Hector frowned. "They're not—"

"They're identical *twins*. Listen, you were up front at the funeral. But I was where I could keep an eye on him. You should have seen him—when she stood up, I mean. Talk about somebody looking like he saw a ghost." Burton laughed. "See, I don't think he realized until then—"

"You think Jes is in danger?"

"Well, if there's this obsession, like Loomis says.

And he sees her at the funeral. And then he picks up this hooker and . . ."

"But you don't know this is where he was headed."

"No."

Hector sighed, looked back past Burton at the road into town. He could be at her place in ten minutes. But it was just speculation, and the tornado wasn't . . . There was a gas station half a block back, he could call her. But the phones were down. He grabbed his radio mike and began trying to raise Millie, through the static.

33

From now on she'd feed him at the kitchen table, not in the dining room. She'd hoped Susie might lick up the splatters on the carpet, but the dog only sniffed at them, turned up her nose and went back downstairs. Jes didn't blame her. This stuff was awful.

Through the dining room window, she caught a glimpse of a car pulling into the driveway, and she grimaced and began dabbing Eddy's face with the wet rag, making him blink and recoil.

She leaned forward, to look out the window and see who was walking up to the front porch. But there was no one in sight. The rear doorbell rang.

She started to pick Eddy up, then decided to leave him there. He was secure in the high chair, and she'd be only a few steps away, at the back door.

It had stopped raining, but obviously not soon enough for the man at the door. There were strands of hair stuck to his forehead, and his pants and shoes looked like he'd waded through a river recently. His jacket looked dry, but the shirt beneath it was nearly transparent. He was standing on the porch with a crooked smile that looked a little manic, and he quickly held up a badge—a Wichita detective's badge. She pushed the screen open.

"I'm sorry I can't invite you in, Detective . . . ?"

"Lassiter." He appeared confused for a moment, then said, "I'm fine here. I wouldn't want to get mud on your floor. Maybe you could just step out here for a moment . . . Ms. Wellington."

She hesitated. There was something a little funny

about this guy, something secretively expectant, like someone playing a practical joke. She'd step out and twenty people would jump out of the bushes and yell, "Surprise!" She looked back at what she could see of Eddy, in the dining room. He appeared content, smearing the food on his high chair tray like finger paint.

She pushed the screen open and stepped out, letting it fall shut behind her. "It's about my sister?"

"Yes. I have some information for you about that. But it's rather involved, and I'll need you to go with me. Also, there are some things you should have. We'll have to go to—"

"You mean, right at this moment? I can't. I've got a . . ." She'd turned her head slightly, toward the dining room, and didn't see him move, only felt his hand close tightly on her wrist.

"Hey!" She jerked away instinctively, knowing it was a mistake as she did it. One of the first things they'd taught her. Move forward, not back. He was trying to cover her trapped hand with his free one, to bend it into a come-along grip.

That first move backward had cost her the balance she needed to use her feet, so she went straight for his eyes with fingernails, screaming, "No!" But he blocked her arm with his, and tried to catch that wrist as well. Instead of pulling back again, she twisted her arm under his and made a short, hard slash at his Adam's apple with the edge of her hand, screaming again, and catching him hard enough to bring a choked sound and to make his grip on the other wrist loosen enough that she could get her fingernails into the back of his hand, digging as hard as she could. He gave a little grunt of pain, but didn't let go.

He was using his greater weight to keep her off balance, not let her get her legs under her, and she thought he might be trying to pull her off the porch, to fall to the ground with her, where his weight would become even more of an advantage. She went with it for a second, then spun a little sideways, a sort of dance move, throwing him off balance, too, and trying to drive one knee toward his groin but catching only his thigh.

She heard a sharp cry, but it came from somewhere else. Eddy cried out again, an inarticulate burst of something more like anger than fear, almost a warning. What was wrong with him?

The man was looking toward the door in surprise—the two of them had frozen—and she yanked her wrist free, falling to one knee at the edge of the porch, afraid she was going to fall off. She fought to get her balance, to fend the man off . . . but he was still looking at the screen, his eyes wide.

The screen suddenly bulged out, like a balloon inflating, and there was a scratching, ripping sound . . .

. . . the dead dog. That's what he thought at first. The dead dog, grown immense and demonic down in hell, tearing right through the black metal fabric to get to him, its great teeth and yellow, hate-filled eyes flying at his face.

He shrieked and took a step backward, missed the edge of the porch and fell. He tried to twist, to protect his head, and his outthrust hand struck mud and slid. One knee banged the concrete block he'd fallen from, and then he was lying facedown, half on the concrete drive, half on the strip of ground between it and the porch.

And then the thing was on his back, pinning him there, its claws digging into his back and shoulder, its jaws biting his neck. He could smell its hot, stinking breath, and hear the pleased growling in its throat, a broken kind of growl that sounded to him like unearthly laughter. *I'm dead*, he thought. *This is it.*

But his body automatically fought for life, rolling, arching, trying to get out from under the weight. Halfway on his side, turning his head to try to keep his throat from the teeth, he had a dreamlike glimpse of the misshapen inverted terrain of the car's underside,

and beyond that things moving back and forth in a
kind of mist . . . shoes . . . people . . .

The dog's teeth clamped his shoulder, making him
cry out and twist. But the pain also seemed to clear
his mind, reminding him suddenly where he was, what
he was doing. He twisted hard, ignoring the pain as
the teeth ripped across the back of his shoulder and
neck, and risked exposing his face and throat for an
instant, in a desperate attempt to get a hand on his
weapon.

He felt the butt, but then had to roll back again, to
escape the jaws, and managed to sweep the dog's
stiffly planted foreleg, rolling it up and making the
dog yelp and retreat.

He rolled after it, came up leaning, on one knee,
the gun in his right hand as his left arm windmilled,
fighting for balance, and fired twice as the dog began
a stumbling move back toward him.

The dog gave a sort of screech that was like no
sound a dog ought to make, and he snapped off a
third terrified shot as the dog dove into him headfirst.

He fought to get free, not realizing that it was finished. Its only movements were the shudderings and
tremblings of death.

He got into a sitting position and stared at it, ap-
palled. He'd *killed* it. This was somehow worse than
the other one . . . the one he didn't remember . . .

A flurry of snowflakes struck his face—no, only
rainwater. For a second he'd been back on that icy
path beside the barn . . . Celia . . . Celia's sister . . .

He fought for clarity. Jocelyn Wellington's sister—
she'd disappeared, run to the neighbors, he supposed.
He looked around for her, found a tall blond man
standing a few feet away. The man put his hands out,
a placating gesture.

"Easy, Detective. I'm not armed. You need some
help? Looks like the dog got you pretty good."

That made him feel the dull, deep pain in his shoulder for the first time, but he ignored it and got to his
feet, keeping his weapon trained on the stranger, who

was just a little too calm to be a civilian. The man took a step backward, his eyes not on the gun but on Lassiter's face. Definitely not a civilian. Lassiter took a quick glance at the dying dog, the empty porch, the ripped screen. He was damned now. Trying to find some way back, he'd only made everything worse, crossed a line that he hadn't before. He was dead and damned. Which meant he had nothing left to lose.

"Where'd she go?" he asked the man.

"Into the house. I imagine she's called the local police by now. Why don't you give me the gun before they get here, not make them have to take it? No need for—"

"Who are you?"

"Tim Haffner. Private investigator. And you're Lassiter, right? We haven't met, but everybody tells me you're a good cop, just having some kind of . . . problem. I don't care what it's about. But look, right now all you've done is shoot a dog. If you give me the gun . . ."

Lassiter gave a grunt of laughter. *Just a dog.* At the same instant, sirens arose nearby, a deafening wail. Storm sirens, not police. Some of the people across the street and in the next yard began moving away, but most stayed, watching. He wondered why he hadn't heard any police sirens by now.

"Toss your weapon," he told the man who called himself Haffner.

"I told you. I'm not armed. I don't like guns."

Lassiter circled him warily, moved to one side, circling him slowly, and Haffner kept turning to face him.

"Turn around."

Haffner shrugged and did so, facing the side of the house. Lassiter moved up close and quickly put the barrel of his weapon against the base of Haffner's skull, then did a quick frisk. No gun. He heard a door slam somewhere, realized it was the one at the front of the house.

"Move!" He marched Haffner a few steps back along the driveway, to where they both could see Jes

Wellington, a bundle that had to be the baby pressed to one shoulder, hurrying toward the red car parked at the curb.

"That your car?" he asked Haffner. "Keys in it?"

"Yes . . . and no. They aren't."

"Where?"

"Left jacket pocket."

Lassiter felt for them warily, keeping the gun barrel pressed against Haffner's flesh. The man still had his arms partway raised.

The siren stopped suddenly, with a squawk, leaving a deep silence broken only by the slap of raindrops on the wet concrete, and then a deep, Godlike voice spoke from somewhere overhead and nearby, making Lassiter jump: "Warning. Warning. This is a tornado warning. Please take cover. This is not a watch. This is a warning. Take cover at once. Warning. Warning . . ."

"We'd better—" Lassiter raised his gun and brought it down hard on the P.I.'s head, above and behind one ear. Haffner went straight down, his legs buckling as if he'd been shot, and sprawled onto his side. Lassiter paused, reflexively, to stoop and check his pulse. Still alive.

Jes Wellington had gotten the baby into the car and was searching frantically for the keys. Lassiter straightened and headed toward the red car.

34

"The blond guy was pretty woozy. He couldn't walk a straight line to get to the other guy's car, but he got right in and drove off after them."

Hector watched the young patrolman—Roberson was his name—struggle to jot the words down on his damp notepad, shielding it with his body from the rain that was coming harder, and at a sharper angle, blown by the wind.

The county deputy who'd also reported to the scene was farther up the driveway, helping Coleman Scott, the vet, put the dog on a stretcher. Hector caught Scott's eye, and the vet shook his head angrily. Hector felt a surge of guilt, as if the anger—justly—were directed at him.

Not because he'd gotten the dog from Scott in the first place, for Jes's protection. Because he'd made the wrong decision once again. Out at the farm on the Cassiday Road there'd been a flattened shed and a chicken coop surgically removed and smashed down a half mile away, minus the dozen chickens that had been in it. Assuming they were dead, those chickens were the only casualties. And if he'd been here, he could have dealt with Lassiter. He was sure of it. He was the only one who could.

He'd told Millie to send someone over to pick up Jes and the baby as soon as someone was free. He was pretty sure it had all gotten through, but maybe not. He wouldn't know until he talked to Millie why no one had shown up until it was too late. Burton had known he was making a mistake. He hadn't said so, but Hector knew it. How could he get so old and still be so stupid?

He surveyed the scene, committing it to memory. One more in his personal Top Ten of all-time terrible moments that were partly—if not entirely—his fault. The moment by the farm pond, of course—but he was no longer sure that had been the worst. There were the two nights in the emergency room—the first, when he'd promised Maria he wouldn't "do anything" to Rafe, and the second, when it had been too late for her to extract any promises. It wasn't a moment he could identify specifically, but there'd been some point at which he'd become aware, more or less, of what was going on between Rafe and the girls, and had decided not to believe it. He knew he'd known it, though, because Jo hadn't had to explain it to him when he'd found her standing there with the shotgun, looking pleased with herself, as if she expected his praise.

"I warned him to leave Jes alone," she'd said. That was certainly the most terrible sentence he'd heard in his life, for it had confirmed everything he knew but didn't want to know. It had been echoing in his mind ever since. Of course he'd helped her get away with it. He was an accomplice.

Funny to think that there'd been a time when he'd thought the worst thing that would ever happen to him was Maria telling him she loved him—like a brother—and wanted him to be godfather to the child she was carrying. Twins, but she hadn't known that yet. And of course Rafe wanted him to be best man. He'd been crushed, obliterated—but that moment seemed happy to him now. Rafe had still been his best friend, a good guy. Maria had still been unscathed, except by love. The new life inside her had been all promise and potential. He'd give anything he could think of, including his life, to go back to that moment and start again. Surely all the rest of them would, too, if they could, including Rafe.

Dr. Scott and the deputy brushed past him, carrying Susie's body to the veterinarian's van.

"You need a ride back to the station, Detective Briseno? Or are you gonna stay?"

It was Roberson. Hector frowned, not understanding, and glanced at the place across the street where he'd parked. His car was gone. Where was Burton? He scanned the scene, realizing he'd completely lost track of him, forgotten he was there.

Roberson was looking at him as if afraid he'd made a mistake. "He said it was okay. He said he knew where they were going."

"Yeah," Hector said. "No problem." *Nice of him to let me know,* he thought. Probably Majors or Loomis would know what Burton meant. Were the phone lines back up? Even if they were, would he be able to patch through to either of them? It looked like the main part of the storm had moved that way. "Let me have the keys to your patrol car," he said. "You'll have to catch a ride with the county guy."

35

"I don't remember," Lassiter said for maybe the tenth time. "I just don't remember."

She glanced at him—this bloody, exhausted man, looking half dead, more than half mad, holding the baby on his lap. But Eddy was content, obviously unfrightened, and she wasn't afraid of him anymore, either. The storm was scarier, this feeling of plunging into a swirling darkness, the car rocking in the wind, flashing past strings of cars and semis that had pulled over to wait it out.

His voice had sunk to a mumble and then stopped, and she took another look. She kept expecting him to fall asleep. She'd been hoping he would, had been carrying on the conversation only to distract him. But now it was past that. She wanted him to stay awake.

She looked over at him again, saw that his head had dropped forward. Eddy had fallen asleep against him, and Lassiter's head hung over the baby's.

"Lassiter."

He gave a start, looked at the window in front of him, looked at her. "What?"

"We're almost to Wichita, I think. You'll have to tell me where to go."

"Sorry." He leaned forward and switched on the radio, but there was still mostly just static, behind which she could hear voices talking about the weather. They sounded like the distant voices you heard sometimes on the telephone. Lassiter switched it off again, straightened a little, gently rearranging the baby against his chest, and drew a deep breath.

"I'll tell you a story," Jes said. "It's a story our mother used to tell us when we were little."

When he didn't say anything she went on:

"There's this Indian family, back in the old days, before the white man. A young couple with a son. And he got to the age where it was time to go out and find his totem—he had to go out in the woods and stay until something spoke to him and told him who he was, his real name, and—you know—what kind of creature he was, you know about that?

"Well, he went out and didn't come back. What happened was, he found out he was a bear, and for some reason he became a bear. I mean, he turned into a real bear and forgot he was human, and stayed out in the woods. Sometimes that happened, our mother used to say. So his parents decided to have another child, and his mother got pregnant, and she had twin girls.

"That was a problem, because the people, whatever tribe it was, they thought twins were unnatural. Animals have litters, humans have single babies. So usually they'd kill one of them, if they found out. Or sometimes the parents would. In this case, the father wanted to, but the mother didn't, and she made him keep it a secret. They'd only let anybody see one of the girls at a time, you know? But after a while, of course, people found out.

"Some people were going to come and take one of the girls, but the mother took them both out into the woods and found a place for them to hide, and told them she'd come back for them. But when she went back, the husband was scared and he was saying she was a witch . . . and so they killed her.

"So the little girls were out there by themselves. And after a while they had to look for food. They were big enough to walk. And they found some berries or something and were eating them, and this bear suddenly appeared, and chased them.

"They found a little tree to climb up, but it was a

small tree and they couldn't climb very far, and the
bear was going to get them . . . but then something
happened. He recognized them, even though he'd
never seen them, didn't even know they existed. All
at once he remembered that he was a human, and he
knew that they were his sisters.

"So he found food for them, and took care of them.
He turned back into a human, but they didn't go back
to where they'd lived before. They stayed in the
woods, just the three of them, and lived there."

She fell silent, thinking about the story, wondering
how much of it she and Jo had changed without knowing it, whether it was really the same story their
mother had told them. "It sounds like there ought to
be more," she said. "But that's how Indian stories are,
I guess."

Lassiter didn't say anything. She glanced at him,
saw that he was awake, staring straight ahead. The
hammering of the rain and the distant moan of the
wind seemed suddenly louder. She didn't think they
were—she thought it was only the silence in the car—
but Eddy stirred restlessly, shifting his position against
Lassiter, as if disturbed by the sound. The Valley Center sign flashed by.

They were at the edge of Wichita.

"Where do we go from here?" she asked.

"To my mother's house, the house where my
mother used to live. There are some things there I
want to give you. You can decide what you want to
do with them. They belonged to your sister."

"And then what?"

He shrugged. "And then you go home. You can
take this car. It belongs to that guy."

"What about your car?"

He seemed to think about it, then shrugged and
said, "I don't care. I don't need it."

Neither of them said anything until they reached
the Twenty-ninth Street exit.

"Get off here," he said. "Go west. Right."

Slowing down on the ramp, she said, "About the bear . . ."

"The bear didn't kill them, did he?"

"No. But what I was going to say, what if he had? What if he killed one of them while he was still a bear, before he remembered he was human . . .?"

"I don't know. He didn't."

"But if . . ."

"What are you trying to do? She was your twin sister, and I killed her. And I didn't just . . ." He closed his mouth, shook his head. "I don't know how much you know, but it was bad. And now you're talking like . . . Look, I just wanted you to know . . . what happened. That's all. I just wanted to tell someone, and you seemed like the most logical one. I'm not looking for excuses or . . . forgiveness or . . ."

"You don't get to decide that. I can forgive you if I want to. It's not up to you."

They'd come to the stoplight at Broadway, and she was waiting for the green.

"Do you?" he asked.

She thought about it, which she hadn't really. She'd only been arguing. "I think I do," she said.

He grunted. "What about the dog?"

That hit her. *Susie*. She remembered the snap of the gunshots, the sound the dog had made, the way she'd looked . . .

She saw that the light had changed, and she put the car in gear and pulled across the intersection.

"That's harder, isn't it?" Lassiter said. "Isn't that funny?"

"Because I saw it . . . and she was innocent. Animals are innocent. And dreams are innocent. There are things I remember as dreams, but they were real. But at the same time . . ."

"What about him?"

She looked at him, saw him indicate the baby with his eyes.

"Look at him," she said.

"Come on. He's a baby. Wait a few years and ask him."

"Why don't you?"

He gave her a crooked smile, but then looked away.

"The thing is, I'm a cop. Not a bear. A homicide cop. That makes a difference. It's who I am. Maybe it's my totem, like you say. What it means is, I don't let killers get away with it. That's what I've got left."

Jes nodded but said, "Nobody gets away with it, though. Jo didn't get away with it."

"She would have, if I hadn't shown up."

"No, I don't mean that. I mean—" She stopped. She'd been assuming Hector had told the other detective that, and that Lassiter would know. Like everyone would know, by osmosis or something.

"What?" he asked.

"She killed him. Our father."

He nodded and said, "Her father." It wasn't a question. "How'd she do it?"

"Shotgun. To the head. Hector helped her make it look like an accident."

"Hector did? Good for Hector." He shrugged. "You said nobody gets away with it, but your sister got away with—"

"You think she did?"

He was silent for a while, and then he said, "Turn right up here. And go slow. I want to see if anyone's waiting for us." He leaned forward, peering into the darkness, motioning her to the left where the road branched around what looked like a park or forest of towering pines. He seemed to be trying to see into the pines. She drove slowly.

"Don't worry about me," Lassiter said. "Worry about the baby. That's your job now. Turn in here."

She hadn't even seen the opening in the trees. It was like a one-lane tunnel, dry and quiet inside.

"Turn off your lights," he said. "Take the turn to the left and drive on around very slowly."

They came out beside a big house—one of those sprawling ranch-style houses that she associated with

California and the fifties. It faced into the trees, seemed to be slightly engulfed by them. On the other side of it was an open space, a large lawn, and then trees came down to the road, right on her left as she curved on around, past what she thought was another tunnel to the outside world.

"What is this place?" she asked.

"That's my mother's house up ahead, on the left. Where she used to live. She's in a nursing home now . . . stop!"

She'd been straining to make out the form of the dark structure, and she noticed the big old car parked along the road near the driveway just as he did.

"That's Hector's car," she said. She felt incredible relief. Everything was going to be all right.

He looked at her, then back at the car. He was silent for a long time. Then he said, "Okay, that's the kind of thing Loomis would do, bring Hector in. It makes sense. So, I don't know . . . what the hell. Let's go on in."

She turned up the narrow driveway that went past the side of the long house and disappeared somewhere in the dark beyond. "Can I turn the headlights on?"

"Not yet. There's a big open area past the end of the garage. A turnaround."

She understood that they were driving past the outer wall of the garage to the original front of the building. What a strange place it was.

At the turnaround, he had her swing in tightly and then reverse, positioning the car to go out again. There was a light in one of the upper windows, but otherwise the house looked dark. When she turned off the engine, he took the keys and handed her the baby, who'd begun to awaken and was fussing a little. Lassiter leaned toward her, to look out the driver's window at the lighted window. He didn't seem to like it. In the dark of the car, she could see a large gash on one side of his neck where Susie had torn away a chunk of flesh, exposing muscle and tendon.

"Jesus," she breathed. "You need to go to a hospital."

He ignored her and straightened up, fiddled with the ceiling bulb. "Okay," he said. "Go ahead and get out. I'll come around." When she pushed the door open, the inside lights didn't come on. She closed it as softly as she could, infected by Lassiter's caution, although one of the garage doors was open and she could see there were no cars inside. Nobody here but Hector. Lassiter came up beside her, his gun in his hand.

"What's that for?" she asked in a whisper.

He looked at it as if he hadn't realized he had it, and then slipped it into a holster beneath his jacket. "Force of habit," he said. "I'm not used to being the perp."

He went ahead of her, pausing to study the garage interior before going farther, then leading her to the door that went into the house.

As he was reaching for the knob, the door swung in suddenly, and lights inside came on. She had a quick impression of a hallway extending inward past doors to stairs at the far end. But the man who'd opened the door wasn't Hector. He smiled broadly. "Hey, Floyd. I thought you'd come here. How you doing, Ms. Wellington?"

"Fine . . ." She craned her neck to look past him down the hallway. "We're fine. Where's Hector?"

"I'm afraid he couldn't be here. He had a case to work. But he loaned me his car."

"This is Detective Burton," Lassiter said. "From Los Angeles." Something had happened in Lassiter's face and voice. All the doors inside him had closed. She hadn't realized they'd been open until then.

"Pleased to meet you." Burton doffed an imaginary cap. "Call me Sandy."

"Nice to meet you, too," Jes said automatically. "This is all just a big misunderstanding. As you can see, the baby and I are fine. It's Detective Lassiter who needs some attention. He was attacked by my dog."

Burton nodded, studying Lassiter, then looked back at her. "Well, I'm relieved to find that everything's okay. But we have a problem here. Come on, I'll show you."

He turned and headed down the hall, stopping at the first door on the left. "Take a look," he said.

Lassiter stepped ahead of her, blocking her with his body, and looked through the door. He stared for a while, then took a breath. "You don't want to look," he said to her.

"You remember this one, Floyd?" Burton asked.

She pushed forward enough to get a glimpse of the naked body of a black woman sprawled across a small bed. She gasped.

Lassiter pushed her back gently. "We can handle this," he said. "You'd better just take the baby home. Here are the keys—"

Burton leaned forward suddenly and snatched them away from him. She noticed that he was holding a gun in his other hand, letting it hang loosely at his side. Had he had it all along?

"I'd say she's a material witness," Burton said. "So unfortunately, I think you'll have to stick around, Ms. Wellington. Probably shouldn't be driving with the baby in this weather, anyway. You don't mind, do you?"

Jes kept quiet. She didn't believe that Lassiter had killed this woman. All she knew was that she didn't know what was going on here.

"She doesn't know anything about this," Lassiter said. "You and I can handle it, can't we? Sandy." There was a coldness in his voice that Jes thought should have frightened Burton, but he only gave a half smile.

"Floyd, the truth is, I'd sooner let you go than her. But you're gonna have to stay, 'cause there's someone here who wants to meet both of you. Now . . ." He raised the gun suddenly and pointed it not at Lassiter but at Eddy. Jes pivoted automatically, putting her body between the baby and the gun barrel. Burton didn't seem to mind. "Now, Floyd," he said, "let's have that service revolver before something unfortunate happens."

36

"Zach," Annie said. "Put your groceries away before they spoil."

Majors glanced at Vincent, who was sitting in the armchair. He looked up at Annie as if he didn't understand, then down the hallway at the two brown sacks on the kitchen counter. He got up and went down the hallway.

"Must be sort of like déjà vu for him," Annie said.

"Except there won't be a body this time."

"You keep saying that."

"They're safe with Floyd. I don't know exactly what's going on with him, but I know the girl and the baby are safe with him."

Annie seemed about to say something but didn't. She got up and followed Vincent to the kitchen.

He knew she thought he was in denial, but she didn't know what he knew. Annie had been at the division when they'd gotten the call from Sand Creek, and he'd let her ride along as a payback for the help she'd given him—and also because he wanted to make sure the truth got told, whatever it was. He didn't know yet exactly what it was, but he was a lot more optimistic about it since talking to the Art Theft Detail.

They'd been just as evasive as he'd expected when it came to giving him the names of the victims. But things had started to change when he'd asked if they had a copy of the original inquiry Lassiter had sent. He hadn't been able to find a copy.

"What inquiry?" the guy he was talking to had asked.

"The one your Detective Burton called about. The one—"

"Our Detective who?"

They'd been a lot more interested after that, and so had he, in a different way. It had turned out that the LAPD had a Sanders Burton—but he was a sergeant in property, not a detective. As far as they knew, he'd never had anything to do with the Art Theft Detail, let alone the Celeste Mundy case.

By the time someone had tracked down a copy of Lassiter's inquiry in the computer, Majors had been talking to an assistant chief who had him describe the "Detective" Burton he'd met, and who didn't seem happy about the description. It seemed that their Sergeant Burton had taken some personal time a few days earlier, and nobody knew where he was.

It had taken a while to find the inquiry because it didn't mention Celeste Mundy. It only asked for any information they might have on Jocelyn Peete. Which meant Floyd had already known who Celia Staircase really was. But it also meant there'd been no reason for anyone in L.A. to associate the inquiry with Celeste Mundy—unless someone was making it his business to know the names of the detectives working the case in the cities the bulletin had been sent to, and to monitor any contacts from them. That seemed a little beyond the powers of a glorified property clerk— someone higher up passing the information on to Burton. But that part was L.A.'s problem, as far as Majors was concerned. He'd been telling Loomis about it when the call from Sand Creek had come, on the landline. The storm had pretty much knocked all the smaller departments off the air.

They'd been able to think of only three places Lassiter might be headed for. It was possible he'd taken the two into custody to protect them, in which case he'd probably be headed for the division. Loomis had people keeping an eye out for him there. Then there

was his house, and Binkley and Davidson had that
staked out. Majors had come here, to watch the apartment across the way, whose doors he could see from
where he sat, through a space in the blinds. It was
frustrating—he yearned to be out in his car, going
somewhere, doing something, but where and what?
There were APB's out on all three cars, but in this
weather the odds went way down. Most of the patrol
officers had plenty to do already.

What was especially frustrating was this thing about
Burton saying he knew where they were going. If he
meant someplace other than the three places they'd
already thought of—and it seemed like he must
have—then Majors thought he ought to be able to
come up with it himself. But so far he was drawing a
complete blank. If he had any idea at all, he'd be in
his car right now, going somewhere, doing something,
not just waiting. He'd tried to reach Kay in Atlanta,
but had gotten only the answering machine. Loomis
had said he'd have someone keep trying every so
often.

Hector Briseno was also out there somewhere, in a
Sand Creek patrol car, and Majors had told dispatch
to send him here if he popped up—unless, of course,
he knew where the others were.

Annie came back from the kitchen, carrying two
cans of Dr Pepper. She offered him one and he took
it, but put it down on the floor beside him. He could
tell there was something she wanted to say, or ask,
but wasn't sure how he'd react.

"What? Say it."

"You think Floyd really did it?"

"There were witnesses . . ."

"You know what I mean."

He took a deep breath and let it out again, thinking
about what to say. He knew what the answer was,
inside himself, but it was different saying it out loud
to someone you didn't want to lie to. He shook his
head. "No, I don't. I never did, but . . ." He shook

his head again. "On the other hand, there's *something*. I don't know . . ."

"The way he looked that night," Annie said.

Majors nodded, shrugged. That was part of it. But maybe Floyd had realized that the killer had found Jocelyn through him. Maybe everything he'd done and not done since then had seemed necessary to him to protect the other twin. Maybe he'd known all along about Burton.

He liked looking at it that way, but he kept coming back to the same question: If it was something like that, why hadn't Floyd told *him*?

He heard the sound of footsteps outside, and then the doorbell rang. Vincent emerged from the hallway, looking hopeful, heading for the door.

Majors held up a hand to stop him, put a finger to his lips, stepped to where he himself would be out of sight from the doorway, and then motioned Vincent to open it, letting his hand rest on the butt of his weapon, beneath his jacket. The doorbell rang again, several times, impatiently. Vincent opened the door.

It was Hector. He came in quickly, closing the door behind him, and looked at Majors.

Majors shook his head, moved back to where he'd been sitting.

"Do you know anything?" Vincent asked. "Has anything . . . ?"

"No, son." Hector patted him on the shoulder, looked at Annie, who put her hand out to him.

"Annie Babicki, *Mid American*."

Hector looked at Majors.

"She's all right," Majors said. "She's a friend."

Hector gave a little shrug and took the hand Annie offered. "Hector Briseno."

"I know who you are, Detective. I'm glad to meet you finally."

Hector nodded.

"I heard that Burton said he knew where they were going," Majors said. "We've got his house staked out. You know of any other place . . . ?"

"Not unless he's heading for the P.D. That P.I. hasn't called in or anything? He went after them, in Lassiter's car, so he's got a radio."

Majors frowned. He should have thought of that. Maybe they could raise Haffner. What about the other two cars? Burton had Hector's, so he might be monitoring the Wichita frequency. Majors picked up the phone and called the outside line in dispatch. Loomis answered. Majors explained the situation and suggested trying to raise Haffner on the scrambler.

"Already tried," Loomis said. "No response. He may not be monitoring, or he might not know how to operate it, at his end."

"Or he might be out of the car."

"You sure about this guy?" Hector asked when he hung up.

"He seems to check out, all the way around."

Hector nodded. "Witnesses said Lassiter frisked him, but didn't take a gun from him."

"He's got Floyd's shotgun."

"If he knows where to find it. Does Floyd keep it under the dash?"

"In the backseat."

Hector shrugged. "If he has any sense, he'll search the car for a weapon before walking into anything."

"You don't remember anything at all that might give us a hint what Burton meant?" Majors asked. "I mean, from back then."

Hector shook his head. "The thing is, I never really knew him very well. That kind of thing, it doesn't make you best pals."

"Even just a name . . . a relative . . ."

"You'd be the one to know that kind of stuff," Hector said. "He came to Wichita from some department up north somewhere, but I seem to remember that he'd grown up in Wichita. There ought to be family, friends."

"There ought to be. His father's dead. His mother's in a nursing home with Alzheimer's. No brothers or sisters. No friends. I mean, there are people in the department, of course, and a lot of them like Lassiter, especially the women, it seems like . . . but nobody knows him. It's funny. I'm his partner, and I didn't realize till now how much of an outsider he's always been."

"Can I use my phone line?" Vincent asked.

Majors looked at him. "Sure." He picked up the phone to hand it to him.

"Not that one. I mean, my computer line upstairs. I have an idea."

"About what?"

"If he grew up here, he's got to be in some local database somewhere."

"You mean the Internet?"

"No, not exactly. I'm talking about things like . . . oh, the county clerk, election commissioner, motor vehicles . . . register of deeds, school board . . . there's a lot of stuff."

"You can get into all that?"

"Some of them." He gave Annie a glance. "If I still had my newspaper log-on, I could get a lot more. In fact, the newspaper's own archives would be the fastest way to search the agate stuff . . . and they've got links to other—"

"What's agate?"

"Five-point type," Annie said. "He's talking about all that stuff in little type that nobody reads. Marriages, divorces, lost animals . . ."

"I could search that kind of stuff pretty fast," Vincent said. "If I still had a newspaper log-on."

They all looked at Annie.

"Open our files to the cops? They wouldn't just fire me. They'd lynch me."

Nobody said anything.

"On the other hand," Annie said, "it's a good story. Where's the computer?"

37

As they were moving down the hallway toward the carpeted stars, Jes heard a car pulling into the garage behind them. "Stop," Burton said. "You. Face the wall. You get over here." He flicked a wall switch, putting their end of the hall in darkness, and grabbed her arm, pushing her in front of him, between himself and the door at the other end. Lassiter was standing against the wall, his hands on his head. Watching the door with Burton still holding her by the upper arm, she tried to imagine possibilities, to think what to do. If it was the police, if there was gunfire . . . maybe try to fall, with the baby beneath her . . .

The door opened, revealing Tim Haffner standing just outside, peering in cautiously, obviously unable to see them. His hands were empty.

Burton let go of her and she spun sideways, out of his line of fire, shouting "Don't come in, Tim!" She fell to her knees facing the wall, hunching her shoulders instinctively, to try to surround Eddy with her body. It was a couple of seconds before she heard them laughing.

"You can make the rules at your place, Jes," Tim said. "But not here. Get up."

"What kept you?" Burton asked.

Tim didn't answer. "You got Floyd's piece?" he asked.

"Yeah. You want it?"

Climbing to her feet, her back against the wall, she watched Haffner take the gun, inspect it, spin the chambers and heft it in his hand. He stepped up behind Lassiter, who still stood silently facing the wall, and brought it up hard against the side of his head. She gasped, and Lassiter flinched at the last second, but not quickly enough. His left leg buckled, and his hands grasped weakly at the wall as he slumped to the floor.

"Now we're even," Tim said. "No hard feelings."

Burton laughed. "Told you you'd need it." He looked at Jes. "Miles is a method actor. If Haffner doesn't carry a gun, then neither does he." He seemed to expect her to laugh.

"Wouldn't have done me any good," Tim—Miles?—said. "Anyway, I haven't seen anybody here so far I couldn't handle without one. I didn't expect Floyd to coldcock me like that." He examined the gun again, then slipped it into his waistband. "Mr. B?"

"Upstairs. I'll go tell him everybody's here." Burton walked off toward the stairs.

Tim/Miles knelt beside Lassiter, who was sitting with one shoulder against the wall, his eyes glazed. "We'll give him a moment." He stood again. "He'll be all right. I didn't hit him as hard as he hit me. You can kill somebody that way if you're not careful, you know. It's not like in the movies." He bent slightly to look her straight in the face. "Is one of my pupils any bigger than the other?"

She shook her head.

He turned back to Lassiter, who was moving a little. "So Miles is your real name?"

"Close enough. Kind of like with your sister."

"Is there a real Tim Haffner?"

"Oh, yeah. There was. Very much like the one you met, if I do say so myself."

"What happened to him?"

Bending toward Lassiter, he gave her a blank look that chilled her. "At the bottom of a farm pond near the airport."

"What pond?" Lassiter asked, slurring the words. "Where is it?"

Miles gave a soft laugh. "If I were you, that isn't

what I'd be worrying about, Floyd. You ready to try to get up?"

"What's your last name?" Jes asked.

"So many questions. Come on, Floyd." He put a hand under Lassiter's arm, but Lassiter shook it off and struggled to his feet by himself, leaning into the wall as he did so.

Miles smiled. "That dog did a job on you. No offense, Floyd, but you look like hammered shit. You need a drink."

"Don't drink."

Miles laughed. "Well, we'll go sit down, anyway."

Lassiter swayed, moaned, put a hand to his head.

"Headache's a bitch, isn't it?" Miles said. "Come on."

He steered them on down the hall, the way Burton had gone, and halfway up the carpeted stairs to a landing that opened on a kitchen. At the top of the stairs Jes saw a big, dark room, devoid of furniture. She remembered Lassiter saying the house was empty, although there'd been a bed in the room where the black woman's body was, and there was a breakfast table in the kitchen, with three chairs. Lying on the table was what looked like a TV remote. Miles put Lassiter at one end of the oval table, his back to the landing, and motioned Jes into the side chair. He sat down facing Lassiter and slid the TV remote nearer to himself, and to the side away from her. It occurred to her that the gun was still in his waistband. She ought to be looking for an opening. Except that his confidence was somehow more intimidating than the gun would have been. She was pretty sure she'd have no chance with Miles. Unarmed, Lassiter probably wouldn't, either.

Anyway, what would she do with Eddy? Fling him aside and attack? He'd been awake for a while—she wasn't sure how long, probably at least since she'd shouted that foolish warning—but he hadn't made any noise. Zach and the nurses had mentioned that about him, but she hadn't realized it went this far. There was something a little spooky about it. He sat on her lap, his head pressed between her breasts, his hands clutching her T-shirt, staring up at Miles, as if even he realized Miles was the one to keep an eye on. She had both arms around him, and she squeezed him softly, making him wriggle a little, but not let go. If anything, he seemed to be trying to burrow deeper into her. At that moment, she realized that she was prepared to do whatever it would take to get him out of here alive. Whatever it took. It wasn't a decision; it was just a fact. *Jo*, she thought. *That's Jo.* The thought made her feel stronger, less afraid. She grasped at it, suppressed the urge to analyze and dismiss it.

"You've been a big help, Floyd," Miles was saying. "Assaulting private investigators, kidnapping women and children, stealing rental cars . . . even a typed confession. Not to mention providing us with the late Ms. Diamond. That's a great touch. What were you up to there?"

"Which one of you killed her?" Lassiter asked, his voice clearer but still a little weak.

"Sandy. Who else? I figured you knew that, since you ran. Didn't you see him . . .?"

"I don't mean Diamond."

"Ah." Miles gave Jes a quick glance. "Well, on balance, I think I'd have to say Sandy again. 'Cause if it had been left *entirely* up to me, she wouldn't have died when she did. She would have given up the stuff first. Burton's not a pro. I practically had to fight *him* to keep him from, umm, you know. Taking advantage of her. And that was the whole idea. I mean, we were expecting you to leave a little more evidence than you did at that scene, Floyd, and we didn't want to mess it up. That was a disappointment. What's up with you, anyway?"

"I've got them," Lassiter said.

Miles looked confused for the first time. "What? You've got what?"

"I've got the jewelry, the stamp with the upside-down airplane, and the little painting."

"Well, well." Miles sat back in his chair, regarding Lassiter. "You're just one helpful son of a bitch, aren't you?" He turned his thoughtful gaze to Jes for a moment, then back to Lassiter. "Let me guess what you want."

"She drives away with the baby. When she's gone I give you the stuff. Simple as that."

"Hmm. What about the confession?"

"What about it? You want me to sign it?"

"That'd be nice. Also if you could include Diamond—"

"No problem."

Miles was silent for a while, then said, "I might be able to make that work. I'll pass it on. I wouldn't get my hopes up, though. These are the kind of people who don't always do what's in their own best interest. By the way, when we talk to the old man, I'd just as soon you didn't mention anything but the painting. That's the only thing that matters, but if you mention that other stuff he'll want it, too, and I don't need any more complications. Neat and clean. The painting for the girl and the kid. Okay? And the signed confession."

Lassiter nodded.

"This is all about a painting?" Jes said. "My sister, and this other woman, and—"

"It's not really the painting," Miles said. "It's real valuable, sure. But she could have taken a whole lot of other stuff that would have been easier to move, and the old man probably would have just let it go. Probably. You never know for sure. But the painting . . ." He shook his head.

"Why?"

Miles studied her. "You know," he said slowly, "this arrangement Floyd and I were discussing kind of depends on you not knowing too much."

She digested that. But didn't she know too much already? Suppose she left right now and went to the

police, and told them everything she knew and
brought them back here? She could tell them that
Miles and Burton were fakes, but they'd be gone.
What would the police find? The body of the black
woman, the confession . . . But what good would that
be if Lassiter—

She understood for the first time exactly what Lassiter had been offering to trade for herself and Eddy—
his life. A suicide probably, which was what she was
sure he'd been planning anyway. Except that now he
knew he hadn't really killed Jo, so there was no reason, except for her and Eddy . . .

But what good would the confession be if *she* was
still alive? She looked at Miles, then at Lassiter, who
seemed to have withdrawn inside himself. He was
barely holding himself together, she realized. He
might really believe Miles would go for the deal . . .

But she could see that Miles was only entertaining
himself, keeping them in line by holding out a false
hope. There was no way he'd let her out of here alive.
Knowing that made things more clear.

"There's no reason to kill Eddy," she said. "You
left him alive before."

Miles looked at her. There was something . . . as if
they *recognized* each other. Like what Lassiter had
said about himself and Jo. Lassiter and Jo. Herself
and Haffner. Somehow, it made sense to her.

"No argument," he said.

Lassiter was frowning, looking confused. The TV
remote buzzed, making her jump. Miles reached for
it, pressed a button, and they heard Burton's voice.
"Bring 'em on up."

"Want to hear something funny?" Haffner asked.
"Burton really is a cop."

He grabbed Lassiter's arm and pulled him to his
feet. Lassiter didn't resist.

The big bedroom had obviously belonged to Lassiter's mother, and he had obviously left everything as
it was. The only thing out of place was a rocking chair

lying on its side, across the entrance to a big, open closet.

The old man standing beside the bed in a bathrobe and slippers, leaning heavily on a cane, greeted her with a smile, then reached out one hand. Miles nudged her a step farther, within the old man's reach, and he lifted one of her hands and kissed it. "So good to see you again, Celeste."

Miles muttered something inaudible under his breath.

"My name is Jesamyn," she said.

The old man's smile disappeared, and for a second she was looking at the face of a corpse whose flesh had melted and molded to the skull beneath. Then he smiled again, and the disconcerting image fled. "Of course," he said. "I know that. I hope you will indulge an old, feeble man. I knew your sister by that name, and I was really quite fond of her. We had much more than a business relationship. I do believe that. We are all forced by the contingencies of life to do things we might not wish to do, and I believe that was so with Celeste, so I have tried to forgive her. And I do regret very much all that has happened." He looked at Burton, who suddenly dropped the smirk he'd been wearing.

"But we can't change the past, and I hope you will not mind too much if I address you as Celeste. Call it an old man's habit."

"And what do I call you?"

"Forgive me. I was rude not to introduce myself. It comes from spending too much time alone, with only my servants." He took a couple of stiff steps backward, the cane pinned hard against the side of his left leg, as if it couldn't bear any weight at all, and gave a half bow. "My name is Bannerman, my dear. At your service."

Miles made a disgusted sound, loud enough to hear, but Bannerman either didn't hear it or pretended not to. "Now we must attend to business. I think you know what your sister did to me?"

"I know she stole some things from her customers."

He actually looked hurt. "What a cold word that is. Customer. But lamentably accurate. At any rate, there is one thing in particular—"

"Lassiter says he has it," Miles said.

Bannerman's eyes went to Lassiter, his whole demeanor changing. "You have it with you?"

Miles nudged Lassiter, who shook his head. "Buried. Had to bury it. It was cold." He swayed slightly, put a hand against the wall to steady himself, then put the hand to his forehead. "Headache," he said.

Bannerman looked at Miles. "You struck him, yes?"

"Not that hard, sir. It's something else. I think he's a little delirious from being mauled by the dog. Might have an infection."

"Hmm, perhaps. But I'm sure being struck in the head did little to improve his condition." Bannerman studied Lassiter critically, then sighed and said, "You'd better start."

"I tell you when they're gone," Lassiter said, his hand still covering his eyes. "That's the deal."

"Yes, of course." Bannerman spoke slowly, thinking. "I tell you what, Detective. Miles will take you back to the kitchen now and make some coffee for you. We'll get you to feeling a little better and then, as a show of good faith, you'll finish the confession and sign it for us? Yes? Does that sound fair? And then we'll talk about the rest."

Lassiter started to say something, but Miles shoved him toward the door. "Come on, Floyd." Jes could see that Miles was annoyed, and that frightened her. The door closed, and she and Eddy were alone with Bannerman and Burton.

"Take the child," Bannerman said.

"No." She turned, squared to face Burton. She was near enough the bed to toss Eddy there if she had to fight. "No one takes Eddy."

"Please," Bannerman said softly. "We mean him no harm. I have made a place for him here, you see? To

make things easier." He turned and hobbled stiffly to
the overturned rocker. "You see? There is a blanket
on the floor, to make it soft. It is a sort of . . ." He
looked at Burton, who frowned, and said:

"Playpen?"

"Playpen," the old man said. "Exactly. Unfortunately, we have no toys . . . but he will be safe and
comfortable here while we conduct our business."

"What business?" Jes asked. "I don't know anything about those things she took."

"No, of course not. Please . . ."

It occurred to her that she might be endangering
Eddy by keeping him with her. "I'll do it," she said.

She stepped to the closet and put Eddy down carefully on his feet on the other side of the rocker, making sure he had a grip on the back slats. "You'll be
okay," she murmured to him. "I'll be right here." He
stared back at her, looking a little worried but making
no sound.

"A charming child," Bannerman said. "And so well
behaved. A rarity these days. I congratulate you."

"I didn't raise him." Jes felt anger rising in her, that
dangerous anger that she had been managing all her
life to swallow. She had to swallow it this time. She
had to stay cool. She thought she could take Burton,
except for the gun. She returned to where she'd been
and a couple of steps farther, putting a little more
distance between herself and the baby.

Bannerman didn't seem to notice. "Burton," he
said.

"Yes, sir."

"You have your dagger?"

"Of course, sir."

"Show it to our guest, if you will."

Burton, smirking again, reached under his jacket
and drew out a knife with a gleaming blade, a black
handle and wide silver pommels. He held it up for her
to see.

"Let her have a closer look."

Burton stepped forward. She wasn't afraid of him, but she took another step away, as if she were.

"Please do not be alarmed," Bannerman said. "Burton will not harm you. Will you, Burton?"

"No, sir." He moved nearer, holding the knife out. She could have taken it from him, and she could see he didn't expect anything like that. But there was still the gun.

There was something engraved on the dagger blade, in some kind of ornate lettering. The handle, which she'd thought was metal or plastic, was wooden and unpainted. Ebony? There was a silver ball at its end, above the pommel, with something like a lightning bolt . . . paired lightning bolts . . .

No. A double S.

Bannerman was smiling. "This is a very special knife. It was my own, which I earned long ago, with great difficulty. Now I have passed it on to Burton, who has also earned it. This makes us two of a very small number of men remaining in the entire world who have done so, and most of them are nearer to my age than to his. There is a bond between those who have earned this dagger that is stronger and deeper than any other. In earning it, Burton has become something like my brother and something like my son . . . but far closer! Do you understand?"

She didn't say anything.

"No. Probably not," Bannerman said sadly. "Burton."

"Yes, sir."

"Bring me the left ear of that child."

As Burton turned, Jes shouted "No!" and launched herself after him, but stumbled as Bannerman's cane struck her shin.

"Halt!" Bannerman barked.

She half fell, caught herself on her hands and came back up, then saw that Burton had stopped at Bannerman's command. He was standing and looking at her, the knife held loosely at his side, the way he'd held the gun downstairs.

"Put it away," Bannerman said.

Burton slipped the knife back and straightened his jacket. He was smiling, but not like Miles. Why didn't he frighten her? The eyes, she thought. Miles watched. He paid attention. Miles would have been more careful, showing her the knife.

"Only a demonstration," Bannerman said. "You understand, do you not, that Burton will do what I tell him, no matter what it is, instantly, without question? He will not hesitate out of any ordinary human sympathy. He has learned the hardest discipline of all—to do what one's own conscience condemns for a larger purpose. That is the truly difficult thing required to earn that dagger, and not many are capable of it. Not many understand that sacrifice. But it is necessary, for the welfare of the child, that you understand it right now. Do you?"

Jes looked at him and nodded.

"I beg your pardon?"

"Yes, I understand what you mean. He'll do anything you tell him to do."

Bannerman gave a half smile. "Well," he said, "I think that because you are my guest, I will not insist that you address me as 'sir.' Nevertheless, I am your elder, as well as your host, and it is only common courtesy to address me with respect, by my name. 'Yes, Mr. Bannerman.' That would be appropriate. Is that too much to ask . . . Celeste?"

She didn't respond.

He sighed. "Very well. Burton. The child's ear."

"Yes, Mr. Bannerman," Jes said evenly.

The old man laughed, gave Burton a wave that halted him again. "I think you must mean, 'No, Mr. Bannerman.' No, that it is not too much to ask, that you address me that way. Am I right?"

"Yes, Mr. Bannerman."

He nodded approvingly. "You see, it is not really a large thing. We come to large things by small steps. Now, here is another thing that you must understand and believe. This will be the rule. If you misbehave, it is the child who will suffer."

He looked at her silently, waiting.

"Yes, Mr. Bannerman," she said.

"Good. I have no wish to harm the child, nor does Burton. I am trying to protect him, in fact, by making sure that you understand the situation. His welfare is entirely up to you. To keep him unharmed you must understand that my commands are to be followed promptly and without resistance." He paused again.

"Yes, Mr. Bannerman."

He nodded. "Yes. I think he will be safe, my dear. I think you will do what you must to protect him." He gave the sash of his robe a yank with his free hand, letting the robe fall open, revealing that he was naked beneath it.

"You see," he said, "it was really you I came here for. Miles and Burton could easily have handled it without me. It was only when Miles described to me his first meeting with you that I knew I must meet you. Miles disapproves. I can tell. But that is his job. To worry about my welfare. He is very good at it, and I allow him to do it—within limits, of course. He is the servant not a soldier. Miles's only bond to me is the bond of money, but that is sufficient for men like Miles." He paused, seeming to have lost the thread, then looked at her and said, "I imagine you are pleased by my particular interest in you. Are you not?"

"Yes, Mr. Bannerman."

He laughed, then leaned forward slightly on his cane and slapped her. She saw it coming, but didn't try to avoid it. It had little force behind it, but she blinked and gave a little cry, as if it did, and raised a hand to her cheek.

"Put your hand down! Of course you are not pleased. Do you think me a fool?"

"No, Mr. Bannerman."

"I am not. Nor do I wish to pretend that you are pleased. In fact, it is my hope that you detest my attentions greatly, that you are only obeying my commands because you must. And that is true, is it not?"

"Yes, Mr. Bannerman."

"So you see, no acting will be required. Our dealings this evening will be completely honest, without deceit or pretense." He was silent, thinking. "With your sister . . . it was all pretense, all acting. Very professional, but pretense nonetheless. Her betrayal made me face that, but I think I had already begun to understand the terrible irony . . . The one thing she had made me want most was the one thing she would never give me. Herself." He paused, frowning. "That is not right. That is cruel."

He grew silent. She glanced at Burton, who smiled when their eyes met. He was having a good time.

"But I think you are different" Bannerman said. "Celeste . . . and yet not Celeste." He shrugged. "Perhaps it is only wishful thinking, but I could not let the opportunity pass."

He spoke brusquely, "So if you do everything I tell you, instantly, without resistance—making no attempt to pretend to enjoy what you don't enjoy—then I will leave both you and the child alive. Do you believe that?"

She hesitated, then shook her head. "No, Mr. Bannerman."

He smiled broadly. "*Very* good. Of course, you would be a fool to believe that. Nevertheless, this much is true. If you do as I say, I will leave the child alive. Beyond that . . . I suppose, if the experiment should prove to be a great success, if I believed I could . . . manage you, keep you alive . . ." His voice faded away, and he became thoughtful, then shook his head. "A fantasy, of course. And Miles would be difficult about it. Never mind. Here is what I will promise you. If I am greatly pleased—and remember, there must be no pretense—your death will be as quick and painless as possible, and neither Miles nor Burton will be allowed to . . . harm you. You understand?"

"Yes, Mr. Bannerman."

"I quite like you, my dear. You may not believe it, but I do. I liked your sister, too, but I couldn't trust her. I feel that I can trust you—within the limits of our arrangement, I mean. If Burton were not here, if you had a weapon, you'd kill me and attempt to escape, wouldn't you?"

"Yes, Mr. Bannerman."

"Of course you would. That's why I like you. Nothing underhanded. No sneaking around, pretending to be my friend. It's really too bad . . . well . . ." He shrugged. "Sit down, please. On the edge of the bed, facing me."

She did so.

"From now on," Bannerman said, "you must keep your eyes open at all times, and look at me . . . unless I give you other instructions, of course."

She looked up at him. "Yes, Mr. Bannerman."

"All right. Take off your shirt."

She crossed her arms, grasping the hem of the T-shirt, began to pull it up, then stopped and looked pointedly at Burton, who was grinning at her.

Bannerman looked annoyed, but then said, "Of course. Sorry, my dear. Burton. Give us some privacy. Go see if Miles needs help. I'll call if I need anything."

Burton hesitated, belying the instant obedience Bannerman had bragged of earlier.

"I have my device," Bannerman said impatiently, pulling a remote like the one she'd seen in the kitchen from the pocket of his robe, holding it up for her to see as well as Burton. "If this ferocious monster attacks me, all I need do is push a button and you will rescue me—and of course carry out the order I gave you with respect to the child." He looked down at Jes, then put the remote back in his pocket, keeping his hand on it.

"Perhaps I would not be able to push the button in time," Bannerman said to Jes, when Burton was gone. "But it would be a grave risk to take with the life of the child, would it not?"

"Yes, Mr. Bannerman."

"Proceed."

She pulled off the T-shirt and dropped it on the

floor beside her feet. Bannerman stood leaning a little on his cane, watching, the other hand in his robe pocket.

"And now the brassiere," he said.

As she reached behind her to unhook it, he moved a little nearer, and suddenly slapped her again. It caught her by surprise this time, and even stung a little. She jerked back, looked for the hand, saw that it was already back in the pocket. He was smiling broadly.

"Just to show you that I am not completely the helpless old man I may appear to be," he said.

"Yes, Mr. Bannerman." She finished unhooking the bra and dropped it on the floor.

"By the way," he said, "did you enjoy that? The slap, I mean?"

"No, Mr. Bannerman."

"Good. Now clasp your hands together behind your head and sit up straight. Lean toward me, keeping your chin up."

She pushed her chest forward. He took his hand from the pocket again, watching her, and grasped one of her breasts, then the other. His fingers felt like leaves or dry sticks. The touch made her want to scratch. He took the hand away and put it beneath his robe. "Stay like that," he said. "Before we go further, I must prepare myself. This is necessary because of my age. I will . . . begin things, and then I will need some assistance from you."

His hand moved in quick, short strokes beneath the robe.

"Look at my *face*," he said.

38

Hector knew it wasn't going to do any good. Majors and the woman reporter hovered over Vincent as he punched the keys. It gave them something to do, but all you had to do was look out the window to know how pointless it was.

The rain was whipping by in waves, as if they were at the bottom of some vast, rushing river. He could barely make out the form of the other building, except when lightning flashed, and then it was more like some ghost of a building—a whitish, ancient ruin, part of another world.

It was another world out there, but it revealed itself only occasionally this way. Most of the time it was this comfortable world of order, of laws and computers, that was more visible, that seemed to extend everywhere. But every now and then there would be this darkness, this mad rush and fury, and people would huddle inside little cubes of light like this one, cut off from each other, waiting for it to go away. Thinking they were safe.

One of the things you finally learned, if you spent long enough being a cop, was that that other world wasn't evil—it was just indifferent. It didn't care. Even after you began to understand that, it took a long time to realize that that was worse, because there wasn't any way to fix it. Punishing the bad, protecting the good—those things didn't even make sense in that other world. Some suffered, some prospered. That was all you could say in the end. Law, science, all this stuff they kept using to try make that other world behave the way it should, were just games played by frightened people who imagined those things gave them some control of the darkness. But all you had to do was look out a window to see how foolish an idea that was, how feeble those tools were. How impossible it was to think you could use them to find and rescue someone swept up by that darkness. They were gone, that was all. The sun would come out again, the illusion of order and light, and the bodies would be found somewhere, and all those things that had been no good at preventing anything would be used to explain it, perhaps to punish someone, and everyone would feel safe again for a while.

He turned around and looked at the three people huddled around the computer, talking urgently, looking as if they were doing something that would make a difference. They might as well be three savages around a campfire, rolling bones, reading entrails. There were going to be bodies. Hector knew that in his own bones. In the end, there would be only the bodies.

"The news stories aren't gonna give us anything," the woman was saying impatiently. "Let's try the obits."

"But he's not dead . . ."

"Survivors. Maybe a name. A cousin, something like . . ."

"His father's dead. What was his father's name? If we search for Floyd's . . ."

"That was in the seventies, though. Before computers. We'd need . . ."

"I'll try it anyway. Maybe someone else . . ."

There was a brief silence broken only by the rapid clicking of keys.

"Tell me if you get a hit," Majors said. "I can't watch this. I'll go blind." He turned away, looked at Hector, and shook his head the way people did who didn't work much with computers. He wasn't discouraged. He was hopeful. The clicking keys, the flashing lights on the screen had made him hopeful. Vincent was punching the keys in a kind of rhythm, doing the same thing over and over, pausing to look, doing it again. Click, click, click. Pause. Click, click, click. Now and then an unintelligible mutter. Ritual and incantation, Hector thought. It was supposed to make you feel hopeful.

"How's the weather doing?" Majors asked.

Hector gestured at the window, noticing that the roar of wind and water had died down some. Majors stepped past him and looked out. "Stopped raining, anyway," he said. Hector turned and looked, saw it was true. He could see the other apartment clearly. Everything was silent, gleaming with water.

"So what now?" the woman asked. "Voter registrations?"

He heard Majors sigh softly. He knew what Hector knew . . . or at least he feared it.

"Did he and his wife get a divorce?" Vincent asked.

"I don't know."

"Yes," Majors said, turning around again. "They did. What would that give us?"

"An attorney's name, maybe."

"Oh, right . . ."

"Not in our listings," the woman said. "You'd have to go to county . . ."

Hector turned back to the window. Majors gave him a pat on the arm and went back to the computer. Reassuring the old man.

The ground below turned white. Hector gave his head a shake and blinked, thinking his eyes were doing something funny. They were getting that way. But it was real. He could see the little white balls bouncing on the old driveway like popcorn popping. "Oh, shit," he said.

The others grew suddenly silent.

"What?" Majors asked. But then it began coming down harder, and they could all hear it hammering the roof overhead.

"Hail," Vincent said needlessly.

"There! Try that!" the woman said.

"What? Oh." The clicking began again.

The hail stopped, and there was a greater silence than before outside the window. *Oh, shit,* Hector thought. Then the wind came back, suddenly, like the roar of a seashell turned up full volume. Bits of trash swept from somewhere else began tumbling through the long courtyard, from street to alley, like animals fleeing a forest fire.

Sirens erupted, not quite in sync. He'd always hated that sound, but now he felt like he could go out there and wail along with it. It was a sound that suited him.

"Christ!" Vincent said. "I just hope . . ."

All the lights went out, and there was a cascade of clicks from devices all around the room.

"Shit!"

Turning around, Hector was surprised to see the computer screen still lit, and the form of Vincent moving quickly in the darkness, turning off other lights that still blinked.

"The UPS'll keep us powered for a while," he said, sliding back into his swivel chair. "But we got knocked offline and I don't know if I'll be able to get back." He glanced at Hector. "I assume it's not just us."

Hector looked. "No," he said. "Everybody's out."

"Cross your fingers," Vincent said, and began punching keys again.

There it is, Hector thought, staring at the lightless, unpopulated darkness. *The real world.* A dead city. And somewhere out there, the bodies.

39

"Now I am ready for you," Bannerman said. "That is as much as I can do on my own. You must fellate me now until my penis is completely erect."

He put his hand back in his pocket and began moving nearer to her, sliding his useless left leg a bit at a time, leaning on the cane each time he did so.

"May I look down?" she asked.

"Yes . . . no! Keep your eyes on mine. Use your hands to . . . find the way."

She took her hands from behind her head, keeping her eyes on his, and leaned forward, feeling with her hands for the open flaps of his robe.

When she found them, she gripped one in each hand and gave a firm tug.

It wasn't enough to make him fall, only to throw him a bit off balance.

"What . . . ?" The hand in his pocket shot out, to the side, like the arm of a tightrope walker, and his body began to turn that way, as he tried instinctively to lean backward against the tug and at the same time put his weight on the cane, which jumped forward a couple of inches, leaving behind the leg it supported. He turned farther, trying to keep any weight off the leg, his arm beginning to windmill. As he began to fall, he groped at her, found her head, tried to get a grip on her hair.

She didn't try to avoid his hand. She even leaned a little to help him. She had the odd sensation of being off somewhere above her own head, watching critically and dispassionately, everything moving slowly, seeing what would happen next, and what to do about it. She saw the sticklike fingers entwine themselves in her short hair, the side of the robe swing forward from the weight of the remote in the pocket. She let go of the robe and plucked the remote out, tossing it behind her on the bed, well out of his reach.

Seeing the movement, what she was doing, he let go of her hair and made a desperate grab, far too late, and fell. She slid out from under him, grasping the cane with both hands as she did so, and ripping it from him.

He corkscrewed, his arms flailing, and screamed something as his weight came down on the bad leg. She thought it was Miles he was trying to call for, but by that time she'd gotten her own balance with one knee on the floor, and she swung the cane across the back of both the old man's legs. The bad one, the one nearest her, caught the brunt of it.

His scream turned to a screech that froze her. She listened for footsteps, thinking they'd surely heard it—surely people on the other side of town had heard it—but all she heard, for the first time, was the sound of the storm outside. How long had it been like that? There was a pounding on the roof overhead that could have been either hard rain or hail, and a moaning sound that had to be the wind, although she'd never heard it sound quite like that before.

There weren't any footsteps coming. Bannerman had fallen almost straight down, leaning over the bed, so that the edge of the mattress had caught his stomach and knocked the wind out of him. He was gasping, trying to get his breath. She watched, indifferent.

His gasps were like the hiccupy sounds a baby might make, hurt so badly it has to gather all its breath for a scream of sufficient magnitude. The slippered foot of his good leg was pawing spasmodically at the hardwood floor, trying to push him farther onto the bed. The other leg hung down, not quite to the floor. It was slightly bent now, but not quite at the knee.

In fact, he didn't seem to *have* a knee on that leg.

It was only a of tube of flesh, and perhaps bone, now bent in one place. She felt suddenly nauseous, was sure she was going to vomit, but then fought it back and swallowed, acid burning her throat. The old man made a weak lunge, gave a strangled cry . . .

The nausea fled, leaving her feeling clearer than before. She leaned toward him, grapped the nape of the robe and hoisted him up onto the bed. He was so unexpectedly light that she nearly threw him across it. The bent leg straightened as he landed, made a soft crunching sound.

Or maybe that was only her imagination, for he didn't scream. He lay still. Passed out. She took a look at his face. His eyes closed as if he'd fallen gently to sleep, and he was breathing more evenly.

She looked at the closet, thinking she'd heard the baby call her name . . . or some name . . . but of course he hadn't.

He was standing again, grasping the slats of the rocker, looking at her in silence. Maybe he'd given a little cry. The sight of him grounded her, brought her up to some new level of clarity. When she smiled, he smiled back and raised his arms to be picked up.

"Not just yet," she said. He seemed satisfied to hear her voice, and seemed even to understand, dropping his small hands back onto the rocker. She thought for a moment about closing the closet door. She didn't know yet what else was going to happen in this room, but it was likely to be disturbing. Still, it seemed to her that shutting this baby in the closet, listening but not seeing, would be worse. She hadn't let herself think about what he might have heard the night his mother died.

She turned her attention back to Bannerman, whose eyes were open again but not quite focused. He was struggling again, as if still trying to crawl up onto the bed. The remote was in his path, although she didn't really think he was trying to reach it—or was even aware of it. But she leaned past him to retrieve it and put it on the dresser.

When she went back to look at him, she saw that he was weeping, the tears rolling out of the corners of his eyes, which had cleared a little. She realized suddenly that he was trying to get away from her, that he expected her to kill him now. Hadn't she said she would, if she had a weapon and the chance?

Do it. It was the same voice she thought she'd heard before, a voice from somewhere off to the side, not quite audible. She remembered that voice now. She'd decided a long time ago, in college, that it had been only her imagination, or some kind of dream, a fantasy of childhood.

You're not even here, she thought back at it, and was a little relieved when there wasn't any response.

So . . . whether or not to kill Bannerman. It would be the easiest thing, but then it occurred to her that it didn't matter until she'd figured out what to do about Miles and Burton. That's what she needed to be thinking about. She examined the room quickly, not finding anything that looked especially useful. She had the cane and the remote . . . and Bannerman himself. Those were her resources.

She went back to Bannerman, lifted him on one side, and pulled the sleeve of his robe loose. When he realized what she was doing, he tried to resist, but she gave him a slap on the rump. "Be still!" She pulled the robe loose from his other arm and tossed it aside. He lay facedown on the bed, naked except for his slippers. When she began rolling him over onto his back, he tried to kick her with his good leg, and she slapped him again. "Next one'll be somewhere else," she said. He subsided, allowed her to turn him, then lay on his back with his eyes fixed on her, his lips twisted in a sneer. His face had that skull-like appearance again, but it only looked like the thin, transparent skin of any old person, fallen close to the bone. There was something in his eyes that was familiar to her the way that voice in her mind was familiar.

He was afraid, but not of death. Of humiliation. It was the same fear she'd seen before in other eyes, in the darkness, silently pleading with her to keep quiet, to go along, to have pity . . . to think of it only as a dream.

Maybe it was death they were all afraid of, after all. Maybe they thought that if they got some control over that most mysterious, most troublesome part of life— the part that was most like death, that most swallowed up the self, most mixed pleasure with terror—they would have some defense against death itself.

It wasn't only men, she realized, if you thought about it that way. What had Jo been doing but trying to master that same thing, to gain control of it and not have to be afraid of it anymore? What else had she herself been doing, in her different way? She had been thinking she could keep death out of her house, if she kept life out.

Jo had abandoned all that once she had Eddy to worry about and not just herself.

She looked at Bannerman. His breathing was more even than it had been. She knew he was getting his strength back, and probably some of his false confidence with it. He was hiding now, waiting for an opportunity. Pretending to be weaker than he was. *You can't play that game on me,* she thought. *I'm the champ.*

She sat down on the bed beside him and pulled off her sneakers, and then her anklets, which she wadded into a ball. When she straddled him, pinning his arms with her knees, he made a feeble resistance, looking astonished, and then bit at her, his dentures clicking and making funny little sucking sounds, as she tried to poke the anklets into his mouth. She slapped him a couple of times, across the face. Tears came to his eyes again and he stopped struggling, but he shut his eyes and his jaw tight.

"If I have to," she said, "I'll use the cane to break your dentures into pieces, inside your mouth . . . or maybe just break your jaw . . . You realize it would be easier to just kill you to keep you quiet."

He opened his eyes and stared at her for a second.

Then his gaze slid away from her and he opened his mouth. She put the socks in.

But she could see at once it wouldn't be enough. He could spit them out easily, even with his arms restrained . . . and she couldn't keep sitting on him like this . . .

So just kill him.

She saw the sense of it, but shook her head. She climbed off him. He lay still, looking at the ceiling. She knew he was thinking about the situation. Miles and Burton were still between her and freedom, and she didn't want to kill him. And he could get rid of the anklets anytime he wanted to.

She considered her bra, still lying where she'd dropped it. She could tie it around his head, across his mouth. She thought about that for a moment, but then, instead, began taking off the rest of her clothes.

He was watching her, looking afraid again, because he didn't understand. She smiled at him as she straddled him again, naked now herself. "This ought to give you a thrill," she said. "Open wide."

He did so, his eyes uncertain. She stuffed the panties in on top of the socks, pushing the whole wad back far enough and hard enough that it made him gag and begin to struggle.

She stayed where she was, her knees on his arms, and watched his eyes bulge. When he finally began breathing through his nostrils and getting control of his panic, she showed him the cane and pressed it with both hands against his throat.

"How much more pressure do you think it would take?" she asked. "Not much to stop you breathing at all. Not much more to break your neck. That's what I think."

His eyes were bulging again, and he was struggling. She took the cane away, waited for him to subside again. "You hear the storm?" she asked him when he did. "Listen to it. They didn't hear your scream awhile ago, when I hurt your leg, because of the storm. They still can't hear you. Whether I kill you or not is entirely a matter of my own convenience. I could probably do it with my bare hands without much trouble, but the cane would be faster. Don't you agree?"

He swallowed, nodded.

She thought about making him say something. Yes, Ms. Wellington. But that was stupid.

He lay still again when she climbed off. His cheeks bulged slightly, although he still probably wouldn't have much trouble clearing his mouth, especially with his arms free. But that was okay.

Not bothering to put her clothes back on, she went to the dresser and studied the remote. She was pretty sure she knew which button made the others buzz. And that was all she cared about. She could just push all of them, for that matter. What if they both responded? No point in worrying about a worst-case scenario. One of them would have to stay with Lassiter probably. With luck, it would be Miles who stayed.

She put the cane on the floor, up against the overturned rocker, at the door of the closet, then went to the door of the room and looked at it, trying to tell whether she'd notice it there if she'd just come in, just glanced that way, didn't expect to see it there . . .

She went and changed its position slightly, looked again. It was the best she could do.

She went to the bed and rolled Bannerman onto his side, his face away from the door. He offered no resistance. She pulled out the bedspread and the top sheet around him, moving him back and forth to create a rumpled place in the bed with him at its center. She leaned over him and whispered, "If you make a sound, I'll kill you."

She wasn't sure he believed her. She leaned nearer, their eyes locking, a few inches apart. "You need to understand me now," she said. "If I can't be sure of you, I'll kill you first."

He nodded. She saw in his eyes the belief that she'd kill him. Maybe it would keep him quiet.

She went to the dresser, picked up the remote and pressed the buzzer button, let go for a moment, then pressed it again. She tossed it back onto the bed, still a little out of Bannerman's reach. She positioned herself midway between Bannerman and the closet, facing the door, and put her hands behind her back, wrapping the bra around her wrists as tightly as she could, with the loose end tight in one hand. She looked at Eddy. "Here goes nothing, kid."

Only one set of footsteps came running along the hall. She had to keep herself from smiling when it was Burton's head that came through the door, the dagger held in one hand, preceding him. She didn't think Miles would have galloped that way.

Burton frowned at her, then looked at the old man on the bed.

"I think there's something wrong with him!" she said. "I think maybe he had a heart attack or . . . I don't know . . . He was moving and then he just stopped . . . and then . . ."

She stopped talking, making her eyes go wide, as Burton stepped up to her and pressed the knife against her throat. He peered over her shoulder at her hands, then gave her a pat on the rump and stepped back, giving her an appraising look. "Just like your whore sister," he said. "Nice ass. Not much up front."

"Don't you want to check Mr. Ban—"

"Did he come?"

She looked away. "I . . . I don't know. He was moving and then . . . he just stopped . . . he just kind of . . . went all limp . . ."

Burton laughed, put the knife away and retrieved his gun. "Shit," he said, "you can see he's breathing. Just passed out. Actually blowing his load, that's big stuff for the old guy. Probably kill him one of these days. But what a way to die, huh?" He gave her another appraising look.

She took a step backward, toward the closet. Burton grinned.

"So how come you didn't untie yourself and put your clothes on and try to get away? How come you buzzed? Must have been kind of frustrating when the old guy just stopped like that, huh?"

She took another step backward. "Where would I go? You and Miles were down there. He said if I was good—"

"I know why," Burton said. "Get back on the bed. Don't worry, he won't wake up."

Instead, she took another step backward, pretended to stumble against the rocker, and fell to her hands and knees, one of her hands only an inch or so from the cane.

"That's good, too," Burton said. "Just stay like that."

Holding the gun on her, he unzipped his pants and began working his belt loose. She kept her eyes on his, trying to hold his gaze while her hand edged toward the cane.

Bannerman finally made the sound she'd been waiting for him to make since Burton had come through the door. She'd begun to think he really had passed out.

He didn't say anything. He only coughed, and his body jerked. His hands started scrabbling at the sheets, his back arching.

Burton glanced at him, irritated. He leaned a little, trying to see Bannerman's face.

He caught the motion of the cane at the last second and tried to back up, but it caught him squarely across the wrist of his gunhand. He shouted, "Jee—!" and grabbed at the wrist with his other hand, the gun flying loose and spinning on the hardwood floor as it slid under the bed. Jes had hoped to grab it, but she heard it bang against the wall beyond the bed, then hit something else.

"You fucking *cunt*!" Burton screamed. "You're dead!" He held the damaged arm tightly against his body while his right hand went back into his jacket, groping for the knife. Jes took a step forward, startling him, feinted at his face and then swung backhand and low, catching his left knee. It made an odd popping sound—not what she would have expected—and Burton screamed again. He hunched forward, then began hopping away from her frantically, still trying to get the knife out. She followed him, the cane cocked like a softball bat. He pulled the knife free and slashed at her with it, just warding her off, not near enough to cut her. She thought he'd finally figured out that she was dangerous.

He was in a bad spot and he knew it. No gun. Only one arm and one leg. Cane against knife, but she had the reach on him, and he'd have to put the knife down to get at his remote, wherever it was. The storm was making too much noise for him to shout for Miles.

She watched him think about it, saw the anger and amazement as he realized just how bad it was.

He looked toward the bed, where Bannerman was, still making weak jerking movements. But it was Bannerman's remote Burton was looking at. Too far away.

"Give it up," she said. "Toss the knife."

He licked his lips. "Come get it, cunt. I'll break your fucking knees for you . . . and I'll fuck you. I'll cut your heart out while I'm fucking you in the ass . . ."

He was backing up, though, and he bumped against the bed and sat down hard. The knife fell on the bed beside him. He looked at it, then went for the remote. She took two quick steps toward him, feinted again, making his head jerk back, and slashed the cane across his throat.

Burton made a squawking sound and raised his hand to his throat, even tried to raise the one that hung useless from his wrist. He turned away from her, his reddening face falling into the bed, his knees folding, sliding off onto the floor.

She took another step, more deliberately, not hurrying. She spread her feet a little, fell into the batter's stance, her knees bending, her eyes on the back of his head. It seemed to move toward her like a pitched ball, and she stepped into it, meeting it solidly, feeling that old rush of pleasure, expecting to see it fly off, high into the sky, out toward the fences . . .

But of course it didn't. It was still there. She swung the cane again, and a third time. The fourth time she whiffed as the head dropped suddenly, making her stumble. She got her balance again, the cane resting on her shoulder, then realized it was over. She heard Eddy crying and looked at him in surprise. Crying.

She looked again at Burton, prodded him with the metal tip of the cane, but he didn't move.

Passed out? It was like some sarcastic voice, mimicking her. She went to Eddy and picked him up, held him against her. She was surprised to find that she had no clothes on, then realized she was getting goofy. She'd thought Burton's head was a ball. She held Eddy away from her a little, to look at him, to tell him that his Aunt Jes was getting goofy, and was startled to see a tiny smear of blood on his cheek.

"What happened?" She examined the cheek, but it seemed all right. She kissed him there, put him down, then noticed the cold stickiness on her shoulder. She touched it, came away with blood. But there wasn't any pain. She looked at the bed, saw the cane leaning against it, the shaft darkened by the blood and . . . *was that hair?*

She looked at Burton, moved nearer, saw that the back of his head was oddly indented and matted with blood. She moved cautiously around his legs, which stuck off the bed a little, to get a look at his face. His eyes were wide and staring.

"Jesus," she said aloud. "He's dead."

Home run.

She remembered swinging the cane . . . she looked at it again . . . her mind began to reconnect everything. Just a few minutes ago. But it felt more like something she'd dreamed. But there he was. There was the cane . . . and all the blood. A wealth of DNA evidence. No problem figuring it out . . .

She looked at Bannerman.

He wasn't breathing anymore. His old, yellowish

skin was cold to the touch. He was dead, too. How the fuck . . .? The stuff she'd put in his mouth hadn't been enough to suffocate him. Maybe he'd really had a heart attack. She shook her head. Christ. Her *panties*. Talk about evidence.

She laughed, suddenly on the verge of hysterical giggling. It was surprising how good she felt, considering. But she kept having the nagging feeling that there was something important she was forgetting, that she ought to be thinking about. She looked at Eddy. That wasn't it. She looked at the door.

Miles. Oh, yes. She definitely needed to start thinking harder about him. But that wasn't it, either.

She began putting her clothes back on—except for what was in Bannerman's mouth. No, thanks. Anyway, it was evidence. This was a crime scene.

That thought made her start to giggle again. But it was serious. When the police . . .

Lassiter. She'd forgotten about him. That was it. But now that she remembered, she wasn't sure what to do about him. Of course, she wanted him to get out alive, if possible, but it was even more complicated than that. There was something about Lassiter she needed to figure out, something she didn't understand. And she wasn't sure it had anything to do with all this. Not exactly. Nothing to do with her immediate problem of getting Eddy out of here anyway. And herself. And Lassiter, if possible. But mainly Eddy. That was the main thing—the *only* thing. Lassiter would agree.

She reviewed her resources. Burton's dagger lay beside him on the bed. The two remotes, Bannerman's and Burton's, lay on the bed. Gingerly, she moved Burton's body enough to probe his pockets, and came up with some money in a clip, a fingernail cutter . . . and Hector's car keys. She'd forgotten about Hector's car being out front. Had Burton done something to him? Was he dead *too*? Everybody but her and Eddy?

There was something . . . and then she got it. That

was what her mind had really been nagging at her about. Burton's gun.

It wasn't where she expected it to be, though. At first it seemed to have vanished. It was only when she got down on her hands and knees, to look under the bed, that she saw it lying against the baseboard beneath the huge upright armoire facing the foot of the bed.

It took her awhile to realize that she really couldn't get it. It seemed too ridiculous. But her arm was just a little too thick and the space beneath the armoire just a little too narrow, the armoire itself a little too deep. She tried using the cane to fish it out, but only succeeded in pushing it back and forth along the baseboard. None of the things she might hook it with— her bra, the sash of Bannerman's robe, Burton's belt— were long enough to manipulate, once she created enough of a loop to snag the gun. There were no hangers in the closet. And she couldn't budge the armoire, couldn't even rock it forward, get it to fall over. It might as well have been bolted to the floor and there weren't any good handholds.

She sat on the bed at last, looking at the armoire with great dislike—why had anyone ever built such a monstrous thing?—making herself accept that she couldn't have the gun.

Okay. So we can't have the gun. Fuck it. We don't need no steenking gun.

She smiled grudgingly. Right. Nobody left but Miles. Piece of cake.

She got up and went to the closet, looked down at Eddy. "Any ideas?"

He gave her that serious look in return. As if he did—and would let her know what they were just as soon as he could talk.

40

"Floyd, there *isn't* any fucking dog's grave. The fucking dog hasn't been buried yet. Get off the fucking dog, okay?"

Jes heard Lassiter say something, but couldn't make it out. It sounded like he was mumbling. Jes sat with her back against the dining room wall, right around the corner from the steps that led down to the landing, with Eddy on her lap. She'd intended to put him in one of the other rooms while she scouted out the situation, but had found she couldn't let go of him again. Anyway, she had an irrational conviction that he knew she needed him to be quiet. She'd also positioned herself so that she could see down the hallway to the bedroom. They were both dead—she knew that. No danger could come from that direction. But she felt more comfortable with it in sight.

"You need some coffee or something," Miles said. "So do I." Lassiter mumbled something, to which Miles responded only, "I wish we had some fucking coffee."

Every now and then, she'd noticed, a ghostly kind of light, like some kind of phosphorescence, ran across the windows on the opposite side of the living room. She'd decided it must be the residue of lightning flashes filtering down through the branches that twitched and shifted against the glass, making a constant swishing, scratching sound that she had to listen hard to hear beyond the constant drumming overhead. That restless movement, she supposed, like the ghostly light, must be only a hint of how the trees were thrashing above.

None of the rain was getting through. The windows looked dry.

That low fitful sound she heard when she knew Lassiter was speaking could just have easily been the filtered sound of thunder, or the growls of some animal trying futilely to speak like a man.

"Okay, okay," Miles said, cutting it off impatiently. "For the millionth fucking time. Celia is dead. You went to her funeral. Burton was there, and . . . No, not her. That was her *sister*. Her *twin* sister. See? Looks just like her. Her name's Jes. You came here with her tonight, for christsake. You kidnapped her and brought her here . . . right. There's a baby, too. That's Jocelyn's baby . . . Celia's baby. I know. It's confusing. All those names. It's confusing for all of us. The main thing is, we're trying to find the stuff she stole . . . Celia.

"Right. Exactly. It belongs to her sister and her baby. I absolutely agree. That's why we're trying to find it, Floyd. To *give* it to them. And you're the only one who knows. And if you remember and tell us, then we can forget all about the kidnapping charge, see? 'Cause you didn't hurt them, and we know you didn't meant anything bad. You were confused. You were sick. You need some kind of treatment. You're not a criminal. You're a good cop. Everybody knows that. You were trying to protect . . .

"No. She's dead, Floyd. Celia's dead. She can't tell us where it is. You're the one. You want to help, don't you? Of course . . ."

Jes wished she could see into the kitchen. She felt that if she could, she'd be able to tell whether Lassiter was faking it or not. But she couldn't. And she probably wouldn't really be able to tell. And he probably wasn't faking it. Which meant it was all on her, which she already knew. Time to forget about Lassiter and get busy.

She stood, picked up Eddy and carried him across the big dark room to the coat closet adjacent to the old front door, which had turned out to be bolted shut. She'd left the knife and the remote at one end of the closet shelf. The closet had no door, but it was wide, and the wall hid it by about a foot at each end.

She flattened against the interior wall, put Eddy down again, and felt for the knife. Listening carefully, she found that she could still hear Miles's voice, but not distinctly. It was sharper and higher-pitched than Lassiter's—more a bark than a growl. She couldn't hear Lassiter at all.

She bent and slid the knife point down into the back of her right sneaker, the blade and handle flat against her heel and the back of her calf. She pushed the tip down into the sole of the shoe, to anchor it, and then secured it further with the sweat pants' elastic leg band. She wouldn't be able to get it very quickly, but if she wound up in a direct confrontation with Miles, she didn't think that would matter much. It was a last resort.

She pulled the remote down, stared at it and took a couple of deep breaths.

"Ready?" she whispered to Eddy. She pushed the button.

The buzz from the kitchen was louder than she expected, and it startled her, made her draw back against the wall. At the last moment, she remembered to press the device against her, to muffle the sound of Miles responding. When he stopped speaking, she pressed the button again, and heard him say, "God damn it!" quite distinctly, not through the remote but from the kitchen. Then he said something in a lower voice, and she heard his footsteps coming up the stairs. He was walking quickly but not running, as Burton had. She put the remote back on the shelf, shoving it far out of sight into the corner.

When she knew Miles was most of the way down the hallway, she released her breath, not realizing she'd been holding it until then, picked Eddy up and headed quickly for the carpeted steps. She took a glance down the hall as she passed it, half expecting

to see him looking back at her. But he hadn't quite
reached the bedroom yet and still had his back to her.

Even though she'd made up her mind that Eddy
was the priority, and that she wouldn't endanger him
to save Lassiter, she had to take a look at the cop
when she reached the landing. He stared back at her,
as if not sure who she was.

"Come on!" she hissed. "Let's get out of here."

To her relief, he stood up at once and came to her.
He wasn't hurrying, though, and when she reached
impatiently to grasp his arm and pull him along, he
balked.

"What about Jerry?"

"Who's Jerry?"

"My partner." He looked doubtful. "We're looking
for something. He went to look—"

"That's not Jerry, Lassiter. Jerry isn't here. The guy
who was here is one of the bad guys. Trust me on
this. We have to get out."

He gave her a troubled look and his hand moved
beneath his jacket. Then he looked surprised. "My
weapon's gone."

"They took it."

He licked his lips. "Something's happening," he
said.

She fought to keep calm. "You're confused," she
said. "You just need to follow me."

She turned away and went on down the steps to the
lower hallway, not looking to see if he was coming
until she'd nearly reached the door to the garage. He
was a few feet behind her.

As she opened the door, a buzz came from the living room.

She nodded, pleased. He'd thought she would be
dumb enough to keep it with her. Now he'd probably
waste some time looking for it.

"Come on," she said to Lassiter, then saw that he
was standing and looking into the room where the
black woman's body lay.

"You didn't do that!" she whispered at him. "They did. Let's go!"

There was a second buzz, and he looked back that way. She started to call to him, then saw Miles's feet appear on the landing. "We're going!" she hissed at him, and went on out into the garage.

"Floyd!" she heard Miles say jovially. "Where you going? Don't you want some coffee?"

She felt along the wall beside the door, at the same time peering at the other walls, trying to figure out where the button was that raised the garage door. Not knowing where it was made her feel stupid, angry with herself. Why hadn't she noticed when they'd arrived? Was it back inside, in the hallway? She didn't think so, but wasn't sure. Could she have gone right past it? She looked at the car, trying to make herself think clearly. Miles was still talking to Lassiter, his voice moving slowly nearer. He was being cautious.

The car. It was Lassiter's car, the car that usually was parked here. She hurried to it and bent to peer through the driver's window. The garage door opener was clipped to the sunshade she reached for the door handle.

"Jes?"

Miles was right inside the door to the hall, standing back out of her sight. But he could take one step forward and shoot her if he wanted, and she'd have no chance to get away. She bent low, putting her body between Eddy and the door, and slid around to the front of the car, edging behind the fender. She leaned against the bumper, crouching, and peered at the door, then scanned the walls, looking for anything that might be of help, might give her an idea. She felt angry and frustrated. All she'd had to do was get out of the fucking garage before he got there.

"I haven't heard the garage door open," Miles said, "so I know you're still there. Things are different now, Jes. We need to talk. We need each other's help now, to get out of this."

She wanted very badly to believe that reasonable,

pleasant voice. The voice of the man she'd just met and the man she'd heard talking with Lassiter. Tim Haffner's voice. But Tim Haffner was dead. She'd never really met him at all.

All she could see that looked even remotely useful was a bunch of gardening tools leaning against the wall right beside the door to the house. She couldn't see how to make any use of it, though. To reach it, she'd have to expose herself, about two feet from where Miles stood. And then what? She'd have a shovel or a rake or a hoe—a longer reach than the knife, but not as long a reach as a bullet.

"Come on, Jes. Talk to me. Let's put our cards on the table. I know you have Burton's gun. It's a Mexican standoff. We can have a shoot-out . . . but why? It's just you and me and Floyd now . . . and of course the baby . . ."

"So talk."

She could hear him talking—to someone else in a low voice. Then he said, "Okay. Here's what I'm thinking . . ."

"Who's there? Who were you talking to?"

"Floyd. Who else? I just told him to go on back to the kitchen. No sense in him—"

"He went?"

"Sure. I like Floyd. Wouldn't want him to catch a bullet. I like you, too. I don't even really mind all that much that you put me out of a job. I was getting sick of those assholes anyway. Thing is though, I've gotta move fast now. If I can get back to Bannerman's place before the cops in L.A. find out what's happened here—see, he's got a lot of the same kind of stuff your sister took. Stuff nobody knew he had. And cash, too. It's a fucking gold mine. And I'm the fucking security chief!" He laughed. "I can set myself up real good and do a fade and everything's cool. So I can't afford to waste too much time here. But I need you and Floyd to help me out."

"In return for which . . ."

"Nobody gets killed. How's that? Especially the

baby, which I know is your main concern. And Floyd's
got that stuff your sister took. It could be worth—"

"Lassiter's a cop."

"Like that makes a difference. Okay, say he's an
honest cop—even though you got to admit he was up
to some funny stuff—the truth is, he's gonna believe
pretty much whatever you tell him, once he comes out
of his trance. Did you know he really thought he killed
your sister? I didn't, until I read the confession he
wrote. What a—"

"So why not stick to the original plan?" Jes said.

"What?"

"You know. The plan where Lassiter kills me the
same way he did Jo and that black woman, and signs
a confession and shoots himself."

Miles laughed.

"Like a movie, huh? Burton thought that was so
fucking clever, but it was also pretty obvious, don't
you think? Especially once we had that confession.
Talk about luck . . . but see, there's two extra bodies
now . . . your bodies. They don't quite fit into the
plan." He laughed again.

My bodies, Jes thought, not understanding for a second what he meant. Oh, yes. To people who knew
Burton only as a cop who'd come here looking for
things her sister had stolen, how would it look?

Eddy squirmed, gave a soft cry. She jerked her head
up, startled, finding she'd been holding him too tightly.

"No!"

"No what?" Miles asked.

"I mean, I'm not going to do that anymore," she
said.

"You're losing me."

"This is all some bullshit fantasy. You've got to kill
us. We know what you look like. We know how you
were connected to Bannerman and Burton. We know
you killed Jo, and this black woman, and Haffner . . ."

"Did you think Tim is *dead*? Hell, Jes, I just intro-
duced him to a lady I know . . . up near K.C. And I
haven't killed any—"

"No sale, Miles. What I want to know is how Eddy gets out of this. Seriously."

He didn't respond, and his silence grew long enough to make her wonder what he was up to. She yearned to find an angle from which she could look into the hall, see where he was, but that was probably exactly what he wanted. She looked around the garage again, and then at the car.

She had the cars a little mixed up, she realized, and she needed to think more clearly about them. She and Lassiter had come here in Miles's rental car, which was probably still sitting outside, pointing at the driveway. But Miles had taken the keys back. He'd arrived in *this* car, which was Lassiter's, the one that had pulled into her driveway . . . this morning? Jesus, it seemed like a month ago. But that meant it was a detective's car, like Hector's. There'd be a radio, or at least a walkie-talkie. There'd probably be a shotgun.

She moved farther back, to the wall, and then along that side of the car, peering over the bottom edge of the passenger window. There was the radio, but she didn't see anything else. No shotgun clipped beneath the dash or above the windows. Hector kept his in his trunk. Probably Lassiter did as well. Miles had the keys to this car, too, but had he locked the doors? She tugged gently on the nearest door handle. It didn't budge. She looked in again, trying to see if the lock button on the opposite door was up or down, but it was hard to tell in the dark. Up, she thought. But that wouldn't get her into the trunk.

Staying quiet, waiting for Miles to speak, gave her a small odd pleasure. *Our Indian genes.*

But when he spoke, it was a new voice, one she hadn't heard before, and it scared the shit out of her. She felt that if she looked down that hallway right now, she'd see something terrible. Not a human being . . . not even a proper animal . . .

"Okay, Jes. Seriously. You're right. I can't leave you alive here. Or Lassiter. If I ever trusted anyone

that much, I'd be in prison right now. Or dead." He
paused. "You listening?"

"Yes. You can trust the baby not to talk."

"But only if he's the only one still alive. You see
that?"

"Yes."

"Fact is, it would be a waste of time and effort to
kill him, and it's the kind of thing that makes them
look harder for you. And I don't particularly like the
idea myself, although that wouldn't stop me."

He fell silent, perhaps waiting for her to say something. When she didn't, he said, "So you toss Burton's
gun in, and then you come in. And the baby stays
alive. It's that simple."

"Not if I don't have Burton's gun." She'd been
thinking that it was an advantage for her that he didn't
know that, but now she had the nub of an idea that
worked better the other way around. She wasn't sure
it made sense. She was feeling her way to it. But it
was true—she didn't have the gun

"Jes, this isn't . . ."

"It went under the armoire," she said. "I couldn't
reach it and I couldn't figure out how to get it. You
could go look."

He was silent.

"It's a problem for both of us, isn't it?" she said.
"You can't afford to just believe me . . . but if I really
don't have it, which I don't, then I can't toss it in."

After a moment he said, "All right. Let's pretend
you really don't have it. Here's how we'll do it. You'll
put both hands up, well away from your body, and
move out to where I can see you, with your back to
the door."

"What about Eddy?"

"Leave him where he is."

"On the concrete floor? I'd like to put him in the
car, where he'll be safe."

"Jes . . . okay. Fine. Put him in the car. On this
side where I can see you."

"I need the keys."

She heard what sounded like a laugh. "Jes," he said. "You're a smart girl, but you're a civilian. If you're making this up as you go along, I'm always gonna be there ahead of you. Everything you could use as a weapon is in the trunk, and the driver's door is unlocked. So put him in the fucking car, and get your ass over here, all right? No more games."

"All right." She stood up and went around to the driver's door, in full view now. "Can I put him in the backseat? So I can put a seat belt on him?"

"Do it."

She could tell from his voice that he was standing in the doorway, watching her. Either he believed she didn't have the gun or he didn't care. She unlocked the rear door from the inside, and put Eddy back there, buckling him in with one of the old-fashioned waist belts.

When she closed the door, Miles said, "Stay right there. Put your arms straight up."

He came up quickly behind her, and she raised her hands and closed her eyes, bracing herself, expecting pain. The "plan" she'd been forming seemed suddenly so foolish, so much a fantasy . . .

She felt the cold barrel of his gun against the base of her skull.

"Oh Jesus, oh Jesus . . ."

"Relax," he said, putting his other arm around her, slipping it beneath her T-shirt and patting her stomach and sides, then running it quickly over her breasts.

She opened her eyes, startled, then realized that he was only searching her. His touch was as economical as a doctor's. His hand went to her back, still beneath the shirt, explored her shoulders, then plunged down inside her sweat pants, feeling down along the back of each thigh, and then pushing between her buttocks, making her gasp.

"Spread a little," he said.

She moved her legs farther apart, and the hand explored her crotch briefly, then went around to the front again, searching her abdomen, the fronts and sides of her thighs, gripping her crotch briefly before being withdrawn.

"Like that?" he asked.

She hesitated only a second. "Yes."

"Good. Turn around."

Maybe he wasn't so different from the other two, after all. She began to feel a small hope.

He was grinning, his head cocked to one side. She smiled back at him.

"Now let's see how much you like this," he said. He shoved the barrel of the gun against her stomach, making her gasp and cry out again. She closed her eyes.

He laughed, and she realized he was crouching in front of her. The gun continued to press into her stomach as his hand patted her calves, found the dagger behind her right foot, and pulled it free. He stood up, still grinning, holding the knife up for her to see. "Did you think I forgot about Burton's SS dagger?"

She didn't say anything. They looked at each other for a few seconds, his smile fading away. "I could just go ahead and shoot you now," he said. It was almost a question.

She swallowed, made herself speak. "You don't want to shoot me here. You don't want to shoot me at all. I'm supposed to look like the others."

He studied her. "Clever girl," he said softly. "Maybe I ought to just shoot you."

"There are other things you want to do first." She made herself hold her eyes steady on his.

"You never give up. Can't help but like that." He pulled the gun back, used it to motion toward the door to the house. "The main thing I want to do first is make sure I know where Burton's gun is. Show me."

She put her arms down and walked past him into the house. *I'm really going to die now,* she thought. It didn't bother her as much as it ought to—or maybe she didn't really grasp it. She wasn't sure how sane she was, how well her mind was working. She was going to die now. And Lassiter was going to die. Two more bodies. There were so many. The house would be full of bodies. It would take him all day to lug them out to the trees and hide them.

She'd reached the landing, and she took a quick glance sideways. Lassiter was sitting passively at the table, his back to her. No help there.

"Okay, Floyd," Miles said. "We're all going up to the bedroom now. We're just about finished here. Bring the confession along."

Lassiter's chair squeaked against the tile floor as he moved back from the table. It seemed unusually loud to her—all the sounds did . . . the branches scraping the front window, the rain on the roof, which she hadn't been hearing for a while . . . and there was thunder rumbling way off somewhere, and the occasional crash of lightning . . . and the wind, which seemed now to be screaming rather than moaning, a high-pitched wailing like the ululation of mourners, fading in and out . . .

"Well, where the hell is it?" Miles asked irritably. "It was right there on the counter."

"It's in the drain trap," Lassiter said.

Jes blinked. Lassiter was back. Miles must have heard it, too.

But he hadn't. "Jesus, Floyd. Can't leave you alone for a—hey!"

There was a quick shuffle of feet on the tile, some grunting. The gun went off, and she heard something strike the wallboard behind her, opposite the kitchen.

She turned. The kitchen chair Lassiter had been sitting in was lying upside down at the bottom of the stairs. Then the two men came flying out onto the landing, Lassiter with his head and shoulders down, leaning into Miles, whose back slammed into the same wall the bullet had struck.

Miles still had the gun clutched in one hand, but Lassiter's hand was on his wrist, holding the arm straight out. The gun swung and flopped as they struggled, pointing in every direction. She tried to keep an eye on it. Miles looked dazed and out of breath, but he was in better shape than Lassiter, who was using his bulk, burrowing into Miles, his legs digging into the carpet of the landing, keeping the other man pinned. He was grunting with the effort, and it sounded like a kind of low growl, the kind of sound Susie made sometimes.

Miles's other hand suddenly appeared, coming free from wherever it had been, and he hammered Lassiter's back and shoulders and head with his fist. Lassiter's hand followed it, tried for a moment to block it, then reached for Miles's throat instead. Miles squirmed, gasping almost soundlessly, clawed Lassiter's hand for a moment, and then lowered his fist and swung it up into Lassiter's torso.

Lassiter grunted with the blow, his body jerking, and Miles hit him again. Miles was winning.

There was a thud against the side of the house, somewhere up toward the bedrooms—something heavy banging against the outer wall. Glancing that way, she suddenly heard the odd, rhythmic screaming of the wind again, and then realized it wasn't the wind. It was a tornado siren.

She looked at the two men, amazed. What was she doing, standing here and watching? She stepped forward, ducking under the gun waving in Miles's hand, locked her fingers together, and swung the double fist into Miles's kneecap.

He screamed something unintelligible and the gun went off again. She heard glass break in the living room, and the landing was washed with a cold spray, a hard wind blowing suddenly toward the garage. The storm was instantly louder. It was in the house. There was the sound of more glass splintering.

Lassiter had somehow improved his grip, raised his shoulders. His face was turned toward her, and his eyes were distant and unfocused, looking at her but not really seeing her. But they were clear. "Go on," he said in a level voice. "Take the baby. Get away."

"I can help—"

"Help—uhh." Miles was flailing at Lassiter's head

with his free hand again, swinging wildly but landing an occasional solid blow.

Lassiter reared upward, his head slamming into Miles's chin, the jaws shutting with a loud snap. Miles gave a groan and a thin stream of blood ran down his chin. But he kept swinging his fist at Lassiter's head.

Lassiter's eyes focused on her. "*Help the baby!*" he growled. "*Get him out of here!*"

She looked back into his eyes only for a second, then moved, sliding past the two men, stumbling a little as she came to the steps, and running for the garage.

She looked back when she got to the door, and saw that Miles had his gun hand high above his head now, and that Lassiter's grip had slid from his wrist to his forearm. In a few seconds, the gun would be free.

The knife, Miles had it. She looked down at the handles of the gardening tools leaning beside the door, most long and slender, but a couple short and heavy, like clubs. There was a gunshot, and it was Lassiter who cried out in pain.

"*Don't run!*" Miles shouted shrilly. "*I'll kill—!*" But then he too cried out—a sound that reminded her chillingly of Susie's yelp when Lassiter had shot her. She didn't look to see what Lassiter had done to him. She pulled the door shut and ran to the car, ducking in and punching the button on the sunshade. The big door began to grind upward, letting in the same wind that had come through the broken window, the same spray of rain blown sideways. The siren was still screaming, going up and down, and she could hear cracking sounds out there somewhere, like trees splintering. There was a bright flash, illuminating the garage interior. The lightning crashed close by.

She got out, pulled open the rear door and got Eddy out, her haste surprising him into an uncharacteristic cry of alarm.

"Hang on," she said. She ducked under the rising garage door and sprinted out into the rain, leaning hard as she turned into the wind that came up the

driveway. It was like wading upstream, and she had
to bend her head and burrow into it, clutching Eddy
with both arms against her.

For a long time the far end of the garage seemed
to get no closer. She thought she heard gunshots from
inside the house, but couldn't be sure it wasn't thunder, or trees cracking, or something else. She ran with
her jaws clenched, expecting at any moment to be hit
by a bullet from behind.

Then, all at once, she was there, out of that tunnel
of wind, past the end of the garage and running more
freely across the soggy yard to Hector's car. When she
was only a few yards from it, the sirens suddenly
stopped, running down like a machine being turned
off. Was that good or bad? She didn't know. Then
they started up again just as abruptly.

She heard herself chanting. "It's all right it's all right
it's all right . . ." She closed her mouth, leaned against
the big old car and began probing Eddy's diaper for
the keys she'd taken from Burton. For a second she
thought they were gone.

But they were there. She fumbled futilely at the
keyhole, made herself slow down and move more deliberately. Putting him into the backseat, buckling him
in again, she heard what she was sure were gunshots
from inside the house.

She closed the door and stood there, getting her
breath. The temptation to go around and get in and
drive away was powerful—but she'd known what she
had to do since leaving the bedroom, even before the
"deal" she and Miles had made. He couldn't leave her
alive. If he got out of here, he'd come after her.
Maybe not tonight or tomorrow, but eventually. And
Eddy would be in danger, too. On the other hand, if
she died here, Miles would have no reason to kill the
baby, and she knew he wouldn't bother. Wouldn't
waste the time and effort.

She went to the trunk and pulled it open, holding
it against the wind with one hand while she pulled the
shotgun out with the other. It wasn't the little Fox 4-

10 she'd half expected to find, of course, the gun Jo had used. It was the big pump-action twelve gauge with the twenty-inch barrel and the magazine that held five shells.

She checked it, pumped a shell into the empty chamber and replaced it in the magazine, then grabbed the box of shells that lay beside the spare tire. She slammed the trunk shut and turned toward the house, bending to shield the gun from the rain.

For Eddy to live, she or Miles had to die here tonight.

41

The garage door was still open, and the door into the house was still closed. Everything just as she'd left it. Still, she stopped to listen as well as she could for any sounds from inside, and to let her eyes grow accustomed to the dark of the garage interior.

Satisfied, she raised the gun, cradling it in one elbow, and headed quickly toward the door to the house. She stood there, listening again, but no sounds came from inside. Miles—assuming he'd won the fight with Lassiter—had decided not to chase her, as she'd expected, and was busy trying to arrange things as best he could before making his own getaway.

She threw the door open, holding the gun at the ready.

"Freeze."

She hadn't expected the voice to come from behind her. She jerked, started to turn.

"I mean it, Jes! Don't move a muscle."

She froze, swept with anger at herself. So easily. A step ahead of her, like he'd said. She heard the car door open behind her, listened to him climb out, grunting softly, as if with some difficulty. His footsteps behind her were a little uneven, not like before.

"How did I know you'd come back?" he asked wearily. "You and your sister. What a pair. Okay. Let the barrel drop slowly. Farther. Okay. Now . . . with your left hand . . . wait. What have you got there? Christ, what were you gonna do, kill me ten or fifteen times? Reach 'em back to me without moving anything but your right arm."

She extended the arm behind her, and he took the box of shells. "Okay," he said. "Now the gun. Take the barrel in your left hand . . . be very careful, Jes. I'm not in a good mood anymore. Let go with the other hand. Right. Let it swing down, so the barrel points up. Now hand it back to me, the same way as the shells."

She felt him take it, listened hard to his movements behind her, but wasn't sure what he did with the gun. She heard a faint sound that might have been the scraping of metal on concrete. Had he put it under the car?

"You're good, Jes," he said from right behind her. "But when it comes right down to it, you're still a civilian. Your sister was a pro, like me. She'd have gotten away clean if old crazy Floyd hadn't happened to find her. She just had lousy luck. But you . . ." He sighed. "What really pisses me off is that you keep underestimating me. Coming back like this, to try to kill me . . . I knew you'd do it, but . . . this disrespects me, Jes. Don't you realize that? So now you're gonna have to die sooner instead of later. And—"

"What are you gonna do, talk me to death?"

He grabbed her arm, spun her around, and slapped her. It was a lot harder than Bannerman had slapped her. It rocked her back like a punch, knocked her head to one side. She clamped her jaw shut, blinked fiercely at the tears and turned to look him in the eye.

He put the barrel of the gun against her forehead.

"I'm not like Bannerman and Burton," he said. "I'm not some kind of psycho who gets a kick out of killing people. I can do it. It doesn't bother me. But it's just a job. Except this time . . . I'm gonna really enjoy this one, Jes. I'm gonna make sure I enjoy it. This one is for me. You people . . . you know, you've completely fucked up my life. Everything's gone. I have to start from scratch. A whole new identity, maybe even surgery. Because of you and your cunt sister. And that crazy fucking cop. That son of a bitch . . . I'm lucky to still have my balls. Thanks to him, I'm gonna have to figure out a way to get some doctoring, which is just one more pain in the ass piled on everything else. And my knee . . ." He pushed the gun harder against her forehead, making her stagger backward. "You fucking people," he said.

He shook his head, pulled the gun back, his arm relaxing but still covering her. He laughed suddenly—a startling reappearance of the Haffner persona. "It's been a long day, hasn't it, Jes?"

The smile fell away and he stared at her. Lightning flashed outside, and a gust of wind splattered them with heavy drops of water.

Miles's eyes lost their focus. "That felt good," he murmured. She thought the rain had let up a little. The siren had stopped.

"A cunt," Miles said, still talking to himself. "A couple of cunts. This isn't right." He shook his head, sighed deeply.

She looked at the gun. It was still pointed at her, but the hand that held it was trembling. She looked back up, found him smiling at her crookedly.

"Go for it."

She turned her back on him.

"You can't say I didn't give you a chance," he said. "That would have been a lot quicker. But since you're in a hurry . . ." He put his hand on her back, pushed her hard toward the door. "Let's get to it."

She stumbled and fell to one knee against the side of the door, her shoulder leaning into the frame. Her left hand scrabbled at the short, heavy handles among the tools leaning there. She looked the other way up the hallway at Lassiter's body, hoping her arm was screened by her body. Lassiter lay head downward on the lower flight of steps at the far end. His jacket and the carpet were soaked with blood.

"Oh, my God," she said.

"Get up."

She leaned into the door frame, getting her legs under her and a good grip on one of the wooden handles. As she rose, she hunched her head and shoulders, and pivoted, getting her right hand around it.

"I'm not gonna kill you until you beg me to," Miles said dreamily. "Until you offer me the greatest blow job I ever had, if I'll just . . ."

She surged upward, getting her legs into it, scattering the other tools as she swung the thing up and around. It was pleasingly heavy. One of the other things banged her shin, but she ignored it.

He made a sound of surprise a split second before it hit him. She felt it strike some fleshy part—his side or thigh—seeming to sink in a little deeper. He screamed and jerked away, and she opened her eyes to see him limp backward, the gun jerking in his hand, making a metallic clicking sound.

He stared at the gun in disbelief. She looked to her own weapon and saw with an odd chill of pleasure that it was an ax, the head now bloody. Miles's left thigh was drawn in at an odd angle. Blood soaked his trousers on that side, and his face had gone white. He clicked the gun at her again, as if thinking it might fire now, then threw it away with an angry croaking sound.

Lightning flashed again. She saw him moving in jerks in the strobing light, seeming to turn and fall toward the side of the car. She heaved the ax up, began to swing it in a circle, like a hammer thrower, her legs bent, her back turning toward him as she brought it around. She had a glimpse of him leaning down, beginning to reach for something under the car.

She went with the ax, wanting to speed it up but unable to without throwing herself off balance and falling. It seemed an eternity before she could turn her head back toward him, over her other shoulder, the ax coming around finally, to see him clutching the shotgun in both hands, trying to balance on one knee as he swung the barrel around toward her.

They were looking into each other's eyes when ax and gun met, the loud metal clang overwhelmed by the roar of the gun as it flew from his hands—an explosion, a wave of heat, the ripping, crackling sound of scatter shot tearing into the wall behind her, splintering the wood of the door, shrieking against metal and concrete, and then, behind it, the sound of the gun itself bouncing away. She couldn't tell if she'd been hit or not. She felt nothing, and that was good enough. Again, he was out of her sight for a moment, as she swung the ax in a circle, but it was quicker this time, and when she came back around to him, she saw him fumbling, one-handed, with the SS dagger, trying to get a grip with his right hand, while his left hand hung bloody and useless at his side, looking thinner than it ought to be.

She tried to turn the ax head, to aim it at the knife, but the effort threw her off balance, made her miss him entirely, and the ax flew from her grip, sailing off into the darker end of the garage, the same way the shotgun had gone. She stumbled after it, carried by its momentum, and righted herself in time to see him moving toward her with the knife clutched in his fist, swinging upward at her.

She leaned backward, away from it, still not quite balanced, as lightning struck again somewhere near, a short, sharp sound without any flash of light. A splotch of blood appeared on Miles's chest, and the knife fell from his hand. He looked down at himself in surprise, and then knelt down, as if to search for the knife. But he collapsed onto the concretelike a marionette.

She stared at him, frowning, mystified.

"Jes?"

She jerked. Hector was standing beside her, holding a gun. Behind him there were other men wearing rain slickers.

"Are you hurt?" Hector asked.

She stared at him. "I don't know." Then she looked down at Miles. "I was going to kill him."

"I'd say you did." Hector put the gun back in his holster. "He just needed to die a little faster. So I helped." He looked at her. "That's fair, isn't it?"

She didn't understand what he meant, but she nodded. People were going into the house, and she wanted to explain it to them, before they found it, but it was so complicated. She heard them calling out to one another inside, and more people went in. Someone inside was shouting in anguish, a sound that tore her heart. She and Hector looked that way.

"Lassiter's dead?" Hector asked. "Why did he kidnap you?"

She frowned. "He didn't. I mean . . . he was trying to save me. He tried to save us. He made me go . . ." She stopped, remembering. "Eddy's in your car."

"Yeah, we found him. So it was Haffner—"

"Miles. His name was Miles. He killed Haffner. He killed Lassiter and . . . I don't know. There are lots of dead people in there. I killed the ones upstairs. Those are *my* bodies."

"Your bodies."

"I didn't mean to kill the old man . . ."

She found that she was sitting in the open door of Lassiter's car, but she couldn't remember sitting down. Hector crouched in front of her, holding her hand, squinting at her. Then another man squatted down beside him—a cop. He took her free hand, to put the cuffs on her, only it was a blood-pressure cuff. He wrapped it around her bicep, pumped it up, let it hiss down, then put a stethoscope to her chest. "Where does it hurt?" he asked.

She shook her head. "Nowhere."

Hector muttered something to the man, and he shrugged and straightened up and went away.

Another cop in a slicker came and squatted in front of her, took her free hand between his. But it wasn't a cop. It was Zach.

"What are you doing here?" she asked him. Then she thought maybe she understood. "Is this a dream? Are you a cop in my dream?"

"You better take her out," Hector said to Zach. "Don't let her answer any questions. Cops or reporters, either one. She's not ready."

"I'll get her past the crowd," Zach said.

The crowd? She wondered what he meant. She let

Zach pull her to her feet, then held onto his hand, following him out of the garage and into the long driveway. It was hardly raining at all now, and it was easy this time because that wind had stopped. There were people and lights at the end of the driveway, and lots of cars, lots of voices.

"At least three bodies," she heard someone say. "Maybe more." She didn't know where the voice came from. Another one said "This terrible massacre in a north Wichita neighborhood while the storm . . ."

Then Annie Babicki came from somewhere, holding Eddy, who reached out to her. Annie seemed to be trying to give him to Zach, but he said, "Let her hold him. He wants her."

She took the baby, glad it was Annie who'd had him, and that he was okay. He gripped her T-shirt with both little hands, and she felt bad because he'd come to her instead of Zach. But Zach didn't seem to mind.

"Thanks, Annie," she said. But Annie had already gone.

Zach took her arm and steered her off the driveway, out onto the wet grass, toward the cars. She kept feeling light, and far from everything, as if she could fly if she wanted, or as if none of the other people were real . . . She had a sudden strange memory of spinning . . . spinning around in a circle, holding onto something . . . It made her feel dizzy and a little sick.

"Get in," Zach said. He was holding open the door of one of the cars.

"Whose car is this?" she asked.

"Mine."

She looked back at the driveway, the people at the end of it—reporters and photographers, she realized, and TV people. All the cops were inside. She frowned.

"I don't think I should go. But you should take Eddy."

"They can talk to you tomorrow."

"They'll think I'm trying to get away. I need a lawyer, don't I?"

"For what? What are you talking about."

"My bodies. The two in the bedroom. And Miles, too, I guess. Hector said I killed him. So that's . . . that's three, isn't it? The black woman, I didn't kill her . . . and . . ." She stopped, confused. "I'm not remembering all of them."

"Don't try. Just get in."

"They'll think . . ."

"No, they won't. We'll just sit here and wait for Hector, okay?"

She thought about that, then nodded and got in awkwardly, holding Eddy against her chest with both arms. Then Zach got in, too, so she had to slide all the way over.

Eddy was asleep. "You want to hold him now?" she asked.

"If you want me to."

She handed the baby to him, and felt a flood of relief when Zach took him. Eddy was safe with Zach. He'd survive with Zach. It was so simple and obvious.

She turned her head to look out the window, but all she could see was her own face hanging out there in the darkness. Or a face that looked like hers, anyway. It was hard to tell in the rain . . . and it had been such a long time . . .

She looked once more into the eyes of that face that was so much like her own. *He's safe,* she said to it in her mind. *He's safe with Zach.*

The other didn't say anything, but she didn't have to. They agreed.

Jes closed her eyes and laid her head back. *We did it. We saved him.* It was what she was thinking, but it came out double in her mind, like two voices speaking at once. *This time we won.*

Epilog

During the month that followed, there were inquests in Wichita and in Los Angeles, and Zach kept Eddy while Jes was giving testimony. Both juries decided there was nobody left to charge with anything. Then the California attorney general subpoenaed her for a grand jury looking into Bannerman's connections in the state legislature, and she got another from the L.A. County D.A.'s office, which had added the question of Bannerman's influence to an existing probe of the LAPD.

Zach hadn't figured it up, but he was pretty sure Eddy had spent more time with him than with Jes since the night at Lassiter's house. Not that he minded. The baby's presence was forcing him to be more organized than normal, and that was something he'd planned to do for a long time anyway. And he liked having somebody to talk to besides himself.

When someone knocked on his door the morning after Jes flew out the last time, he saved his work and went down the stairs expecting it to be Annie Babicki, who'd appointed herself to check on him every now and then when the baby was there. But it was Hector.

"Come in," Zach said. "Eddy's asleep."

He wasn't quite sure whether he and Hector were now friends, exactly. He liked Hector and was glad to see him, and he sort of suspected Hector liked him. But it was really more like he'd become Hector's assistant in looking out for Jes. Which was okay with Zach.

Hector sat down on the sofa.

"Coffee?"

"No, thanks. How is it, taking care of the baby full-time?"

Zach shrugged, a little surprised by the question. Hector generally wasn't one for chitchat. "Not as bad as I would have thought, actually. I have to be more orderly. Have to clean up a little more than I'm used to. Get more female visitors." He laughed.

Hector nodded, not changing expression.

"So, hypothetically, you wouldn't mind having him permanently."

Zach didn't say anything for a moment, then shook his head. "No, I wouldn't mind. But that's pretty hypothetical."

Hector sighed. "Jes has a plan," he said. "She asked me to lay it out for you, see how you react."

"A plan."

"Yeah. It goes like this. You get married. Then you adopt him—"

"Married? To Jes?"

"Right. Then you adopt him. She wants him to take your name, by the way. No more Wellingtons. Then you get a divorce and she grants you sole custody. What do you think?"

"I think this is either some kind of joke or it's fucking nuts."

"It's no joke. She's very serious. She's extremely serious. In fact—"

"Wait." Zach held up a hand, shook his head. "Is the idea just that he winds up staying over here all the time, and with her some of the time . . . I mean, just kind of switching . . . ?"

"Nope. She won't see him at all, she says. Complete separation."

Zach fell silent. Hector looked away from him, surveyed the apartment's living room as if he'd never been there before. It was obvious that he'd known Zach would dislike the idea of complete separation, for reasons having nothing to do with Eddy. Did Jes know that?

"Neither of us is gonna talk her out of it," Hector said. "I've already taken my best shot. She's been working it out for a while, practically since the day after. She's been talking to this retired judge she knows. Says it'll take about six months."

When Zach still didn't say anything, Hector added, "You understand, this is her idea. I'm just passing it on. She said it's like a green card. That means, just 'cause you get married they don't automatically let you adopt him. Women sometimes marry assholes. That's what I'm told. So there's a waiting period, and they drop in on you every now and then."

"Well then, they're gonna see that we don't even live together."

"That's what I'm saying. She knows that. You'd have to move over there for the six months."

"To her *house*?"

"You see what I mean. She's serious about this."

"Hmm." That was something he needed to think about, not least because it made the idea seem suddenly more attractive to him.

"So what do *you* think?" he asked finally.

"I think it's your problem," Hector said.

"Great. Thanks for the sage advice."

Hector gave a half smile. "Truth is, I don't know. Nobody knows what's gonna happen in the next six months."

Zach stared at him. That could be taken for encouragement, or just the opposite.

"This is the kind of thing," Hector said, "it'll probably affect all your lives from now on, whatever you decide."

"Jesus, Hector. Thanks for pointing that out to me."

"The best advice for something like that," Hector said, unruffled, "is not to just think about right now. Or just a year or two. You should think about what it'll mean in, say, thirty years. How you'll feel then."

"And how am I supposed to know that?"

"You aren't. But I guarantee you, thirty years from now you'll know whether it was the right thing to do or not." He gave a grunt that might have been a laugh, although he didn't smile, and stood up. "You got a week or so to think about it before she gets back. If you need any more sage advice, let me know."

They were married by the retired judge she'd been talking to, in his home office. Hector was there as best man, and the judge's daughter, who'd been a childhood friend of Jes and her sister, served as matron of honor. Eddy also attended, but was more interested in the judge's cat than in the wedding.

Then they all three went to the house. Zach had already moved most of his stuff over by then, but it was still different—the three of them going there as an official family. He hadn't told his mother or his sisters he was getting married and would soon be a father, although not in the usual way. He hadn't quite figured out how to explain it.

He and Eddy had the room that had belonged to the twins when they were young. Jes slept in the master bedroom at the far end of the hall, beyond the bathroom and her office. That first night he noticed the sound of her closing the bolt lock on her door, and wasn't sure whether to feel insulted or not.

But in a short time he stopped noticing things like that, and it all began to feel more or less normal. He'd grown up in a household full of women and knew how and when to keep out of the way. The only thing that bothered him, at first, was having to work down in the windowless, wood-paneled rec room where Jes's sister had killed their father. At least there wasn't any ghost, unless you counted the dog who had had a near-death experience and who obviously regarded the rec room as her territory. But he and Susie quickly became den mates. For the first few weeks he was there, she had bigger problems than him to worry about, like the full-leg cast she still wore and the huge plastic cone she had to wear around her neck until the cast came off.

She never seemed to get the hang of it, and he became her friend largely by helping her navigate the basement and stairs, by taking the cone off now and then when Jes wasn't around to see, and by taking her out when Jes didn't. According to the vet, she'd taken three bullets, but none had hit a vital organ. One had broken her leg and another had shattered her collarbone, throwing her into deep shock—essentially a coma. Zach had the impression that the normal procedure would have been to put her down, but that Dr. Scott had made the extra effort to bring her back and patch her up just because he was so pissed off.

For a while he made a point of taking care of Eddy and staying out of Jes's way, letting her go on about her life as if they weren't there. But that was more trouble for both of them than it was worth, and gradually they began eating together, watching TV, playing computer games, grocery shopping with Eddy sitting in the cart. Apart from not sleeping together, and the awareness that it was temporary, they became pretty much the kind of family the adoption agency wanted to see.

Zach found, a little to his surprise, that he liked it. It wasn't *that* hard to think of Jes as a sister. There were even a couple of times when he forgot she wasn't, and came close to embarrassing himself. He began thinking of suggesting that they continue the arrangement beyond the six months, but he was a long way from working up his nerve to broach the subject to Jes. He wasn't sure she was as comfortable with it as he was.

Things changed in the fall, when Eddy began walking. He was babbling by then, too, and even crying sometimes—not only when something was really wrong, but when he didn't get his own way, or just when he wanted attention.

Jes decided that he ought to have his own room, and Zach helped her move her office stuff into the big bedroom where she slept. Zach didn't say anything about it being a wasted effort, since the adoption was

less than two months away. She was trying to help
him prepare Eddy for that, and was willing to give up
her office to do it. He'd also decided to leave it to
her to bring up the subject of what happened after the
adoption was final. It was her plan, and he'd agreed to
it, and as far as he knew there'd been no change in
it. It was partly cowardice. He didn't want to suggest
a change and have her reject it.

One morning in late November, over breakfast, Jes
told him she was going away for a while. She said
she'd realized that it was really her mother she ought
to be writing about. She'd already made some calls
and collected some research notes, but mostly that had
only shown her more clearly how little she really knew
about Maria Peete, the orphaned girl who'd become
Maria Wellington.

She said she was working on the assumption that
her mother had been at least part Navajo, although
she didn't really know that to be true. There were
Peetes—with spelling variations—in the part of New
Mexico where her mother's parents' license plate had
been issued, but there was no way of knowing which
if any of them were related, and she'd been given
to understand that there were more who didn't have
telephones, living on one of the reservations in that
area. So she was going to New Mexico to see what
she could find out.

How long? She didn't know. Maybe quite awhile.
"All I really know about that area is from reading
Tony Hillerman novels," she told him.

He assumed she remembered that the adoption
would be final in less than a month, and that if she
wanted any change in the original plan she'd say so.
It was obvious that finding out about her mother
wasn't just a ploy. It was very important to her. But
it was also true that it would be easier on all of them
if she were gone when he and Eddy moved out.

He expected it to be different, of course, but he was
still astonished by how empty the house felt without

her. Both Eddy and Susie were fretful and out of sorts, needing more of his attention than usual. He looked forward more than he had to Hector's occasional visits, for their sakes as well as his own.

There were a couple of postcards, cheerful but brief and distant, from towns in New Mexico and Arizona. She phoned from Farmington, New Mexico, on the morning of the day after the adoption agency called to say that everything was approved. There were things to sign, but he could sign them now and his wife could sign them when she got back from her business trip. But Jes only said "That's good," and changed the subject. She now knew that she'd be there beyond the end of the year, and she'd been thinking about missing Christmas at home. She'd thought about returning for a couple of days, but then had thought that maybe they could come out there instead. She could show it to them. She sounded excited by the idea, and a little anxious about what he'd say. He told her they'd come. Unsurprisingly, she had all the details worked out—which flight to take, where to stay. He realized she'd found a better way to bring things to an end.

He made arrangements to board Susie with Dr. Scott, bought the plane tickets, made the motel reservation, in Farmington, packed a few gifts he'd gotten for Eddy and for her, and shipped the rest, paying a fortune to be sure of getting it there in time.

Jes met them at the airport in Albuquerque, in a secondhand Jeep she'd bought, and drove them through the strange warmth of the desert, excited and uncharacteristically chatty, pointing out historical sites, describing the tribes that lived on the various reservations they passed through or near. Most of it had little to do with her research, as far as he could tell. She just liked the place. She looked to Zach like someone who'd found a home.

She'd also found a little of what she'd been looking for—enough to form what she called a theory, but which sounded to Zach more like a conjecture, although he didn't say so.

She'd determined that Maria Peete's mother's maiden name had been Cruzado, although she hadn't yet linked her to a particular family by that name. It now seemed unlikely that her maternal great-grandparents had had any Navajo blood. But, on the basis of some things that seemed pretty flimsy to Zach—one was the absence of twins in her father's family; another consisted of what she thought were significant differences between stories her mother had told her and her sister, and otherwise similar stories that were well-known here—she'd decided to pursue the possibility that her grandmother had been a twin, born on the reservation and secretly given to an off-reservation Hispanic family to raise because, Jes said, the Navajos considered twins unnatural.

Her apartment in Farmington consisted mostly of a clutter of paper and books and maps and an unmade bed—more evidence of her involvement in what she was doing—but it turned out she'd taken the room right next to theirs at the motel, with a connecting door, so that they could approximate what Eddy was used to.

In the days just before Christmas, she took them to the restaurants she liked, took them for drives in the desert and into the mountains to the west, to some of the more remote places, and showed them promontories and wind-shaped rocks and the ruins of old trading posts, deserted places known by everyone here to be occupied by ghosts. She pointed out figures of strange creatures carved into the stone high above stone pathways leading to places where people had once lived within the stone itself. She told them of places even more remote, to which they couldn't take Eddy safely, or for which there just wasn't time.

Zach could see how much she wanted him to like it all—and he did. But he also felt a little off balance down inside, a little too aware of the guarded, watchful eyes of the people who never seemed to be looking back when you looked at them. The Christmas lights draped on the flat roofs that never had to bear the weight of snow, the crèches standing in yards of sand and rock and cactus—it all made him feel more out of place than he might have at some other season. He realized again, and with the same surprise, what he'd discovered in Boston: He was a Kansan. He couldn't have explained that to anyone, except maybe another like himself. It meant nothing to him until he went to other places.

Jes had come up with a small tree that looked enough like an evergreen to make a Christmas tree, and they'd put it in a corner of his room and decorated it simply with tinsel, and strings of cranberries and popcorn, and a few ornaments, and put under it the presents he'd shipped, along with some that Jes had bought. It turned out that the Vincents and Wellingtons had had the same family tradition of letting the children open a single gift on Christmas Eve, and he and Jes decided to regard themselves as children on this occasion.

Jes didn't want to do it in the motel room, though. It would be all right to have Christmas morning there, she said, but somehow . . .

He understood what she meant, although neither of them could quite put it into words. They needed to go somewhere else, someplace that felt more home-like, for Christmas Eve. He thought she meant to take them to her apartment, but instead, when they got into the Jeep that evening, she drove out into the desert again, going west, all the way to Shiprock and beyond, into the darkness, turning off the highway and climbing on roads Zach wasn't sure he could have made out in the dark, ending up at a high, flat place that seemed to look out over the whole world but from which they couldn't see a single light other than the stars.

It was cold, too. Not the cold of a Kansas winter, but enough to require jackets and something for the ears, to make the Jeep a welcome windbreak when they spread out the big blanket Jes had brought, to eat their supper of turkey and rolls, mashed potatoes and gravy, cranberry sauce—all the things they'd both grown up with. Even a pumpkin pie, of which they both dutifully ate a piece, although neither of them liked it.

As it grew darker, Zach built a fire, using the wood Jes had brought for the purpose, along with what bits of wood and dry brush and tumbleweed he could find within range of the Jeep's headlights. The desert stuff burned fast and hot, giving them a light for opening their gifts.

He'd bought Jes one of those multipurpose machines—printer, fax and copier—something he'd decided she needed while lugging all her separate, somewhat antiquated peripherals from one room to another. But he'd left it in her office, with a ribbon and a funny card. The thing he'd brought for her to open tonight—a turquoise pendant—seemed a little foolish once he got to New Mexico, where there was turquoise stuff everywhere, and where he realized that he couldn't remember ever seeing her wear any jewelry, even back at the newspaper.

But she seemed genuinely pleased, and genuinely surprised. When he mentioned his doubts after buying it, and that he'd never seen her wear jewelry, she said, "Only because nobody ever gave me any."

She put it on, posing with it in the firelight, and he felt befuddled for a moment. It wasn't the pendant itself, it was her expression putting it on, and the way it looked on her, and what she'd said. For a moment he could only look, as if unable to form a thought or speak a sentence.

She handed him a large, flat, heavy box, and then watched apprehensively as he opened it. It turned out to be an old-fashioned cast-iron skillet—exactly the kind his mother had had, and obviously secondhand. Briefly he wondered if she'd somehow gotten his mother's skillet. "How did you know I always wanted this?" he asked, examining it. He believed it *was* his mother's skillet.

She smiled, relieved. "You said there were some things that couldn't be cooked right in anything else. Remember? We were having breakfast."

It was something he knew he'd said now and then during his life, and he nodded, although the truth was he had no memory at all of saying it to her. "But how did you get it?"

"It wasn't easy. I went to a bunch of secondhand stores and some garage sales, and I finally found it at an estate auction. Not too far from here, in fact."

He looked at her, not understanding. Then he got it. It wasn't his mother's skillet. Of course it wasn't. What an idiot. "This may be the best Christmas present I ever got," he said.

She smiled, looking a little embarrassed, and said, "Time for the main event."

Breaking tradition all to hell, they'd each brought two things for Eddy to open, although he seemed more interested in the boxes and wrappings than in some of the gifts. The thing he seemed to like best was a plastic box with large keys that made sounds like different musical instruments when he banged on them, and that could be set to play familiar tunes.

They sang along with them, singing as loudly as they wanted in the empty dark. Eddy was clearly delighted, looking back and forth between them. When they stopped, he banged on the box again.

They exhausted the toy's repertoire and began singing Christmas carols. Eddy babbled loudly and shouted. Zach and Jes began vying to see who could remember the most Christmas carols. Jes was the first one stuck. She frowned down at Eddy, who was sitting in her lap, and whispered, "You know any?" He laughed as if he understood the joke. "It doesn't actually have to be a Christmas carol, does it?" Jes asked. "Just a children's song."

"Absolutely," Zach said.

She nodded and began singing again.

> *She is handsome, she is pretty,*
> *She is the belle . . .*

She stopped, seeming to choke, looking down at Eddy, whose eyes were wide, his expression solemn. Zach wasn't familiar with the song, but Eddy was. The baby gave a sudden lunge, just sort of rocking his body in place, and made an impatient sound.

"I think he wants you to sing it," Zach said.

She looked at him. The movement of the firelight made it difficult to read her expression, but he could see she'd been thrown back a little, toward the nightmare.

"It's all right, Jes," he said softly. "It's just a song. You can sing something else."

She looked at Eddy again, gave her head a little shake, and began again:

> *She is handsome, she is pretty,*
> *She is the belle of Belfast city.*
> *She is courting, one-two-three.*
> *Please won't you tell me, who is she?*

Her voice faltered and she looked at Zach again. He nodded. She sang again, more softly:

> *Al the bully says he loves her,*
> *All the boys are fighting for her.*
> *They tap at her door, they ring on*
> *her bell.*
> *Will she answer? Who can tell?*
> *Out she comes, as white as snow,*
> *Bells on her fingers, bells on her toes.*
> *She is courting, one-two-three.*
> *Please, won't you tell me, who is she?*

Eddy had begun trying to sing along, more loudly than Jes. "Ba ba ba, ba ba ba . . ."

She clutched him to her and stopped. He made a

soft sound of protest, and she relaxed her grip. Zach saw tears on her cheeks.

Eddy suddenly became interested in a large bow on a box set beside them. He leaned, reaching for it.

"He's right," Zach said. "Time to start cleaning up." He climbed to his feet, brushed off his jeans, and began gathering things up and loading them into the Jeep. Eddy had gotten hold of the box and the ribbon, and was examining them with a grave frown. Jes sat looking into the fire, which had settled down to a few small flames flickering on the blackened remains of the wood she'd brought.

When she finally got up, she got into the passenger seat with Eddy and his box on her lap. "You don't mind driving back, do you?"

He shook his head, although he wasn't completely confident about the narrow roads they'd come up here on.

It wasn't so bad going down to the highway, though. He drove slowly and kept an eye on the ruts. When they were on the highway again, headed back toward Shiprock, he said, "You really like it here, don't you?"

She looked at him, then nodded. "The weather's great. People apologize when it's windy." She smiled. "Somebody told me that when it's windy here, that means it'll rain in the Midwest tomorrow."

"Or maybe snow," Zach said. "It was starting to get cold when we left. I guess you won't miss the cold. I mean, you *will* miss it, but . . ."

"I think I will," she said. "I do like the people here. They leave you alone. But they're there if you need them. They know who they are. Who they're supposed to be. They think that's normal, and they expect you to be like that, too . . ." Her voice faded away. "It makes them strong," she said after a moment. She looked at him. "But this isn't my place," she said. "I'm a Kansan. That sounds kind of silly, doesn't it?"

"No."

There was a silence which went on long enough that Zach was surprised when she spoke suddenly.

"Are you and Eddy still going to be there when I get back?"

He looked at her in surprise. "I thought you'd expect us to be gone. I thought . . ."

"If you think that's best."

"Me? It's your plan."

"I know, but . . . You never said anything . . ."

He gave a soft laugh, shook his head. He drove in silence, then asked, "Do you want us to be there?"

"Yes."

"Then we will."

She sighed deeply. He glanced at her, saw her leaning back on the seat, her eyes closed.

He felt like doing the same, but he drove on, trying to sort out what had just happened and what it meant. She wanted them to stay, at least until she got back. That was all she'd said. Best not to start thinking beyond that. Still, he felt so much better than he had only a few moments before—better than he had in a long time. He hadn't been aware, until this moment, how much pain he'd been in.

She fell asleep at some point, her arms still gripping Eddy, who was also asleep. He concentrated on driving very carefully.

She woke up when they pulled into the motel parking lot, looked around as if unsure where she was, then gave her head a shake and said, "Zach?"

"Yes?"

"Can Eddy sleep with me tonight?"

"You sure you want him to? He gets up now more than he used to. And he kicks."

"I don't mind."

He laughed. "Okay. I'll move over the stuff you might need."

Later, sometime in the night, he felt Eddy climbing into bed with him. Same old, same old. He started to go back to sleep, but then remembered that they'd closed the connecting door. He turned over and sat up, looking at it. It was closed.

He looked down at Eddy, but found himself looking into Jes's eyes. Eddy wasn't there.

She reached a hand out to him, and he took it in his, studying her face. "Are you sleepwalking?" he asked. "Do you know where you are? Do you know who I am?"

She only looked back at him for a moment, as if she hadn't heard. But then she said, "I know that you're my friend Zach. I know that you're Eddy's father, and my husband."

There was a silence between them, and then she said, "I'm not sure I know who I am, though. Do you know who I am, Zach? Do you have any idea?"

He thought about it, not wanting to give an easy, quick answer. He thought about the woman he'd met in the computer class . . . the woman he'd met again at the Children's Home . . . the woman who'd walked with him through the park and back, with the baby in a stroller . . . the woman who'd walked with him from that house of death, holding onto his hand, trusting him . . .

And the one he'd lived with these last few months. Eddy's mother. That's what he'd told Hector, and it was true. Truer now than it had been then.

And his wife. That was the tricky part, the part he wasn't at all sure he understood. But maybe it was always that way, with everybody. *Please, won't you tell me, who is she . . .?*

He smiled. "I have an *idea*," he said. "But there's a lot I have to figure out."

"You want to try?"

He lay back down, on his side, still looking into her eyes. "Yes. Definitely."

She smiled. "How long you think it'll take?" She edged slightly nearer to him. They were both whispering.

"I'm never much good at estimates like that," he said, moving a little nearer to her. "I'd say . . . oh, maybe thirty years or so. I should have a better idea by then."

"That quickly," she said, moving closer.

PENGUIN PUTNAM INC.
Online

Your Internet gateway to a virtual environment with
hundreds of entertaining and enlightening books
from Penguin Putnam Inc.

*While you're there, get the latest buzz on
the best authors and books around—*

Tom Clancy, Patricia Cornwell, W.E.B. Griffin,
Nora Roberts, William Gibson, Robin Cook,
Brian Jacques, Catherine Coulter, Stephen King,
Ken Follett, Terry McMillan, and many more!

**Penguin Putnam Online is located at
http://www.penguinputnam.com**

PENGUIN PUTNAM NEWS

Every month you'll get an inside look at our upcom-
ing books and new features on our site. This is an
ongoing effort to provide you with the most
up-to-date information about
our books and authors.

Subscribe to Penguin Putnam News at
http://www.penguinputnam.com/newsletters